must have been love

CARRIE ELKS

MUST HAVE BEEN LOVE by Carrie Elks
Copyright © 2025 Carrie Elks
All rights reserved
1404252

Edited by Rose David

Proofread by Proofreading by Mich

Cover Designed by Najla Qamber Designs (www. najlaqamberdesigns.com)

This book is a work of fiction and any resemblance to persons, living or dead, or places, events or locales is purely coincidental. The characters are fictitious products of the author's imagination.

All rights reserved.

No part of this book may be reproduced in any form or by any electronic or mechanical means, including information storage and retrieval systems, without written permission from the author, except for the use of brief quotations in a book review.

one

SKYLER

Have you ever known you're making a bad decision at the *EXACT* time you're making it, yet still you won't back out? That's me, right now. To be honest, that's been me for the majority of my life. The last twenty-nine years of my existence have been one bad decision after another.

But this one could definitely be the worst.

I'm sitting in my car, the wipers working overtime to push the rivers of rain away from the windshield, staring out at an ocean that looks so foreboding I'm surprised anybody willingly drives down this road and onto the ferry that's waiting at the end of the jetty.

"You promised me sunshine," I say out loud, my voice echoing in the empty car.

A chuckle blasts out from the speakers. "I said I remember the sun shining there," my sister says through the phone line. "It's just one bad day. It'll get better, Skyler."

It's ironic that Lee's the one who's being all optimistic and rah-rah-rah. She's been against this from the start. So has our mom, which is a huge part of the reason I'm here right now, staring out at the rivers of rain pouring down the road to the dock. I'm the family mess up. The black sheep.

And for once, I want to prove them wrong.

A baby starts to cry from the other end of the phone followed by Lee's cooing. She has her daughter Cora, her husband, James, who's made it big in business, and her own career as an entertainment agent that is thriving. She's been on maternity leave since my squishy little niece was born but she'll be back at it soon enough.

"I should let you go," I tell Lee.

"No, please don't. You're the only adult I've spoken to all day." She sighs heavily. "Describe exactly what you can see."

I lean my head forward, trying to squint out through the blur of the rain, but I only succeed in obscuring the glass even more with my misty breath. "I can see the ferry," I say. It's currently unloading the cars who have sensibly left the island.

It's called Liberty, or at least that's what everybody calls it. Its full name is Cape Liberty Island but according to Lee, nobody has ever called it that. It's a pretty little island off the East Coast, lined with beaches and a main street that used to attract tourists by the boatload in the early part of the twentieth century, before the commercial airplane was invented and the rich moved on to foreign resorts.

But, from what I have gathered, there's been some investment that has improved the town, as well as the hotel and bed and breakfasts that are there. I guess I'll find out in a few minutes.

"What else can you see?" Lee says, sounding almost

desperate. I know how much she loves her little girl, but I also know how much she hates being isolated at home.

"Um, I can see the island in the distance," I lie, because I sense she needs this. "Just barely though." There, not too much of a lie.

"It's so pretty there," she tells me. "You'll call once you get to the bar, right?"

"Of course," I say.

"And it's usually sunny, I promise. I remember that visit with your dad…" she trails off. Mostly because she doesn't like sad things, and this is definitely an upsetting subject. We have different fathers, but for a couple of years mine was a parent to both of us. She can remember him in a way that I can't. Can remember who he used to be before the alcohol took over and changed him.

Whereas I can only remember bad times.

Because he's been absent for most of my life, and now he'll be absent forever.

The last car is off the ferry. A guy in one of those yellow rubber capes and hats gestures at the cars waiting to onboard. There are only two vehicles ahead of me. The one at the front belongs to an air-conditioning company. The second is another van, this one with the words *The Grand Liberty Hotel* written across it.

I lift my hand to the steering wheel, my bangles making a jangling sound. "Looks like it's my turn to drive on," I tell her. "I should probably go."

"No!" she says quickly. "Don't hang up. Let me hear what's going on."

"You know there's a big thing on the wall of your living room that's much more exciting than this," I tell her.

"I hate watching television," Lee says. "It reminds me too much of work."

The guy in the yellow raincoat beckons to me and I drive onto the metal ramp that leads to the small ferry, the wheels groaning and clanging as I pull into the space ahead of me.

As I press on the brake, the bedraggled man knocks on my window and I lower it, the wind pushing a sheet of rain inside the car and wetting my face.

He glances at my clothes and I inwardly squirm. I'd taken Lee's rose-colored memories at face value and dressed for a beautiful summer island day. I'm wearing a white gypsy style top and a floaty cotton skirt that I found at a thrift shop in Manhattan, along with sandals that show off my freshly pedicured – by myself – toes.

"Put your car in park and shut off the engine," he shouts over the thunder of the rain. He brings his gaze up to my face. "You come to work at the hotel?"

I shake my head. "No."

"I hope you're not a visitor. You picked a bad day for it."

He's telling me. But I kind of like the way he's chatty despite the weather. "My dad used to own the bar on the island," I tell him. "The Salty Dog." And now I own it, thanks to his will.

"You're Wayne's kid?"

Of course he'd know my dad. The island isn't exactly huge. There are only a few hundred full time residents, though it's a tourist haven during the warmer months, when the population surges by the thousands on a daily basis. Most come for the day, though there are guest houses in the town center along with the stupidly expensive hotel that opened late last year. I checked out the prices before realizing I could barely afford one night there.

"That's right," I shout back at him and he blinks, opening his mouth then closing it, like he's thought better of what he was about to say. Instead he shouts out to a second man dressed in a yellow rain slicker. "Hey Jesse!"

The man who turns around is younger than me. "Yep?"

"This is Wayne's daughter, the one who inherited The Dog." The older man grins. "That's Jesse," he says to me as though I should know who he's talking about.

Jesse walks over, leaning down until his face is next to the other guy's. "Hey." He gives me the biggest smile.

"Hi." I smile back, trying to be friendly, but he seems disappointed by my response for some reason.

"I'm going to lock up the gate," he tells the older man. "We're ready to go."

"Okay." The man frowns again, then looks at me. "Once we get to Liberty, the bar is on the right as you drive up. It's been empty a while."

I take a deep breath, trying to ignore the guilt that washes over me. I'd had no idea my dad was sick. I hadn't heard from him for years. Didn't even know he'd gone back to the little island off the Atlantic Coast to run a bar.

He and my mom separated when I was a baby and Lee was five. I barely remember him, save for the occasional visit when he was sober enough to remember he had kids and for Mom to let him into our nice house in Hollywood Hills. Lee remembers a bit more – the visit to Liberty before I was born, the way he and mom would throw things at each other during every fight.

Theirs was a passion that burned hot and fast. Looking back, their relationship was so alien to the way I see my mom now. She's the ultimate responsible parent, and he was a free spirit, never willing to settle down.

She says I take after him in that way, and I know it exasperates her. I just don't know any other way to be. I've lived in dozens of different places and had a lot of different jobs. It's not the life she hoped I'd have.

"Thank you," I tell the older man. I'm feeling nervous about seeing the bar for the first time. There's something portentous about it, especially with this rain streaming down.

He nods, still giving me that strange look, then tells me to roll the window back up. Not that it matters, my face and neck are already soaked.

"Who was that?"

Lee's voice comes as a shock. I'd forgotten we hadn't hung up our call.

"The ferry captain and Jesse, his assistant, I think."

She laughs. "You'll know everybody's name within a week. There are no secrets in small towns."

And yet it feels like the opposite. We didn't even know my dad was here for the last few years. He'd inherited the bar from his own mother, and had been running it for the last five years before he became ill. But he hadn't bothered to let us know.

That had hurt more than anything. The fact he'd finally settled down for a few years. Enough to have a little business he could leave to his daughter.

"As part of the bequest he would like for you to stay on the island for a period of six months," the lawyer told me as he read me the contents of the will. Apparently – according to my mom, who's a paralegal – that clause is easily contestable.

But I'm not sure I want to contest it. I'm not sure of anything really. I have nowhere better to be and I need to see the island my dad grew up on, the island that everybody in my family can remember except me.

And then I'll make some decisions.

It takes twenty minutes for the ferry to cross the little channel of the Atlantic Ocean between the mainland and Liberty Island, and for the entire journey I can see nothing but rain. The only indicator we've actually reached land is the way the boat slows down and the crew starts to rush around, preparing for us to dock.

The ramp groans as they let it hit the concrete of Liberty's jetty, then the van at the front starts to pull away.

The younger man – Jesse – waves at me as I start up my engine. I wave back and turn my wipers to high, thankful that the bar is in the main town, just up from the dock, so I don't have to try to find my way around this place in the pouring rain.

It takes less than a minute to drive up the road and make the right to where a low roofed building overlooks the water. I park in a graveled spot next to the overhanging canopy that shades stacks of outdoors chairs and tables, and stare out, feeling stupidly emotional.

This was where my dad grew up. And where he spent the last years of his life. Did he think about me? Did he think about calling me?

I would have visited. I *should* have.

"I'm here now," I tell myself.

"Excellent."

Dear God, how is Lee still on the line?

"I'm gonna hang up," I tell her. "I need to put my phone away if I'm going to dash through the rain to the bar."

"Take photos. Send them to me. Call me once you're situated."

I will, but I feel like I need to be alone right now. I hang up and grab my purse, deciding to leave my luggage in the car until the rain lightens up. I want to explore before I decide what to do next.

According to the lawyers, there's an apartment at the back of the bar. The same apartment my dad lived in until he relocated to the mainland when he got sick. I'll be staying there for a while.

"Here goes nothing," I murmur to myself as I open the car door and the sound of rain hitting the tin roof of the bar fills my ears. It's a short run from the car to the canopy, but I still manage to get soaked, the thin cotton of my skirt and top clinging to my flesh like it's afraid.

I have to dig through my overstuffed purse – way too full of fliers and tissues and a half-eaten bag of M&Ms – to find the code and keys the lawyers gave us. I key in the numbers then unlock the three rusty locks, hearing the groan of metal scraping against metal. When the last one is unlocked the door swings open and I quickly close it behind me, taking a look at the place that I now own.

The bar consists of one room with tables and chairs piled neatly across the wooden floor, like whoever was here last thought they'd be back in the morning. There's a large wooden counter at the end of the room, along with liquor bottles attached to optics that haven't been used in a while.

It feels almost ghostly in here. For a second I consider leaving. Just turning my back and agreeing with my mom that the best thing to do is contest the clause.

But then she'll be right and I'll be wrong, the way I always am.

I walk over to the bar, running my finger over the sticky wooden countertop. Dust clings to the pad, turning it a dark gray. Drops of rain fall from my hair onto the dust, moistening it, as a shiver wracks through my body.

I'm not sure if it's because I'm soaked to the bone and it's cold or because it feels like there are way too many memories in this place.

I'm just about to pull my phone out and call Lee back – for moral support more than anything – when the door I closed securely behind me is shoved open. The sudden noise makes me jump and I shiver again, goosebumps breaking out on my body as I turn around to look at the doorway.

And the man framed inside it.

Holy hotness, he's good looking. I blink, taking in the expensive suit, the white shirt buttoned to the top, and the perfectly knotted tie, all packaging the tall, broad body that wouldn't look out of place on a viking. One with brown hair though, because he has the thickest, glossiest, brushed back hair I think I've ever seen.

But it's his face that draws my gaze. He has one of those straight, strong noses that leads down to the perfect lips – not too full, not too narrow, just perfectly balanced and currently pressed together.

I've always been a sucker for a man with a chiseled jaw. But those jaws are usually stubbled, belonging to a guy with long hair, a suntan, and no 401K or designer suits to his name.

This guy though. He has an aura about him. If I had to categorize it, right now it's screaming 'don't mess with me.'

My breath stutters at the way he looks ridiculously angry and handsome at the same time. His jaw is twitching, his lips pressed into a mean scowl, and his ocean-blue eyes are glaring at me.

My heart starts to pound. I can't remember the last time I had such a visceral reaction to somebody I've never met before. Especially not an angry guy in a suit. I'm all about happiness and free love.

Shame my body doesn't seem to remember that right now.

Luckily, he goes and spoils it all by opening his mouth.

"How many fucking times do I have to tell you people? This is private property," he rasps. "Get out of here. You're not welcome."

I've had a lot of server jobs in my life. Dealt with thousands of annoyed people whose meal was cold or wrong or they're just having a bad day and decided to take it out on me.

I know how to deal with angry people, but right now I'm cold and I'm wet and damn it, I could do without this right now.

"No," I say, shooting him as dirty of a look as I can muster. "You get out. This is *my* bar and *you're* not welcome."

two

SKYLER

Of course he doesn't move. He looks like the kind of man who doesn't take orders kindly. Instead, he stares at me like he'd like to wrap his huge hands around my neck and wring it, slowly taking in my face and my wet white gypsy blouse that's turned translucent from the rain and is broadcasting the fact that I prefer not to wear bras, and the skirt that's clinging to my thighs.

He pays special attention to the ink that swirls from my left ribcage down to my hip.

I wait for him to apologize to me, for walking into *my* bar and ordering me around, but of course he doesn't.

He looks like the kind of man who isn't used to apologizing to anybody. In his expensive clothes, with his perfectly styled hair and his tight jawline, he probably spends most of his days around corporate ass-lickers telling him he's the bees knees.

"Aren't you leaving?" I ask him. "I think I made it clear that I own the place."

His eyes narrow and yet somehow his sexiness isn't diminished by his annoyance. "You're Wayne's kid?" he asks, frowning like he doesn't believe me.

"What's it to you?" I ask, my pulse still racing. I fold my arms across my chest for good measure, because if he's going to be an ass he doesn't get to look at my nipples while he's doing it.

Especially since they seem to have minds of their own right now.

"I live on this island. Making sure it's safe is my job." He even looks handsome when he scowls. "So are you Wayne's kid, or do I need to call the cops?"

He doesn't look like he needs to call the cops at all. One flex of his biceps and he'd have me over his shoulder and marching me back to the ferry without taking a breath.

"Yes, I'm Wayne's kid," I say, because as good looking as this man is, I don't want to be hoisted over his chest right now. Or anywhere else for that matter.

He nods, looking slightly mollified.

"I'm sorry for your loss."

Oh boy. We've gone from evicting me to offering condolences. I'm starting to get whiplash.

"You knew my dad?" I ask him. And it doesn't come out as strong as I want it to. There's no way I want to show any vulnerability to this oaf, even if he is the first man to set my pulse racing in a long, long time.

"Yes." He nods. "I assumed you'd be selling this place."

I shrug. "I'm not sure what I'm doing yet. I just got here." I pull my lip between my teeth. "Not that it's any of your business," I add, just to make him grimace a little more.

It works.

"Of course it's my business," he says, still not walking out of my damn bar. "I plan to buy this place as soon as it's on the market."

I immediately bristle. Oh hell no, that's not happening. "It's not for sale."

Technically, that's true. I won't be putting it up for sale until I've had a chance to go through all the things that are still in here and in the living quarters. I owe that to my dad. Even if I don't end up spending the next six months here.

But if it takes my last breath, I'll make sure this guy never gets his hands on this place.

"What did you say your name is?" he asks.

"I didn't." And he knows that as well as I do. He's got that ability that only rich men seem to have of putting me on edge.

And then he glances at my chest and I realize my nipples are still pushing against the translucent top that seemed like a good idea only a few hours ago.

I'm not attracted to him. Yes, in my past I've been a bit of an asshole magnet, as Lee would put it. But I'm older. I'm wiser.

I just need my body to get the memo.

"You're Skyler," he says, suddenly surprising me.

"How do you know that?" I narrow my eyes at him, feeling exposed in more ways than just having my damn nipples pressed against my top like traffic lights.

"Your father had a daughter and a stepdaughter. Skyler and Lee. Lee has a husband and a house and lives in LA. You..." he trails off. "Don't."

"He talked about us?" My voice comes out small. Not only because this man had some kind of connection with my dad, but because his knowledge of who I am must come from Dad too.

Which means Dad talked about us.

For some reason that makes my throat tighten so hard I find it difficult to breathe.

"He did." He nods.

"What's your name?" I ask him.

"Hudson Fitzgerald."

He doesn't offer me his hand, and I'm grateful for that. Mostly because I don't feel that charitable to him, despite the lowering of his tone. But also because I'm not sure I want to touch him.

"And there's really no need to be here," he tells me. "Whatever offer you get, I'll top it. I'll buy this place as is. You can leave and enjoy the money."

He says it so easily, like we're talking about a simple transaction, not my dead father's bar. I can't walk away from it like that.

"Thank you," I say. "But I won't be taking that offer."

Because now an idea is forming in my mind. I look around at the chairs stacked on the tables and the dust clinging to every surface. But in my head I see a bar full of people, laughing, ordering drinks, maybe a singer on the podium at the far end, a couple dancing to the music next to him.

And I see my dad behind the bar. Not the man who died of cirrhosis, but the man he was before. The one in the photographs I've seen from when Lee was young and I was a baby.

In a stupidly strange way it feels like home.

"I need to change out of these clothes," I say, aware that I'll have to run through the rain again to get to the car to get my luggage, but it has to beat being wet. And exposed.

This time he doesn't look down at my body. Instead his gaze dips to my lips, to the stud in the top left corner. I part them, exhale, and there's a flash in his eyes.

"Very well." He nods. "But I'll be back." It sounds like more of a threat than a promise. He holds out a card. "If you change your mind, call that number. My assistant will answer day or night."

I bite down a smile. "And what if I only want to talk to you?" I ask him.

"My assistant is more responsive than me," he says.

"I bet."

He shakes his head and goes to turn his back on me, before changing his mind. "This is a small island. Extremely boring. You're going to hate it here," he tells me, his voice certain. "I guarantee within a week you'll change your mind."

"Well if I do," I say giving him a sour smile, "I'll make sure you're the last to know."

* * *

HUDSON

The rain is pouring down in sheets as I head back to my car, wrenching the door open and climbing in before I close the umbrella. I slam the door hard for good measure before letting my head fall back against the leather upholstered headrest. I'm furious, because I should have known she was coming. I pay good money to know exactly what's going on all over this island.

I don't like surprises. Especially not in the form of a

soaking wet woman who has the most perfect breasts I think I've ever seen.

Not that I was looking. I don't think I've met anybody who's less my type than her. I'm not keen on tattoos. I don't like facial piercings. Fuck only knows what other surprises she's hiding under those clothes.

You'd like to find out though.

I blink that thought away. Because that voice sounds way too much like *her*, and she was fucking infuriating. Beautiful, poised, and extremely fucking annoying. Not my type at all.

And yet if I close my eyes, I can still see her behind my lids. That wet hair stuck to her face, those white clothes clinging to her perfect curves. I try to push that image away, because even a few minutes in that woman's presence tells me she's trouble with a capital 'T'. And something I don't need is trouble.

"Is everything okay?"

My sister's voice brings me out of my dark mood. She's sitting in the backseat, next to Ayda. My six-year-old daughter is asleep, and has been since we left the hotel earlier. Autumn – my sister – volunteered to come with us while I drove into town to check on a few business arrangements. This rain has made everybody feel antsy. I think both of them needed to get out of the house, along with Barney, the huge Irish Wolfhound that is Ayda's shadow. He's currently curled up in the back of the car, snoring.

It was only when I drove by that I noticed the lock open on The Salty Dog door. We've had trouble there, since Wayne passed. Kids breaking in to drink from the optics, visitors from the mainland camping out and making fires in the center of the room.

MUST HAVE BEEN LOVE

And yeah, it's not mine yet, but it will be. And I protect what's mine. I don't want the place burned down – I just want to own it.

"Everything's fine," I say tersely.

"Who was in there?"

"Nobody important." I start up the car, but I can tell by the way Autumn shifts in her seat that my answer hasn't satisfied her. My twenty-six-year-old sister is nosy as fuck. Honestly, my whole family is.

As the oldest of six, it's always been my job to protect them. And sure, Asher, Wyatt, and Zach are grown men – as tall and as strong as I am – but Autumn and Eden are always my top concern, along with my daughter.

Even if Autumn is married to my best friend, she's still my responsibility.

I back out from the parking space and curse when a car screeches to a halt behind me. Fuck it, I wasn't looking and I always look.

I always do everything right. It's how I've gotten to where I am in life.

"Be careful," Autumn murmurs. I look back to check that they're both okay. Barney, Ayda's wolf of a dog – is lounging in the trunk, his head perched on the back of the seat like he's standing guard. The sudden jolt has woken Ayda up. Her lips purse as she looks around, trying to work out where she is.

And all I can think is that *maybe this is the day she says something*.

But no words escape her lips. They haven't for the past year.

I turn back around to pull out onto the road and head back to the hotel. I have more meetings this afternoon, and

Autumn has offered to watch Ayda for me. I have a babysitter on call for when Autumn and my best friend Parker aren't available, but I prefer my daughter to be looked after by family whenever possible.

By the time I park outside of the hotel the rain has eased a little. Enough for us to make a run for it to the huge oak door that leads to the Liberty Hotel. Autumn holds Ayda's hand, the two of them running through puddles like it's actually fun to get wet, Barney chasing them with delight because at heart he's a working dog. Ayda gives a silent giggle and my jaw tightens, because her inability to speak is my fault.

I lost control of her mother. I almost lost Ayda. And now she's lost her voice.

"I'm going to be a few hours," I tell Autumn. "Then I'll pick Ayda and Barney up. Is that okay?"

My sister gives me a beaming smile. "Of course. I have a commission to work on, she can help me with it."

Autumn is an interior designer. She used to be based in New York, but since she and Parker got together, they both moved here. They live in the refurbished lighthouse on the edge of the hotel grounds. About a ten minute walk from where Ayda and I live in the Captain's House that's been in our family for generations.

I'm still getting used to being based here on Liberty permanently. It's a slower pace of life, but a protected one, too. I know – or at least I usually do – exactly who's coming onto the island. I nearly lost Ayda once and I'll be damned if anybody gets close enough to her without warning again.

That's why I'm so pissed about Wayne's daughter turning up without me knowing. For a second her image flashes behind my eyes. The white top and skirt that had turned translucent and clung to her body. The vivid ink that covered her bare waist, curling up her side. And that fucking lip stud.

I hate lip studs.

So why am I imagining what it would feel like against my tongue?

Christ, I need to get laid. I run the palm of my hand over my face. That's easier said than done on Liberty.

I stalk past the reception staff who call out a hello, through the double doors to the private area where there are two apartments and a business suite, at the back of which is my office. I push the door open and stride in, yanking the plush leather chair from beneath the oak desk before sitting down on it. I look at the three monitors on my desk that are always on, showing the NASDAQ, the S&P 500, and the Dow Jones.

A quick glance tells me not much has changed since this morning as I hit the call button on my phone that connects directly with my lawyer.

"Hudson, how are you?" Richard booms out.

"I need you to run a check on somebody," I tell him.

"Sure." He doesn't blink at my brash tone. Probably because I pay him a hell of a lot of money not to. "What's his name?"

"Her name is Skyler Brown. I want all the background."

"Brown as in Wayne Brown?" Richard knows about my desire to buy The Salty Dog. If he were my therapist and not my lawyer he'd probably remark that it's part of my need to be in control of everything. But luckily he isn't and he knows better than to question me.

"Yep." I'm still thinking about that fucking stud above her lip. I have no idea why I'm so fixated on it. "She's just arrived on Liberty. I want to make sure she's not bringing trouble with her."

I glance out of my window. The rain has eased even more as I've been sitting here. It's a light mist now, enough to give some visibility out of the window. We're only a few weeks away from spring turning into summer and reaching our busiest time of the year. It's our first full year of being open since the huge renovation project that took place on the nineteenth century hotel last year. Guests will be paying a hell of a lot to stay here on Liberty. Every suite in the hotel has been decorated to the highest standard.

We're delivering luxury, privacy, and the promise of good weather. Luxury will include a bar near the center of town that will help my guests feel at home.

Not The Salty Dog. And not a bar run by a manic pixie dream girl with a stud in her lip and an attitude on her mouth.

That mouth though...

Swollen, pink, delicious. Christ, I could show her how to use it.

"Anything else?" Richard asks. He sounds amused.

Was I actually staring out into space then? Thank god we're not on a video call. I don't stare out into space, I don't fantasize about sex. I have it hard and fast and then I move on.

"That's it," I say. "Make it quick, please."

"It'll cost," Richard points out.

"And you know that I can pay." Because yes, we extended ourselves with buying all the available real estate on the island, but after this year it will start to pay off. I have investors, I have money. What I don't have is the time to think about women who are of no interest to me.

"On it," Richard says, and I end the call without saying

goodbye. I'll have the report in my hands by the end of the week and be escorting that damn woman off the island shortly after that.

Then everything will be calm and under control. The way I like it. And I'll never have to think about lip studs again.

three

SKYLER

Everything in the apartment at the back of the bar is neat and tidy. I suspect that somebody came in after my dad died – or once he went to the hospital – and cleaned it up, maybe expecting him to come home and wanting the place to be ready for him.

I feel like I'm intruding as I pull open the closet and see his clothes hanging in there. I grab a sweater – old and chunky with some holes in it from overwashing – and sniff the sleeve.

It smells clean, yet there's also a hint of the salty air. Like he pulled this on and walked along the ocean. My chest tightens, because I'll never see that.

I'll never get to see him again.

I know so little about him, really. My mom never talked about him when I was growing up. He'd flit in and out of my life like some kind of distant relative, arriving unexpectedly, leaving quickly, and never letting me get to know the man who supplied half of my genes.

I manage to find some fresh bedding and change the sheets, then I unpack my suitcase and hang my clothes in his closet, where there's plenty of space because he was apparently a man of few clothes.

I still don't know why he requested that I stay here. Did he want me to have somewhere to finally lay down some foundations? Maybe he knew that I'm just like him, never able to settle, always moving onto the next thing.

From the earliest age I drove my mom crazy by never sticking at one thing for long. We tried ballet and t-ball and every other hobby you could give to an elementary school kid, but none of them seemed to fit me.

And then, at school, I was a daydreamer. She'd roll her eyes every time I brought home a progress report.

Skyler would be doing much better at English if she didn't spend most of the class staring out of the window.

"You're just like your father," she told me after she read that one. And I knew from the way she said it, that it wasn't a compliment.

Maybe that's why I'm here. This was the one place he kept coming back to. The place he grew up in and the last place he lived before he died.

The rain has stopped and night has fallen, the ocean an inky black mass of liquid as it laps against the shore. The smell of damp air lingers, like the weather can't quite bring itself to move on.

Lee calls and we talk for a while, but then I spend the rest of the evening exploring the bar, the outside porch, and searching through the drawers in the apartment to try to find the reason I'm here. The reason he wants me to stay here.

But there's nothing. Just sad piles of clothes and old letters and photographs. I find one of him. It's faded but you can still see him smiling at the camera. He's leaning against an old car, wearing a pair of jeans and no shirt.

He looks to be in his mid twenties – the same age he was when he met Mom at a concert in LA. I can see why she fell for him. He has this easy grin and a handsome face.

He was her only rebellion in life. And the one thing I think she regrets, though she insists that she doesn't regret having me. Even if I am her problem child.

And then a rush of exhaustion comes over me. Maybe it's the day of travel or the storm. Or maybe it's the angry man with eyes the color of the ocean on a sunny day. I've only met three people so far, and each of them has treated me strangely. The ferry captain, Jesse, and now this man.

Hudson Fitzgerald.

Even his name sounds stuffy. I hate the way he acted like he owns this bar when it's mine. I sit down on the freshly made bed and let out a sigh.

I don't think I've ever felt more alone in my life than I do right now, sitting in this empty apartment.

Do you think I've made a mistake?

I type quickly and send it to Lee.

She replies just as fast, her name on my screen making me feel wistful.

No, I don't. You're right where you need to be. Now go to sleep.

How many times did she tell me that when I was young? Being six years older, she was like my second mom sometimes. Bossy, overbearing. And completely loving.

You go to sleep. You're the one with the baby.

She sends back a heart. And I heart her heart.

A couple of hours later, I finally do as my sister tells me

and fall into a fitful dream about an angry man with piercing blue eyes.

* * *

When I walk out of the bar area onto the deck the next day it's as though the storm never happened. The sun is beating down, golden rays sparkling as they bounce off the waves in the ocean. I lift the cup of black coffee to my lips and take a long sip.

It tastes stale. I found an old unopened jar of coffee in the tiny apartment kitchen, and last night and this morning it's all I've had in my mouth. I brought enough food to see me through until I could make it to the grocery store, but I'm not hungry.

I lean against the pole holding up the overhang of the bar, breathing in the salty ocean air. I was so happy to get up and put on some shorts and a midriff tank, because those are the only clothes I packed to do cleaning. I'd hate to soil any of my vintage ones. They have too many memories in them – mine and so many others.

Thinking of memories, as I look at the bar area from my vantage point on the deck, I can almost see Hudson Fitzgerald – the angry man from yesterday – standing there, as he berated me.

I frown, angry at the memory, because I would never treat anybody like that. I'm new, my father died, and he pretty much told me I wasn't welcome.

When I told Lee about him she'd thought it was hilarious.

"Oh my God," she gushed. "It's just like those small town Hallmark movies. The two of you are going to end up doing it."

Ha! As if. I can think of a dozen things I'd rather do than let his disdainful mouth come anywhere near me. Like pull my nails out of their beds one by one.

Angry sex is great if you want to get off, but the older I get the more I've learned that relationships should be about caring, mutual trust.

Love.

When I finish my coffee – which involves pouring half of the cup into a nearby planter full of dead leaves – I walk back into the bar area to decide where I'm going to start with the clean up. I need to get supplies, both for the cleaning and so I have something other than stale black coffee to keep me going.

I walk behind the bar and go to pull the nearest cupboard open, only to scream out loud when my foot hits something on the floor, sending it scurrying across the dirty tiles.

Jesus, Mary, and Joseph, is that a rat? I swear it has a tail. My stomach turns as my heart starts to hammer against my chest like it wants to get the hell out of here.

I know the feeling.

"Oh my God," I whisper. When I look down, the rat hasn't moved. Not one inch. "Please don't be dead," I say. Because then I'll have to feel sorry for it.

Did it die alone? Was it wishing it had somebody there holding it's hand. Okay, it's paw. Whatever, nobody should die alone.

Putting my big girl pants on, I prod the animal with my toe.

It still doesn't move.

My stomach turns. Am I going to have to bury it? I don't even know if there's a shovel here. And I'm not throwing it in the trashcan. Even a rat deserves better than that.

Before I can make a decision a sound comes from the door. Like it's being opened. Then a dog rushes in. Or at least I think it's a dog. It's huge and furry and looks more like a wolf than a friendly mutt.

Before I can say a word it rushes past me, behind the bar and lets out a low growl before it picks the rat up between it's bared teeth.

I'm not gonna lie. I actually scream.

"Don't eat it!" I shout. Because dead rats usually mean poisoned rats.

The dog, calmer now that it has the rat in it's jaw, turns to look at me. If animals could look disdainful, this one would be the champion. It drops the rat and that's when I see it's actually a stuffed toy. A dog toy, I guess.

Belonging to *this* dog?

"Hey," I say, my heart rate finally calming. "Is this yours? You could have taken it before it gave me a heart attack."

The dog lets out a low sound. Somewhere between a bark and a purr. And yes, I should be afraid. It's an unknown beast, it could be dangerous.

And yet to my female-logic, it's less scary than a dead rat that turned out to be a stuffie.

The dog nudges my leg with it's nose.

"What is it?" I ask him.

He nudges me again, like he's trying to push me out from behind the counter. And because I'm not an idiot, I let him.

"Okay," I say as I back up. "But I'm only doing this to be nice. We've just met and I've already made one enemy on the island. I figure we should be fri— oh shit!"

I jump at the sight of a little girl standing in front of me, like she's just appeared out of nowhere. She's staring up at me with wide, saucer like eyes. She's in a pair of shorts and a t-shirt and her dark hair is neatly pulled into a pony tail.

"Hello?" I say warily, looking around for her parents. "I think you came in the wrong place, sweetie."

The dog walks between me and the girl, the toy rat forgotten, like he's trying to guard her.

"Is he yours?" I ask her.

The little girl nods. I'm not great with kids' ages, but she looks like she might be five or six.

"Where are your parents?" I ask her, looking hopefully at the door. Surely they must be close.

She doesn't reply. It's kind of unnerving how direct her stare is. She has the most beautiful blue expressive eyes.

"Are they outside?" I ask her. "Because we aren't open yet."

She shakes her head.

Okay then. I guess she's been told not to speak to strangers, which is good. But it's not going to help me figure out what the heck she's doing here.

"Well shall we try to find them?" I ask, holding out my hand. The dog lets out a low warning growl. And the little girl pats his head like she's calming him down.

Instead of taking my hand, she walks around me and the dog. Her faithful hound follows her as she heads behind the bar like she owns the place. It would be funny if it wasn't so weird and I wasn't scared that any minute her parents are going to run in and accuse me of child abduction.

"You can't go behind there," I say, because even if she won't speak to me I know she can hear me. But she completely ignores my words, opening a drawer next to the refrigerator.

And she pulls out a coloring book and a box of half-stubbed crayons inside an old ice cream tub. The interior is covered with scribbles that the crayons have made as they've rested in the box. Her tiny lips are pressed together as she carries them back around the bar and reaches up to put them on the counter.

But she's too short.

She tips her head and looks at me like I'm some kind of idiot then shoves them toward me.

"What?" I ask.

Her lips part and she lets out what looks like a sigh, then points at the bar counter.

"You want me to put these up there?" I ask.

She rolls her eyes and nods at the same time. This kid has chutzpah. And for some reason I end up doing exactly as she asks. Once they're safely on the counter, she pulls out a bar stool and climbs on it.

"Wait," I say, realizing she's planning on hanging out at the bar. "You can't stay here."

She lifts a brow. A weird memory flashes in my mind, like I'm trying to connect her expression to something but I don't know what.

"Kid, you need to go." Except I can't throw her out. I let out a long sigh, then hold my hand out to her, planning to help her down from the stool.

The dog barks loudly.

"I'm trying to help here," I mutter to him. "You should be thanking me, not barking at me."

He tips his head to the side, his eyes not leaving my face.

"I'm friendly," I tell him, holding up my hands. "See?"

Then I hold a hand out once more to the little girl. This time she takes it, and I smirk at the dog.

He doesn't look amused.

"We're going outside to look for a responsible adult," I tell her. "Okay?" Because I'm anything but responsible. Nobody should put their child in my care.

She shrugs. Well okay then.

I don't let go of her hand as we walk to the front door and I push it open, sunlight flooding into the bar. She's wearing little sparkly sneakers, and they squeak against the wooden deck as we walk to the steps, the sound of steady dog paws behind us.

He nudges my ass with his nose, as if to remind me not to do anything funny.

"Wasn't planning on it," I promise him.

There are no adults outside looking for a missing little girl. No sign of people at all. Apart from the guys working on the ferry which looks like it's just about to leave for the mainland.

"Do you live around here?" I ask the little girl. "Or are you a visitor?"

She shrugs. Well that's helpful. I look up the hill, at the building next to mine. *Eileen's By The Sea* is painted on a brown wooden sign affixed to the wall. The front door is open and a woman is kneeling on the stoop, scrubbing the front step.

"Hello?" I call out to the woman. She turns to look at me. Her hair is a steel gray color, tied into a severe bun. She's wearing what looks like a housecoat, though it's the first time I've actually seen one in the flesh.

Slowly she stands up, and if I'm being honest it's painful to watch. I swear I feel every twinge and ache reflected in her expression as she straightens her legs.

"Hello." She offers me a smile. "You must be Wayne's daughter."

"I am." I smile widely at her. "Do I look like him or something?"

"No." She shakes her head, and I feel deflated. "You're all the talk on the island WhatsApp. What are you doing with Ayda?"

I look down at the little girl. "Is that your name?" I ask her. "Ayda?"

She nods.

"She walked into the bar. I'm trying to clean it up," I call out to the woman. "Do you know where her parents are?"

"Well her mom's dead." The woman shrugs.

My mouth drops open. This is the brutal island honesty that I was promised, but somehow it feels bad. I think about putting my hands over Ayda's ears, but she doesn't look perturbed at all by this woman's words.

"And her dad is probably at work. Her aunt looks after her mostly."

"Do you know where her aunt is?" I ask, trying to sound patient.

"No. You could try calling her." The woman winks at Ayda.

Who winks back.

"That would be a great idea," I say. "If I knew her name or had her number."

"I tell you what, I'll text her," she says, and finally I let myself relax.

"Great. Can I leave Ayda with you while she waits to get picked up?" A rush of hope goes through me.

"Oh no, dear." She shakes her head. "I have things to do." She pulls a phone from the pocket of her housecoat and taps on it like an expert. "There," she says. "I've told her that you have Ayda at the bar. You two might as well go back there and wait."

"But you don't know me," I say. "I'm a stranger. I could mean danger."

"You're Wayne's girl," she replies. "Now why don't you two go get to know each other?"

"She won't talk to me."

"She won't talk to anybody. I wouldn't take it personally."

I glance at Ayda, who doesn't look at all upset at being talked about so directly. "You want to come back to the bar?" I ask her, warily.

She nods, a smile lighting up her face.

"Well okay then." I look at the woman. "Thanks..." I trail off.

"Eileen," she says, pointing at the sign on the guest house. "Obviously."

"Thanks, Eileen," I say, then under my breath I mutter. "*Obviously.*" Taking Ayda's hand in mine once more, the three of us – Ayda, me, and the hound from hell – head back to the bar to wait for her aunt.

four

SKYLER

"Oh my god, oh my god, oh my god," a pretty brunette shouts out as she rushes into the bar ten minutes later. Ayda is at the counter happily coloring a house with a red crayon. Her dog is lapping at a bowl of water I gave him, still standing guard over his little ward. The only time he's let her out of his sight is when he decided to go around the counter to grab his toy rat.

"I'm so sorry," the brunette continues. Wait, is this Ayda's aunt? I frown, because I expected somebody more like Eileen. Somebody older and more… responsible. Not someone who looks like she's my age or younger with her hair flying behind her, a t-shirt reading 'please don't make me do stuff' printed across her chest. It's knotted at her waist, revealing her perfectly toned stomach, and like me she's wearing cut-offs.

She grabs Ayda, who still has a crayon in her stubby fist,

and hugs her tight. "You monster, you were supposed to be in the grocery store. I've been looking for you everywhere."

Ayda shrugs and goes back to her coloring.

"You must think I'm a terrible person," the woman says, giving me a rueful smile. "I'm Autumn, by the way." She holds out her hand and I shake it. "You must be Skyler. You're the talk of the town."

"In a good way, I hope."

She wrinkles her nose, but is clearly too polite to tell me the truth.

"You can't keep running off like this," she tells Ayda. "Your dad will kill me. Do you want him to hire a full-time nanny?" she asks.

Ayda looks like she couldn't give a damn.

Autumn takes a breath. "Honestly, I'm usually better at taking care of her than this. I just got distracted by a call from a client. They wanted me to check something and when I turned around she was gone. I've had half of Liberty out looking for her." She looks around the bar. "Damn, this place looks sad."

"It needs a bit of work," I agree.

"And then you're selling it, right?"

"I'm not sure," I tell her, her question reminding me of Mr. Sexy-But-Angry from yesterday. "I'm still thinking about what to do."

A smile pulls at her lips as she looks at me, and I realize just how pretty she is. "That would be amazing," she says. "There aren't enough women my age on the island. I'm so bored here. Do you know I even thought about joining the knitting circle? But they refused to let me in because I can't knit."

"Knitters can be very territorial," I say solemnly and she laughs. Then she catches sight of my tattoo.

"That's so pretty," she says. "I've always wanted a tattoo. But my brothers would have a meltdown if I did." She tips her head to the side, as though a thought has just occurred to her. "Maybe I should. Did it hurt?" she asks.

"Like hell," I admit.

"And how about your lip piercing?" she asks, her eyes on my mouth.

"That didn't hurt at all," I say. "The tattoo took hours though. The worst part was needing to use the bathroom when he was doing the intricate parts."

"You've put me off." She ruffles Ayda's hair. "Okay, miss, you've been bothering this nice lady long enough. We should head home."

Ayda carries on coloring.

"You can take the book with if you'd like," I tell the little girl. "I don't really need it."

Ayda slides off the stool, her little feet landing on the wooden floor with a thud. She has the book in her hands, but instead of heading out, she walks around the counter and opens the drawer, putting it back in.

"Honestly," I tell her. "It's yours."

She shakes her head and I look at Autumn.

"She's stubborn," Autumn tells me. "Just like her dad. And she has plenty of coloring books at home, it'll be fine."

"Okay then."

Autumn clasps her hands together. I notice a stunning engagement ring and gold band on her wedding finger. "Hey, would you like to... I don't know... meet up some time?" she asks me. "We could get coffee or something."

It's weird, but I can see how much effort it's taken for her to say that. Like she's not used to asking.

"I'd like that," I tell her truthfully. Because I'm already feeling pretty lonely too.

"Great. Let me take your number." She pulls her phone out of her pocket. But before I can give her my number, the door to the bar flies open once more.

For an abandoned building, it sure gets a lot of unannounced visitors. I open my mouth to tell the interloper we're closed until I see who it is.

The angry man from yesterday.

Looking stupidly sexy in a gray suit and blue shirt.

"I haven't changed my mind," I tell him, in case he's here to rant about me selling the bar again. But instead of looking at me he strides straight toward where Autumn and Ayda are standing, scooping the little girl into his arms and hugging her tight.

"You got my message then," Autumn says. "I was about to call you and tell you she's safe."

He's actually shaking. I frown, realizing that he must be her dad. Autumn's brother. Damn, well that puts an end to that friendship. "Of course I got your message," he says, his voice low. "I came straight here." He puts Ayda down and holds her at arm's length. "Is she okay? Is she hurt?"

"She's fine," Autumn tells him. "Skyler's been taking care of her."

It's like he's only just realized I'm here. His gaze moves from Ayda to me. "You should have called me when she got here," he says thickly.

It takes me a second to realize he's talking to me. "What?" I frown. "How would I know who to call? She wouldn't tell me who she is."

"Of course she wouldn't," Autumn says, her voice soothing. "And it's okay. Skyler went to Eileen. She messaged me." Then a thought occurs to her. "Wait, you two know each other?" She looks from her brother to me.

"We met yesterday," I say.

MUST HAVE BEEN LOVE

He lifts an annoyed brow at me. My heart starts to speed. I hate the way I react to him. Like I want to lick his face. Ugh, he's so not my type.

And yet my body still isn't getting the memo.

"You're welcome," I tell him. "It was a pleasure looking after your daughter." Because seriously? He hasn't even thanked me.

He lets out a long breath, his gaze not leaving my face. "Next time you'll know to call me," he says, taking his daughter's hand. "Come on, let's get you home."

Autumn frowns. "Wait. I'll take her home. You have meetings."

"Not anymore," he says brusquely. "I canceled them."

From the surprised look on his sister's face, I suspect that's not something he does often. So he's an angry, sexy workaholic. Definitely not my kind of guy.

"You didn't need to do that," Autumn tells him. "I got this. I just turned my back for a minute. She's fine."

His face softens as he looks at his sister, and a weird feeling of envy flashes through me. "It's not your fault," he tells her. "We both know what she's like." He tickles his daughter's face and she laughs, then with the hound from hell behind them, he sweeps out of the bar, back through the door.

Wait. What? So it's not Autumn's fault, but somehow it's mine for not being able to read his daughter's mind and work out that he's her dad? The envy is replaced by a strong sense of injustice. He didn't even thank me.

Autumn screws her face up, as though she knows exactly what an ass her brother is. "I'm sorry. He's not usually like this."

"Yes he is," I say and she actually laughs.

"He's had a bad couple of days. Ayda's not been

sleeping well and..." she shuts up, as though she's thought better of making excuses for him. "Okay, he is always like that. But I'm nice, I promise."

I start to laugh, too. I like this woman. "I believe you," I tell her. "I'm nothing like my sister, either."

"Then we have lots in common." She leans forward to hug me, taking me by surprise. "Thank you for taking care of my niece."

"You're welcome."

"And here's my number," she says, passing me a card with *Autumn Designs* written across it. "Call me if you fancy having coffee and don't hate me too much by association."

As she walks out of the bar I notice she has the same strong, determined stride as her brother. Hopefully that's all they have in common, because I get the feeling she might be my only friend on this island.

I take a deep breath, looking at the abandoned stuffed rat laying legs up at my feet.

"I guess we're both staying for now," I tell him. "But you might be more welcome here than I am."

five

HUDSON

"Well that was an asshole move," Autumn says as I close the car door on Ayda and Barney, who might be a dog but his expression at me is cutting. "You could have been nicer to Skyler," she points out.

"Why?" I ask. "What is she to me?" Christ, I'm exhausted. Not because of Ayda's nightmare last night, which is the excuse I gave my sister. She doesn't need to know that I also had an annoyingly disturbing dream about a certain owner of a mouth stud. Mostly of me doing unspeakable things to those swollen, beautiful lips.

And today I got a glimpse of her bare stomach to add to the library of Skyler Brown images that seem to be accumulating in the dark recesses of my brain. The way it's tan and taut, the tattoo curling around to lick at her navel. And I'm not going to fucking think about those long, lithe legs that look like they go on for miles.

"She took care of Ayda for one," Autumn says, interrupting my thoughts, thankfully. "And she's new and she doesn't know anybody."

"She obviously knows Eileen," I point out, trying to ignore the pang of guilt pulling at my abdomen. I don't have time for guilt and I definitely don't have time to worry about the feelings of a woman who's hopefully leaving the island very soon.

The sooner the better. Because I don't like the way I want her.

"She doesn't know Eileen," my sister corrects me. "She went to Eileen for help. With *your daughter*. If you want to be annoyed with anybody, be annoyed with *me*. I'm the one who was watching her when she disappeared."

I take a deep breath, pinching the bridge of my nose. From the corner of my eye I see Ayda pick up one of the many picture books strewn across the backseat. She can read and understand every word we say to her.

She just doesn't speak. And it's killing me.

Because she used to speak. As a baby she babbled away to her heart's content. She cooed and smiled and started to say words at the right age. Younger, actually, because she's an intelligent kid.

Dada was her first word, said with intent at the age of ten months. It annoyed her mother to bits, but the doctor told us she wasn't only hitting every milestone with gusto, she was smashing them to pieces.

By three she was speaking in full sentences.

Now she just sits passively and says nothing and it's all my fucking fault.

That's the truth of it. I let out a long breath, because all of this has absolutely nothing to do with the woman whose father's died and left her his bar.

She's just gotten into the middle of something she shouldn't have.

I toss the keys to my sister. "Can you drive Ayda home?" I ask.

She frowns at me. "How will you get home?"

"I'll call a cab."

Autumn grins at me because we both know that's a lie. The only cab driver on the island is Simon and this is his day off because his wife insists that he takes her to the mainland to the local market.

"I'll walk. It's a beautiful day."

She blinks, surprised. "Walk? You never walk."

"I've been doing it for the last thirty-six-years," I point out.

This time she laughs. I love my kid sister fiercely, the way I love all of my family. Part of the reason I've invested so much money on this island is to bring us all together again. Autumn is already back for good, and Eden will come when she's ready. As for my brothers – I have three of them – they visit for holidays and parties and I know at least two of them hate leaving every time.

It's not just an island it's a haven. It's where we all feel safe after being adrift for so long. It's where I can bring up my daughter without fear of losing her.

Again.

"Just go," I tell her. "I'll find my own way home."

"Okay, whatever." She shakes her head at me. "I hope you're going to apologize to that nice woman. I don't have many friends my age here, and I'd like her to fill that gap."

"You can't just be friends with her. You don't know her. She's an out-of-towner," I tell her, using the word the people of Liberty use for tourists and visitors.

"She's Wayne's daughter. That makes her one of us,"

Autumn counters, and I can see that stubborn look in her eye. She's ten years younger than me, but damn she can be recalcitrant when she wants to be. Like when she fell in love with my best friend and the two of them got married.

I've come to terms with that. Maybe I even like it a bit. I know Parker will take care of her, and I need the headspace to stop worrying about her constantly.

"She'll be leaving soon," I point out gently, because I know Autumn has the tendency to get attached. "Don't put too much hope on being besties with her."

But the truth is, I don't like my kid sister being lonely. Sure, she has Parker and her business which is growing. And she takes great care of Ayda. But I also know she's an outgoing woman. She craves female company.

So I'm going to go apologize even though I don't want to. And then I'll forget about this woman and her fucking lip piercing for once and for all.

My life is finally on an even keel after being rocky for way too long. I need to concentrate on Ayda's recovery and nothing else.

"But you'll still apologize?" Autumn says hopefully, giving me that wide-eyed stare she knows will work every damn time.

"I'll try." My reply is short. "But don't expect miracles."

* * *

SKYLER

It's been almost twenty-four hours since I arrived on Liberty and I'm already thinking about leaving. So I decide it's time to start rage cleaning and forget all about that handsome ass who thinks he owns everything and everybody on the island.

But because *I'm me*, and easily distracted, I decide I need music to get motivated. I walk over to the old-style jukebox that's covered in a film of dust and hunker down to plug it in.

As soon as I flick the switch I wait for the sparks to fly and the whole thing to explode in front of me; after the morning I've had, it really would be the icing on the cake.

But instead, the lights on the Wurlitzer glow in pinks and whites and purples, forming an arch over the huge wooden case. I lean forward to look at the music options, smiling as I see them.

I remember finding some vinyls and an old record player Dad left behind in Mom's garage, years after he left us. They were in a tattered box on a shelf and it was a little bit like finding a treasure trove. I can still remember my excitement at listening to Fleetwood Mac for the first time, dancing in the dusty garage, feeling like I was free.

I still love Fleetwood Mac. Stevie Nicks is my queen.

Along with Fleetwood Mac, there are other singers I recognize on the jukebox's list. Bruce Springsteen, Journey, Tom Petty. My dad's musical heart belonged in the seventies and eighties, the same place my own soul belongs. And that makes me feel warm inside.

Hitting the second button I choose Tom Petty's "Free Fallin'", and the strum of his guitar echoes out from the speakers on either side of the jukebox, the familiar riff making my heart feel wistful.

Then the vocals start. His voice rasps out, making me shiver. Telling me that she's a good girl and she loves her mama.

I start to sing, feeling stupidly emotional, as I walk

behind the counter to locate the cleaning supplies I was looking for earlier. There's so little there. Just a bottle of bleach, a bag of clean cloths, and a spray bottle that's seen better days.

I'm going to have to go shopping. I grab my purse and keys, still singing along with Tom, my heart starting to beat faster as he gets to the part about being a bad boy because he's breaking her heart.

Then his voice lifts as he reaches the chorus. He's free fallin', he tells me, as I sing along. You can't help it with this song, you just have to go for it. I start to dance, singing my heart out, feeling more like Tom than the girl he's written the song about.

I'm not the good girl my mom wanted me to be. I'm the wayward one. I don't know how else to be.

I sing louder, loud enough to push away those dark thoughts. I've spent a long time trying to be the person my mom and sister wanted me to be. I never could do it. I can't conform, but it doesn't mean there's not a little part of me that wishes I could.

Wishes I could be the good girl that fits in with the rest of my family.

I wipe away a tear, because I'm not here for that, as Tom launches into the second chorus and I sing along.

I'm free. That's what I want to be. That's what runs through my veins.

Maybe that was the same thing that ran through dad's veins, too. The need to be different. To not conform.

I put my hands up in the air, swaying, singing like my heart depends on it. I'm going to be okay, I always have been.

And then I just about jump out of my skin, because I'm

not alone in the bar. *He's* standing there, in the door way watching me.

Hudson Fitzgerald. His jaw tight, his eyes dark, and his hair still perfectly styled. What wouldn't I give to mess it up and piss him off?

My heart slams against my ribcage.

"Jesus, you gave me a heart attack," I tell him, my eyes wide. "How long have you been standing there?"

"Long enough to know how much you love Tom Petty," he says, deadpan.

I run my tongue along my bottom lip. "I was trying out the jukebox." Not that I owe him any explanation. Truth is, despite the fact that I'm a free spirit this man is a little intimidating.

Okay, a lot intimidating. It's not just his broad stature, or the way he always looks like he's about to go for a quick shoot with GQ magazine. It's his dark brows and stormy blue eyes.

"Did you leave something here?" I ask him, pretending to look around. "Like your manners?"

The corner of his lip twitches. "I just came back to speak to you."

"About what? Want to take me to the cop shop for child abduction?" I put my hands on my hips, and his gaze follows the movement. Then it dips to my legs.

"No." He lets out a breath. "I've come to apologize for my response earlier. Thank you for taking care of Ayda."

I blink. Well I wasn't expecting that. I wait for him to start laughing but he doesn't.

"I'm sorry, I'm not sure I heard you," I say.

"You heard me perfectly well."

"Tom's very loud," I point out. "And I'm pretty sure I didn't. Say it again."

His lips twitch harder. He opens his mouth but no words come out.

"Oh come on," I say. "Apologies should be like proposals."

"In what way?" he asks. "They're nothing alike."

"You should mean them for one," I tell him. "And the person you're saying them to should actually get to hear them."

"And apart from that? What are the similarities?"

I shrug. "I mean if you want to give me an expensive diamond ring..." Of course I'm joking.

This time the corner of his mouth actually curls. Could this man actually be smiling? I wasn't sure it was physically possible.

"I'm very sorry for accusing you of not being trustworthy," he says, his eyes locked on mine. "And I'm very thankful that you took such good care of my daughter. Is that okay?" He doesn't sound like he cares if it's okay or not.

"I would have preferred the on one knee thing, but sure." I shrug. Tom finishes singing, and the silence echoes in the room.

"My sister would very much like to be friends with you," he suddenly says, his voice a decibel too loud.

"You want to arrange a play date for us?" I arch a brow.

"Of course I don't want to arrange a playdate. Autumn is my sister, and she's a little lonely here on the island. For some reason she likes you."

I can't help it, I laugh. "Why does that feel like criticism and not a compliment?" I ask him, though secretly I'm thrilled. I liked Autumn too. It would be nice to have somebody to talk to other than Lee, who as lovely as she is, can be a little too inquisitive.

"It wasn't supposed to be either. Just a statement of

fact." His gaze flickers over my tattoo, exposed right above the waistline of my shorts.

"And how do you feel about that?" I ask him. "Are you worried I'll lead her astray?"

"She's an adult."

"You don't treat her like one. You don't treat anybody like one," I tell him. "You seem to think you're the king of the island and we're all your subjects."

"King of the island?" He lifts a brow. "That's a very interesting way of describing me."

"How would you describe yourself?" I'm closer to him now. I'm not sure whether it was him or me that took a step toward the other. God, I hope it was him.

"I wouldn't." He shrugs. "Why would I? I'm not interested in being described."

"Because I know how you'd describe me," I say, my voice low. There's a crackle in the air between us.

"And how would that be?"

This time I do take a deliberate step toward him. He looks down at my face, his expression unreadable. He's so annoying. And I want to annoy him.

I try not to think about why I want to do that. Because that way madness lies.

"I'm not one of the good girls you're used to, am I?" I say. "I don't wear sweet little skirts or designer jeans. I don't talk about houses or babies or whether the polo club's ball will be a *Pretty Woman* theme this year."

He tips his head to the side, saying nothing, just listening. And I'm annoyed. By the way he treats me, by the way he thinks he can own this place when it belongs to me.

And the way my body responds when he's near.

This time he takes a step closer. He looks down at me, our gazes locking like they're ready for battle. His close proximity makes it hard to breathe. My heart starts banging against my chest, but I refuse to look away.

He can't intimidate me. And he won't be intimidated by me, either.

We're at a deadlock. And it's never felt so physical.

I part my lips to exhale and his gaze dips to my lips. He leans down and for one drawn out moment I think he's going to kiss me.

My breath catches. My heart pounds. His jaw twitches like it's on speed.

There's a sweet pulse between my thighs that I swear he knows he's causing. My body wants to rub itself up against him until the aching disappears.

My mind, though, wants to claw at his face.

It's a strange juxtaposition. One I'm not used to.

I lift my chin, my eyes screaming for my lids to close. I swear they're more dry than the desert. But I won't be the first to blink, I won't.

Then he lets out a long sigh and steps back, the weird connection between us breaking. I'm not sure whether to be relieved or disappointed.

All I know is that my skin tingles for him.

Running his fingers through his hair – like even an inch of it is out of place, he takes a long breath and frowns.

"Have a good day," he says, as though we didn't just have a battle of wills with our eyes. "I'll tell Autumn to call you."

"She doesn't have my number," I point out.

"No, but I do."

He has my number? I frown, because I didn't give it to him. How the hell has he gotten it?

Because he's King of the island, dumb dumb.

He's out of the door before I can say anything else. He

walks past the window to my right, and for a second he pauses and adjusts his pants.

Oh. So he did feel it too.

This is Tom's fault. Or his song at least.

And okay, it's a little bit mine too.

The only good thought is that I'm pretty sure I'll never see Hudson Fitzgerald again after that little exhibition. Which is a good thing.

Or at least, that's what I tell myself.

six

SKYLER

Lee can't stop laughing as I describe my latest encounter with *the man who thinks he rules the island*. Which I guess is a good thing, because I expected her to be appalled. To tell me I need to get away from this place before I upset all the rest of the locals.

Instead she makes me describe his expression in full detail as I hear her tapping on her laptop.

"Hudson Fitzgerald," she says, glee rounding her syllables. "I've got him. Ooh, he's a looker."

"He's an asshole."

"An asshole you practically slept with in your imagination," she says.

"I didn't sleep with him. I just refused to back down."

But Lee is too busy mumbling something to her baby to hear me. Instead she lets out a sigh. "Oh god, that's so sad."

"What's sad?" I ask her. "The fact I practically garroted him with his tie?"

"No, there's all these photographs of him carrying his daughter and trying to shield her face from the paparazzi in London. God they're assholes. I'd hate to be famous and live in that country. At least here we all drive around in cars and it's harder for them to get a picture." There's a click. "Ooh, there's an article about him. He had to fly to London last year to regain custody of his daughter."

"Custody from who? His wife?"

"No," Lee murmurs, and I know she's skim reading. Another of her superpowers. "According to this article, Ayda's mom died in a car accident shortly after she and his daughter arrived in England. And they weren't married so it complicated things. Her parents refused to let him have his daughter back after the accident, so he had to fight them through the courts."

My throat tightens because that is really sad. And also because I feel guilty. The man lost the mother of his child and then lost his daughter and I've been calling him an ass. Even if he is, I can feel some sympathy for him.

"She died in a car accident?" I ask.

"Apparently," Lee says, sounding distracted. I can picture her trying to feed the baby while scrolling through her laptop at the same time as talking to me. She really is a superwoman. And a good girl.

The type of woman that Hudson would probably hold in high esteem. Unlike my messed up self.

"Ooh," she says, sounding excited. "Wanna know how much his business is worth?"

"Not really," I tell her, because I'm already feeling inadequate. But then curiosity gets the better of me. "Okay, how much?"

"Fitzgerald Enterprises is made up of a conglomerate of businesses," Lee intones, like she's reading off her computer. "Though the exact valuation isn't known, estimates put the net worth of these enterprises at just over two billion dollars."

"I bet none of it's liquid," I say, trying to make myself feel better.

"Maybe you should ask him what he'll offer for the bar," she says. "Make him pay big."

"I'm going to head to bed," I tell her, not wanting to think about him getting his hands on this place. "I'm exhausted."

"Of course you are. All that salty air. Make sure you call me tomorrow."

She hates when I don't call. And I'm really terrible at remembering. But then I know if I don't she'll call me anyway.

"I'll try," I promise. We end the call and I stare at my phone for a moment. Then, in a fit of madness, I open up my incognito browser and type in Hudson Fitzgerald's name.

Photographs load up slowly. And in each one of them he's unsmiling, his eyes stormy and piercing.

Like he can see right through the screen to me ogling him.

I touch my lip stud, remembering the way he looked when he stared at it, his eyes the same vibrant color of the ocean.

He's rich, he's arrogant, and he doesn't know how to talk to people without antagonizing them.

So why is my heart beating like it's about to fly out of my chest?

* * *

HUDSON

"I hear you've been making friends with the locals," Parker says sardonically as I walk downstairs after reading Ayda a bedtime story.

Tonight it felt like I needed to make things up to her. I was an asshole earlier and she got to see the whole thing.

Parker is one of my closest friends – and also a business partner. We met in college during freshman year and for more than a decade he and West Abbott, the third of our triumvirate at college and our other investor, have been the only two non-family members I'd trust with my life.

And right now he's smiling at me like he's just won the lottery.

"She isn't a local," I say, annoyed that I'm having to think about Skyler Brown again. Because every time I do all I can think about is those lips and that metal stud and all the things I want to do with it.

That's it, the next time I go to the mainland alone, I'm going to get laid. It's been a long time and there's no way I'm getting involved with anybody on Liberty. I'll call up an old friend, one who knows the score, and fuck this annoyance out of myself.

Then everything can go back to the way I like it. Calm, normal. In control.

"She kind of is," Autumn says, breezing in. She and Parker have been married for six months.

I'm happy that they're happy. I'm also annoyed that they got together behind my back.

"Of course she is," Parker agrees happily, giving me the side eye to watch my reaction. "Her dad was Liberty born and bred, right?"

"Right," Autumn nods, and I know these two have been talking about this all evening. That's the problem with living on a small island, the gossip is fucking rife. And my sister thrives on it. "She's pretty though, isn't she, Hud?"

I let out a long sigh. "It's Hudson. And I guess, if you like that kind of thing."

Her lip curls into a grin. "I do, I really like her. I'm hoping to see a lot more of her."

"Just be careful," I say. "You don't know her."

"She's Wayne's kid. She's practically family," Autumn says. "And you should be nicer to her. If you want to buy the bar you're going to have to win her over."

"Of course I don't." I frown. "I'll make a good offer."

"Not everything and everybody can be bought," Autumn says pointedly, taking a seat on my sofa and kicking her shoes off. She crosses her legs into a yoga pose that tells me this isn't just a flying visit. She and Parker live in the lighthouse that came with the hotel. She's worked hard with an architect to make it perfect for them.

I just wish she was there right now, because I have work to do tonight.

"Is there something I can help you with?" I ask pointedly. "Or is this a social visit?"

Her grin widens. She's used to my mood swings. "Actually, I'm here to talk about Ayda's birthday party."

"What birthday party?" I ask. Ayda's birthday is early next month. But I haven't arranged a party.

Autumn rolls her eyes. "It's your daughter's sixth birthday. It's a big deal. You can't treat it like it's another day."

"I wasn't planning on treating it like another day," I tell her. "I thought we could go to the mainland. Maybe take her out for dinner."

"She's six, Hudson, not thirty-six. Where were you

planning to take her? To some five star swanky place where she'll have to behave like she isn't a kid?"

Truth is, I hadn't thought that far ahead. Maybe I don't let myself. Having fought so hard to get her back with me, I've learned to take each day as it comes. "A party really isn't a good idea," I say.

"Why not?" Autumn reaches into the bag next to the sofa and pulls out her tablet. "I've already started planning the theme. You know how into *Frozen* she is. I thought we could use that as the theme. Or maybe go a bit wider and do Princes and Princesses."

"It's spring," I point out. "Almost summer." As far as I can remember, *Frozen* takes place in winter.

"Exactly. It means we get to play with decorations and outfits. There's this company that sends princesses to run the party, with games and gifts and pretty cakes." She shoves the tablet toward me, but all I see is a sea of pastel blues and pinks. "I called them and paid a deposit."

"Isn't there a small problem?" I ask, because I really don't want to throw a party. I love my daughter more than I love anything in life, but I fucking hate being surrounded by people I don't know.

"What?" Autumn asks, tipping her head to the side and glaring at me.

"She has no friends to invite," I point out.

From the corner of my eye I see Parker watching us. He doesn't step in between us, mostly because he knows that my kid sister usually has me wrapped around her little finger.

"Of course she does," Autumn counters. "There are kids on the island. And adults too. They're all her friends."

"What if she doesn't want to have a party?" I ask, grasping for straws.

"What kid doesn't want a party?" Autumn runs her finger over her bottom lip, like she's cooking something up. "And anyway, aren't you always the first to tell us we should be treating her like a normal kid? And normal kids have parties, Hudson. With pretty dresses and pink cakes and other kids throwing up because they eat too much sugar." Autumn's on a roll now. "So stop being an ass and just say yes."

I let out a long breath. "Let me run it past Dr. Methi the next time I see him." I take Ayda to a psychiatrist for therapy on the mainland once a week.

"I already called him," Autumn says smugly, making me regret putting her on the list of approved people for Dr. Methi "He thinks it's a great idea. I've already ordered the invitations for us to hand out."

Parker coughs out a laugh, because he knows I've lost this battle. And maybe that's a good thing, I don't know.

I want Ayda to be happy. I want her to talk again.

"Okay," I say, already regretting it. "We'll have a damn party."

Autumn claps her hands together and grins at me. "Thank you. It's going to be the best day ever."

seven

SKYLER

I wake up the next morning determined to finish cleaning out my dad's closet, just as soon as I've hunted down a good cup of coffee. Not that I've even started going through it yet. My plan to get everything done is going a little awry, much to Lee's amusement.

Timetables and lists have never been my thing. On the plus side, I've been through every record Dad had and listened to each of them. I worked out how to change them over in the Wurlitzer so I get to dance in the bar alone to them, thinking of how he might have done the same.

In a weird way, I feel closer to him now more than ever. Maybe that's why I'm putting off cleaning out his clothes. I'll never get him back, but it just feels so final.

Because I'm the ultimate avoider, instead of facing my task I slide my feet into a pair of sandals that are decorated with shells and head up the road to the main town. The sun is out in her full late spring glory, her rays bouncing off the ripples in the ocean, making them sparkle like diamonds. By the time I reach Main Street there's already a healthy number of visitors here, all talking excitedly and popping in and out of the *Island Treasures Thrift Shop* and the *Liberty Book Nook*, two shops that I make a note to visit later when I have more avoiding to do.

But right now I head straight for the coffee shop that stands proudly at the top of the hill, my lips twitching when I see the sign hanging above it.

Brewed Awakenings is painted in swirly gold letters, with little beans scattered around on the sign. Whoever named it is a fellow pun lover at least.

The café is busy, filled with the hum of conversation and a radio playing softly in the background. The aroma of roasted beans is enough to set my blood racing in anticipation of caffeine.

"Hello," the familiar woman behind the counter says as I walk up. "What can I get you?"

"Hi," I say smiling at Eileen. She looks even older than I remember as she stands behind the counter, which isn't a huge surprise. Is the woman so poor she has to run a guesthouse and a coffee shop? Maybe Hudson Fitzgerald should concentrate on making the people of Liberty's lives easier rather than making mine harder.

"Hello." She doesn't smile back and my own grin falters. Oh, is she annoyed with me about Ayda? Did Hudson say something? Maybe the whole town hates me now.

Still, I'm nothing if not a trier. "Thank you for your help the other day with the little girl," I say.

Eileen frowns. "I have no idea what you're talking about."

Not only is she overworked, she's losing her memory.

"With Ayda Fitzgerald," I remind her. "You messaged Autumn for me when I found her."

"No I didn't." She sounds completely sure about that.

"You did." Now I'm starting to doubt myself. "You were on the guest house porch."

"I haven't been on that porch in years," she says. "Horrible place. So many bad memories."

Somebody behind me laughs softly. I turn and Autumn Fitzgerald stares at me with an amused gaze. "Hey," she says. "How are you doing?"

Not great, but I won't tell her that. Or that I think I might be the one losing my mind. "Um... in need of caffeine."

"Well I can help you with that, dear, if you'd just give me your order," Eileen says, sounding peeved.

"An iced latte, please." Because I've decided I should go for a walk to clear my head, and it's already warm outside. Spending too much time in the bar must be addling my brain.

"Of course."

"I'll have the same, Mylene," Autumn tells her.

Wait. What? "*Mylene*? I thought your name was Eileen."

Eileen – or Mylene – looks like I've just slapped her with a cold dead fish. "Never say that name in here." Her voice is almost a growl. Conversation in the coffee shop stops dead.

"What name?" I'm so confused now.

"It's okay," Autumn whispers, touching my arm with her warm palm. "Just get your coffee and I'll tell you."

When our coffees are ready, Autumn and I walk outside to sit at one of the white painted metal tables on the sidewalk. Autumn sits, crossing her legs, a smile still playing at her lips.

"Okay," she says, looking delighted that she can share

some gossip with me. "So Mylene and Eileen are twins but they haven't spoken to each other in decades."

I look back to see Mylene serving another customer. Surely this is a joke, right? A way to tease the newcomer.

"There are two of them?" I ask her, suspiciously.

Autumn nods. "Yes. Apparently, they left the island for a few months when they were twenty-one and when they got back they weren't talking to each other." She leans forward. "It's been almost forty years. They're both pretty stubborn."

"But they live on this tiny island." It's so weird. "They must see each other all the time." I point at the guest house, with the sign clearly visible. *Eileen's By The Sea.*

"They ignore each other completely. It's like they can't even see each other."

"And nobody's ever tried to reconcile them?"

"Oh hell no," Autumn says, taking a sip of her iced coffee. "They're both way too fierce and scary. We all just pretend it's fine."

I try to imagine not talking to Lee for forty years and the thought makes my chest feel tight. We can barely go a day. "That's so sad."

"Ah, they thrive on it. Just never get them mixed up again. Mylene will give you one chance, after that she'll probably poison your coffee." Autumn looks cheery about that. "Anyway, I'm glad I caught you. I meant to come over yesterday to say sorry about my brother." She wrinkles her nose. "Maybe I should stop talking to *him* for a few decades."

"You don't have to apologize for him." It's weird how my mouth feels dry at the mention of Hudson Fitzgerald. "He's a big guy, he can apologize for himself."

"He did say sorry, right?" Autumn asks. "Because he

told me he did, but I wouldn't put it past him to make things worse."

The memory of his half-assed apology and my stupid flirting make my cheeks feel hot. "Um, yeah. Kind of."

"Ugh, I knew he didn't." Her brows knit. "He's such an ass."

"Honestly, he did," I say quickly, because if there's one thing I don't want it's to bring Hudson Fitzgerald's fury down on me once again.

I like Autumn. She's funny and chatty and so easy to get along with. It's not her fault her brother is a grade A dick.

"He better have," she says grimly. "I do a lot for that man. He owes me."

"Do you watch Ayda a lot?" I ask, changing the subject because I really don't want to talk about her brother anymore. Every time I think of him I break out in hives.

"Yeah," she says, a soft smile pulling at her face. "We all try to help out. When Hudson isn't in meetings he has her with him. And she has tutoring a couple of times a week."

"She's so young for that," I say.

"She's almost six," Autumn says. "Most kids her age are at school. And Hudson's determined that her lack of talking won't hold her back." That soft smile is still there. Another thing we have in common, we're both doting aunties.

"Is that where she is today?"

"Oh no." Autumn shakes her head, nodding to the dock. "They're heading out on the ferry, see? It's her therapy day. She and Hudson go to the mainland for it once a week. They dropped me off here on the way."

I follow the direction of Autumn's gaze, to the Liberty Ferry at the end of the jetty, where Hudson is climbing out of the expensive car parked at the back, all black shiny metal and gleaming grilles. He lifts Ayda out of the backseat, swinging her into his arms and making her laugh loudly.

And then he laughs too and I swear my heart stops.

Hudson Fitzgerald knows how to laugh? *Seriously?* I wasn't even sure he knew how to smile.

But that's all I see because the next minute the boat is revving up, the crew untying the ropes and taking their positions.

I let out a long breath, wondering what I've got myself into by coming to Liberty. It's an island full of secrets. Twins who don't talk to each other, a little girl who doesn't talk at all, and the most attractive man I think I've ever laid eyes on who only scowls whenever I'm around.

And then there's my dad. The reason I'm here, even though I have no idea why he was so insistent I stay.

Maybe I shouldn't have come. I'm not sure anymore.

* * *

HUDSON

"Do you really think this party is a good idea?"

Dr. Methi, the psychiatrist who's been monitoring Ayda since we came back from England and moved to Liberty, lifts a brow at me. He practices on the mainland, in a pristine office at the top of a shiny steel-and-glass building overlooking the water.

"As I told your sister, I think it's a wonderful idea," he tells me. Nothing phases this man. Not Ayda still remaining mute after months of therapy. Or my outbursts when we're alone because I'm so damn frustrated that nothing is helping.

Today's session has followed the usual pattern. Ayda and I come in and either color together or play with Legos at the center of Dr. Methi's office as he talks to us. Then he focuses on Ayda for thirty minutes, where he interacts with her and asks her to point at pictures to show her emotions.

And then she gets sent out to color with his assistant while I sit here and am grilled about how my week has gone, because he has some stupid idea that I need therapy as much as Ayda.

The first week we came I tried to leave at this point, but he insisted that he couldn't treat her without treating me. If I wanted her to keep coming here I had no choice but to comply. He's the most highly recommended child trauma specialist within a thousand mile radius. My daughter will always get the best.

"I did have one thought though," Dr. Methi says, steepling his fingers so the tips are all touching.

I look at him like a drowning man looks at a life raft. "That we should do it next year instead?" I hate parties. I hate small talk and I hate having to be nice to people I don't like and I particularly loathe dealing with people who've been drinking too much.

And yeah, this is a kid's party, but I know that Autumn wants to invite adults too. I already saw a charge on my card for ten crates of wine.

He laughs like I'm joking. "No, this year is good. I just think you should be the one to go with Ayda to hand out invitations."

He has to be joking. "I'm too busy. Autumn can do that." It's her damn idea after all. The least she could do is help Ayda decide who's coming to this hellish gathering.

"She could..." he muses. "But from a therapeutic point

of view it would help Ayda feel more relaxed if she knows you want this party as much as she does."

"How do you know she wants this party?" I ask, because as much as I pay this man, I'm pretty sure he's not a mind reader.

"When I asked her about it she lit up." He shrugs. "And then she saw your expression and the light immediately went out."

Ah fuck. "She did?"

He nods. "She loves you. She wants to please you. I don't know if you realize how often she looks at you for approval, but I see it all the time. Maybe next week I'll video our session and show you."

My jaw tightens. "It's just been a bad week."

"How so?" Dr. Methi leans forward, suddenly interested. The man thrives off actually breaking through my barriers.

"Nothing. Just work and island issues." I cross my arms over my chest. "But back to the invitations, what if we just address them together? I have meetings all week."

"Do you think that would work?" Dr. Methi asks, turning it back on me. The asshole looks smug, because he knows the answer.

"I don't know," I say, pinching the bridge of my nose. Another fucking headache is threatening. "Isn't that *your* job to know?"

He says nothing for a moment. I look out of the window at the blue sky with little wispy clouds, wishing I was anywhere but here.

But I have to be here. Ayda needs it, and I need her to heal. To get over the trauma of being taken to a different country, losing her mom, and then being brought back here to a life she can barely remember.

Christ, I hate this. I hate that she's been through so much at such a young age. I hate myself for letting it happen. She's the center of my fucking world and I let her down.

"Is everything okay?" the doctor asks, his voice more gentle than I've ever heard it. "You seem more... tense than usual."

I bring my eyes back to his. Is he being serious right now? "Of course I'm tense. I'm running a multimillion dollar business. I have a daughter who won't speak, a sister who seems to think inviting strangers into my house to celebrate my daughter's birthday is a great idea, and a fucking woman who seems to have a personal mission to drive me to distraction."

The words come out in a stream of consciousness. Methi doesn't even lift his brows.

"What woman?" he asks.

"I'm sorry?"

"What woman is driving you to distraction? Are you seeing somebody?"

I frown. "Of course I'm not."

Immediately the image of her mouth comes into my mind. The way her lips were so fucking soft as she clashed eyes with me.

The way I got hard in response. Once upon a time I would have fucked her out of my thoughts. I'd have shown her that I'm not the stuffed up asshole she thinks I am.

But that was then. This is now.

Dr. Methi tips his head to the side. "It would be okay if you were. It might be good for you. And for Ayda, in time. I'd be very happy to work with you on the best way to introduce her to a new romantic attachment."

"I don't have any romantic attachments," I tell him

firmly. "And if I did, I wouldn't need to work with you on them." The mere thought sends ice through my veins.

"Maybe that's the problem," he murmurs. "Maybe you should be having attachments."

Jesus Christ. As if my week hasn't been bad enough. "How much do I pay you?" I ask him.

"I don't know," he says, not even blinking at my question. "But I can have my billing department resend you the invoices if you'd like."

This is the problem with an emotionally intelligent man like Dr. Methi. He knows exactly how to respond to me.

He'll never engage in a back and forth with me. He'll just diffuse the situation and move on. That's what he's trained to do. And it pisses me off.

In every battle we have, I'm the loser before we get started.

"There's no love interest in my life," I tell him, just to make myself clear. "The woman I'm referring to is the one who has inherited the bar I want to buy on the island. Ayda wandered off earlier this week and she ended up in the bar with her."

"Ah yes, your sister told me about that, too. When she called about the party. I hear Ayda was missing for a good while. How did you feel about that?"

"Annoyed. Afraid. Mostly annoyed."

"Why annoyed?"

"Because Autumn knew better than to let Ayda wander off."

"But the island is safe. You've made it that way."

Yes I have, as much as I can. I know nearly everybody who lives there. Plus the people who come to stay at the hotel are extremely rich and vetted. But it's not exclusive. Anybody can get on the ferry and arrive at their own whim.

In the summer it's full of tourists and I'm already uncomfortable about that.

"I didn't know about this woman coming to stay at the bar," I say. "I was blindsided."

"I imagine that made you feel uncomfortable."

"Mostly annoyed," I say, my throat feeling itchy.

"But Ayda was okay, yes?"

"She was fine."

"Autumn says this new woman is about her age. Is that right?"

"I guess so. Is that it? Can I go now?"

"This isn't a prison, Hudson," Dr. Methi says mildly. "You're always free to leave. Whenever you want."

"But it's not about what I want, is it?" I reply. "It's about what's best for Ayda. I don't come here for me, I come here for her. So I guess what I'm asking is if it's okay for me to leave now, and still bring my daughter back next week so that we can work on getting her talking again."

Christ, my blood pressure feels like it's peaking. I need to get some exercise. Hit the gym or go running.

Or fuck somebody until we both collapse on the bed, sated and spent. Like I used to, before my life became... *this*.

"Of course it's okay," Dr. Methi says. To my immense relief he stands and walks over to the door, gesturing me to follow. When I reach where he's standing, I wait for him to open it, but instead he puts his hand on my arm.

"It is okay for you to think of yourself sometimes," he says gently. "I know that you want Ayda to speak again. That's what we all want. But you've both been through trauma and you both need to heal."

He pats my arm softly, and for some reason that makes my throat feel tight. I'm not used to being touched. I don't like it.

I'm used to being the one in charge, in control. I prefer it that way, because then I know where I stand.

"Just be kind to yourself," he murmurs as he opens the door. "You deserve to heal as much as Ayda does."

As soon as she hears the door open, my daughter's face lifts from the page she's coloring and looks up at me. And then I see it, that fucking lit-up-face that Dr. Methi talked about.

The twist in my stomach tightens even more, but I ignore it, smiling at my girl as I walk toward her and pull her into my arms. She laughs – along with crying and coughing it's the only sound she makes, so it feels very damn precious. I hold her tight and she buries her face against my neck, the smell of her strawberry shampoo filling my senses.

"Ready to go?" I ask her.

She nods happily.

"Good." I glance at Dr. Methi. "Because we have work to do. Tomorrow we're delivering your birthday invitations."

He smiles at me, then turns and walks back into his office.

Dr. Methi 1. Hudson Fitzgerald 0.

The story of my life right now.

eight

HUDSON

We make the last ferry back to Liberty by the skin of our teeth. I had to make some business calls from the car after our therapy session and then we went to Ayda's favorite diner for dinner, where she proceeded to fall asleep over her half-eaten sundae. So I carried her back to the car and fastened her into her car seat and let her rest while I made the trip back to the dock. Once aboard, I made a couple more calls and replied to some emails that my assistant marked as urgent.

Ayda lets out a soft snore – another sound that isn't talking – and I look back at her to check that she's okay. Her eyes are closed, her eyelashes fluttering against her pink cheeks. She looks so damn peaceful it makes me feel wistful.

I don't think I've ever been that relaxed in my life.

Needing some fresh air, I open the door and climb out

of the car, inhaling the night ocean air. It's warm and salty and somehow centering.

From the corner of my eye I see Jesse wave at me. He's one of the island kids that stayed here – there aren't many of them. Most leave at the first chance. I know I did. I went to college then grad school and ended up in New York working for an investment firm before striking out on my own.

And one by one my brothers and then my sisters left too. Now Autumn and I are back.

"Nice night," Jesse shouts out.

"Sure is." I nod at him. I don't know Jesse that well. He's more Autumn's age than mine. But I know his family and I know they have their secrets the way all families do. But they're not my concern, not really.

"Gonna go get ready to moor up," he calls. "Last run of the night."

"Sure." I nod, taking one last breath of the freshest air before I climb back into the car and close the door softly so I don't disturb my kid. I look out of the windshield at the approaching island. The houses are all lit up in the center of town, but darkness surrounds it. In the distance, I can see the glow of the lamps that lead to the hotel, and to the right, the lighthouse.

Where Autumn and Parker are. Probably all cozy and in each others' arms. I push that horrifying thought out of my brain.

Bringing my gaze back to the main town in front of me, I see the light blazing in the living quarters of The Salty Dog.

Where *she* is.

If I close my eyes I can see her in picture-perfect detail. The dark, glossy hair that falls in a tumble of waves past her shoulders. The golden skin that comes from genetics, not a spray bottle or too many hours spent in the sun. And those lips that seem to taunt me no matter where I am or what I'm trying to do.

Especially at night when I'm trying to fall asleep.

"Just be kind to yourself."

Dr. Methi's words echo around my head. Right now I'm not sure if being kind to myself would be paying Skyler Brown to leave this damn island for good, or fucking her until we're both breathless and sweaty.

All I know is I don't like this feeling of being out of control. I don't like anything that pierces my strictly regimented life. My only concerns are Ayda and my family, everything else doesn't matter.

I'm so deep in thought that I don't hear the knock on my window until Jesse raps his knuckles on the glass a second time. I press the button to lower it, and he leans in, an easy smile on his prematurely sun weathered face.

"Hey," he says. "I meant to ask you, have you met her yet?"

"Met who?"

"Skyler." His eyes light up as he looks over at the bar.

I follow his gaze to The Salty Dog. "Yes. You?"

"Only when she got on the ferry over here. It was pouring that day so I didn't get a chance to say hi."

It dawns on me. "You didn't tell her?"

He shakes his head. "No."

"Will you?"

"Sometime." He gives me a tight smile. "Anyway, she seems nice, huh?"

"Yeah," I say. "Real nice."

We're almost at the dock now. I look pointedly at it and

Jesse wrinkles his nose. "Best go tie the ropes. Have a good evening."

"You too."

I look at The Salty Dog one more time as I start my engine up. And once the ferry is moored and I drive off onto the main road, I slow down as I drive past the bar.

She's inside. And I'm becoming stupidly obsessed about a woman I have no interest in apart from a fucking lip piercing that annoys me and a body that reminds me what I can never have.

But I can't help but wonder what *she's* doing inside.

Wishing I was in there, watching her. And yes, that makes me a fucking voyeur, I know that. Even if it is only in my mind.

* * *

SKYLER

"Hi," I say breathlessly as I walk into *Brewed Awakenings* a few days later, my thigh muscles protesting because I practically ran up the road to the coffee shop, mostly because I have to pass *Eileen's By The Sea* and I felt guilty knowing I'd be talking to her sister.

I have no idea how the people of Liberty have managed to cope with this bloody feud for so long without spontaneously combusting. Last night when I came back from a walk on the beach to clear my head I waved and called out to Eileen when she was passing the bar, only to realize it was Mylene when she pinched her nose between her thumb and forefinger as she passed Eileen's house.

"The usual?" Mylene asks me as I walk in, which is a

bit of a surprise because it's only the second time I've been in here. Are you even allowed to have a usual after one visit?

And yet I love that I have a usual. I've never lived anywhere long enough to have one before.

"Um, yes please." I hesitate, and then add, in case she has me mixed up with somebody else, "An iced latte please."

She gives me such a beaming smile that I start to wonder if there's a third twin. Or triplet. Because both Eileen and Mylene have been pretty short with me until now.

"I didn't realize you were Wayne's girl," she says. "You should have said something the other day."

I blink. "I thought everybody knew." I put my phone on the card reader, my bangles jingling as the reader beeps. "Who did you think I was?"

"Oh, one of Hudson Fitzgerald's fangirls," she says. "We get a lot of women visiting the island who are interested in him. He hates it."

Laughter bubbles up in my throat. "I'm definitely not one of those," I assure her. Then I see a photograph of him over her shoulder, along with a lot of others on the wall. She follows my gaze.

"Such a good man," she says. "He helped me with this place. I thought I was going to lose it, but then he helped me pay my debts and for the renovations. Now look at it."

I nod, not wanting to hear that he's a good guy. I much prefer thinking of him as the devil.

"And then there's what he's done for the other businesses on the island. He's our angel investor." She smiles. "That's why we make sure he's not stalked by all those wannabe rich girls. Did you know some of them post on that TickyTock?" she asks. "They're looking for a guy in finance."

"I had no idea," I tell her, trying not to laugh at her name for the video app.

Then I feel a warm hand on my shoulder.

When I turn, a tall sandy haired man is looking at me. His eyes look familiar as they crinkle with a shy smile.

"Skyler?" he says, his voice as shy as his expression.

"Yes." He has the kind of rugged face you can only get from working outside. "I'm sorry, have we met?"

"On the boat, when you came over."

Oh, he's the guy in the yellow raincoat from the ferry. That makes sense. I immediately feel myself relaxing because he's not after something. And I hate that I initially thought that but I've lived long enough to know that when a stranger approaches you they usually either want your body or want to con you out of money.

Often, both.

"I meant to stop by the bar to see how you're getting along, but time got the better of me. I had a gig on the mainland and then I had to work."

"A gig?" I ask, immediately interested. "What kind of gig?"

"I play the guitar and sing a little." He looks almost embarrassed. I can see the pink of his skin beneath the sandy scruff of his beard. "I used to play at The Dog before..." he trails off. "Anyway, hi. Have you settled in yet?"

I wrinkle my nose. "It's a work in progress, but it's fine." Truth is, I'm still going through Dad's stuff. Bit by bit. I can't stand to sort through things longer than an hour a day. It hurts, knowing that he bought these clothes to wear, not for me to bag them up to donate to charity.

The weirdest thing is his freezer. It's full of pizzas and

ready meals and every time I look inside I want to cry. He bought them fully intending to eat them and now he never will.

I won't either. It just feels wrong somehow. I'm going to have to throw it all away but it feels like a waste. I don't know what to do with it so I've left it. I haven't told Lee that because she'll think I'm some kind of over-sentimental idiot.

I probably am.

"But I don't know that I'm settled in." Mylene hands me my iced coffee, then pours a cup of drip for Jesse. "I guess I might never be. Depends how long I stay."

His brows pinch as though he doesn't like that answer. "I hope you do. I hope you open The Dog back up."

I blink, because the man is probably missing the money from his gigs. I've heard a few people speculating on when the bar will reopen. I guess it's important to the island. And the sooner I clean up the sooner I can sell it and the sooner everybody gets their favorite drinking hole back.

"I don't think I can reopen it," I say. "I don't have a liquor licence."

He tips his head to the side. "That's not difficult. The local ABC office is right over on the mainland. You just have to show them your documentation and pay a fee."

"ABC office?" I ask.

"Alcoholic Beverage Control. They issue all the licences for Liberty."

"Doesn't it take forever for them to process?" I ask. I don't know why I'm even considering it. Lee would kill me if I stayed here long term. So would Mom.

"Usually, unless you know somebody with some power there." He shrugs. "Hudson Fitzgerald got the licence for the hotel in three days."

Of *course* he did. "I don't know anybody there," I say. I don't know anybody anywhere. I don't even want to run a bar.

Do I?

"Speak of the devil," Jesse murmurs as we walk out of the coffee shop together. I see Hudson in the distance, one hand holding his phone to his ear as he barks something into the mouthpiece, the other holding his daughter's as she skips beside him.

I take a sip of coffee. "I don't think he'll be any help," I say to Jesse. "He wants to buy the bar. I can't see him pushing the licence through for me."

"He would if we all asked him to," Jesse says. And for some reason it makes me feel warm that at least one person wants me to stay. I don't think it's because he's attracted to me. Or at least I hope he's not. If he is, he's doing a good job of hiding it behind friendliness.

Don't get me wrong, he's a handsome man. Tall, muscled, with the kind of good looks you'd expect on a lumberjack in a Hallmark Movie. Once upon a time – okay most of the time – he'd be my type.

But there's no spark there. Unlike...

Hudson turns around, still speaking fast into his phone, and spots Jesse and me standing outside the coffee shop. His eyes wander over the clothes I'm wearing today – an ankle length brown and pink paisley skirt, with a white tank and a thick vintage leather belt I've cinched at the waist.

When his gaze reaches my face I give him a smirk. He doesn't smile back. Instead, he says something to his daughter and she pulls him into the bookshop on the other side of the road.

"I should go," I say, because that man always discombobulates me. "Thank you for being so kind," I say to Jesse. I think I needed it.

"You're… Wayne's kid," he says, stuttering over his words. "We loved him. And I know for a fact he loved you."

"You knew my dad well?" I ask. A lump thickens in my throat.

"Yeah." He nods, pressing his lips together like he doesn't know what to say next.

"Do you think…" I take a deep breath. "Could you tell me about him sometime?"

Those pale lips curl into a smile. "I'd love to."

"Great," I say. "Thank you."

"If you give me your number, I'll check my work schedule. I can bring those forms over for you, if you like?"

"Forms?" I say.

"The ones for the ABC licence."

Oh God, I'd already forgotten about that. "Sure," I say. "Great idea." I can always tell him I've changed my mind when we talk next. I take out my phone and we exchange numbers. He stands there for a minute like he's trying to make a decision.

Then he puts his coffee on an empty table next to us and reaches for me, folding me in his thick, muscled arms, burying his face in my hair.

The sudden embrace takes me by surprise. Which is stupid, because nobody on this island behaves the way I assumed they would. Still, there's a warmth in the pit of my stomach because this is the first physical contact I've had with anybody since I've been here.

I've always been a hugger. And this man is a natural one. I look up at him and smile and he grins back.

"Thank you," I say to him. "I think I needed that."

"Yeah." He nods. "I think we both did."

It's only when he walks away that I feel a weird prickle in my neck like I'm being watched. As I turn to the left, I see Ayda pulling Hudson out of the bookshop and pointing at me.

He says something quietly to her and she shakes her head, looking suddenly furious. It makes me smile, because she's so little yet I've never seen her look more like her dad than now.

Stubbornness is in her DNA.

She drags him across the road, and he reluctantly lets her, his eyes stormy as they meet mine. I've never seen a man like him be so tamed by a little girl.

When they reach me on the sidewalk she grabs a card from him and shoves it toward me until I take it from her and she beams, like she's accomplished her mission.

The card is pink with gold lettering. I lift it up to get a closer look at the foiled words shining out from the front of the expensive cardstock.

Miss Ayda Fitzgerald cordially invites you to her sixth birthday party.

The theme is Cool Princes and Princesses. Please come dressed appropriately.

* * *

HUDSON

"You don't have to come," I say to Skyler, when Ayda runs into the coffee shop to give Mylene her invitation. "It's a week away, you'll probably have left by then."

And I should be relieved at that thought. I *am* relieved. *Mostly*. Up close I can see a line of freckles on her shoulder. They look like a constellation. She tips her head to the side and her hair covers them up and I'm relieved.

"I'm planning to stay for a while," she says. "So I'll still be here."

Of course she fucking is. Why make my life a little difficult when you can make it a lot difficult? I think of the report I got back about her last week. About her transient lifestyle, her poor academic results, the way she dropped out of college and has never held down a job. But she also has no criminal record or anything that stains her past.

And I still fucking want her.

"Aren't you bored of being here?" I ask.

"Bored of learning about my dad?" she replies. "No, not at all. It's pretty here. I love the beach and the people are nice. Mostly." She smiles as she adds the last word. "And I love parties, so…I'll be there."

Ayda comes out right as I open my mouth to tell Skyler that I'll pay for her to stay away.

"Thank you for the invitation," Skyler says to Ayda, who's staring up at her like she's some kind of queen. "I'd love to come to your party. I can't wait to choose an outfit."

Ayda jumps up and down excitedly, then throws her arms around Skyler. And I feel that weird twinge in my chest again. I need to make an appointment with my doctor. I'm clearly having heart issues.

My phone starts to buzz and I see that it's our London office calling back. A deal we've been working on for months is on the verge of collapse and the head of investment needs my go-ahead to up the offer.

"Excuse me," I say, but neither my daughter or the woman who's driving me up the wall are looking at me.

Skyler is leaning down, whispering something in Ayda's ear. And Ayda nods, her eyes wide, like Skyler's just suggested they go to Disneyland.

"Fitzgerald," I croak into the phone.

"They rejected it," Damien, the head of our London office says.

"Then go for the final offer," I say, because we all know they can't do it without my say so.

"What if they reject that?" he asks.

"Then we walk away, but you call me right away and we'll work out how to fuck them over good and proper," I growl. "But they won't because they know they have no other choice."

It's only when I look up that I realize both Skyler and my daughter heard me.

"Sorry for swearing," I say quickly.

"It's okay," Damien says, even though that wasn't meant for him. "I'll keep you updated."

"You do that."

I take a deep breath. "Come on, sweetheart," I say to my daughter. "Let's go home. Autumn's taking you to see the horses this afternoon."

Instead of listening to me, my kid looks up and sees Eileen outside the guest house and snatches another invitation out of my pocket before I can point out what a bad idea that would be.

She runs past Skyler, who watches her open-mouthed, before she turns to me.

"Eileen and Mylene?" she says. "In one place?"

I pinch my nose between my fingers. Skyler is new and already knows what a bad idea this is.

"I fucking hate parties," I mutter. Her laugh is so breathy it sends a shot of desire right down to my dick.

"Well if I wasn't going to come before, I definitely am now," she says. "It'll be the party of the century, how could I miss it?"

"Maybe it'll rain," I say. She smells of damn flowery glades and it makes me want her even more.

"What you said about maybe staying a while, you were kidding, right?" I ask her.

She rolls onto her tiptoes until her mouth is close to my ear. I automatically reach out to steady her, my palms curling around her waist.

"In your dreams," she whispers. I turn to face her and her lips are so close to mine I can feel the warmth of her breath on my mouth. It takes all the restraint I have not to close the fucking gap and kiss this woman in the middle of the street. Because I want to kiss her. I want to dominate her. I want to show her she's playing with fire.

Thankfully she rolls back, pulling out of my hold and my hands hover in mid-air like they miss her already. I let out a sigh. Near miss averted.

"I'll see you at the party," she says, flicking her hair over her shoulder. "I'll be the one dressed as a slutty princess."

Yeah, I'm almost certain she will, just to drive me out of my mind.

Weirdly, it's the only part of the party I might actually look forward to.

nine

HUDSON

It becomes increasingly obvious during the run up to the party that I've been duped about it being just a casual kid's celebration. I'm in crisis mode thanks to the London deal, which means not only being in video calls at stupid hours of the morning, but going over to the mainland to catch a helicopter to New York to meet some investors who are getting itchy feet.

I've also had three calls from the local Alcohol and Beverage Commission wanting my opinion on an application for a liquor licence for The Salty Dog bar, as the main land owner of the island.

I told them I have no objection and I'd appreciate it if they pushed it through. Not because I'm interested in her, I tell myself, but because it will help the hotel if all the surrounding establishments are open for the summer.

She's not leaving. That much is obvious. So I've asked Autumn to resurrect the design plans I had her draw up when I planned to buy the place. If the bar is going to be open, I'd like it to have some luxury about it. She's promised to mention it to Skyler in a delicate way.

Whatever.

Despite everything on my mind I'm still present enough to notice the huge delivery trucks that pull up to the hotel every day, bringing food, decorations, two huge covered tents and a full-size fairground carousel with pink horses and carriages that makes Ayda jump up and down when she sees it.

"Can I have a word?" I ask Autumn, two days before the party when I get a message from Eden – our other sister – saying how sorry she is that she can't make it to the party of the year but she hopes to visit soon.

Autumn is wearing yoga pants and a t-shirt, with her ear pods in because she's obviously making calls as she works, and has that tablet that goes everywhere with her. She's currently talking to a man with Hal's Hog Roasts written on his t-shirt.

As soon as she clocks me standing there, a guilty look comes over her face. "Oh, hi." She takes a deep breath. "Can it wait? I'm kind of busy."

I tip my head to the side. "When can you fit me into your busy schedule?" It comes out more sarcastically than I'd hoped. But she knows how fucking overwhelmed I am. The thought of this weekend's impending doom is making my teeth grind.

She presses her lips together, like she's weighing her options. "Okay," she finally concedes. "I guess I have five minutes." She looks at the Hal's Hog Roast guy. "Can you start unloading in the back? Near the far tent. I'll be right out."

"Sure."

Taking her elbow, I lead her into the reception area of the hotel, then through the door marked 'private' where we have offices.

Mine is at the end, overlooking the ocean. I open the old oak door – restored from the original turn-of-the-last-century hotel, and usher my sister in.

"Exactly how long have you been planning this thing?"

"What thing?" she asks, her voice faux-innocent. She gives me that doe-eyed look she thinks works with me every time.

"This party. I might be a novice at event planning, but even I know it must have taken you a hell of a lot longer than fourteen days to arrange everything that's happening outside."

She shifts her feet. "I'm very good at organizing things."

"Not that good," I growl.

She looks like she's about to laugh. Why is it that the women I interact with think they can grab me by the balls and twist?

"Relax," she says, patting my arm like I'm a child. "I've got it covered. And I scored us some pretty great deals."

"How much is this costing me?" Truth be told, that's the least of my concerns. It's my kid's birthday, I have the money, I'm okay with paying whatever it takes to make her happy. But still, I'm pissed at being kept in the dark.

"I haven't totaled it up yet, but I set myself a really challenging budget," she says. "And Parker says that if you don't want to pay, we can. We're her godparents, after all."

"You're not a godparent, you're an aunt."

"Po-tay-to po-tah-to," she says. "Why are you such a grumpy pants? Do you know how hard I've been working at this? I've saved so much money by not hiring an event planner. And you'd better buck your mood up by the weekend. Everybody's looking forward to seeing you."

I blink. "Everybody?" My voice is weak.

As soon as I repeat the word she realizes she's messed up. She swallows hard, saying nothing.

"How many people are coming to this party?" I ask, my voice ominously low.

"Just family..." She pulls her lip between her teeth. "And friends. And some people that West and Parker suggested would be good to have here."

"You've invited business acquaintances to my daughter's princess party?" For fuck's sake. I hate being blindsided. Autumn knows this.

She looks over my shoulder at the door, like she's trying to figure out how quickly she can escape. "It kind of grew," she admits.

"Seriously," I tell her, because I'm losing it here. "I need to have a complete list of who's coming. You shouldn't have invited people without my say so."

"You didn't even want to hand out the invitations with Ayda," Autumn protests. "If I'd run the guest list past you, we both know that you'd have vetoed everybody."

"And where are they all sleeping?"

"We've booked rooms in the hotel and Eileen's guest house, plus a lot of them are coming by yacht and sleeping out there. The accommodation is all covered, Hudson." She's smiling again. "All you have to do is show up and enjoy it."

That's asking way too much. I let out an agonized groan.

My phone starts to buzz and I glance at the caller, seeing it's Damien in London reminds me that I was supposed to join a video call five minutes ago.

"You should go," Autumn says, looking delighted at the interruption. "By the way, you don't even need to worry about a costume. I've ordered a fabulous one for you."

"What costume?" I ask, as I quickly type out a message to Damien to tell him I'll be on our call in two minutes.

"For the party. Princesses and princes, remember?"

"Hell, no," I growl. "I'll go to the party, and I'll pay for the whole thing, and I'll even attempt to smile when I remember. But I'm not wearing a fucking costume."

She laughs. "We'll see." Then she turns on her heel and walks out of the room, her body language telling me she thinks she's won this round.

Probably because she has.

* * *

SKYLER

"Okay Slutty Princess," Lee says, her face beaming at me through the screen of my phone. "It's time for the big reveal. Show me what you've got."

"I told you, I'm not going as a slutty princess to a children's party," I say, rolling my eyes at Lee. "It was just something I said to rile the man up."

"You seem to enjoy riling him up," she says, looking suddenly interested.

"That's because he's an ass with a stick up his behind." Though I think we both know that's not the reason why.

"He has a great behind though." She sighs. "Have you seen how good he looks in a suit?"

"No," I lie. "And nor have you." Truth is I haven't seen much of the man for the past few days. A couple of times

I've seen his expensive car drive past and felt my heart race, but he hasn't stopped.

This is a good thing, I tell myself.

"I've seen photographs," Lee says.

"You're married, you're not supposed to be looking at other men," I point out.

"Shut up. And show me your costume. I'm dying to see it."

"Okay." I put the phone on the little shelf next to the mirror in the bathroom, angling it so that when I take a few steps back she can see a full-length image of me dressed as a princess.

I got the costume last week when I went over to the mainland to file the application for a bar licence at the ABC office. Jesse brought it over and helped me fill it in, and we'd ended up making an evening of it, playing songs on the jukebox and drinking cans of beer from the local liquor store – who told me they can't wait for me to re-open the bar because they're beyond busy and they can't keep up with the demand.

"Oh, my God," Lee says, starting to laugh. "That's not what I expected at all. Where's all the pink ruffles and tiara?"

"You really think I'd wear pink?"

She's grinning at me. "I guess not. But you were wrong about one thing. You look super slutty."

"I do not." My mouth drops open. This outfit is far from slutty. It's powerful and yet pretty. It has 'not taking shit from anybody' written all over it.

Not literally. It's a kid's party. But it sends the message, or at least I hope it does. And to a certain person.

The top half of the dress is a leather bodice, laced tight at my waist and sides, and so snug at the breasts that they're practically lifted up to my chin. The skirt is made of a delicate cream cotton that skims my hips and falls gently to my ankles. My hair is down, a leather band – my crown – tied across my brow.

"A Warrior Princess," Lee says approvingly. "I wish I could be there when you walk into that party."

"I wish you could be too," I say. Because I miss her face.

"But that ferry guy – Jesse – is taking you, right?"

"He is." We've hung out a few times over the last week. And when he heard I was going to the party, he offered to drive. He has to leave early, but assured me that there are shuttles running from the hotel to the ferry every half hour, so I can jump on one of those to get home.

There's a rap at the door, and I grin at my sister. "Speak of the devil. I have to go."

I grab my bag from the counter then rush to open the door. Jesse is waiting on the step for me. A huge grin pulls at his lips as he takes my outfit in.

"You look amazing. Like that woman on that TV show in the nineties. I've seen reruns."

"You don't look bad yourself," I say. "Flynn Ryder, right?"

"You know him?"

"I used to nanny for a little girl a few years ago. I can't tell you how many times I've watched *Tangled*."

I pull the door closed behind me and lock up. Next week, if I hear back from the ABC office, I'll need to start getting everything ready to open the place back up. I'm still not sure if I'm doing the right thing, but I'll worry about that tomorrow.

Jesse's car is an old rusty clunker that apparently belonged to his mom before he bought it off her. I like that it's unpretentious. Just like him.

"So have you been to a party at the hotel before?" I ask as he drives along the country lanes out of the main town, toward the less populated part of the island, which he tells me all belongs to the Fitzgerald Company.

"Not for years. Or that I can remember," he says. "Back when Hudson and Autumn's dad lived here, he used to throw huge parties all the time."

"What happened to him?" Autumn hasn't mentioned her dad, even though she's popped into the bar a few times to say hi in the past week. She wants us to get together for a girls' night soon. She also says she has some ideas for the bar which sound intriguing.

"He died," Jesse said. "But by that time he had no money left. Lost the whole island gambling."

"He lost the island?" I frown. "How much of it did he own?"

"Nearly all of it. His great-great-grandfather won it in a poker game back in 1896. He built the original hotel and renovated the captain's house where Hudson lives. And for about a hundred years nothing changed. Their dad got married, had six kids here, and then he got into a gambling spiral. His wife left him, he lost the island, and he never really recovered."

"I didn't know that."

"Hudson always wanted to buy the place back. He spent years making so much money it was coming out of his ears so he could do it. A couple of years ago it came up for auction and he snapped it up. And here we are."

I look up, realizing he's talking about *our* journey, not Hudson's. We've stopped behind a line of cars entering the gates to the hotel. Town cars, expensive sports cars, and the occasional rusty sedan like Jesse's, which I assume belong to islanders who are invited to the party.

I take a deep breath, readying myself, because I'm not great in crowds. I'm not great with people at all, really. And one thing's for sure, I'm really terrible when it comes to the unsmiling, handsome host of this party.

I have a feeling it's going to be a long day.

ten

HUDSON

There are people everywhere and the party hasn't even officially started yet. Not just staff – though Autumn has hired a whole army of them, thank god, because I've seen the full guest list and it's huge. But my family and closest friends arrived last night, and our close-knit band are together having one glass of champagne before the party officially begins.

I look around, my throat tight, because I'd lay down my life for each and every person here. There's Autumn and Parker, of course. But Autumn is too busy adjusting Ayda's braid to drink her champagne. Ayda is dressed as Elsa from Frozen – though a brunette version, because she tried the wig on and hated it.

"You look like you could do with a whole magnum of champagne to cheer you up," West murmurs. He's flown in from LA to be here. Which is a minor miracle because he's the only man I know who has more meetings than I do.

"Just trying to get in the party mood," I mutter, taking a big mouthful of my champagne.

"Don't worry, I brought someone to cheer you up. Her name is Sylvie. I think you'll like her." West gives me a grin.

"You brought a date for me to my kid's party?" I frown, not liking that one bit.

"She's here as my plus one. But don't worry, she's very sweet. She loves kids. She's from a good family. Just your type." He winks. "And it's time, my friend."

I never should have told him how long it has been since I've touched a woman. I open my mouth to tell him I can manage my own love life, thank you very much, when I see my brother, Asher, staring at something to my right with such an intense look on his face it makes me jump.

All of us are dressed up to one extent or another. Autumn and her best friend, Francie – who also arrived from the mainland for the party – are in full Disney princess regalia, and West had gone full Prince Charming because the man can pull anything off.

Parker, who I know has been fighting with Autumn as much as I have, finally conceded to wearing a pair of blue dress pants and a brocade jacket, so he looks a little like Prince Charming to Autumn's Cinderella.

Asher and I, on the other hand, have had the same idea. We're both wearing suits – because we decided to come as Prince William and Prince Harry.

Basically, we look normal. Or we did until Autumn, who can read us like a book, gave us crowns to go with our designer suits.

Asher's is in his hand at the moment, because he hates the damn thing as much as I do. He's still staring past me with that dark gaze though. And when I see what he's staring at, I frown. Because it's not what, it's who. Francine Salinger. My sister's best friend.

She's part of our extended family, the same way West and Parker are. But I have no idea what she's done to make Asher look like he wants to kill her.

"Okay, people are starting to arrive," Autumn says, patting Ayda's face. Her eyes are shining with excitement. I hate to admit it, but Autumn was right, this party is exactly what my daughter needs.

I have a natural inclination to keep her safe from harm, but I know that can lead to isolation.

Autumn puts her hand to her ear and nods, and that's when I realize she's got an earpiece in. Like some kind of damn Secret Service agent, she murmurs back and stands up.

"Hudson, you need to get to reception to welcome your guests," Autumn tells me. "Ayda, you can come with me, we'll go meet the Disney Princesses," she says to my daughter, because I've paid only god knows what to bring a whole hoard of them over from the mainland to mingle with the kids. "Parker, Asher, West, can you make sure the guests are given drinks as they come in?"

All three of them grin. Being next to the drink servers isn't exactly a hardship. "Sure," West says, winking at me. "Let's go, fellas."

I take a deep breath, walking out of the office to the reception area, where I'm shocked by the number of people who are already milling inside. Luckily, we have enough staff to point them to the ballroom and the double doors beyond which lead to the gardens, where the carousel is running, the bouncy castles are inflated, and a band is playing Disney music from the stage set up next to the dance floor.

For the next half hour I'm greeting locals with their kids, and friends and business acquaintances from all over, who gush about how beautiful the island is, how lucky I am to own this place, and how they'd love to come back to visit when things are quieter.

A blonde wearing a short black dress with a heart neckline, a thick choker on her neck, and sheer tights walks in. Her hair is brushed back from her face, and her heels are like daggers.

"Hi," she says, walking straight up to me. "You're Hudson, right?"

"Right," I murmur.

"I'm your mother," she says. I frown and she giggles.

"Okay, I'm Princess Diana. In her revenge outfit. The one she wore after Charles admitted he was unfaithful." She shifts uncomfortably. "West said you were dressed as William. Her son." She holds out her hand. "I'm Sylvie Armstrong."

Oh fuck. The woman West talked about. And yeah, he's right, she's just my fucking type. A cool blonde, obviously well brought up. And with a killer body.

And I feel absolutely no attraction toward her.

"It's a pleasure to meet you," I tell her.

"And you. Is your daughter here?" She looks around.

"She's with my sister in the gardens." I look at her lips, waiting to feel a reaction. Or at least a stirring. There's nothing.

Dear god, I hope I'm not broken inside. I've always had a healthy sex life. Or I did until my life twisted into what it is now. Sure, I'm discreet but I'm a fucking man.

"I can't wait to meet her. I think you know my father."

It's clicking now. "Your dad is Martin Armstrong?" One of the wealthiest men on the east coast. I've done a lot of business with him in the past. He's in his sixties, and from the looks of it Sylvie must be in her early thirties.

"That's right. We've met before, but you probably don't remember. At one of his parties. We have a lot of mutual friends."

"I'm sure we do," I say. "Half of them are probably here."

She laughs, her eyes crinkling. "I know you're going to be super busy, but if you have a chance later, it would be great to get to know you better." She leans forward to kiss my cheek at exactly the same moment my eyes land on a pair of perfect lips and a silver lip stud and my whole body tightens in response.

Skyler Brown walks in, her stride so damn sassy it makes my dick weep. She stands out like a sore thumb in the sea of pastel princesses, because she's wearing some kind of dark brown leather bodice, laced so tightly it pushes her breasts up so high that I swear she's a breath away from a wardrobe malfunction.

Her skirt is white and gauzy – so gauzy, in fact, that I can see the outline of her legs through it. It takes every fucking ounce of effort I have not to look to see if she's wearing panties.

"Excuse me," I murmur to Sylvie. "I should go greet my other guests. I'll see you at the party."

"It's a date," she says, looking happy at my words.

But I barely hear her over the rush of hot blood that drums in my ears and pumps to my groin. How could I ever have thought I might be dead inside.

I'm fucking alive and kicking. And desiring.

Striding over to where she's standing, I nod at Jesse, who's dressed as Flynn Ryder, which was one of the outfits Autumn tried to persuade me to wear.

But it's Skyler I'm looking at. Skyler who is looking straight at me, her eyes a challenge, her lips curled into a taunting smile.

Fuck, I want her. Like I've never wanted anything else before. I want to make her come so hard the smile melts from her lips, replaced by her screaming my name.

The need is getting almost impossible to ignore.

"You promised me slutty princess," I murmur, as Jesse walks off to chat with somebody else.

Her smile widens into a grin. "At least I'm dressed up. What are you dressed as? Let me guess. Designer business man who needs a personality transplant?"

I grin. "Prince William, actually."

"Close then." She runs the tip of her tongue over her top lip. I've never met a woman so unknowingly sensual.

"And who are you?" I ask her, mesmerized by that mouth.

"Xena, Warrior Princess."

"Of course you are." I can't help it, I smile back. Because there's no way this woman would have come as a Disney princess like all the other women – and girls – here.

"It's suits you."

"Is that a compliment?" Her brows lift. "Excuse me while I faint."

"I'm royalty today," I tell her. "I have to be nice to everybody."

"It's a shame, isn't it? You should have come as Henry the eighth. You could have ordered all the women to have their heads chopped off."

"That's one way of getting the party to finish early," I say. "A missed opportunity."

She tips her head to the side. Her dark hair shines beneath the lights of the receptions' chandeliers. She has a leather crown tied across her brow and around to the back of her hair. "You know," she says softly. "You're kind of fun when you take that stick out of your ass."

"I'm not sure whether that's a compliment or criticism," I reply.

"Maybe it's both."

My gaze dips to her chest. Her breasts look magnificent. My fingers twitch with the need to trace the swell of them.

"Well thank you. And fuck you."

She laughs harder. "Always a pleasure."

"You ready?" Jesse asks, coming back to take her arm. He smiles at me. "Hey, Hudson."

"Hey Jesse." I nod at him.

"Sure, I'm ready," she says, looking at me once more. Her eyes are dark, the same as mine.

Jesse walks off, and she goes to follow, but before she gets too far she turns back to me, putting her hand softly on my chest.

"By the way," she says, her voice so low I have to lean down to hear her properly. "I'm not wearing any panties. So I guess that counts as kind of slutty."

eleven

SKYLER

"What did you say to him?" Jesse asks, as we walk out into the expansive grounds of the hotel, Hudson glaring after us. A huge, perfectly tended lawn stretches out into the distance, eventually ending at the cliffs that border the Atlantic Ocean. Because it's a kid's party, a huge fence has been erected to stop any children from running too close to the edge.

"Nothing," I reply, because I'm pretty sure Jesse would think I'm an idiot for taunting Hudson Fitzgerald. Heck, *I* think I'm an idiot. I don't know what it is about the man that makes me behave like this.

Like a brat.

I'm not usually so mocking. I like to think of myself as a nice person. But with him I feel... I don't know. Judged, I guess. And like an errant child, I play into it to make him more annoyed.

Jesse gives me an interested look, but says nothing

more because we're both too busy looking around the grounds, our mouths opened in awe. There are stalls serving cotton candy and sugar-fragrant funnel cakes, along with non-alcoholic punches and ciders for the kids. Servers are carrying around harder drinks for the adults – champagne and mimosas – plus there's a bar in the corner serving beer, and presumably later, liquor for the adult party.

But it's the entertainment that's breathtaking. Not just the band, or the pretty princesses and princes who are mingling with the children, hugging them, having photos taken, but also the carousel at the center of the party. Like a real, full-size one you'd see at a fairground.

It's painted in pastels, with horses who look haughty and gold-plated carriages that little girls and boys are squeezed into, looking delighted as the carousel turns.

"I'm going on that later," I tell Jesse and he grins.

"You want a drink first?" he asks as a server approaches us.

"Sure."

He grabs a glass of champagne for me and a mimosa for him, and we clink our glasses together. "Listen, there's something..."

"Here you are!" Autumn walks up to us, interrupting his flow. His brows knit and for a second I wonder if he was about to ask me out.

"Hi," I say to her, grateful for the interruption. Next to her is a pretty woman dressed as Belle.

"This is Francie, my bestie. Francie, this is Skyler. I told you all about her."

"I'm so happy to meet you," Francie says, leaning forward to hug me. "I've heard so much about you."

"All good I hope."

"Absolutely." Francie grins. "And Autumn is a great judge of character."

"Francie is here for a few days," Autumn adds. "We were wondering if you're up for that girls' night before she leaves. Maybe on Monday? We can drink, eat, and trash talk men."

"That sounds like a plan," I reply back.

"That sounds like my cue to leave," Jesse says and we all laugh because we kind of forgot he was still here.

"You don't count as men," Autumn says.

"Thanks. *Not*." He wrinkles his nose.

"Seriously. You're one of us," she says, her eyes crinkling as she smiles at him. "I bet you can trash talk like the rest of us."

"Not at a kid's party," he says.

"Speaking of kids, where's Ayda?" I ask, looking around. Because I have a huge soft spot for that little girl. I put her gift on the table at the other end of the lawn when we arrived, but I'd still like to say hi to her.

"Over there." Autumn points, and I see her on the dance floor with some other kids. They're all moving to the sound of "Circle of Life" and they look so sweet it makes my heart clench.

"Are they her friends?" I ask, as one little girl grabs Ayda's hand to dance.

"They are now," Autumn says. "I miss being able to make friends like that."

Ayda looks up, her lips curling into a smile when she sees me. She runs over and throws her arms around my hips.

"Ooh, she likes you," Francie murmurs. "She's never hugged me like that."

"Me either," Jesse adds.

But I'm too busy hunkering down and looking at Ayda's pretty dress to acknowledge them.

"Look at you! You look exactly like Elsa. I love your braid." I run my hand over it and she grins. "Are you having a good birthday party?" I ask.

She nods, then she looks up at Autumn before back at me.

"What is it, sweetie?" Autumn asks. "She has the look on her face when she wants something."

Ayda bites her lip then takes my hand in her tiny fingers, using her other hand to point at the dance floor, where her new friends are now dancing to "I Just Can't Wait to be King".

"You want to dance?" I ask her.

She nods, then pokes my stomach and points at the dance floor again.

"You want *me* to dance with you?" I clarify.

This time her nod is emphatic. I look up at Jesse, Autumn, and Francie. "I guess I'm going dancing," I tell them.

"Have fun," Autumn says, though I can tell by the way her eyes crinkle she's pleased.

"I'll find you later," I tell them all, as Ayda drags me away.

"Don't forget about our girls' night," Francie calls after me.

"I won't," I promise, practically running to keep up with Ayda. When we get to the dance floor, the music has changed again. This time it's "We Don't Talk About Bruno", and I love the song so much that I start singing, taking Ayda's hands in mine as we both dance our little hearts out.

Then I sweep her into my arms and swing her around and she giggles out loud, enough to make my eyes widen.

She curls her arms around my neck, hugging me tightly as we dance. And my skin prickles, as though somebody is watching us.

* * *

HUDSON

"Who's that?" West asks as he looks over at the dance floor we had erected in the center of the lawn.

I swallow hard, watching as Ayda smiles up at the woman I can't stop fucking thinking about, the two of them swinging around. She takes Ayda's hand and twirls her and my girl cracks up as she almost ends up on the floor.

For a fleeting second, Skyler's eyes meet mine and her mouth parts.

"Skyler Brown," I grunt.

He blinks. "Who is she?"

"She's Wayne's kid. He left her The Salty Dog when he died."

His eyes widen. "Oh that's where I recognize the name. You didn't say she was hot as fuck." He watches her lift her arms up and roll her hips in time to the music. Ayda does the same.

"Because I didn't notice," I lie.

He laughs. "You're a dad, you're not fucking dead. Of course you noticed. Every hot blooded male around here is staring at her right now."

I frown, taking a look at the men milling around the party. Business acquaintances, locals, a few investors that wanted to come here and experience the island and hotel for themselves.

They're all watching her. A shot of hot jealousy rushes through me.

"She's not my type," I remind him. And that's not a lie. "Anyway, apparently you're in charge of my love life at the moment." Yeah, I'm still pissed at that. Twice I've caught Sylvie staring at me. I'm going to have to let her down gently. Especially since I do business with her father.

"Have you persuaded her to sell the bar?" West asks, smoothly changing the subject.

My jaw hardens. "No. She has this idea that she wants to run it herself. She's applied for a liquor licence."

He starts to laugh. "Oh shit, she's pretty and she plays hardball." He looks over at the dance floor again. "She has the most magnificent tits."

"And she's completely off limits."

He looks amused at my warning. And yeah, it does sound like a warning. "You sound very interested for a man who says she's not his type."

"I want her to sell me the bar and get the hell off the island," I tell him. "I don't need complications."

I can't keep being distracted this way.

"You should probably get in a better mood," West murmurs. "I spy old man Harrison walking this way."

Stanley Harrison. A legend on Wall Street. One of our biggest investors.

I paint a smile on my face and pull my gaze away from Xena fucking Warrior Princess.

"Stanley," I say, holding my hand out for the older man to shake. "Thank you for coming. And I love your outfit. Let me guess, Good King Wenceslas?"

And as I talk to him, my eyes are on her the whole time. She's fucking mesmerizing.

twelve

SKYLER

The afternoon passes in a blur of appetizers and new faces, along with a glass or two of champagne. Every now and then my gaze catches Hudson's and the two of us have a little staring battle. It's weirdly sexy.

By the time evening arrives, the party slowly morphs into a more-adult focused event, complete with non-Disney music and the disappearance of the paid Disney princesses who depart on their boat. And I'm feeling a little intoxicated.

Jesse comes over and tells me he has to leave, too. He starts work at six in the morning and there's a strict sobriety rule, so I walk him to his car and hug him tight.

"Maybe I should go home too."

"Don't be boring. I need you to report back later about the debauchery," he tells me. "Who ends up kissing who on the dance floor, who throws up in the lawn. Whether Mylene and Eileen come to blows."

"I expected that to already happen," I confess. But somehow Autumn – who has the complete knack for party organizing – has kept them apart. She's even got a timer set on her phone for making sure that Eileen takes the shuttle home an hour earlier than Mylene.

She showed me the whole schedule on her tablet screen earlier. The amount of planning she put into this sends shivers down my spine. I can't even plan what I'm having for breakfast tomorrow.

Jesse drives out of the hotel parking lot and I walk back into the reception area, coming to an abrupt halt when I see Hudson talking to the woman dressed as Princess Diana again.

She's laughing at something he said, her fingers casually tracing the lapel of his suit jacket, though I know enough to tell there's nothing casual about it. And suddenly all those gazing battles seem juvenile.

Rolling onto the toes of her stupidly high heels she whispers something in his ear, her lips curling like a smug cat who just found a vat of cream. Hudson nods, murmurs something back, and she laughs again.

God, she's acting so obvious. And I'm so stupidly jealous it's not funny. There's a twist in my stomach I hate so much.

What's your problem? Are you the only one allowed to tease him?

Yes, yes I am. I'm not an idiot, I know there can never be anything between us. He's him and I'm me and we're so different it's not funny. But seeing this woman – who's completely at his level – flirt so effortlessly, and him act like he's enjoying it.

It makes me want to throw something.

Instead, I act like the fool I am and stomp through the

reception area loud enough for the two of them to stop murmuring sweet nothings and look at me.

"Don't let me interrupt," I say. Then I look at Princess Di. "But you should know, he may look pretty now, but he turns back into Shrek at midnight."

She laughs and he turns to look at me, those dark eyes scanning my face.

I don't let my gaze get caught by his this time, as I try to sidle past them with some level of dignity. But instead – because the world hates me – the tip of my boot hits the corner of one of the velvet brocade sofas that fill the reception area and I lose my footing. My whole body launches forward as I fly through the damn air and land straight down on my face on the marbled tiles.

"Shit," I groan, willing the tiles to swallow me up right now.

"Oh my God, are you okay?" Princess Di clacks over. I feel her shadow come over me.

"Skyler?" Hudson murmurs, hunkering down next to me. "Are you bleeding? Jesus, let me look at you."

I blink, completely dazed. "What?"

"You tripped. Let me look at your face."

"No need." I sit up, then scramble to my knees because I need to get out of here, *now*. "I'm fine. Just a little trip." Somehow I manage to push myself up to my feet without falling back over, because my head is so damn dizzy from the fall. Then I go to walk away. Okay *run*.

Because I can deal with many, many things. But embarrassing myself in front of Hudson and the woman he's almost certainly going to fuck later isn't one of them.

I nearly make it out into the garden – where a couple are eating each other's faces in front of the roses – when a hand wraps itself firmly around my wrist, causing me to skid to a halt.

Some kids party this is turning out to be.

When I turn around, I'm feeling furious. My eyes clash with his. "What do you want?" I ask him. I can deal with him disliking me. But I don't like the look of concern in his gaze at all.

"To see if you're okay."

"I'm fine. I told you I'm fine." I try to pull away.

He sighs, sounding exasperated. "Come with me."

"Where?"

"To my office. Let me check you over."

I look around for Princess Di. "Where's your friend?" I ask, trying – and failing – not to sound bitchy.

"Gone back to the party. Now come with me and let me check you out."

I open my mouth to argue with him, but all that comes out is a soft sigh. I'm tired, I'm embarrassed. And the energy to fight him has disappeared.

Hudson keeps a hold of my wrist as he leads me through a door marked 'private - authorized persons only', then walks me down an empty and dully-lit corridor toward a heavy oak door at the end. He punches in a code and pushes it open, then pulls me inside, flicking the light switch with his free hand.

Then the door slams closed behind me and I'm completely alone with this man.

He's so damn tall I have to incline my head to look up at him. And when I do, all I see is his scowl. He's staring down at me like he hates me.

Of course I stare back. For a moment there's silence – save for the hot thud of my pulse as it rushes through my ears.

I clench my thigh muscles, trying to ignore the way my whole body needs him.

"We have a little problem," he finally says, breaking the silence.

I blink. "We do?"

His gaze dips to my dress, where it's pushing my chest up so high I can practically feel my breasts grazing my throat. Then pulls it up to look at my lips.

I part them, letting out a soft breath. This man is so overwhelming it's hard to breathe.

"What kind of problem?" I ask him.

"I think you know."

"Do I?" I feign innocence.

He won't stop looking at me. His body is only a breath away from mine. Somehow I've managed to back up so my back is against the door.

There's nowhere to run. And I'm not sure I want to.

Then he closes the gap between us, his hard, muscled body pressing against mine.

His fingers graze the underside of my chin, lifting my head up.

"Are you okay?" he asks, his voice low.

It takes me a minute to remember my spectacular fall. "Yes." I nod. "No permanent damage." Then I give him a weak smile. "Nothing more than there already was."

He drops his head like he's relieved, which is quite frankly boggling. His brow presses against mine and I can feel the warmth of his breath as he exhales. Can smell the edge of whiskey tracing it.

"What kind of problem do we have?" I whisper to him. My heart is slamming against my chest at his nearness. There's a steady thrum of appreciation between my thighs at his proximity. At the smell of him.

The damn masculine energy that exudes from him.

He doesn't answer. He just stares at me, his eyes even narrower, like he's sizing me up. His fingers are still under my chin, his thumb grazing my jaw.

And I realize exactly what problem he's talking about. I can feel it pumping through my veins.

"You don't want this," I tell him. "I'm so not your type."

"What is my type?" he asks.

"Princess Di."

The corner of his lips quirk. "The original or the fake one?"

"The one who stares at you like she wants to eat you for breakfast. The one who speaks properly, who looks like she's a walking wet dream of a bank balance." He reaches down to trace my clavicle – from the center of my chest to my shoulder – and I swear I've never been so turned on before in my whole life.

"She's a good girl," I whisper. "She won't embarrass you, or dress wrong, or get a piercing in her lip or a tattoo on her hip."

His fingers dip to the edge of my leather bodice, leaving a trail of fire across the swell of my breasts.

"I'm not like her, Hudson," I say. "I don't wash my dishes right after I've eaten. I don't make my bed most days. I'd drive you up the wall within a minute."

His breath catches.

"I think I can handle you," he murmurs.

The words feel like the softest of knives to my heart. Like a threat and a promise. The truth is, I believe him.

I'm the one who can't handle this. Yes, I put on a good game face. I pretend I don't care. But I've never been one for a casual relationship. For fuck buddies or anything else that doesn't involve emotions.

Out of the two of us, I figure I'm the one who'd get hurt here.

And yet my body doesn't get the memo. Sliding my hands between his jacket and shirt, I feel the warmth of his skin as it leeches through the cotton. And then, because I'm an idiot who has no idea of self preservation, I push the jacket off him, as he pulls off his own tie, then unfastens the top two buttons to give himself room to breathe.

I can see the dip at the bottom of his throat as it meets his ribcage. I want to kiss it, so I do, leaning forward, tasting his skin.

If I thought my heart was pounding before, it's pretty much launching itself on a suicide mission against my ribcage now. My breath is short, my legs are weak, pleasure is pooling between my thighs as he leans down to softly kiss the skin beneath my ear.

"Hudson..."

"Hush." His lips are soft, teasing. "Unless you want me to stop."

I do. I don't. I just... God he knows how to tease. Slowly he kisses his way along my jaw until his lips are a breath away from mine.

"I want to fuck you," he murmurs, kissing the corner of my mouth. "I want to make you come so hard it'll split your soul in two."

Dear God! Before I can respond his lips press against mine, and my whole body heats up in appreciation. My fingers curl around his shirt to steady myself, as he moves his mouth, kissing me softly at first.

Then hard, his mouth opening, our tongues colliding, his hands caressing my hips, my waist, my ass. I hook my arms around his neck, kissing him back like my life depends on it, arching my back until I feel his hard ridge of excitement pressing against me.

The man is big in every way.

I run my hands up his shirt, feeling the ridges of muscles on his abdomen, then the tight points of his nipples beneath the white cotton. He groans as my fingers graze them, the rumbling from his throat sending another shot of pleasure to the neediest part of me, before he slides his hands over my ass again and lifts me up, turning around before he carries me to his desk and slides me onto it, using his palm to push the papers piled neatly to my left until they scatter onto the floor.

My mouth already misses his, so I sit up, reaching for him, pulling him between my legs until he's kissing me again. His fingers dip inside my leather bodice as his tongue teases mine, his warm hands cupping my breasts, his thumbs teasing my nipples until they're so hard and tender.

My own fingers tangle into his thick, dark hair as he kisses his way down my jaw, my throat, to the swell of my breasts. His hands make short work of the lace fastening my bodice, pushing the leather open until my breasts are exposed, and he takes me in with a dark-eyed stare.

"Christ," he murmurs, as I arch my back until my breasts are close to his face. "Do you know how perfect you are?"

I want to laugh. I'm anything but perfect. But this man somehow is making me feel like a goddess.

He dips his head and his lips capture one of my nipples, his teeth grazing as his tongue soothes. His hand slides beneath my back to steady me against him. I scrape my fingers against his scalp and he murmurs something unintelligible in appreciation.

Somehow he's unlaced the last of the eyelets, and my bodice falls to the desktop beneath me, leaving me exposed to him. He takes his time, kissing each breast with appreciation, teasing my nipples and stroking my body like a man who knows exactly what he wants. And then he lowers his mouth to my tattoo, tracing the edges of it with his tongue.

Just when I think I couldn't get any more turned on, he slides his hand down my stomach, along my thighs and dips it beneath the hem of my skirt, pushing it up, exposing me.

And then he grins. A boyish, heart melting smile that makes me realize how rarely he looks happy. "You're wearing panties."

"I know."

Sliding his hands over my legs, he traces the edge of my skin-colored panties. "Maybe you're not the bad girl you think you are," he says, his fingers touching the center of them. Even though there's a layer of cotton between his hand and my aching core, I almost jump out of my skin.

"Maybe I'm worse. Now you know I'm a liar."

He slides a finger under the cotton, muttering a soft oath when he feels how turned on I am for him. "Is this for me?" he murmurs, his middle finger finding the bundle of nerves that are so swollen I swear I'm on the edge of oblivion.

"No," I manage to pant. "Disney music. It always turns me on."

This time he laughs. And damn, it makes my heart ache. There are crinkles around his eyes and his lips are curled up. His lips brush mine, and it feels almost tender.

I bite the inside of my cheek to remind myself that this isn't about love, or emotion. He's a man who wants what he wants, and for some reason he wants me.

When it's over? He's going to walk away. Because no matter how stupid the chemistry is between us, he's an intelligent guy. A rich man. He already knows that we're complete opposites. I wasn't lying when I said Princess Di was the kind of woman he'd want in his life.

I'm always a dirty secret.

But then he starts kissing me again, pushing all those dark thoughts out of my brain. Replacing them with fireworks as he circles his finger against me, his mouth soft, his tongue teasing.

My breath comes in stutters as he pushes a finger inside of me, groaning as I tighten around him.

"Christ," he mutters. "So fucking tight."

I don't bother telling him it's been a while. Truthfully, I'm not sure my lips are able to form a sentence right now. He curls his finger inside of me, presses his thumb against the swollen part of me, and kisses me until I'm so breathless all I can do is cling onto him, my fingers digging into his arms as I feel the muscles flex beneath them, determined to make me feel good.

Then, right as I'm on the edge, he pulls my panties down my legs and throws them on the floor, before dropping to his knees and yanking my thighs apart. Before I can say a word his face is pushed between them.

He runs his tongue along the length of me, his face rough against my tender thighs. Every part of me feels exposed.

"I knew it," he mutters. "I knew you'd taste this good."

I open my mouth to respond, but then he pushes a finger inside of me again, at the same time as he flickers his tongue against me, and my head tips back in pleasure, because this man knows exactly what he's doing.

I slide my hands through his thick hair, tugging it,

scraping my nails. Making him groan louder as he continues his onslaught, with soft flickers and hard long licks.

"Please..." I manage to gasp out.

"What do you need?" he says, looking up at me. His eyes catching mine.

You. All the time. Like this.

"Don't stop."

His eyes crinkle. God, he's so stupidly handsome it hurts. "Sweetheart, if you don't want a man to stop, don't interrupt his dinner."

Before I can come up with a witty retort, his tongue traces me from my behind to the tip of me, then he pushes two fingers inside until my eyes roll back in my head.

And then I feel it. The explosion pulling me from the inside out. My thighs tighten around his head, my fingers scrape his scalp, and I convulse around his fingers so hard that I'm worried he'll never be able to use them again.

Not that he seems to care. He's too busy coaxing the pleasure from me, his fingers moving gently, his mouth kissing every aching part of me, as my body arches from the desk as I chant his name.

And then everything comes crashing down.

"Hudson?" a low voice calls out through the door. He looks up from between my thighs and our eyes lock in panic. For a moment neither of us breathe.

"You in here?" There's a rap of knuckles at the door. And I'm so aware that I'm half-naked on his desk, my body still quivering from the best orgasm I've ever had.

"Just a minute," he calls out to whoever's on the other side of the door. His voice is so calm and controlled. He looks at me again, running his tongue along his bottom lip.

God, he's tasting me. For some reason that sends my heart racing.

I sit up, pulling my leather bodice together. It took forever to lace up when I was getting ready earlier. There's no way I can make myself respectable in time for Hudson to open the door. So instead I hold it over my boobs and slide off the desk, picking up my panties from the floor, then run around to the other side of the huge oak desk and slide underneath it.

There's a rustle of sound, almost certainly Hudson pulling his jacket on, then the steady thud of footsteps as he walks toward the door.

I'm crouched under his desk in the space where his chair is usually, holding my legs to my chest so they don't stick out. My head is pressed against the underside of the desktop. A minute ago I was screaming his name on his desk, now I'm hiding like some kind of bad secret.

And I brought it all on myself. Dear God, what have I done?

thirteen

HUDSON

I storm over to the door, ready to unleash the wrath of God onto whomever is on the other side, while simultaneously willing my hard-as-steel erection to go down.

Running my fingers through my hair in an effort to make it look like the most beautiful woman at this party hasn't spent the last five minutes tugging it, I take a deep breath and open the door.

Parker is standing on the other side. "Been looking for you everywhere, man. Tried to call, but you weren't answering."

My phone is in my jacket pocket. On silent. "What's up?" I ask, distracted by the knowledge that I almost got to slide inside the woman who's been messing up my mind for the past few weeks.

"Ayda fell asleep on Autumn. She took her back to your place. Said to enjoy the party, she doesn't mind staying there and babysitting."

There goes my father of the year award. Autumn had insisted on watching Ayda this evening, along with her friend Francie, because she wanted me to – in her words – *have a blast at the after party*.

To be fair, I'd decided to give it an hour before I scooped my kid up and headed home. But then I got distracted – first by Sylvie who stalked me down, then by Skyler doing the most impressive air dive I think I've ever seen.

And now by her body. By all of her.

It hasn't escaped my notice that I can still taste her on my tongue.

"She should be the one enjoying the party," I tell him, but he's not paying attention. Parker is looking at my waist, which seems a really fucking weird thing to do until I realize my shirt has been pulled out of my pants, and it's more than a little crumpled. Saying nothing I tuck it in. "She's the one who organized it after all," I continue, like nothing has happened.

He's still giving me a strange look though.

"I'll go take over," I tell him. "I'll send her back."

"Sure. I'll walk you over." Parker nods.

Shit. "Actually, I have a couple of things to sort here," I lie smoothly. "It won't take long, but I don't want to hold you up. I'll meet you there."

"It's okay," Parker replies, as easy going as always. "I'm happy to wait." He goes to walk into my office but I block him with my body. He blinks, surprised.

"No need," I insist. "I don't want to hold you up."

But instead of leaving, Parker tips his head to the side. Then he leans forward and picks something off the cotton of my shirt.

A brown hair. He lifts it up and inspects it like it's a diamond ring.

"Ayda's," I say.

He smirks at me. "And did she give you the hickey, too?"

"What?" I touch my neck. "What hickey?"

Parker points at my throat. "That one," he says. "Say hi to her from me, whoever she is." Then he turns on his heel and walks back down the hallway to the door that leads to the reception area.

I'm still touching my neck with one hand when I close the door once more, turning to face my desk.

Skyler is still hiding behind it.

"Did you give me a hickey?" I ask her. Before she can reply, I walk over to the mirror on the opposite wall to inspect my neck.

And there it is. The telltale redness on the skin.

She walks over to where I'm inspecting my throat. Her bodice is laced up again, though she's still holding her panties.

I reach out and grab them.

"Hey!" She tries to take them back but I hold them up in the air. "Those are mine."

"I'm keeping them."

"No you're not." She starts jumping, in a feeble attempt to get them back from me.

"Yes I am. You gave me a hickey, I'm taking your panties."

"I didn't mean to give you a hickey," she tells me, reaching out to touch my neck. And fuck, the rush of desire is pumping through me again. Our eyes lock.

"You marked me," I murmur.

The corner of her lips quirk. "Should I be sorry?"

"Probably. I haven't had a hickey since high school."

This time she grins. "Nobody has stolen my panties before, if that helps."

In a way it does. "I'm sorry you had to hide," I tell her. "I don't like that at all."

She shrugs nonchalantly. "It's not like we want anybody to know what we were doing, right?"

I blink. I don't have an answer for that. My brain says she's right. That we should feel lucky to get away with it.

But my body? It wants more. It wants everything. It wants to take and give until every sense I have is full of her.

If I had a heart, maybe it would, too.

"You should go to Ayda," Skyler says softly. "I bet she'd love for you to read her a bedtime story."

There's no guile to her words. She's looking at me with honest eyes. Because I know for a fact what dishonest ones look like.

"We need to talk," I say firmly. Because yes, I have to go see my kid, but this isn't the end.

"Look, I know I got my rocks off and you didn't," Skyler says. "And that's unfortunate, because I'm a giver not a taker and I absolutely would have followed through if we hadn't been so rudely interrupted. But I think we both know this was a mistake. Let's blame it on the alcohol. Or my major accident." Her eyes crinkle. "Go see your daughter. I promise I don't expect anything. I know I'm not your type."

"I'm getting pretty sick of you telling me who my type is," I say, my voice mild.

"Maybe that's because you know I'm right." She looks over my shoulder into the mirror, adjusting the leather crown across her face. "Now can I have my panties back, please?"

"No," I say stubbornly.

She laughs. "You're so petulant."

"I'll bring them back to you on Monday night."

"Monday night?" She lifts a brow, looking amused. "Two days is a long time to stay panty-less for."

"I assume you have more than one pair," I point out.

She looks at me closely. "You're full of assumptions, aren't you. And anyway, I can't."

"Why not?" I try and fail to keep the annoyance out of my voice.

"Because your sister is coming over with her friend for a girls' night. Unless you want to join us." She lifts a brow.

"Then let's make it Tuesday," I tell her, because that's as long as my patience will last.

"So you can finish what you started," she murmurs.

There's a strange expression on her face. She almost looks hurt.

"No, I want to come over and talk to you. I'll bring dinner."

"Like a date?" She frowns like I suggested we swim in a pool full of sharks with bleeding wounds. "It's okay, you don't have to do that. And we don't have to talk. Let's just agree to never mention this again. You can keep the panties. Whack yourself off with them if that's your thing." She takes a step backward from me, like she's afraid. "Seriously, you made me come. And it was very nice. You don't owe me dinner and you don't have to pretend you're interested in me. What's done is done." She mimes zipping her lips. "It's our secret."

I stare at her. "It was *very nice*?" I repeat.

"Is that what you got from my words?"

"Very nice," I say again. "Damned with faint praise." I'm not going to lie, my ego is a little dented. Because what happened on my desk was far from nice. It was dirty and it was heaven.

But *nice*?

"Okay it was mind blowing." Her eyes lock with mine. "I came harder than I ever came before. You're the King of Cunnilingus. The Earl of Oral." Her brows knit. "The Troubador of Tongues."

"Tuesday night. Seven o'clock."

"Make it eight. And I'm a picky eater." She smiles like she thinks that will put me off.

Before I can answer, she sashays out of my office, leaving me staring after her, open mouthed.

fourteen

HUDSON

It's pouring with rain on Monday morning, which is kind of appropriate for my mood. Because even though my kid is practically jumping with excitement in the car, I absolutely don't want to be anywhere near this fucking house today.

I pull into the driveway and let out a long breath. If I had any other choice, we wouldn't be here. But I'm trying to be the better man here – and more importantly, Doctor Methi thinks it's important for Ayda's healing that we're here today.

She deserves to know where she comes from. That's what all the best therapists tell me. But as I unbuckle my kid's seat belt I still feel that sick impending doom in my stomach.

"Darling!" an expensive English voice calls out. "Come here to Granny."

And Ayda – because she's a kid and she loves her grandparents as much as I loathe them – does exactly that, running into the arms of the elegant woman standing on the doorstep of what is probably her sixth home.

Her husband – Dennis – walks to the bottom step of the porch and shoots me a warning look. Not that it affects me other than making me want to punch his face. But I've been wanting to do that for the last two years.

Ever since they stole my daughter away from me.

Ayda's mother and I dated casually. Or at least I thought it was casual. She thought it was more. She was an English model living in Manhattan and I was a damn idiot.

It was only when I was trying to break things off gently – mostly because she made it clear that she was expecting a ring – that she told me she was pregnant. And then her family got involved.

Turned out the sweet little model with a cute accent came from a hugely wealthy family. Her father is a third generation financial baron. Her mother the daughter of a duke.

"Hudson," Dennis says, not holding his hand out. We're way beyond handshakes now. We were from the first time they encouraged Ayda's mother to flee the US, despite Ayda being a US citizen, and bring her to the UK to 'wear me down.'

And then, when Ayda's mother died unexpectedly in a car crash, they refused to let me bring her home. We fought for custody for almost a year. And at no point did they tell me that my daughter – my vibrant, intelligent, beautiful daughter – hadn't spoken a word since she'd been removed from the wreck of the car that killed her mother and been taken to the hospital.

Those months without seeing my daughter were without a doubt the worst months of my life. Yes, she was conceived under less than ideal circumstances, but from the moment I held her in my arms I knew that my whole world had changed.

I smelled her soft, new baby hair and made a promise that I'd always protect her.

It killed me that I couldn't protect her from her mother's desire to wear me down or her grandparents' desire to keep her from me.

And now, I'm having to face the two people I loathe the most, because Ayda loves them, and even though they hate me, they love her, too.

"Dennis," I acknowledge the tall, thin man dressed in a suit despite being on what I guess is a vacation. When we agreed to the visitation arrangements, I offered that they could meet up with Ayda four times a year. So they bought this house right over the water from Liberty Island.

Thankfully they only come when it's their time to see Ayda. I already know that they're flying back to London at the end of the week. The rest of the time the house lays empty, save for the staff they've hired to maintain it.

I'm wearing a pair of jeans and a Henley today, because I won't be going into work at all. Though Dennis and Catherine hate it, there's no way I'm leaving Ayda here unsupervised.

Yes, her name is on every do-not-fly list that exists, and if they take her I'll bring the full fucking wrath of the law down on them, but I also know the wheels of justice turn so fucking slowly it hurts.

I can't put her through another custody case.

"Happy birthday, darling," Ayda's grandmother says, taking her hand. "Come see the swing set we bought you."

A fucking swing set that she'll use four times a year at the most. And not today because it's raining.

I keep my mouth closed and follow them inside.

MUST HAVE BEEN LOVE

"You don't have to stay, you know," Dennis murmurs to me.

"Yes I do."

Their butler – or whoever he is – closes the door behind us as we follow Ayda and her grandmother through the grand hall and into the living room that overlooks their huge yard.

"Garden's looking nice," I say to Dennis, who's still looking like he's sucking a lemon.

"Cut the bull," he says, making me lift a brow. "What do I have to pay you to let us see our granddaughter without you skulking around?"

I let out a long breath. I should be surprised it's taken him this long to ask. "You know that's not going to happen," I tell him. "And you know why."

"It's not like we can take her anywhere. You've made sure of that."

"Didn't stop you last time," I murmur.

"Come on, dear," Ayda's grandmother says, squeezing her hand. "The cook made you a cake. Let's get some and then you can open your gifts."

She shoots a dirty look at me and takes Ayda along the hallway to the kitchen, leaving Dennis and me alone.

"You have these visits because I offered them," I tell him. "I'm very happy to cancel them if you can't behave."

His already-beady eyes narrow. "If you cancel them, I'll make sure you regret it."

"Not as much as I regret agreeing to them."

"Why isn't she talking yet?" he asks, changing the subject.

"Because her mother stole her from home and traumatically died, then you traumatized her even more by not letting her see me for months," I say, trying to keep my voice even.

"Is she still going to therapy?"

He knows she is. I also allow Dr. Methi to send them a report – heavily edited by me – each month. I'm a fucking saint, if I'm being honest. They deserve nothing from me.

But I'm playing the game. Letting them see her enough that it looks like I'm being magnanimous. If they try to take me to court again, I'll point out how generous I've been.

"She's doing fine at therapy."

"And at home? Are you even there at all? Every time I open the newspaper you're making a new deal."

"I'm keeping a roof over my daughter's head."

"We offered to pay you whatever you need," he says, sounding wheedling now.

This is one of the reasons he hates me the most. Dennis is a man who's used to buying everything and everybody. And I can't be bought.

Nor can my daughter.

During the custody battle they tried everything. To pay me to give up, to pay me to live in England.

And when I made it clear that wasn't happening, they demanded to pay for a full-time nanny – who would almost certainly report back to them – so they could stay in control.

He hates that I don't need them. It's the one advantage I have.

"What's that on your neck?" he questions, changing the subject again.

"What?" I frown.

"Is it a bruise?"

Jesus fucking christ. That hickey. Truth be told, I'd

forgotten about it. If I was wearing a collared shirt, it probably would have been hidden.

"I was wearing a tight shirt to Ayda's party. Probably that," I say smoothly.

"Dennis, come sing "Happy Birthday"," his wife calls out. It's obvious from her tone that she's deliberately excluding me.

Which is just fine. I know they love my kid as much as they hate me. They won't do anything to her, and they can't take her anywhere while I'm here.

"Go ahead," I say, giving my daughter's grandfather a humorless smile. "I'll wait here. I have some phone calls to make."

He shoots me the dirtiest look I've ever seen before he turns on his heel and stomps off.

It should give me some satisfaction, but I'm still annoyed about the hickey. There's no way he should have seen it. I'm off my fucking game.

I reach up to touch it. It's not tender, but it's still a chink in my armor I didn't need to have. My mind wanders, remembering the way Skyler gave as good as she got in my office. The way she scraped her teeth against my skin, her nails against my scalp.

The way she tasted on my tongue.

When I see her I'm going to give her hell for this fucking hickey.

And next time I'm wearing a damn turtleneck.

fifteen

SKYLER

I'm stupidly nervous waiting for Autumn and Francie to arrive. Maybe it's because I don't have many female friends here on the island. Or maybe it's because I'm still on edge about Hudson coming over tomorrow.

Autumn called me earlier, wanting my email address so she could send over some design ideas for the bar. She wanted me to look them over because she says she's already found some contractors who can start right away.

I explained that I couldn't do anything without going to a bank to get a loan, but she told me that the Grand Liberty Hotel company had agreed to fund it as part of their island improvement plan.

Which means Hudson has agreed to pay for it. Along with pushing my licence forward – because she admitted that was him too. It's messing with my mind.

I could take us having a fling when I thought he was an asshole. Yes, I grow feelings too fast, but he's great at making them go away with one scowl and a cutting sentence. But now I know he also has a benevolent side, it's making my chest feel tight.

Everybody on the island raves about how much he's done for the people and businesses of Liberty. Even Jesse tells me that Hudson replaced his guitar when it got smashed last year.

But I can't fall for a man who would never fall for me. And if I sleep with him, I know that's what will happen. So I'm going to tell him that this isn't going to work.

Yes, I feel bad about the fact that he made me come and I didn't do the same for him. But that's life. I'll buy him a sex toy or something.

The thought of him opening a box to see a pulsing cock ring makes my lips twitch. I immediately feel better.

"Hey," Jesse says, walking into the bar, the first to arrive for girls' night. "I thought there was a party. There isn't even any music."

I smile at him, because he has this stupid calming effect on people. I know that my family considers me laid back, but Jesse is something else. He walks over to the jukebox and presses the button to flick through the tracks before he chooses something.

The low sounds of "Superstition" by Stevie Wonder throbs out of the speaker, as he smiles at me and starts to sashay across the main floor.

"I love Stevie," I say.

"Yeah." He gives me a soft look. "Wayne did, too."

The tightness in my chest reminds me that there's still so much more to learn about my dad.

"Do you know what song was my dad's favorite?" I ask Jesse, this need taking over me.

""Go Your Own Way". Fleetwood Mac." His eyes catch mine.

That's one of my favorites too. I love that I feel so connected to him right now.

"Would you like a drink?" I ask, walking behind the bar.

"Beer would be good."

I open the refrigerator, where I've stored some beers and ready made cocktails because until the refurb is done I can't place a big order from the brewery on the mainland. Popping two bottles open, I pass one to Jesse before clinking it with mine.

"Hey hey!" Autumn sings out as she walks into the bar with Francie. "No drinking without me."

She looks amazing in a silver sequined dress. Francie is in a slightly less over-the-top but still sparkly gold shell top and black skirt as they both rush over to hug us.

I look down at my own outfit – a cut-out-lace white top and a silky long flowing skirt, cinched at the waist with a thick leather belt. "I should have worn something more appropriate," I murmur.

Jesse chuckles. "You and me both." He gestures at the black, overwashed Nirvana t-shirt and jeans he's wearing.

As Autumn releases me I spot a pair of dark, brooding eyes over her shoulder.

And immediately my heart starts to race.

He's in casual clothes. A pair of jeans that seem to hug his muscled thighs like they're in love with them. And a gray Henley that's unbuttoned at the neck to reveal a dash of hair on his chest.

I run my tongue over my dry lips, trying to calm my nerves.

"Are you staying for a drink?" I ask him, my voice low and thick.

Hudson has dark shadows under his eyes like he hasn't slept well for days. The corner of his lip pulls up at my question.

"Of course not. It's girls' night. He's just dropping us off while Parker and West look after Ayda for a minute," Autumn says, shooting him a playful look. You can tell from her eyes how much she loves her big brother. "You can go now."

"Jesse's staying," I say. "He's not a girl." Why am I so desperate to keep him here?

"I do need to get back for Ayda," he murmurs, his gaze still locked on mine. God, I'm stupidly attracted to him.

And then I make the mistake of glancing down at his hand. Yes, that one. The talented one that along with his even more talented lips made me forget who I was for a few minutes.

It's curled into a fist. It makes my heart race.

"Can I have a word?" I ask him.

"Ooh, has he done something wrong?" Autumn asks. "Hudson, you promised to be nice."

"Not at all," I say, my voice low. "It's just something about the licence. Go ahead and help yourself to cocktails," I say, pointing at the refrigerator. Jesse's at the jukebox, lining the next song up as I walk past him toward Hudson, then out of the door that leads onto the veranda overlooking the ocean.

"Call me when you're ready to come home," he calls out to Autumn.

"Sure." She's distracted by the cocktails, trying to choose between a sex on the beach and a screaming orgasm.

The night air is cool as we step outside onto the planked veranda. It dropped since Saturday and I can feel it.

According to Mylene when I picked up my coffee this morning, it will get warmer soon. By mid summer even at night the temperatures barely dip below seventy.

But my bare arms are prickling at the icy sensation of the salty air as the breeze hits them.

"You cold?" Hudson asks.

"It's okay. I'll be quick. I just wanted to thank you for pushing the licence forward."

He blinks like he wasn't expecting that. "It only took some phone calls. It's not a big deal."

"It is to me."

Our eyes lock again. "Then you're welcome."

"Autumn showed me the designs for the bar," I continue. "There's no way I can accept you paying for them."

He runs his thumb over his stubbled jaw. He really does look tired. "Is this something we can discuss tomorrow?" he asks.

"About tomorrow..." I trail off. "I don't think it's a good idea.

"Why not?"

"I don't think I have what you need."

"Is this because of the licence?" he asks. "I can call and ask them to rescind it."

"No," I answer.

"The remodel then?"

"I don't think we should mix business and pleasure," I say, suddenly latching onto the idea. "That's all."

"The remodel will be mutually beneficial," he tells me. In the distance the ferry is coming into port. The last run of the night – I've gotten used to the timings. Gotten used to a lot of things around here.

"How will it benefit you?" I ask.

"Because the nightlife on this island is dire. My guests expect a certain level of entertainment. Originally I wanted to provide it by buying this place, but since you refuse to sell..." He gives me a half-smile. "Then the second best option is to pay for it to be renovated. To the standard they expect."

Oh.

"So it's not because you want to have sex with me?"

He frowns. "You think I'm paying for the privilege?"

When he puts it like that it sounds super sordid. "I don't know," I say, confused now. "All I know is that it feels wrong to accept something like that."

He lets out a long breath. "I'm really fucking tired," he says, looking more human than I think I've ever seen him. "It's been a long day, I've had to deal with people who hate my guts and I just don't know what to say to make you understand that these two things are perfectly separate. I can want to improve the bar and want to spend time with you. In two very different, very exclusive situations."

I let out a breath. "You want to spend time with me?" I hate that my heart lights up at that.

"I believe that's what a date entails." He reaches out, his fingers trailing over my jaw. Stupid fireworks explode low in my stomach.

No, no no. I can't let myself respond to him like that. "I'm sorry you had a bad day," I whisper.

He doesn't pull his hand away. Instead he threads it through my hair, pulling me against him until my cheek is pressed against his strong chest, his head is lowered as he breathes in my hair.

"Let's get one thing straight," he murmurs. "You don't

owe me anything. You don't owe me sex, you don't owe me a drink, you don't even owe me a date. But I'd very much like to come over and spend some time getting to know you tomorrow."

I can feel the tenseness relaxing in his muscles as he holds me. And for some reason that makes me feel stupidly soft inside.

"I'd like to see you too," I whisper.

"Good," he says. "Now have a good evening. Try not to let my sister get too drunk, and I'll see you tomorrow." He kisses my brow and it sends my fireworks into overdrive, before he releases his hold on me and walks down the veranda to his sports car.

I watch until he's sitting inside of it, then he gestures at me to go inside, shaking his head because I'm so obviously shivering again.

And of course, he doesn't start his engine until I do exactly as I'm told.

By the time I walk back into the bar, it seems like girls' night is already in full swing. The Jukebox has moved on from Stevie Wonder to Hotel California, and Jesse is singing along with Don Henley, using his beer bottle as a microphone, while Autumn is pouring out what I hope is only their second cocktail.

"How long was I gone?" I ask. Though I completely suspect that Autumn and Francie had a few drinks before they even arrived. They're super giggly right now.

"Too long. You're playing catch up. What's your poison?" Autumn asks me, holding up an empty cocktail glass.

"Actually, I think I'll just go for a beer," I say. The cocktails look far too dangerous. She pops the lid from a bottle of Bud and passes it to me. I take a sip and grin at her. "You seem awfully at home behind the bar."

"I grew up pouring drinks for my dad and his gambling buddies." She shrugs. Then she passes Francie another cocktail and holds up her glass. "A toast. To new friends."

I feel my heart clench. If I'm not careful my eyes are going to go misty. "To new friends," I repeat, clinking my bottle against hers and Francie's glasses, followed by Jesse's bottle, which he's stopped using as a mic for a second.

"What did Hudson have to say?" Autumn asks me. "He wasn't giving you a hard time was he?"

I shake my head quickly. The last person I want to talk about right now is Hudson. I've never been great at hiding things, and I certainly don't want her to know that we have a... whatever it is... planned for tomorrow. "He's fine. Grumpy, but fine."

She laughs. "He's been in a bad mood ever since he got back to the island." She wrinkles her nose. "In fact all my brothers have." She looks over at Francie. "What did Asher say to you earlier?"

Francie blinks, like she's been caught in the headlights. "What?"

"I saw him say something to you then storm off. I meant to ask you earlier." Autumn lets out a breath. "Brothers can be such assholes," she murmurs. "I swear they don't want me to have any friends."

"That's because you keep stealing theirs," Jesse says, grinning.

"I didn't steal Parker," Autumn protests. "He came willingly."

"In more ways than one," Francie quips, making me giggle.

"Stop changing the subject. What did he say?" Autumn has Francie in her sights now. And I actually feel sorry for her. I get the feeling it's hard to hide anything from Hudson's sister. But whatever is going on between Francie and Asher, she clearly wants to keep it quiet.

"He was just annoyed at the fact we were going out tonight, I think, when he's leaving for the mainland tomorrow." Francie shrugs. "Anyway, let's ignore him. You're right, brothers are idiots."

"You should know." Autumn grins. "Did you know Francie has six brothers?" she asks me. "I thought I had it bad with four until I met her."

"Six?" My eyes widen. "Where do you come in that birth order?"

"Last. By far." Francie wrinkles her nose then takes another large mouthful of cocktail. "Believe me, it wasn't fun."

"Remember your eighteenth birthday party?" Autumn asks, clearly enjoying herself now. "How they tried to stop you from kissing anybody?"

"I remember." Francie lets out a sigh. "Let's face it, they haven't stopped trying since."

"You're making me glad I only have one sister," I say, taking a sip of my beer. For a second there's silence, then Autumn lets out a little noise.

"Let's stop talking about our families," Jesse suggests. "How about we play a drinking game instead?"

Autumn's face lights up, and she claps her hands together. "Never have I ever!" she suggests. "That's my favorite."

"That's because you've done everything," Francie points out. "And you get to drink every time."

Jesse splutters out his beer. Our eyes catch and he smiles at me. He's such a sweetie, I like him a lot.

"I'll say something I haven't done. I promise." Autumn says to her. Francie shakes her head, grinning. These two are a riot.

"Never have I ever..." Autumn drags it out, running her finger around her glass. "Kissed one of my brothers." She looks slyly at Francie, like she's waiting for a reaction.

But oh shit. This particular gotcha may not be aimed at me, but it's hit me right in the solar plexus anyway.

"I don't have any brothers," Jesse says. "So I definitely haven't kissed any of them."

"Me either," I say, and for a minute they all stare at me. Then Francie joins in. "I definitely haven't made out with any of my disgusting brothers."

"I mean *my* brothers," Autumn says, shaking her head. "Hudson, Asher, Wyatt and Zach. Do I have to spell this out for you?" I try to hide my dismay, but Francie isn't quite so good at keeping her face neutral. "What?" Autumn asks. "You told me I'd done everything. I haven't done that."

"Luckily for me it's still easy," Jesse says, putting his bottle down on the bar without taking a drink. He looks over at me. "I haven't made out with any of them. None of us have," he says, looking over at me. "Right?"

My breath catches. "Right," I manage to say. It's just a game, I don't need to play it, I tell myself. But I still find myself feeling guilty when I don't lift my own bottle to my lips.

Autumn doesn't seem to notice though. She's too busy looking at Francie. "So what's it to be, are you doing to drink?" she asks.

Francie is still desperately trying to look nonchalant,

but there's a blush stealing its way up her neck to her cheeks. Oh god, the poor girl. I feel stupidly sorry for her. Not least because I think she's probably made out with Asher and doesn't want to admit it to Autumn. But because I'm in exactly the same boat as her.

What is it about these damn Fitzgerald men? I need to create a diversion before this turns into an interrogation.

"Oh my God!" I shout out suddenly. Probably a bit too loud because all three of them turn to look at me with wide eyes, like they think something terrible's happened.

"What?" Jesse says, frowning.

I open my mouth, hoping something will actually come out. "I just realized I forgot my mom's birthday."

Autumn frowns. "Huh?"

"You forgot your mom's birthday?" Francie repeats, her voice sounding like I just committed a heinous crime.

"Yeah. I have to call her." I look over at the jukebox. "Somebody put some more music on," I say quickly, because the Eagles have finished. Talk among yourselves. But definitely don't play this game without me."

Jesse looks at me carefully, like he knows exactly what I'm doing. Autumn pours her and Francie another cocktail. One more of those and she'll have forgotten her name, let alone that Francie never actually answered the question.

"I'll be five minutes," I promise. "Don't move."

"Okay..." Autumn says.

"And you get to choose the music," I tell Autumn. "Make it loud." Enough to blast over whatever thoughts are whirling around her head.

With that I grab my phone, and rush over to the door to the apartment at the back of the bar. I quickly tap out a message before I walk through.

. . .

Distract Autumn. Keep all conversation away from her brothers. Do something stupid if necessary – Skyler.

I send the message to Jesse who pulls his phone out of his pocket when it vibrates. He reads the screen then looks at me and nods. Then as I open the door to the apartment I hear him shout out. "You want to know my most embarrassing moment? I once flashed Eileen and Mylene on the same day!"

I start to laugh, because he absolutely understood the assignment.

"What?" Autumn shouts out. "Have you? When was this? And why didn't I know?" She widens her eyes. "Were they in the same place?"

From the excitement in her voice, I know that all thoughts of brothers and kissing are forgotten.

Was that good enough? – Jesse

When I turn back, he's surrounded by Francie and Autumn who are shouting out so many questions he doesn't look like he knows where to start answering them. And I feel this strange pull in my chest at the sight. I think I could fall in love with these friends, in a completely platonic way.

It was genius. And I need all the details later. – Skyler.

. . .

There are no details. I made it up. – Jesse

That's when I really start to laugh. Who knew lovely, innocent Jesse was such a good liar? Our eyes catch and I mouth a 'thank you' to him. He nods.

Somehow this place is beginning to feel a lot like home.

sixteen

SKYLER

"So you're definitely not going to have sex with him, but you're still having dinner with him?" Lee asks me the next day as I put my makeup on in the bathroom. She's propped up on the counter – or at least my phone with the video chat of her is. She's in the middle of breastfeeding. Cora has slowed to a drink every twenty seconds or so, which means she's almost asleep and we need to keep our voices low.

"I think maybe we can be friends," I murmur, brushing mascara onto my curled lashes. I'm still feeling a bit jaded from last night, even if the evening did end early because Autumn started looking green and Francie called Hudson to ask them to pick them up. It was Asher who arrived, though, and it looked like he and Francie were having heated words again as he helped Autumn out to his car.

"Bullshit," Lee says, bringing me out of my thoughts. "You're doing a full face. That means you want him."

"I'm not doing a full face." I frown at her image on the

screen. She looks so serene in her rocking chair. "I'm just trying to look professional. I'm a business owner now."

She starts to laugh. "Oh sweetie, you can lie to yourself but don't lie to me. You like this guy."

I put the mascara wand back into the tube and let out a long breath. "It doesn't matter if I like him. What matters is we both know I'll be the one who ends up in tears at the end. And I'm over being the one who gets all the feelings."

She gives me a sad smile. I know my big sister wants me to have what she has. But we're fundamentally different. And she hasn't met Hudson Fitzgerald. He's a man who needs a woman who has it together.

I could live a hundred years and never have anything together. But when I try to picture him with another woman – okay, with Princess Di and all her elegant ways – a wave of anger washes over me. I want him. I just... don't want to want him.

Even with the excess cocktails and the awkward first drinking game, last night was exactly what I needed. And Jesse proved he was one of us in the best way. After his genius intervention last night I'm pretty sure the two of us are firm friends now.

Like you and Hudson?

I frown. Because there's a huge difference between Hudson and Jesse. And it's not just money. In fact, I'd prefer it if Hudson had no money at all. I hate that it puts me at a disadvantage compared to him.

And yes, I know that's my hangup to deal with. Any therapist worth their salt could dig into the veneer of 'don't care' that I paint myself with and find a scared little girl cowering underneath. Just because I've never been the type to conform doesn't mean there isn't a part of me that wishes I could.

"Are you sure this is what you want?" Lee asks, pulling me out of my thoughts.

"What do you mean?"

There's that sad smile again. "I know you feel like you have something to prove. To Mom, mostly, but maybe to me, too. But you should know that I love you just the way you are. And so does Mom, even if she doesn't show it."

It's not often that I get emotional. Maybe it's the impending remodel of the bar – which Autumn tells me starts tomorrow and will go on for a few weeks. It's making everything real and I'm not sure I'm ready for that.

"What if I mess it all up again?" I whisper. Because that's my modus operandi after all. The fear I always ignore has somehow slid its way between my ribcage and is squeezing around my heart.

"You won't." Lee sounds so sure it makes me worry more. "It's a bar. You've had so much experience with those. And more importantly, it's your dad's bar. He was born on Liberty, you're half.. I don't know... Libertarian?" She smiles at me. "You have as much right to be on that island as anybody else. And I know you can do this."

"I wish I had your faith."

"I wish you did, too. And I can't help but feel it's my fault that you don't." The baby lets out a soft sigh and she pats her head. "My wedding..."

"We don't need to talk about that," I say quickly.

"Yes we do. Because you chose that day, between me and him. And I know things have never been the same for you since."

Lee being Lee had invited my dad to her wedding. Though they'd never had the traditional stepfather - stepdaughter relationship, he had still been there for a few years when she was young. And my mom had begrudgingly agreed.

And then Wayne turned up drunk to the ceremony. Not a little tipsy either, but falling down, ranting and raving wasted with whiskey.

He'd always been in love with Mom. And seeing her with Bryan at the rehearsal dinner the previous night had made him realize just how much she'd moved on. He'd left the dinner early, and apparently had gone on an all night bender at whatever dive he could find open.

The next morning he arrived at the swanky hotel that Lee had chosen for her dream wedding, reeking of alcohol and looking like he'd been living on the streets for months.

I'd been the first to see him and my heart had dropped. I was only seventeen then. Halfway through my hair being done when another bridesmaid had whispered in my ear that there was a problem, and should we tell Lee?

"No," I'd said firmly. And I'd told them not to tell my mom, either, because she was ruthless and would have thrown him out without blinking.

I was so sure it wasn't that bad. It was the first time we'd seen him in years, after all. He'd never been the type to keep in touch. From the age of ten until seventeen I think I'd seen him twice and spoken to him five times on the phone.

And he couldn't stay sober for one day.

I'd run down to the hotel lobby in my slippers and robe, my hair pinned into curls, only to find him slumped drunkenly on the reception counter, arguing that the bar should be open to the stepfather of the bride.

I'd walked over to him, smiling, trying to work out how to deal with a drunken stranger who I shared blood with.

And then he'd started crying loudly. Telling me he'd

forever be in love with my mom and that he'd messed up so badly.

"Talk to her for me," he'd slurred. "Tell her I love her. You want us back together, don't you?"

"It's Lee's wedding day," I'd hissed. "You need to sober up. *Now*."

"Little Lee. Cute kid. She used to think I was a god, you know?" He'd smiled sadly. "Loved her. Loved her mom." He blinked at me. "Love her so much."

"If you love her, you'll sober up."

He'd blinked at me then, as though he'd only just realized I was there. "I'm gonna tell her during the ceremony," he slurred. "I'm gonna shout it out for everybody to hear."

My blood ran cold. This was Lee's special day. We'd spent more than a year organizing it. Like everything else she touched, it was elegant, beautiful, perfect.

And I couldn't let him ruin it. So I called a cab, paid the driver extra to take him to a bar as far away as possible, then took a deep breath and headed back to the makeup room where Lee and Mom were oohing and aahing about her dress.

It was only later, after the ceremony, when Lee asked me where he was that I confessed he'd been drunk and I'd thrown him out.

I hadn't heard from him after that day. Not until I got the call from his lawyer about his will.

I push those memories away, back down into the dark where they belong. I would always choose Lee above anybody else.

But I hate that I sent him to a bar.

These days, I'm older and wiser. I would have arranged for him to go to rehab, been there for him. But I was too young, too afraid.

And now he's gone.

The baby lets out a loud cry and Lee hushes her softly. "I should go," she says. "Diaper changing time."

I wrinkle my nose. "Good luck."

"Thanks." She gives me another concerned look. "I wish I was there with you."

I wish she was too. But I'm not going to tell her that. "I've got this," I say instead. "Maybe I'm finally growing up."

"You've always been a grown up," she tells me. "Just your own kind of grown up. And I don't want you to ever change."

That's the thing about my big sister. She's always on my side. Even when Mom pulls her hair out over me, Lee is my loudest cheerleader.

"Go change that poopy diaper," I tell her, letting out a breath. Push away the sad, let in the happy. "And once she's clean give her a big kiss from me."

"I will. Love you."

"Love you too." I end the call and look at my freshly made-up face in the mirror. If I can face my demons, having to face Hudson Fitzgerald should be a cinch.

I just have to keep telling myself that.

seventeen

HUDSON

The porch lights above the bar are on, which feels like a good sign. Like not only is she expecting me, but she doesn't want me to trip over my feet and land on my ass on the wooden deck.

It's a low bar, but Skyler not wanting me to break my neck is a good thing, right?

I park the car in the dark lot behind the bar, instead of parking on the strip of grass facing the ferry like I usually do. I tell myself it's because I know she won't like people talking about me being here at night.

When I reach the door, I rap my knuckles lightly on the wood and she opens it.

I have no idea what it is about this woman that sends every sense I have into overdrive. But seeing the way she looks at me with those thick lashes sweeping down makes me want to scoop her into my arms and bend her over the damn bar.

"Come in." She looks at the bag I'm carrying. It has the Grand Liberty Hotel logo on it. "You really did bring dinner." She sounds surprised.

"I said I would," I tell her, following her inside, carrying the food I asked the hotel's chef to prepare for me.

Skyler's wearing a denim dress today. It's western style, with buttons from the collar to the hem that skims her bare thighs. I like the way she's dressed. Casual yet sexy.

It takes every ounce of self control I have not to reach out to start unfastening those metal stamped buttons.

"Where shall we eat?" I ask her, looking beyond her to the private apartment. I've been in there a few times. Mostly when Wayne was in a bad way and I'd carry him to bed.

"I thought here." She points at a table at the center of the bar area. I look at it, frowning.

"Wouldn't you rather be somewhere more private?" I ask.

"I don't think we're about to get overrun by tourists." Her lips curl as she looks at me. "And I think this would be best."

I open my mouth to protest, but then close it again. I've pissed her off enough since she arrived on the island. If she wants to eat in the damn bar, then that's what we'll do.

"Anyway," she says. "It's kind of like a final goodbye to the way this bar looks. Tomorrow it'll be ripped out. There's this guy with way more money than sense that's paying for a full remodel."

"He probably has an ulterior motive," I say, putting the bag on the table and starting to unpack it.

"I'm pretty sure he does. But luckily for him I know what's best for him." She moves over to help me with the food.

"What is best for him?" I ask, handing her the plates and silverware, which she lays out neatly.

"Somebody who doesn't drive him up the wall." Her eyes meet mine and I feel a shot of desire rush through me.

A smile pulls at my lips. "Maybe he likes that." I open up the starters the chef made at my request. A simple shrimp salad made from local catch. Martin worked in Michelin starred restaurants in New York and L.A. before his wife passed and he realized he needed to change his lifestyle, and you can tell by the way he's paid attention to every single detail.

And yet, it's not the food I'm interested in. It's this woman who feels like a fucking dream dancing on a breeze. Something I want to catch but keeps slipping away.

I plate up the food and pass it to her, and she looks at me like she's trying to work me out.

Good luck with that, sweetheart. I've been trying the same thing all my life.

"Is that why you came tonight?" she asks. "To handle me?"

I take a mouthful of the shrimp. Christ, it's good. "Eat," I say after I swallow it down, pointing at her untouched plate.

"And then what?"

"Then you'll be full."

"I mean, then what. For this." She points at me and then herself. "What are you expecting?"

I frown at the insinuation. "What makes you think I'm expecting anything?"

"Because you're you. And I'm me. And I really don't think this is going to work."

This again. I put my fork down and take a deep breath.

"Why do you think I'm here?" I ask her.

"Because you want to have sex with me to get me out of your system."

At least her answer is honest. "You think that little of me?" I murmur.

"No. I just think..." She shakes her head, a frown pulling at her brows. "Don't you *want* to have sex with me?"

I start to laugh. "There's no right answer to that question. Either I do and you're disgusted because I'm only after one thing, or I don't and you're insulted. So I'm not going to answer. And that's still not the reason I'm here."

"Then why?"

It hits me like a damn fist in my chest. This isn't about me. It's about her. About her insecurities. Beneath that chilled out, sexy armor she wears there's something softer. More wary.

"Because I want to have dinner with you. I find you interesting. Funny. You make me smile and you're nice to my kid."

"She's easy to be nice to."

"I still like it." I spear another shrimp. "Now can we enjoy this food? That's the reason I'm here, alright? To eat. To talk. To enjoy each other's company?"

Her lips part as she stares right at me. My gaze locks with hers as I stare back. I have nothing to hide, not with her. I'm being completely honest.

If all that happens tonight is we eat and talk, I'm weirdly okay with that. Yes, I want to kiss her. I want all of her. I want that more than I want to breathe right now. But that's up to her.

For the first time in my life I feel like I'm okay with somebody else making the decision.

She takes a bite of the shrimp. I watch as her eyes widen

and she lets out a groan. Then she swallows it down and smiles at me. "Oh, my God," she mouths.

"Good, huh?"

"It's like an orgasm in shellfish form." She takes another bite. "How does it taste so good?"

"Martin is an excellent chef."

"Is he single?" she says, still smiling at me.

"No," I lie. "Very much taken."

"Do you cook?" she asks.

"I've been known to make toast." Another lie. I know how to cook. I have a kid, she doesn't starve. Yeah, it's basic but thankfully Ayda's tastes are basic too. We like chicken and fish and noodles and potatoes. It's amazing how many combinations of those things you can create.

"I'm not a great cook," she says. "You should probably know that about me."

"I think I can live with that," I say. "What do you like doing?"

That smile is still playing on her lips. I'm stupidly entranced by them. Especially the stud in the corner. I flicked it with my tongue more than once when we kissed.

She tips her head to the side, her hair falling over her right shoulder. "I like music. Dancing. Dressing up as a slutty princess."

I laugh. "You're very good at it."

"I know." She grins. "I like that moment before you fall asleep when your whole body goes soft and it feels like you're about to slip under the surface."

She runs the tip of her tongue over her bottom lip, like she's really thinking hard.

"I like that too," I tell her. "Tell me more things."

Her body shifts forward, like it's being pulled toward

me. "I like the smell of hot concrete when it's freshly rained. The smell of babies after they've just had a bath and they're all warm and cuddly. I like eating breakfast for dinner." She pulls her lip between her teeth. "And the feeling of somebody playing with my hair."

I can almost feel the silkiness of it between my forefingers and thumbs.

"And most of all I like not knowing where life is going. I like the excitement of not being pinned down. I like being free to be whoever I want, whereever I want." Her gaze is soft as she glances at my mouth. "What about you?" she breathes. "What do you like?"

I think about it. Not because I'm trying to impress her but because I genuinely think she won't judge me. "I like knowing my family is safe," I say. "That nobody can hurt or touch them."

She lets out a soft breath.

"I like the way my daughter thinks I'm a hero even though I'm just her dad. Just a flawed man. I like eating good food like this. But I also like eating a slice of toast when it's late and there's nobody around to tell me I'm making poor nutritional decisions."

She laughs at that. And I smile right at her. "Tell me more," she says, looking fascinated.

"I like having enough money to be able to tell people to fuck off to their faces," I continue, waiting for her to wince, but she doesn't. "I like the power it gives. The safety."

"Because it allows you to protect those you love," she murmurs.

"Something like that," I admit.

"What's your favorite childhood memory?" she asks me suddenly. She leans forward across the table.

I have to think about that one. I'm not one for looking

back. There's too much baggage and it's history. But then I remember it. That day.

"Teaching Autumn and Eden how to swim."

"Eden's your other sister?"

"Yeah," I nod. "They're both younger than the rest of us. Asher and I used to be big swimmers. It's hard not to be when you live on an island. We'd race each other every day during the summer. Go down to the beach at first light and spend most of the day there, goofing around."

"It sounds idyllic," she murmurs. Her hand is on the table, so close to mine I can feel our fingertips touch.

"It was." I nod. "Except Autumn and Eden used to constantly beg us to take them. And of course we didn't want to because we were assholes and they were kids who cramped our style."

"How so?" she asks, smiling at me. Our fingers are touching now and it feels weirdly comforting.

"The usual. We'd like to flirt with summer girls. Having our sisters with us made it harder."

"I bet they loved you."

"My sisters or the girls?"

"Both." She laughs lightly. "But I was talking about the summer girls. Is that what you called them?"

"Most people on Liberty call them out-of-towners," I say. "But they mostly came in the summer."

"I bet they did." Her lips curl.

"Are you bringing the conversation back to sex again?" I ask, my voice teasing.

"I'm just trying to picture you as a young punk. I bet you were devastating."

"On the contrary. I had an overbite that took three years of braces to fix. And I was skinny as a rake."

"And I bet they all still wanted you." She steeples her

fingers under her chin. "How old were you when you lost your virginity?"

My brows lift.

"You tell me yours and I'll tell you mine," she says.

"I was seventeen. And it wasn't pretty. You?"

"Sixteen." She wrinkles her nose. "Also not pretty."

"I disagree. Everything about you is pretty."

She traces the veins on the back of my hand with her finger. "Were you born with a sweet tongue or did it arrive with the muscles and perfect teeth?"

"I'm not sure that's for me to say." I turn my hand over and slide my fingers through hers. She doesn't pull away and that feels like a victory. "What's your favorite memory?" I ask her.

"Losing my virginity," she jokes and I laugh.

"Seriously."

"Okay." She nods, using her free hand to rub her jaw. "Let me think. It has to involve Lee because all my good memories involve her."

"Lee?"

"My older sister. Half sister, I guess, but it's never felt like half. She's my you, and I'm her Autumn."

"How is she like me?"

"She's got her life together. She and our mom are two peas in a pod that way. Good jobs, own their own homes, they don't run away to an island on a whim."

"They sound boring," I say, only half kidding. She smiles at me.

"Lee's always been my biggest cheerleader. I guess one of my favorite memories is the time we went camping. The first and last as a family." Her eyes meet mine. "I begged so much that my mom relented. She regretted it the moment we got there and she realized we had no idea how to put the tent up." Skyler's eyes light up as she talks. "She lasted one day before she packed us up, leaving the tent behind, and drove us to a hotel. But that day..." Her face goes soft at the memory. "We had so much fun. Lee is a bit like our mom, a city girl, but she let me lead the way. We swam in the lake, climbed trees. Made a fort with some sticks even though we had tents. And then mom thought she heard a bear and that was that."

"What were you like as a kid?" I ask her.

"Always messy. My head in the clouds." She shrugs. "Pretty much the same as I am now."

I run my thumb over the back of her hand. "Come here."

"I am here," she replies, a smile ghosting her lips.

I pat my lap. She tips her head to the side, her skin flushing. "Is that a good idea?"

"You don't strike me as somebody who cares if things are a good idea," I reply, dodging the question. "Now are you coming here or do I have to come to you?"

I stand, still holding her hand, pulling her up from her chair until her body hits mine. With my free hand I stroke her hair. She inclines her head to look at me, her heart-shaped face so fucking lovely I want to remember it forever.

"I want to kiss you so badly it's killing me," I whisper.

Her lips part. "I want you to," she says. "But..."

"But?"

"If we're going to do this," she breathes, "we need to agree to some rules."

I trace her jaw with my thumb. Her skin is so soft it makes my body heat. "Okay," I agree. "But I thought you hated rules."

"I do." She traces her fingers over my shirt. "Other people's at least. But I think we need them."

She does, I can tell that much. And if she needs them, she gets them.

"I'm ready. Hit me with them." I lean down to kiss the soft spot on her throat beneath her ear. Her breath catches.

"We keep this between ourselves. I don't want people talking about us."

"We can do that," I say, kissing the shell of her ear. "Agreed."

"We use birth control."

"Goes without saying." I kiss the underside of her jaw. She curls her fingers into my shirt.

"And we don't use a bed."

That one makes me stop for air.

"What?" The corner of my lip quirks. Maybe I misheard her.

"We can have sex anywhere but in bed," she whispers.

"Why?" I'm genuinely interested. I have a feeling I could know this woman for a hundred years and still never be able to guess what will come out of her mouth next.

"Because we both know this isn't going to last," she says. "And I need to protect my heart. No beds, no staying over. Just sex."

"And friendship," I add.

"Friendship?" She looks at me, skeptical.

"Yes." My voice is firm. "I'm not going to walk in here, have sex with you anywhere except a bed, and walk out again. I like this. Talking to you. Holding you. If you want bedless sex, I want friendship."

"Bedless sex and friendship," she murmurs.

"Apparently the basis for any relationship."

"Is that what this is? A relationship?"

"If I'm going to be inside of you, then yes," I say.

"I thought it was every man's dream to have no-strings sex. Wham, bam, thank you for not asking for a ring, ma'am." She lifts a brow at me.

"I was right. You do have a very poor opinion of me." I tip her head up with my finger beneath her chin. "First of all, there'll be no wham bam. There'll be, oh my God, Hudson, don't stop." I say the last bit in a falsetto. Her smile widens. "And secondly, if I want meaningless sex, I have a perfectly good hand and shower to provide it for me. So if we're doing this, that's my one demand. We have dates. I take you on them. If the mood strikes, we have sex."

"And if the mood doesn't?" she says, her eyes dark as she stares at me.

"I don't think that's going to be a problem. But then that's fine too."

"You're very unexpected, you know that?" she asks me.

"Pot meet kettle."

She reaches up to take my tie off, then unfastens my top button. "Sit back down," she says.

I do what she asks, and for a minute I think that's it. My one request is a deal breaker.

Which is pretty fucking funny if you think about it. I've spent most of my life avoiding intimacy.

But this woman is different. I don't want to be free. I want to capture her.

Most of all, I want her to want that.

She's still standing as I look up at her. I can feel the power differential thrumming through me. If this was a business negotiation there's no way I'd be sitting and letting her stand.

But this isn't business. This is... I don't know what it is.

And then, right as I think she's going to tell me to leave,

Skyler does the unexpected once more. She reaches for her own top button, sliding the metal stamped disc through the eye, then repeats it for the next and the next, until her dress is gaping at her chest.

My fingers twitch with the need to take control. To be the one unbuttoning her dress. To be the one kissing her until she's breathless. But I've been in enough negotiations to know when to push and when to hold back.

She needs to equal the power differentiation between us – the one that exists in her head at least. I curl my fingers around the armrests of my chair to stop myself from reaching for her.

Her gaze is fixed firmly on me as she unbuttons four more metal discs until her dress falls completely open, revealing her luscious curves, encased in black lace lingerie. Her dragon tattoo is curled around her hip, and I'm so fucking desperate to trace it with my tongue that I almost launch myself out of my chair.

"You're so beautiful," I manage to rasp.

"Take your jacket off," she whispers. So I do. I have a feeling I'd do whatever the fuck this woman asked of me right now.

And when I'm sitting there in my shirt and pants, she shucks her dress off, leaving her in her heels and lingerie and nothing else, to the delight of my already-aching cock.

"You're so beautiful," I tell her again.

"So are you," she says, walking toward me, straddling my thick thighs until she's sitting on my lap, her half-naked body curling around me.

Threading my fingers through her hair, I pull her closer, until her lips are an inch away from mine.

"You could have asked for more," I tell her.

"I would have agreed to less," she confesses, smiling at me.

That's when I know I'm fucked, in the most literal of ways. And when I realize I don't give a damn that I am. All I want to do is taste her lips and fuck her senseless, apparently not in a bed.

So I press my mouth against hers, and it's on.

eighteen

SKYLER

I'm not sure I've ever been more turned on in my life than right now, as Hudson Fitzgerald kisses me hard and fast, his breath warm against my lips, his tongue teasing mine. I feel powerful yet completely at his mercy at the same time. It's confusing and perfect in every way.

He tightens his hold on me, his hands sliding down my body, then up my stomach, my ribcage, his fingers pushing at my bra.

I break the kiss, desperate to feel his body against mine. "This needs to come off," I say urgently, tugging at his shirt. It takes us a moment of teamwork to unfasten the buttons and throw the white cotton garment on the floor. But then he's bare chested and I'm almost naked as he pulls me against him with his strong arms.

His skin is warm, stretched across taut muscles. A contrast to my soft curves. I run my hands over him, feeling the ridges and dips of his abdomen and chest. His eyes are dark, following my movement.

Then he reaches behind me and takes my bra off.

"Fuck," he mutters, looking at my breasts. "How the hell are you so perfect?" I open my mouth to tell him I'm not, but he's already standing, lifting me with him, my arms around his neck, my breasts pressed into his chest.

"Where are we going?" I murmur as he starts to stalk through the tables and chairs. Our dinner is forgotten, and I feel a momentary pang about that because that shrimp was so good. But then I have a feeling the main course – Hudson – will be even better.

"I need to look at you," he mutters, sliding my panty-clad behind onto an empty table closer to the bar. I can see the thick ridge of his excitement clearly through his pants. "This would be much easier on a bed."

I smile coquettishly at him. "You strike me as a man who never takes the easy way."

"I take the easy way when it doesn't lead to back problems," he mutters, but then he leans forward to kiss my waist, his breath hot against my tattoo and any sassy retort I might have made dissolves on my tongue.

As his tongue starts to trail across my skin.

He kisses my hipbone, my stomach, then slowly drags his lips up to the swell of my breasts. There's a deep rumble in his throat as he kisses each one in turn.

"Gonna dream of these," he mutters against my skin.

"In your bed," I manage to gasp as he closes his mouth around my nipple.

He chuckles against me, then lashes his tongue and my eyes just about roll into the back of my head. I reach down, running my nails over his scalp and he groans in response.

This is happening. I'm going to have bedless sex with

Hudson Fitzgerald and I don't think I've ever wanted anything more in my life.

I'm splayed out on the table and he's standing in front of me, my legs hooked around his shoulders as he teases my body. It's awkward and it's hot and right now I'm reconsidering my requirement about no beds.

And then he pulls me toward him and kisses me softly and I remember why I made it in the first place.

This man would be so easy to fall for. I know it's an abrupt change in direction after all my hatred of him, but I didn't know him then. I do now. I know his favorite childhood memory. I know how fiercely he loves those he's closest to.

I know he'd do anything for them. It touches me so hard that I can feel my heart already aching.

"Take your pants off," I tell him, needing him to be as naked as me.

"Need to make you come first," he tells me.

"I think that's a pretty foregone conclusion." I'm practically vibrating here, without any form of energy except the desire his mouth is creating as he kisses me hard, his thumbs brushing over my nipples before he moves his hand lower, sliding it underneath the elastic of my panties.

"Fuck, you're wet."

"It's your fault." I'm getting a cricked neck from leaning up to kiss him. And he's so damn awkward as he leans over me. Yet pleasure is radiating from my body every time he brushes his thumb over my clit.

"Pants off," I say again, tugging at them this time, my fingers unbuckling his belt to slide the tailored wool over his hips. His cock is jutting out from his boxers, the head thick and swollen as it escapes from his waistband. I curl my hand around him, my thumb brushing him. "You're wet too," I murmur as he kicks his pants across the floor.

"Your fault," he replies, brushing the hair away from my face. "Last chance," he says. "Sure you wouldn't like to take this to a bed?"

I would, I really would. But I'm stubborn and I'm turned on and I'm kind of liking the way he's so desperate to get me horizontal. I want him to remember tonight for a long, long time.

So I push him away, then slide off the table to my feet, before dropping to my knees. I look up at him, my eyelashes sweeping over my face.

His lips part as I pull his shorts down, a soft breath escaping them as I curl my fingers around his thick, stiff excitement. I push my tongue out, slowly circling it around him and he groans.

"Sky..."

I slide my mouth over him as he grunts out my name, tasting his warmth, feeling his fingers tangle into my hair. All suggestions of beds and bad backs disappear as I move my lips over his skin, my tongue flicking as he almost escapes my mouth, before I engulf him once more.

It only takes a minute for his breath to turn ragged. I love the way I'm on my knees, yet I feel so in control. This huge, muscled man has his eyes trained on me as I look up at him, sucking him, teasing him.

Then I flutter my tongue against his head and he lets out a growl. Before I can swallow him down again, he's leaning down, lifting me up onto the table once more, pushing me back so I'm splayed out on the surface and he's the one on his knees, his stubble scraping my thighs as he parts them with his face, burying it between them.

Dear God, this man knows how to make me squirm. His

tongue is weaving some kind of black magic against my clit as he slides a finger inside of me, making me arch my back against the table.

And yes, it's hard and cold and I'd so much rather it be a bed, but this is pretty damn hot, being ravished in an empty bar.

He slides a second finger inside, murmuring in approval as I tighten around him, pleasure coiling deep inside my body, ready to explode. He pulls my clit between his lips, sucking, flicking with his tongue, and then he scrapes me with his teeth and I'm done.

"Hudson!" My eyes widen as the strongest orgasm I've felt in my life overtakes me. My hands clutch at the air, my body convulses, my breath escapes in little torn up bursts, as he carries on plundering me with his mouth.

"You have to stop," I manage to get out. "You're going to kill me."

I'm only half joking. I read about a woman who couldn't stop orgasming. It seems like a dream, but it turned into a nightmare pretty quick. She'd go to the grocery store and collapse in a pile of goo while disapproving old ladies expressed disappointment.

What if I don't stop? What if that becomes me? Hudson damn Fitzgerald has a lot to answer for.

Thankfully he does stop, his eyes dark as he pulls himself reluctantly away from my thighs, kissing his way up my body to my lips as he softly presses his mouth against mine. They're warm, they taste of me. It's weirdly decadent.

"I want to be inside of you," he murmurs against me.

Oh god, I need that too. Praise be, my orgasm is waning, dissolving into a soft, warm pleasure that radiates through my body. I nod, and he pulls out a condom, sliding it easily on, before he pulls me against him. I don't tell him I'm on the pill – he doesn't need to know that I take it for bad periods. I just like that he's taken my requirements seriously. His heated excitement is hard against me as I wrap my legs around his hips and he lazily thrusts inside.

The air rushes from my lips. This man is big. I hold onto his shoulders, trying to get used to his size.

"Okay?" he asks me, our gaze locking.

I want to tell him to stop being nice to me. To stop checking on me. To stop snapping my soul in two. But instead I nod again, and he pulls out then pushes in, his eyes looking down at the connection between us as he moves in and out of my body, his rhythm creating a burning need inside of me, and sating it all at the same time.

"Better than I imagined," he mutters. "So much better."

He's imagined me like this. My cheeks heat up at the thought.

"Fuck me until you break me," I whisper.

A half-smile pulls at his lips as he takes me at my word and starts to thrust harder, faster, his hands trailing over my body as I cling onto his. He kisses me, his hand sliding down until it's between us, his thumb finding where I need him, the movements matching the rhythm of his thrusts until I swear I'm going to combust.

"Hudson..."

"Come," he murmurs, kissing me. "Come for me. All over me."

So I do. Every muscle in my body tightens as pleasure washes over me in a wave. Softer, this time, but no less sweet. I bite his shoulder to stop myself from screaming, and then he's muttering my name, stilling as he spills inside of me, his breath rough and sharp as I scrape my nails down his back.

We stay like that for a minute, my arms tight around him, my mouth against his skin, his face buried into my hair. I'm almost afraid to let go. I don't know what happens next.

I lift my head up to catch him staring at me, an unreadable expression on his handsome face. Neither of us says a word, we just stare.

And then he reaches between us and pulls out of me, his fingers keeping the condom secure, before he grabs something from his pants and strides unabashedly naked over to the bathroom, the door swinging closed behind him.

I immediately miss his warmth. But it's only a second before he's back. He has something in his hand, something white.

It takes a moment before I realize it's a handkerchief that he's dampened under the tap.

"It's clean," he tells me, as he slides it between my legs, the warm cotton cleaning up the mess he's made of me.

My throat is tight as he takes care of me, cleaning me up before he stands and kisses me softly. I sit up, watching him as he pulls his shorts back on.

"You have no idea how much I want to take you to bed right now," he tells me.

My chest tightens. "You just did."

"I mean to snuggle."

For some reason him saying that word makes me laugh. Snuggle and Hudson Fitzgerald aren't two things I'd ever put together.

"I'm not a snuggler," I lie, swinging my legs because I like the way he can't stop looking at my naked body. "I'd annoy you by being restless." I reach for him, wrapping my arms around his neck, as he stands between my legs.

"You're annoying me by not letting me take you to bed," he mutters.

I tip my head to the side, running my fingers through his hair. It's soft and silky against my skin. "It's better this way," I murmur. "Now you can go home and sleep in your own bed and not worry about when it's a good time to leave or if I'm going to demand that you stay all night. No strings, no worries."

His eyes narrow. "Who says there's no strings?" He sounds almost pissed off now.

I swallow hard. "Isn't that what you want? Your life is complicated enough without me." I try to smile. "And I promise, I'm always a huge complication."

"Maybe I like complications," he mutters. "And you said no bed. You didn't say no strings."

Oh, he looks really annoyed.

"Isn't that every man's dream?" I ask him. "For a woman to offer up sex without expecting anything from him?"

"I have no fucking idea," he says shortly. "But it's not my dream. There are definitely strings here. A goddamned web of them."

"What kind of strings?" I rub the pads of my fingers against his scalp. He closes his eyes, his face relaxing.

"Obviously I want to see you again," he says when he opens his eyes. "Next Tuesday. And every Tuesday after that."

"Tuesday?" I say. "That's very specific."

"Autumn has Ayda sleep over at her place on Tuesdays."

My heart does a little leap. "Okay," I breathe. "What else?"

"We don't see anybody else." His eyes catch mine.

"I guess I'd better break things off with Mylene," I say sighing. "Shame, she makes a mean coffee."

"I'm serious, Skyler. I don't share."

Of course he doesn't. "No sharing," I agree.

"Good. And maybe I'll need the occasional massage," he says grumpily, picking up my dress from the floor and putting it over my shoulders like he's worried I'll get cold. "Because I'm going to end up with a fucking slipped disc at this rate."

My breath catches. "Just how long is this thing going to go on for?" I ask him, sliding my arms through the denim. Because he's making it sound like a long term thing.

"Maybe we should make it less bedless..." he murmurs.

"It's non negotiable," I say firmly. Because I need to have some power here. I have a feeling that not only would this man walk all over me if I let him, I'd actually enjoy having his foot in my face.

Not literally. I'm not a foot fetishist. But I still need to assert my authority, or what little of it I have. And keeping this relationship out of bed is all I've got.

"I'll bill you for my chiropractor," he says, pulling his pants on. "I'm way too old for this."

"Shut up, you're in your thirties. You're not exactly at death's door." I smile at him and he shakes his head.

"I'll get you into a bed if it kills me," he mutters.

"Not going to happen," I say lightly, secretly enjoying the way he looks so grumpy. My dress is still gaping and he can't stop looking. *Good.* "But you can use your imagination. Just because we won't be having sex in a bed doesn't mean you have to give yourself sciatica. Don't be a killjoy. If you want me, you'll have to take what I'm offering."

He reaches out to trace my lips with the pad of his thumb. "I want you," he says gruffly.

Another thrill rushes through me. "Then work for it," I whisper.

Something about my words makes his eyes darken further. "Christ, you're aggravating."

"Right back at you." I lean forward to kiss him softly, and his mouth yields against mine, the scowl on his face replaced by a warm gaze. "Now let's finish getting dressed and eat dinner. I think we might need the calories."

nineteen

HUDSON

"You're in a weirdly good mood," Autumn says the next week when she brings in a stack of bills for me to sign off. They're mostly for the bar renovation, for the building supplies and the first installment for the contractors.

The lead contractor is a good guy. Sam also worked on the hotel when we were remodeling it. I know for a fact he has a soft spot for the bar. He and his workers spent every night there back when they were working on the hotel.

"Am I?" I ask.

"Yes you are. You haven't even bitched about the increased costs."

"Wait," I say. "There are increased costs?"

My sister grins at me. "No, but it was fun to watch you freak out. So what's got you smiling like that?"

I roll my eyes at her. "I'm not smiling. I'm just not frowning."

"Isn't that the same thing for you?" she teases.

Truth is, it's the thought of tonight that's making me feel relaxed and not constantly fucking stressed. After I left Skyler last week, I've spent more time thinking about how to get her into my bed than I have about the spreadsheets on my screen and the deal we're about to close in London.

I've also called her every night. The first time she sounded confused when she answered. Like she couldn't figure out why I was taking the time to call her. But somehow we've gotten into a rhythm – I call her after Ayda is asleep. It's the highlight of my day if I'm honest.

She's like a wild bird. I have to approach slowly to make sure she doesn't fly away. And yeah, I like that challenge. It's made all the more difficult by the fact that I can't simply go and see her every evening. I have Ayda to take care of, which means I've had to be more creative in my wooing.

It hasn't escaped my notice that Skyler's usually in bed when I call. I made her go onto video last night and yes, after talking for almost two hours the conversation got dirty. And I talked her into making herself come in front of me. It's the closest I'm going to get to having her on a mattress, at least for now.

But that doesn't mean I don't have some ideas to make her bedless sex demands easier on my back. One of which I'm putting into practice tonight. Because fuck it, I want that woman in my bed.

But that will have to wait.

I sign the last invoice and ask Autumn to send them over to my accountant. She only has to upload them to the system and he'll make sure they all get paid.

"Listen," she says as she takes the papers back from me. "Can I drop Ayda off a little later tomorrow?"

"Why?" I ask. Though truth be told that would make my life easier too.

"Because I'd like to take her over to the mainland in the morning." My sister fiddles with the hem of her shirt, a surefire indication that she's nervous. "There's a children's author talking there. I thought it might be good for her. You know how much she loves books."

Yeah, she does. "Which author?"

"Emma Salinger. Francie's sister-in-law, you remember her?"

I shake my head because I really don't. Francie has so many brothers and sisters-in-laws that I lose track.

"She's married to Francie's youngest brother," Autumn reminds me, not noticing my complete apathy. "Brooks. He's the real estate guy."

Oh yeah, actually I do know who she's talking about. I've had dealings with Brooks in the past. He's a good man.

"Okay." I nod. "She'd like that."

Francie claps her hands together. "Perfect. Oh, and I confirmed an end date for the renovations. They should be done in ten days. I'm going to tell Skyler to start preparing for the grand opening."

"I'll tell her," I say far too quickly. Then immediately regret it. "I need to talk to her about something else anyway," I add.

"What do you have to talk about?" Autumn asks. "I thought you didn't like her."

"I like her enough to pay for the damn renovations."

My sister grins at my annoyance, though she has no idea *why* I'm annoyed. Maybe it's because I feel like it's so damn obvious that I like that woman. And that she at least tolerates me. Yet somehow I feel like everybody else in the world would find our almost-relationship hard to understand.

And sometimes, I fucking long to be understood.

twenty

SKYLER

I'll be there at six. We're going out. Bring a sweater. – Hudson

My lips curl as I read the message on my phone screen. Even though it's just black letters on a white screen the grumpiness is so obvious – I can actually hear it in his voice.

And I know why he's so grumpy. He's spent the whole last week trying to persuade me to spend tonight in bed with him. My bed, his bed, he doesn't care. He even offered the honeymoon suite at the Grand Liberty Hotel, as if that wouldn't sent the tongues rolling all over town.

Despite his bitching – and then his soft cajoling which is much harder to withstand – I've held firm all week when we've talked. It's weird how I've gotten used to him calling. And how much I've missed being in the same room with him.

Which is a good reminder that I can never get into a bed with him. If I can just avoid snuggling, I can avoid getting my heart broken.

"It's looking good, huh?" Sam, the head contractor brings me out of my thoughts. I slide my phone into my jeans pocket and follow his gaze.

They've been working on the outside today, because they're waiting on the new flooring to arrive. The deck has been stripped and the first layer of stain put on the wood, and the roofers are putting new shingles on the porch overhang. Autumn called me today and told me that the new tables and chairs will be arriving early next week, and that she wants to discuss the reopening plans.

I let out a long breath. "It looks amazing," I tell him. "I can't believe how quickly you're getting things done."

Sam shrugs. "We were given a timeline. Autumn can be fierce if anybody disagrees with her."

Just like her brother. I can't imagine how much this whole renovation is costing him. And I feel stupidly guilty about it. I've tried to bring it up with him multiple times over the past week – wanting to agree to a repayment schedule – and each time he's batted me away.

Sam and the other contractors pack up for the evening, loading their tools into their trucks as they head down the hill toward the dock where the ferry is waiting for them. In the distance I can see Jesse opening up the ramp to allow cars on. He lifts a hand up at me and I wave back.

He's taken to dropping in to see the progress of the renovations on his way home from work. When he saw the new stage in the design – much bigger than the old one, able to hold a band rather than just two people at a push – he smiled.

I'm going to ask him if he can perform on opening

night. Just as soon as I run it past Autumn, because I feel like this is her baby too.

"Well this is looking different," Eileen says – or at least I think it's Eileen – as she walks up behind me.

"Hi." I don't say her name just in case. I smile though. "It's a transformation, isn't it?"

Even half-finished the difference between the peeling paint of the old Salty Dog and the freshly repaired deck with dark stains and white painted pillars is stark. Autumn showed me the furniture she liked before she ordered it, wanting my opinion. I'd oohed and aahed over the rustic white painted chairs and stools, plus the sofas that Autumn tells me will be perfect for day tourists who want to spend the afternoon drinking cocktails while overlooking the ocean.

"It's very pretty. I was wondering, do you have an opening date yet?" Eileen or Mylene asks. "With the summer season coming up I've had a lot of inquiries about rooms and some of them are asking if there's a local bar."

Ah, it's definitely Eileen. Crisis averted. "Autumn is coming to talk with me about it tomorrow. She wants to have a grand opening as soon as the renovations are done, but I'm not so sure. I don't have any employees."

"Oh, you can get the old staff back in. And I'm sure Jesse will help you if you ask him. I've been seeing him popping in here most nights." She waggles her eyebrows at me.

"There's nothing going on between us," I say quickly. Because I don't want her to get the wrong idea.

She smiles. "Of course there isn't. There couldn't…" She shakes her head. "Can I ask for a favor?" she says, beaming at me in a way she never has before.

"Sure," I say, because if I'm going to be running this

place I need to make friends with the other business owners. "What is it?"

"Invite *me* to the opening party. Not *her*." She wrinkles her nose, looking up the hill at *Brewed Awakenings*. "She always gets in first and it's infuriating."

"Mylene?" I ask.

She widens her eyes as though I've just said Beelzebub. "*Her*," she says. "Yes."

"I can't ask you and not her," I say, shifting my feet.

"Why not?" Eileen frowns.

"Because it would be rude."

"It would be rude to ask her," Eileen counters. "Because then *I* wouldn't be able to come." She looks put out as she smooths down her dress pants. "You want me there, don't you?"

"You were both at Ayda's party. Why can't you do the same here?"

Her jaw twitches as she leans forward. "That was a mix up. I thought it was my turn. When I realized we were both there, Autumn came over and asked me to put my feelings aside for one day. It was hell," she whispers.

I'm still dying to ask her why she and Mylene don't talk.

"If you could do it for Autumn can you do it for me?" I give her my best puppy dog eyes, but she still shakes her head.

"Never again. If I die without seeing that woman's face for the rest of my life I'll die happy."

I don't point out that she must see it every time she looks in the mirror, because that would just be catty, even if it's true.

"Maybe Mylene won't be able to come," I say hopefully. Eileen winces again when I say her sister's name.

"Oh, she'll be there. Just to spite me." She rolls her lips

over her teeth, bearing more than a casual resemblance to a rabid dog. "That hussy."

Before I can make another attempt at reconciliation, she turns on her heel and stomps away. But not before a sleek black sports car drives past her. She stops and stares at it, and I swallow hard because I should have realized that everybody would see him arriving in daylight.

She lifts a brow then carries on walking to her house, and I take a deep breath, readying myself for a Hudson Fitzgerald onslaught.

"No beds, no snuggling, no falling for him," I mutter to myself.

But I fear it might be too late.

* * *

"So where are we going?" I ask Hudson as he steers me toward the open passenger door of his car. His palm is splayed against my back, which means his skin is touching my skin because I'm wearing a pair of vintage embroidered flares and a white lace cropped blouse. Goosebumps break out over me.

"I told you, it's a surprise," he says.

"A good surprise?" I ask, sitting down in the bucket seat. "By the way, why do you have such a nice car on this island? Isn't it a waste?" I look around at the sleek interior of the car. The console gleams like it's been polished by an army of elves.

"A waste? Why?" he asks, looking confused.

I pat the smooth-as-butter cream leather seat next to his thick thigh. "This must've cost hundreds of thousands. And you probably don't clock more than five miles a day in it."

"I drive it to the mainland," he tells me. "And what makes you think it costs hundreds of thousands?"

"Because it's a sports car."

"It's an affordable sports car," he says. "A Subaru. I hate to shatter your dreams, but I'm not the kind of guy who throws two hundred thousand dollars down on a car."

I turn to look at him. He has a smile on his face. I wrinkle my nose at him and he smiles harder.

"Okay, I used to have a Porsche," he admits, looking sheepish. "But the salty air isn't great for it. I sold it and bought this."

Of course he had a Porsche. He probably had a whole army of them. Wait, what's a collective noun for Porsches? A Pickle?

"And I have the Range Rover, of course. That's more expensive, but more practical for driving Ayda around. Autumn has that one tonight."

"How many cars do you have in total?" I ask, still imagining that Populace of Porsches.

"Three. Plus my dad's old Jag that's sitting undriveable in the garage at the house. Once I retire I want to restore it."

There's a dreaminess to his voice that surprises me. "You want to retire one day?" I ask.

"Doesn't everybody?" He starts up the engine with a push of a button.

"I don't know," I say. "I kind of imagined you being at the helm of your company until your dying day. Falling face first into a pile of unread memos. Like that guy on *The Simpsons*."

"I'm assuming you're not talking about Homer," he says, pulling out of his spot and onto the road.

"I am not. Mr. Burns," I say, clicking my fingers. "That's who I meant."

"What a compliment," he murmurs. "Now my life is complete."

I roll my eyes at him even though he's too busy watching the road ahead to notice. There's a smile playing at his lips and I like it way too much. It gives him a boyishly handsome look that sends warning claxons in my ears.

Don't fall for him. Don't snuggle. No beds!

Once we're off of Main Street he takes a right, which means we're definitely staying on the island for our date – if that's what this is. As we progress along the country road, buildings disappear into nothing, replaced by trees and bushes that line the edges, framing the view of the sparkling ocean beyond.

"Are we going to your hotel?" I ask suspiciously.

"No."

"Then where?" I ask. "Or are we going to have to play twenty questions?"

"Patience," he tells me. "All will be revealed." He looks ridiculously smug as we pass both the road to the hotel and the one to his house.

"If you wanted to drive me off a cliff you could have done it closer to town," I say when he takes a sharp right turn, onto a rocky road that makes the car rise up and down like an amusement ride.

"I figure your body is less likely to be found out here," he says.

"Oh," I say as the road gets even rockier. "Are you taking me to a lookout point? Are we going to make out in the car?" I look around the tiny interior. "Because I'm not sure it'll do wonders for your bad back."

Hudson sighs. I wonder if I can annoy him enough to make him not want me. Maybe that would be better all around.

The problem is I *want* him to want me.

This whole attraction thing is very confusing.

The trees that overhang the road part, revealing a cluster of old houses that look like nobody's been living in them for years. And the most glorious view of the Atlantic Ocean as its white tipped waves lap against the golden sand in the secret cove below.

"Wow," I whisper.

"I know." A smile pulls at his lips. "Come on, let's take a closer look." He cuts the engine outside the house closest to the cliff and climbs out, walking around to open my door. "Wait, where's your sweater?" he asks.

Oh damn. "I'm not great at taking instructions," I tell him. He should know this by now. Truth is, I'd completely forgotten about it.

He sighs again. I wonder how many more sighs I can get out of him today. And then he opens the trunk and grabs two old pieces of fabric from the car. It takes me a minute to realize they're blankets.

"It's not even cold," I tell him.

"It will be later. When the sun goes down."

"We're staying here that long?" I ask him.

He ignores me, grabbing an insulated cooler from his trunk. The same one as last week, with Grand Liberty Hotel written on it in swirling script.

"A picnic?" I ask him.

"Unless you want me to take you to dinner at the hotel, or back to my place. Otherwise this is our only option," he says, inclining his head at the cliff. I follow him, wishing I'd worn more appropriate shoes. My heels keep sinking into the grass as I follow him.

"You only want to feed me in your house because it has

a bed in it," I tease, and I swear I see a hint of a smile pull at his lips.

"Luckily for you, there are no beds on the beach." We arrive at the cliff edge. There are some old stairs carved into the stone at the top, leading to wooden ones that twist and turn down to the beach, into a little cove that is completely deserted. Even in the fading light it looks perfect.

"How beautiful," I say. "Do you own this too?"

"All this land from here to the town," he murmurs. "Yes."

He leads the way down, and I follow gingerly behind, taking off my stupid shoes because even with the threat of splinters in my soles I'm still more likely to survive than if I try descending to the beach in my heels. Hudson, on the other hand, manages to carry the blankets in one hand and the cooler in the other, not having to touch the wooden banisters once before we reach the sand.

If it was pretty from above, right now this little cove is breathtaking. The water is lapping gently against the golden sand, and there's a copse of bushes growing up from a dune on the left. You can't see the rest of the island from here at all, just the ocean. We could be stranded on a desert island with how quiet and secluded it is.

"What a place," I say, looking back up at the cliffs. "Are you planning to build here?"

"We are. An exclusive retreat." He nods. "But tonight it's ours."

He lays out one of the blankets and tells me to sit down and wrap the other around my shoulders, before he puts the cooler down next to me and starts to wander off.

"Hey, where are you going?" I call out, alarmed. Because we're a good couple of miles away from town and there's no way I can find my way back in the dark.

"Collecting firewood," he shouts out, pointing at a pile of sticks and twigs next to the sand dune. "Well, strictly speaking I got one of my staff to collect it earlier. I'm just bringing them over."

I start to laugh, because it feels so like Hudson to have his staff do personal things like this. He shakes his head and brings the firewood over, then starts to stack them expertly.

"Couldn't you have asked your staff to build the fire too?" I ask, still amused, as he flicks a lighter and puts it to the edge of a rolled up piece of newspaper. "Hell, you could have had them come and join us. Bedless sex all round."

"Shut up. I had too many meetings today. Otherwise I would've done it." He slides the lighted paper between the sticks and softly blows on the flame as it licks against the pile of wood he's created. To my shock, they ignite. He smiles at his own skill as the orange flames light up his face, making it glow.

"You look so damn proud of yourself right now," I tell him.

"Still got it." He winks at me.

"What is it about men and fires?" I ask him, tipping my head to the side. It's funny seeing him this way. Genuinely relaxed, with a smile on his face.

My heart does this weird little twisty thing. I'm almost getting used to it now.

"We like to provide," he says. "It's genetic. You should just let us."

"Very caveman," I say. But I have to admit, it's kind of sexy seeing how easily he can light a fire. "What made you decide to bring me here?" I ask him, still trying to reconcile this fire-building, picnic loving man with the devil-in-a-designer suit he usually is.

He sits down next to me, then deliberately lies back.

"Mostly this," he says, smiling over at me. "Horizontal bedless sex."

My mouth gapes open. "You'll do anything to get around the rules, won't you?"

He sits up, still grinning. "I thought of this place the other day. Remember when you asked me about my favorite memory? It was here. Me and my brothers and sisters used to come here to swim when we wanted to be away from the crowds at the main beaches during the summer. I guess I wanted to show it to you."

A wave of emotion washes over me. I look at him, blinking. So not just about horizontal sex.

"Come on," he urges. "Where are your smart ass remarks? You can tease me about how skinny I was as a kid if you like."

"You were skinny?" I ask him, my throat still feeling tight.

"As fuck. Filled out in junior year, thank god. We were all the same, Asher, Zach, Wyatt."

"More genetics," I murmur. "I've only met Asher, right?"

"Yep. My tech bro."

"He's a tech bro?" I grin. "I didn't know that. What do your other brothers do?

"Wyatt runs a charter boat company down south," he tells me, tracing my skin. "And Zach runs an art gallery in Chicago, but I'm pretty fucking sure he makes most of his money gambling but he hides it from me."

"You don't like the idea of him gambling?" I say, remembering the way his dad lost everything to poker.

"Not much. But I dislike him hiding it more."

Of course he does. One thing I know about this man is that he dislikes being blindsided. Like me arriving on the island without him knowing. "Maybe you need to relax a little about it," I say.

He lifts a brow. Okay then.

"I thought you were going to feed me," I say, changing the subject as I lean forward to grab the cooler. He snatches it from me and starts to get the food out, like he's affronted that I should lift a finger on this date.

I watch, my stomach rumbling, as he lifts out the Tupperware containers full of food.

This time it's true picnic fare. Sandwiches and cut up veggies plus some potato chips.

"Did you make this picnic?" I ask him, because it doesn't look like restaurant food. I'm surprised that he had time. Not that I care, I love proper picnics. Finger food is my jam.

"Some of it." He shrugs, like he's embarrassed. But the truth is, I like it. He surprises me in the weirdest of ways. He's like an iceberg, so much of him is beneath the surface. And I want to dive down to discover it.

"That explains it," I say, taking a bite of an egg sandwich. "You've brought me here to poison me and get rid of my body. Nice work."

* * *

We spend the next hour eating sandwiches and tiny cakes and talking. Hudson adds the occasional log onto the fire when it starts to wane, and I try not to fangirl over what a great fire tender he is.

The night starts to come in, the inky blue of the sky turns the ocean a dark gray, though the tips are still white as they kiss against the shore.

"Okay, this is what I really brought you here to see,"

Hudson says, when we've finished our food and the dishes are packed away. "Come here."

"I knew it," I say. And let's be honest, I'm ready for a bit of bedless sex with the suave businessman who apparently could come in handy when Armageddon hits. "Wait, let me rinse my mouth out with some water. I taste of egg salad sandwiches."

He shakes his head and pulls me toward him, but instead of kissing me, he pulls me down until my back is against the sand, and he's laying prone too, both of us staring up at the sky.

My mouth drops open when I see what he's talking about. There are a billion stars sparkling against the velvety black of the sky above us. It looks like a black velvet pincushion with a light shining behind it, through the tiny holes in the heavens.

"Keep watching," he murmurs. "I used to see shooting stars all the time when I was a kid."

"You used to lay here like this?" I ask, still staring up at the sky above us. My fingertips brush against his and he slides his hand into mine.

"Sometimes."

"I used to as well," I say, surprised because this is probably the one thing we have in common. "Not here, of course. Back in California. I loved being outside at night. Looking at the stars somehow made me feel less alone."

His thumb brushes against my hand, sending a little jolt of electricity through me.

"Wait, there!" he says urgently, pointing up with his free hand. I follow the direction, seeing a flash of light sliding against the sky, then disappearing.

"Oh my God," I say, my eyes lighting up with excitement. "We should make a wish."

"What kind of wish?" he murmurs.

"I don't know. One we can't tell each other or it won't come true."

"Okay." His voice is thick.

For a minute we're both silent. I stare up, my brows knitting as I send my wish up into the sky.

I hope Ayda Fitzgerald can learn to talk again.

I don't know where that came from. I could have wished for anything. For Lee and Cora to be happy, for the bar to be renovated in half the time. But somehow it came into my head and now there it is, out in the heavens.

When I turn my head Hudson is staring right at me, his gaze so intense it makes my body feel like it's on fire. I roll onto my side and kiss him hard, my fingers twisting into his hair.

And when we part there's darkness in his eyes. "What was that for?" he murmurs.

"For showing me a shooting star."

The corner of his lip quirks. "Strictly speaking, it was a rock or a meteor."

"Don't spoil it," I tell him. "You're getting me in the mood here. Seduction by stars."

"Remind me to bring you here when the Perseids are on show," he says, reaching out to cup my face.

"When are the Perseids here?" I whisper as he traces my jaw with his thumb.

He glances at my lips. "In the height of summer. August is the best time to see them."

I hate the way my body tightens at the thought of us being together here in August, watching the sky. He's not supposed to make me fall for him. By August we'll probably hate each other again.

But that doesn't stop me from leaning toward him and brushing my lips against his.

This time as we kiss he holds my face softly, his gaze on me as our mouths connect, before he finally releases me to taste me all over. The flames lick against the charred wood as he starts to kiss his way down my neck, his fingers deftly unfastening the buttons on my blouse before he kisses my stomach, my hip, the tattoo that curls across my abdomen.

Then he pulls at my jeans, dragging them down my hips, before he reveals my white thong. Like he's too impatient to take that off too, he pushes it aside and kisses me right there.

A gasp tumbles from my lips.

"You're not wasting any time," I whisper.

He chuckles against me, his tongue trailing a line of fire across my clit. "I don't want to rebuild the fire. Plus, we're gonna have horizontal sex. I've been dreaming of it."

"It's still bedless," I manage to say before he sucks me between his lips. He doesn't reply – he can't when he's doing that. And he's so damn good at it that it takes me less than two minutes to convulse against him, my fingers pulling at his hair because this man already knows how to make me feel good.

When my moans have calmed into regular breaths, he lifts his head up, kissing his way back up to my mouth. We're a blur of fingers as we both pull at his clothes, my feet pushing at his jeans in an attempt to magically get them off his body.

And finally he's naked and hard against me, his elbows resting on either side of me like he's caging me in. He kisses me softly, dragging the tip of him against me. I'm still so sensitive that I gasp. As he rolls on a condom I can't help but look at the way he is so magnificently hard. He's mouthwatering.

"Fuck me horizontal," I whisper as he lines up against me. He laughs, but he does exactly that, sliding inside of me, filling me so well that all the air rushes out of my body.

He rolls his hips, staring at me like I'm some kind of mystery. I stare back, my mouth falling open as he drags himself against my achiest part.

I can't fall in love with this man. It's just sex. But damn, the sex is so good, I'm already vibrating underneath him.

I tighten around him and he lets out a low oath. "Christ."

"You're going to make me come again," I whisper.

"You're going to make *me* come," he replies, kissing me.

But there's no doubt who's in charge here as he slides in and out of me, causing the pleasure to build deep inside of me as he cups my face with his hand and murmurs my name.

This time when I orgasm I call out his name, scraping my fingers down his back, making him groan. I'm still fluttering around him when he follows me into oblivion, capturing my mouth with his as his back arches with pleasure.

When he finally pulls out of me, the fire is already embers. It feels like a metaphor I can't quite fit into my mind. All I know is that I'm so happy I made some boundaries between us. Those rules are the only things that are going to shield me from the full onslaught this man creates inside my body.

Sex and love. They're two separate things.

So why does my heart feel like it's falling?

twenty-one

HUDSON

"What time are you heading over to the party at the Dog?" Autumn asks, walking into my office wearing a silver form-fitting dress. She's been spending every free moment she has over at The Salty Dog, which in any other lifetime would be great because it would mean my sister isn't nagging me to death.

But actually, it's made my life harder. Twice last week I drove off the ferry, intending on stopping at the bar to see Skyler before I headed home to my kid, only to see Autumn's car parked outside.

This keeping our relationship secret from everybody else is getting tiring. And annoying. I said as much to Skyler this week during our date.

This time she insisted I come to the bar again, even though the renovations weren't finished. She cooked for me, then we fucked, and she sent me home annoyed because goddamn it, I want her in a bed.

I've never had to work so hard in my life to get a woman to want to see me. When we're together it's perfect. We have fun, we talk, she makes me laugh like nobody else ever has. Mostly because she likes to tease me, which is good because nobody else does that either.

I make sure she's satisfied. Multiple times. And yet it still feels like I'm trying to catch a cloud whenever I think of her.

"I'll be over there at eight," I say to my sister, remembering she's actually standing there and asking me when I'll be going to the opening night. Truth be told, I'm a little pissed because when I was messaging – okay sexting – with Skyler last night, she made it clear that I was going as an investor and not as her date.

"But it starts at seven."

"I have a meeting at six, and then I have to go home to see Ayda," I say patiently. And she pouts.

"But I want you to see the bar before everybody arrives, it's spectacular. Honestly, Hudson, your guests are going to go crazy over it." She beams at me, and I almost tell her I've already seen it, but then I remember.

Nobody can know.

Ah, fuck that.

"I'll see it," I tell her. "When I get there."

"Who has meetings at six anyway?" she asks. "Are you telling the truth?"

I usually have an infinite well of patience for my sister. But it takes an act of will not to bite back at her.

"My lawyer wants to talk to me," I say.

"What about?"

"I don't know. I guess I will as soon as I speak to him." I lift a brow.

"You will be at the party, right? You got a babysitter, didn't you?"

"Yes." One of the women who works at the hotel is looking for some extra cash to save for her wedding. Turned out she was a nanny before she came to work for us in reception. I've introduced her to Ayda and the two of them got along. Of course, I'll have the nanny cams on too.

I'm not an idiot.

"I'll be there," I say firmly. "I wouldn't miss your grand opening."

"It's not mine, it's Skyler's." She tips her head to the side. "Are you sure you can't sneak out and come with me now?"

"I'm sorry," I tell her. "I really have to make some phone calls before this meeting if I want to make it to the party at all."

"Okay. But be there by eight. I mean it." She widens her eyes at me.

Since when did I let myself get bossed around by my kid sister? I've no idea, but it's clearly catching, because now I'm being dragged around by my balls by a pretty little daydreamer who makes me explode every time I'm inside of her.

I'm a fucking goner and I know it. But I'm still putting up a fight anyway.

* * *

"The answer is no," I say firmly to my lawyer. "I don't even know why you had to ask that."

"Well first of all because you're the client not me, and I take my instructions from you." He looks amused at my outburst. But he shouldn't. I'm fuming at the presumptuousness of the letter Ayda's grandparents have sent him.

They're demanding that Ayda stay with them during the summer for six weeks. In England and without me.

Because they feel it's important for her to learn about her heritage without the influence of *the other party*. Their words, not mine. Because clearly they can't even stand to say my name.

"You know what happened the last time they took her to England," I say, my voice thick. Because I still haven't gotten over it. Strictly speaking, they weren't the ones who took her to England. That was her mother, right before she was involved in an accident that took her life and completely turned Ayda's upside down. But after the funeral, instead of releasing Ayda back into my care like any normal fucking grandparents would, they refused to give up custody and made me wait for months, fighting through the courts for the right to bring up my own daughter.

"I already let them see her four times a year. That's more than they deserve. Tell them no, and tell them if they make any more idiotic requests, they'll be lucky if they see her again before her eighteenth birthday."

He shakes his head. "I think I'll leave that last part out."

"Whatever. It's not happening. Now I have to go. I'd like to see my daughter before she goes to bed tonight."

He ends the video call and I stand up wearily, more ready to go to bed than to a damn party where I have to share the woman who I desperately want to have more of.

But first I'll go home and read my daughter a book, kiss her goodnight, and thank God that she's here on the island and safe.

Once upon a time, that's all I wanted in life. Now I want the fucking fairytale.

The only problem is, I'm no Prince Charming.

***

SKYLER

The entire population of Liberty seems to be squeezed into The Salty Dog for the opening party. There are five of us behind the bar – me, Jesse, Autumn, plus the two prior employees she introduced me to who used to work for my dad. And still we're being run ragged trying to serve everybody who's lined up at the bar.

After tonight we'll provide table service, but for the re-opening Autumn suggested we have everybody line up for their drinks, because we don't have enough staff – or tables – to deal with individual groups.

In an hour we'll lose Jesse to the stage, but I'm hoping by then everybody will have a drink in their hands and be chilled. Still, as Autumn tells me when she reaches past me to grab some bottles of soda, this is a good omen.

"What can I get you?" I ask Eileen, who's across the bar in front of me. She was the first here – she was literally standing on the porch waiting for us to open. A little while ago I saw Mylene stand at the door then walk away as soon as she spotted her twin inside.

"A club soda, please." Eileen looks around, her brows knitted. "I'm not one for drinking alcohol."

"Club soda coming up," I say, grabbing the wand and starting to fill the glass.

"Actually," she says, leaning in like she's about to tell me a secret. "Put a little vodka in there too."

Biting down a smile, I put a shot of Grey Goose in and

pass her the drink. As she takes it, I glance over her shoulder, the way I've been looking over every customer's shoulder when I serve them, waiting to see his black, broody stare and stupidly perfect suit storming through the bar.

Because Hudson Fitzgerald definitely storms everywhere he goes. I'm getting used to it. In fact, I find it a turn on.

Making him laugh is almost as enjoyable as making him come.

A group of men walk in, jostling and laughing, and I lift my hand up to wave hi to the contractors I invited after they finished, because I believe they should get to enjoy themselves after all their hard work. And they did work hard – they finished the final few snags at four this afternoon.

It's past eight by the time I see Hudson standing at the door, nodding at one of the locals. They're talking to him and he's listening patiently, even though he has his resting bastard-face on.

And yeah, a shiver runs down my spine because I know what that face can do. I know what that body can do.

I let out a long breath.

"There he is!" Autumn's face lights up when she sees her brother. "Hudson! Want a beer?" she shouts out.

He looks over at us, his jaw tight as his gaze roams over to me. My chest tightens as our gazes lock.

I know he has a babysitter for Ayda tonight. It would be so, so easy to ask him to stay over with me tonight. In my bed. To wake up with his arms around me.

"I'm gonna head over to the stage," Jesse whispers in my ear. His warm voice makes me jump. I turn to look at him and we both smile.

"What's your opening number?" I ask him.

"It's a surprise." He grins at me. We really are fast friends now. It's strange how close I feel to him in a non-amorous way. So it doesn't annoy me one bit that every woman who's not staring at Hudson is staring at my friend as he saunters over to the stage and picks up his guitar, sitting down on the stool and forming the chords he uses to tune the strings.

"Imma take a quick bathroom break," Autumn says, since the line at the bar has dwindled down to pretty much nothing. Everybody's too busy getting excited about the live music to order drinks right now.

"Of course." I hug her. "Thank you. You can go enjoy the rest of the party with Parker. You're the one who did all the hard work to make this happen."

I gesture around us. The walls are painted a soft, ocean blue, the oak stained floor gleaming in contrast. And the tables with their cream leather upholstered chairs add a luxurious touch. But she's still kept the heart of the place. The jukebox – in full working order – is in the corner, and when there's no band playing, it will be echoing the music my dad loved.

I wish he'd seen it. I wish he knew what this place was like now. But I push that thought away because today is for happy things.

"I loved every minute of working on this place." She winks at me. "You're so much nicer than my last boss."

I laugh because we both know her last boss – and her next one – is her brother. After the bar she's scheduled to start designing the interior of the retreat center he has planned on the north of the island. In the little fishermen's cottages he showed me before we made love on the beach.

And now I'm blushing. I lean on the bar as Jesse introduces himself to the crowd – who he pretty much grew up with and know exactly who he is. They give him a loud cheer anyway and I can't help but grin.

"This one is for our new resident and the owner of the bar." He winks at me and leans in, his fingers softly strumming before his low, graveled voice starts to echo through the microphone. I swear my whole body turns to goosebumps as he starts to sing the first line of "Rhiannon" by Fleetwood Mac.

Jesse loves seventies rock as much as I do – another fact we've discovered since we've been sitting around, listening to music whenever he visits. And he knows I love this song most of all. About a woman who's taken over by a free spirit. Nobody can pin her down. Nobody can really have her.

I love the way Stevie Nicks sings this song, especially live. The way she twists and turns on the stage. The way she's so beautiful and untouchable and is like a goddess.

When Jesse reaches the part where he sings that she's been taken by the sky, he looks over at me, and for some reason my throat feels tight. I love that he's sung this for me. I love that we have this friendship.

This place is starting to feel like home. Something I never knew I needed.

I take a deep breath and turn to see Hudson staring at me too. Then he looks at the door marked 'private', the one that leads to the apartment I've been living in but have never let him in.

Then he inclines his head at it, and my heart starts to slam against my chest.

I still can't quite work out this hold he has over me. Maybe I don't want to work it out. All the best magic is spoiled by peeking behind the magician's curtain.

Sometimes people come into your lives for a reason. I wonder if I needed this, the ache, the desire. If it's what keeps me anchored here long enough for me to grow roots.

That thought would usually make me panic. If I'm being honest, it still does a bit. I know I've effectively put down roots by keeping this bar and starting to run it, but I also know that Hudson would buy it off me in a second if I wanted to leave. At a profit, too, thanks to the investment he's put in.

"I'm going to grab something I forgot," I whisper in Maud's ear. She's one of the two seasoned bar staff who've come back to work here. She doesn't blink an eyelid at the fact that for a little while there'll only be two of them behind the bar.

There's a security monitor in the apartment living room, so I'll be able to see if an unexpected crowd forms. But right now everybody's dancing between the tables as Jesse segues into a faster song – "Jesse's Girl" – which really makes me grin.

As soon as I hit the code on the door to my apartment and walk inside, I can *feel* him right behind me. He's not even touching me, yet I'm shivering.

The door clicks closed behind him, and without saying a word he's cupping my face and kissing me hard, pushing me against the wall until his body is pressed hard against mine.

His tongue slides against mine, his palm digging deep into my hip as he hitches up my skirt with his other hand, his fingers tracing a line of fire on my thighs.

"Hudson," I breathe, when he reaches my panties. His thumb brushes me there, through the cotton and my eyes roll into the back of my head.

"I just need you," he says, his voice thick. And for some

reason that hits me right in the heart. It's like an arrow, piercing me deep.

He needs me.

When has anybody ever needed me? When have I ever wanted anybody to? I've spent most of my life actively avoiding that kind of attachment. And the few times I've let it happen I've gotten hurt.

I love my sister and my mom, even if I don't understand them. But they don't need me. They never have.

But this man does. He dips his head to my neck, kissing it until I feel like I'm on fire. My nipples harden against the cream paisley cotton dress I'm wearing, making me feel needy.

Through the wall he's currently got me pinned against, I can hear the vague beat of the song. It's almost as fast as my heart. Hudson drops to his knees, pushing my skirt up around my waist, burying his head between my thighs.

And he inhales, long and slow.

I twist my fingers into his hair, feeling so on edge even though he's barely touched me.

"That song," he murmurs, kissing one thigh then the other. "That's you. Exactly you." He looks up at me, from his place on the floor. "You've bewitched me."

I scrape my fingers through his hair.

"Let me stay tonight." The way he's looking up at me makes me ache in places I didn't know I could ache. "Let me hold you. Let me stay."

My chest clenches. "You know you can't."

He doesn't move his gaze from mine. "For somebody so free spirited you have a lot of rules."

"For a reason," I say softly. For more reasons than he knows. He's the only person I need to have rules around right now.

If I break them, I'm afraid I'll break myself.

"You're afraid," he murmurs, sliding his thumb along my panties. Then he slides it under the elastic, touching me, making my legs buckle. "But you don't need to be afraid. I'm not going to hurt you."

He circles his thumb, the shocking pleasure he creates sends all thoughts of words out of my head. "Let me take care of you," he says softly, and I don't know if he's talking about right now or something else. I'm not sure I care. I'm so fixated by the teasing sensations created by his thumb and the way he's still staring at me, those dark eyes locked on my face. He quickens his movements and my inner thighs tighten in response.

He slides a finger inside of me, followed by another, coaxing pleasure from me with one easy movement. His thumb circles, his fingers curl, and my body starts to quiver with the impending orgasm I know he's determined to give me.

I tighten around him and his gaze narrows. "Come for me," he whispers, curling his fingers hard, kissing my thigh as I start to fall over the edge. I have to steady myself on his shoulders, and still nearly fold in two, the orgasm so strong he has to put his hands on my hips to keep me upright.

When I finally gain control of my body, he stands up and kisses me. "One day, we're doing this in a bed," he tells me. "Even if it kills me."

Before I can answer him, he's stalking out of the apartment door, looking every inch the grumpy, furious man he was when we first met. He's annoyed at me. At my rules.

Maybe I'm annoyed at myself.

I lean against the wall, trying to catch my breath. My body still feels the aftermath of my orgasm, all shaking and full of pleasure.

Sometimes it feels like that man uses sex as a weapon. But right now, I'm not sure I want to declare a ceasefire.

twenty-two

SKYLER

"Oh my," Autumn whispers in my ear a couple of hours later. "Eileen's drunk as a skunk."

I follow her stare, looking over to see the older woman dancing in front of the jukebox. My eyebrows lift up, because that woman can dance. Like seriously dance. I can sway and move my hips but she's absolutely mesmerizing.

"How much has she had?" I ask. It's weird, but now that I'm a business owner I actually want to make sure I follow the rules. "Should we cut her off?"

Eileen does a perfect pirouette and then stumbles into Jesse, who unfortunately has his hands full with his guitar. Somehow he manages to catch her with his free arm, but for a second it's touch and go whether he's going to drop the expensive instrument.

Thankfully he doesn't. I let out a long breath and look at Autumn. "Can you make some coffee?" I ask. "Strong?"

She nods. "On it."

I lift up the hatch in the counter and walk around to the main bar. The party is starting to thin out now that Jesse has finished his last set. Most of the tables are taken, but there are less people to weave my way through, which I'm thankful for.

And of course, over in the corner, leaning on the wall, is Hudson. The man who for some reason seems to be determined to get me into bed even though I've offered him sex everywhere else. I can feel the heat of his stare as I reach Eileen. For a second I allow myself to look over at him.

A smug I-can-make-you-come half-smile pulls at his lips. I lift my brow at him then turn away. I'll deal with Mr. Bed later. Right now I have a drunk bed and breakfast owner on my hands.

"Hi Eileen," I shout over the music. "Why don't you come talk with me at the bar?"

She reaches out for my hands. "Dance with me." She looks around, frowning when she realizes she's the only one swaying right now. "Where's everybody at?"

I take her palms in mine. They feel dry and cool, despite the fact she's moving like a demon. "We can dance later," I shout. "Let's go sit down."

"Don't be boring." She shakes her head. "I thought you were a free spirit."

I bite my lip in an attempt not to laugh. She's the second person tonight who's questioned if I really am as free as I think I am. But I'll worry about that later. "My legs ache," I lie. "I just need to sit down. Come and chat with me, we can dance later."

She actually pouts which makes me want to laugh even more. "Okay, spoilsport. But only a short rest. You young people need to get more exercise."

I lead her back to the counter, managing to maneuver

her onto a stool just as Autumn finishes making the coffee and slides a mug toward her.

"What's this?" Eileen asks, frowning at the black liquid steaming from the glass cup.

"Irish coffee," I tell her. "Full of whiskey. It's only for our special customers so don't tell anybody else."

I hear Autumn snort behind me. She's no help at all.

"Take a sip," I urge Eileen. "Don't be a spoilsport."

Turning her words back on her is all it takes for her to actually do as she's told. She lifts the cup to her lips and wrinkles her nose as the smell of hot coffee assails her. "Haven't drunk a coffee I haven't made for myself in years," she says.

I'm guessing that's due to Mylene owning the only coffee shop in town.

"This one is specially imported," I tell her. "From Brazil."

God I'm getting good at lying. But it's for a good cause.

"Oh my, I can taste the whiskey in this," Eileen adds, taking another, longer sip. "You're a bad girl."

"So people keep telling me." I smile at her.

She looks around the bar, her eyes trying to focus on the optics behind me. "Your dad would be so proud of you."

"He would?" My throat tightens.

"Oh yes. Look at what you've done. This was always his dream, to have his family here. And now he does."

"If I count as family."

"Well of course you do. And..."

"Is that Mylene I see?" Autumn says quickly.

Fast as a whip, Eileen turns around to look. "Where?"

"Oh, it was just a mirage," Autumn says. I frown at her. What's she trying to do here? Make Eileen dizzy?

Thankfully Jesse chooses that next moment to walk back in and over to where we're all standing at the bar.

"Hey," he says, taking the three of us in. "I think I'd better head out. I have to work in the morning."

I give him the brightest smile. "Thank you so much for all your help. And for playing tonight. I'm going to book you so many gigs your head will spin."

His eyes are warm as he leans forward and kisses my cheek. "Thank you for letting me be a part of it."

It isn't enough. I hug him tight, smelling the low notes of his cologne as he holds me, dipping his head into my hair and kissing it softly.

Then he says his goodbyes to Autumn and Eileen before he leaves. Eileen takes another sip of coffee and lifts a brow.

"You two are very friendly," she says, sounding approving.

"Not like *that*," I tell her.

"Of course not. He's not the one I see sneaking around your place desperate to see you." She grins at me, and panic suddenly washes through me.

"What?" Autumn asks.

"Nothing," I say quickly. "She's confused. She probably sees Jesse come over most evenings after work. It's only to chat." I look at Eileen. "There's nothing going on between us."

"I know that, silly." She wrinkles her nose. "That would be ugh. Especially when he's your..."

"Eileen!" Autumn shouts out, her voice lifting an octave. There's something in her panicked tone that makes me do a double take.

I look from Eileen to Autumn, who is pointedly not meeting my gaze.

"What's going on?" I ask, completely aware that they

both know something I don't. Autumn lets out a strangled groan.

"Oh God." Eileen takes another sip of coffee. "She didn't hear me, did she?"

"I didn't hear what?" I ask Eileen. I'm confused, but it's the kind of confused that you're on the edge of de-confusing.

Like the darkness right next to the light.

"What were you going to say about Jesse?" I demand.

"I should go home," Eileen says, putting her cup down. "I'm very drunk."

"No." I put my hand on her shoulder, gently, but firm enough to stop her movement. "You said Jesse is my…" I trail off. "What is he?"

Autumn lets out another groan and I turn to look at her. "Who is he?" I demand. "What was she about to say?"

"I'm sorry." Autumn shakes her head. "It wasn't supposed to be like this."

"Like what?" I'm so confused. I feel like an animal, cornered and unable to move. "Who is he?" I ask again. "What are you all trying to say?"

"Oh honey," Eileen says, patting my arm. "I knew it was bad, everybody keeping this from you. I said from the start that secrets can only lead to trouble."

"What's the secret?" I demand, my voice low and thick.

She takes a deep breath, looking like she'd prefer to be anywhere but here, drunk on my bar stool. "Please don't be angry," Eileen says. Over her shoulder I can see Autumn's face wrinkle in angst. "But Jesse is your brother."

twenty-three

SKYLER

From the way Autumn winces I immediately know it's true. Jesse is my *brother*. All this time he's been coming over to see me and he's known and he hasn't told me. Nobody has told me. I've been living here on the island, a few hundred yards away from somebody whose blood is the same as mine and I had no damn clue.

"You've been hiding this from me too?" I ask Autumn, feeling betrayed.

"I'm sorry," she whispers.

"Why didn't you tell me?" I ask. Then a horrific thought comes into my mind. "Does everybody know?" And of course by everybody I mean Hudson. Did he know I was being lied to while we had sex in this bar? As he made love to me on the beach?

While he made me come in my apartment only hours ago?

Of course he did. I can tell that by the way Autumn

shifts her feet. I feel sick. Like I'm some kind of experiment everybody has enjoyed watching.

How could they? How could they let me go on with my daily life not knowing?

"How could you all say nothing?" I ask again, unable to keep the sob from my voice.

Autumn's face crumples in sympathy. "Jesse should be the one to tell you."

Except he's been lying too. He's the worst liar of them all. Oh my god, I think I'm going to be sick for real. I put my hand over my mouth and rush past Autumn and Eileen, who looks remarkably sober compared to a moment ago. I need to throw up.

I need to not *be here.*

"Honey, please..." Autumn calls out. "Let me explain."

I shake my head, running to the private door, entering the code. As soon as the lock clicks I thrust down on the handle. I can feel Autumn right behind me. I turn to look at her and tears are streaming down her face.

"I want to be alone," I tell her.

"No." She shakes her head, mascara running down her cheeks. "You don't."

There's a lump in my throat so big I'm finding it hard to breathe. "I wish everybody would stop deciding my life for me," I say. "Please leave me alone." I step inside my apartment and slam the door, blocking out the noise from the bar beyond. It's only then, when I'm in almost exactly the same position I was earlier when Hudson made me see stars that I allow the tears to fall.

Pain overwhelms me as I slide to the floor, sobs wracking my body.

* * *

I cry until I feel completely wrung out and empty, sitting on the floor, my face covered by my hands.

I still don't understand it. I have a brother I never knew about. My dad had a son and didn't tell me.

Nobody told me.

I need to talk to Lee and my mom, but I have no idea how to ask them if they knew. I'm ninety-nine percent sure that they don't know either. If they did, if they lied to me too, I don't know what I'll do.

Maybe that's why I'm afraid to call them. Not knowing is sometimes better than knowing the truth.

The music stopped playing almost as soon as I disappeared from the bar. I think most people have left – I heard the regular thud of car doors and engines rumbling as people drove away.

They must all think I'm terrible, not saying goodbye. Disappearing from my own opening party. Maybe it doesn't matter. Maybe I should disappear altogether.

Suddenly the town that seemed so welcoming has turned into a darker place. One full of secrets.

And I hate it.

Every now and then there's a tap at the door that I ignore. I know Autumn is a kind person but I can't deal with her right now.

It's another ten minutes before I hear a louder knock.

"Skyler. Open the door," Hudson says.

I ignore him, because he's a liar too.

"For fuck's sake," I hear him mutter. The next minute the door opens and he walks inside.

"How did you get in?" I ask him, aware of how much of a mess I must look. On the plus side, it'll probably put him off wanting bed sex with me for good.

"I watched you punch in the code a couple of hours ago," he says. "It's nothing sinister."

The man has a photographic memory to go with the money and power. Of course he does.

"I don't want you here," I tell him thickly. I manage to push myself up from my sobbing position against the wall, but my legs feel unsteady.

He stands in the center of the living room, clenching and unclenching his hands. "I understand that," he says. "But there's no way I'm leaving you alone."

I sit down heavily on the sofa, as he stands there, looking at me with the kind of emotion I wasn't sure he was capable of having. "I just came back from talking to Jesse," he says. "I told him about Eileen blurting everything out. He's devastated. He wants to talk to you, but I suggested he give you some space to get used to the idea."

"I don't want to talk to him," I say, the tears starting to fall again. "I don't want to talk to anybody," I sob, lowering my head into my hands. "How could you all lie to me? I thought he was my friend. God, at one point I worried he was attracted to me? What if I'd kissed him? Jesus..."

A pair of strong arms wrap around me. Hudson kneels in front of me, pulling me against him. I'm too tired to resist, and maybe I need some comfort, from anywhere I can get it right now. My head lowers against his shoulder and I start to sob hard. The kind of messy, dirty sobs that lead to snotty noses and chest convulsions. And all through it, he just holds me, never letting go. Not talking, not moving, just letting me fall apart.

"Why didn't Dad tell me I had a brother?" I mutter against his shirt, once I've finally cry myself out once more. I've managed to make his shoulder completely damp with my tears.

"Jesse wants to explain that to you," Hudson says more gently than I've ever heard him talk. "And I think you should hear him out when you're ready. I can tell you if you want, but really this part is between the two of you. I know if it was something between me and my sisters…"

I sniff loudly. "I don't know that I want to talk to him."

"He's a good kid. He cares about you. Please don't shut him out."

"He's only a couple of years younger than me," I say. "Hardly a kid."

"I know." There's a ghost of a smile on his lips. "But he still seems like a kid to me. I grew up with him."

I let out a long breath, thinking of Jesse with his golden hair and shy smile. The way he's been here so much. The way he always looks so happy to see me. Then I remember him on the boat, that first, rainy day when I arrived on Liberty. How he leaned in, looking delighted I was there.

My heart clenches. I have a brother. Somebody of my own. Somebody who knew Dad more than I did, more than Lee or Mom did, maybe.

"I'll talk to him," I say. "Tomorrow. I'm just so tired right now."

Hudson pushes the hair that's sticking to my wet cheeks behind my ear. "Of course you are," he says. "Let's get you to bed."

Before I can say a word, the man is scooping me into his arms like I'm as light as a feather – something I know for a fact I'm not. And I'm not going to lie, it feels good. Way too good.

Like he cares for me. Like I'm something more than a challenge for him.

He carries me to the bedroom, laying me on top of the

covers. Then he gently pulls off my shoes and unbuttons my blouse.

"I should brush my teeth," I say.

"Tomorrow." He pulls the blouse from my arms then turns his attention to my skirt. There's no lust in his eyes. Nothing but care.

"And wash my face."

"That can wait, too." He helps me out of my skirt until I'm laying in my underwear on the mattress. "Get under the covers," he says.

"Okay."

I do as I'm told, finding comfort in just *being*, not thinking. I curl up under there, and he takes my hand in his, sitting down on the floor next to the mattress.

"What are you doing?" I ask him.

"Holding your hand."

I almost laugh. "I know that. But what are you doing *here*?"

"Making sure you get some rest. And keeping you company while you do."

"You should go home to Ayda. She'll be wondering where her daddy is."

"Autumn has gone to my place to help the babysitter. I don't have to be anywhere but here."

I frown. "You're planning to stay here all night?"

He tips his head, a smile playing on his lips. "I am," he says solemnly. "I'm staying right here, next to your bed, not on your bed. There will be no funny business, no snuggles. No bed related sex."

My cheeks pink up. I want to ask him why. Why would he stay here when there's nothing to offer? But the fatigue is overwhelming. It's like my body's had too much and it just wants to shut down. To dream of something other than small towns full of secrets. I let out a yawn and he smiles at me, and it hits me right in the gut.

"I'll be okay on my own," I say.

"I have no doubt. But you don't have to be on your own. So you won't be."

My eyes close against my will. My breathing evens out. And he's still holding my hand as I slowly drift into the oblivion my aching heart craves.

But as I teeter on the edge of sleep, all I can think about is the fact that this feels more vulnerable than sex in a bed or anything else I've been building walls around. I feel raw and hurt and he's here holding my hand, keeping me safe.

And I like it way, way too much.

twenty-four

SKYLER

When I wake up in the morning Hudson is still here. He's looking disheveled from sleeping the night on my floor, and it makes my heart ache to see him.

"You didn't leave," I say, sitting up.

"I said I wouldn't," he replies simply. And that's probably all I need to know about this man. He makes a promise and he keeps it.

I let out a breath. "You should go. Ayda will want to see you. And you have to work."

"There's no rush. Let me get you a coffee and then we can see how you feel."

I run my hand through my hair. I can tell that it's as much of a mess as the rest of me. "I need to talk to Jesse," I say.

"Yes you do." He gives me the softest smile. "He's messaged me about a hundred times."

"Can you ask him to come over?" I ask. "At eleven."

"Eleven? It's going to be a long three hours."

"I'm going to need that long to make myself look respectable," I say. Between the tears and the tossing and turning I hate to think how terrible I look. But Hudson's face is soft as our gazes meet.

"You look perfect."

"Shut up."

He leans forward and kisses me softly. It makes my toes curl.

"And now I'm going to get those coffees," he says, standing up and stretching. He took his shirt off at some point during the night, so he grabs it and slides his arms through it. "You going to be okay?"

"I'm going to be fine." It's weird how strongly those words come out. Because I am, I know it. "I'm going to take a shower, drink that coffee, then go for a walk on the beach before...

"Before Jesse comes over," Hudson says.

I nod. I was going to say before I talk to my brother. What a weird word. All this time I've thought I only have one sister. But he was here all along.

So many thoughts are whirling around my mind. But right now I need to get up and face the day.

"Thank you," I tell this man who is so hard and yet so tender. "Thank you for being here for me."

His gaze rakes my face, like he's trying to take everything in. "I wasn't going to let you deal with this alone."

* * *

Jesse lets out a long breath, his face full of emotion as he looks at me later that morning.

It's a beautiful late spring day. The sun is beaming down from a cloudless sky, the ocean is sparkling and we're sitting out on the bar's deck, at the far end so we can't be seen from the road. We're both drinking coffee because Jesse brought me one – I guess as a peace offering.

It hasn't escaped my notice that my love language is apparently caffeine. Or that the two new men in my life seem to understand that. I've gone from being a loner – albeit with a small family that I love – to having this extended network of people who care about me. If I think about it too long it'll make me feel uncomfortable. I know how to be alone.

I don't know how to be part of a community.

"It's what Dad wanted," he says. "For me to tell you when the time was right. It just..." he shakes his head. "It never felt right."

He called into work sick for the first time since he's started working there, apparently. And I can see why. He looks so pale he's almost ghostly. There are dark rings beneath his eyes like he didn't get any sleep.

And his eyes themselves are full of regret.

Hudson and I walked and talked for an hour along the beach this morning before he took me at my word that I felt better and agreed to go home.

We talked about my family – the one I knew and the one I didn't. About my dad and how I feel more upset about him not telling me than about Jesse and the rest of the island keeping it from me.

I have so many questions I started losing track of them. Hudson gently suggested I write them down in my phone so I could have them ready for Jesse.

He looked almost shocked when I did as I was told and got my notes app up on my phone and typed in a dozen questions in one go. Like he expected me to ignore him. But he was right. I'm starting to think he's always right.

And now I'm going through those same questions methodically, feeling almost like the adult I should be as I ask Jesse each one.

"How long have you known about me?" I ask him. That's question number two. The first was why my dad didn't tell me. Jesse's answer was as honest as he could be without actually knowing the answer. Because my dad took a lot of secrets to his grave.

"So you need to know a little about my life for me to answer that one," he says. "I didn't know Wayne was my father until I was sixteen."

I blink. "Seriously?" I would have been eighteen or nineteen. After the wedding. I wasn't speaking to Dad by then.

Jesse takes a deep breath, his brows knitting. "My mom never told me. Or Wayne. They apparently had a short fling, then he left the island for a while and she went back to my dad. It was only years later when my dad died that she finally admitted that Wayne was my biological dad. He was back on the island full time by then, running the bar. We did a DNA test." He shrugs.

"Were you close to him?"

"As close as anybody gets to him I guess." He presses his lips together. "He was a drunk. You know that. And even when he tried to get his drinking under control he was sick."

"A dry drunk?"

"Along with the liver disease and everything else that comes with abusing your body for that long, yeah." Jesse's jaw tightens. "He encouraged me to play the guitar. Gave me gigs here. But he was more of an uncle than a dad to me."

"And you went to his funeral." My chest tightens.

He nods. "I was hoping you'd be there."

"I was avoiding…" I let out a long breath. "Everything." Our eyes meet and there's so much understanding there. "I guess the apple doesn't fall that far from the tree."

"You're nothing like him," Jesse says firmly. I lift a brow and he smiles. "Okay, you're only like the best parts of him. He had his moments. He loved to sing and dance. When you got him talking he'd tell you all about his travels. He had a restless soul but that was a good thing. How boring would it be if we were all settled down from an early age?"

"Having a restless soul can hurt people," I say. And I think we both know we're not talking about my dad anymore.

"It can also inspire. Light up the world. The sun isn't always here. She has places to go, but when she does show her face…" He tips his head, the warmth of her rays illuminating his skin. "She makes you feel good like nothing else can."

A smile steals across my lips. "Are you comparing me to the sun?"

"I'm just saying, you're you. And Wayne was Wayne. He spent a lot of time fighting who he was. Drank a lot of alcohol to try to forget who he was. If he'd just accepted it…"

"He would have been happy?" I say, completing his sentence. My little brother is wise. I like that a lot.

"I don't know." He shrugs. "But anything is better than fighting yourself, isn't it?" He looks at my phone, still open on my lap. "What's your next question?"

"Does everybody on the island know that he's your father? And have they always known?"

"Once we took the DNA test it wasn't a secret that I was his son. They knew that Wayne wanted me to be the one to tell you, and they honored that wish." He swallows hard. "Don't blame anybody else for this, it's all my doing. I should have told you earlier. I wanted to. I was just..."

"Afraid?" I ask.

"I don't have any other siblings. My mom moved back to the mainland. It felt... I don't know... *big*, having you here. My sister. I was scared that if you took it the wrong way I'd be left with nothing. I heard a lot about you from Wayne. He followed you, you know. Your Instagram, he had that on his favorites."

"He followed me?" I whisper.

"He was so fucking proud. And I was so in awe of you. You seemed so together. So in love with life. You weren't afraid of anything."

"I'm afraid of everything," I tell him. "Social media is a bitch. It lies constantly. I only ever put up the good stuff. The happy stuff. Mostly to make my mom and Lee feel like they didn't have to keep saving me."

"I'd like to meet them sometime," he says. "I know we're not actually related but..."

"They want to meet you. I spoke to them this morning." I called them right after Hudson left. I had to be sure in my head that they hadn't been keeping this from me, too.

Lee was just as shocked as I was. Mom was... not surprised. I guess she knew my dad better than anybody and she knew that he wasn't an angel.

"Of course you're family," I tell him. "Family isn't just about blood. Or titles. It's about being there for each other.

Taking care of the other person." I take his hand. "You've always felt like family. I just couldn't work out why until now."

His face lights up. "You felt like family too." He chuckles. "I mean I know I knew you were. But there's been this connection..."

"At first I thought you were attracted to me," I admit. "But it was a different kind of pull, wasn't it?"

"I love you, but not like that." He wrinkles his nose.

His words hit me so hard that tears form in my eyes.

"What? What did I say?"

"You love me?"

"Of course I do." He takes my hand, squeezing it tight. "You're my sister. You're my friend. But most of all, you're you. I feel like I knew you before we even met. How can anybody not love you?"

The tears start to fall. But this time they feel like good tears. Cleansing ones. I don't fight them – because maybe my brother's wisdom is seeping in. You don't fight, you accept. And here's my accepting.

There's a reason my dad brought me to this island, even after his death. And now I know what it was. He'd made errors. Ones he couldn't admit to my face. But he wanted to clear them up. He wanted me to meet my brother.

And he made it happen.

A part of me will always wish he'd done it when he was alive. That he'd tried harder to tell me about Jesse. And that maybe I'd be a little more willing to listen.

But regrets are like fighting against your nature. They eat you up. And I can't let that happen. Not when my younger brother is here, looking up to me, wanting me to give him the same acceptance he gave me.

"Right back at you," I tell him, hugging him tight. "I love you too." And it's true, I do. A weird sensation of protectiveness washes over me, and that's when I realize that I'm not the youngest in the family anymore. Not the baby in the corner.

"Oh my God, I'm a middle child," I say to him. "That makes so much sense."

He starts to laugh.

But it's true. I'm that wandering soul that they say middle children are. Always looking for something I can't have. Always moving on to the next thing, hoping it will be *my* thing.

"And also," I tell him, my voice turning serious. "I want a veto on every girlfriend you have. Because they're clearly not good enough for you."

"Jesus, don't make me regret you finding out. Ask me another question before I run away." He shakes his head.

So I do. I ask nine more before I get to the big one. The one that makes me hesitate, because I don't want to hurt him, but I also know that it will hang between us for as long as I let it. And I don't want anything bad between us.

Not now that we've found each other.

"The last one," I say solemnly, and he smiles, like he's ready for this to be over. I take a deep breath. "Why did he leave the bar to me and not both of us?" I ask him.

Jesse looks like he's been expecting this one. He doesn't shift, doesn't break our gaze. Just gives me the softest of smiles. "Because I asked him to."

"Why?" I ask, completely confused. "This place is worth a lot of money. You could have sold it to Hudson and been set for life."

"I don't give a damn about money," he says. "And I think you're the same. Yes, I need enough to keep a roof over my head and food in my stomach, but more than that? I don't know..." He shrugs. "It doesn't seem to make Hudson happy, does it?"

I swallow hard, remembering how Hudson looked this morning, all crumpled up on my floor. I have no idea what time he fell asleep, but he was dead to the world as I looked at him, my stomach tight because even at my lowest he kept to his word. He didn't get into my bed.

I'm still processing that. I'll think about it later, because there is a lot going on in my world right now and I need to concentrate on one thing at a time.

"Money can definitely help," I say. "And it doesn't matter, I'm signing over half of the bar to you."

"No." He shakes his head. "You don't have to do that."

"You just said yourself that money doesn't make you happy. But do you know what does? The thought of co-owning a bar with my baby brother." I give him a broad smile. "Plus I might get a day off if you have to help too."

"I work on the ferry," he points out.

"And that's fine. You can come here when you want. Or we can employ more staff. Whatever, we'll work it out."

A sense of peace falls over me. It's like I'm slotting a jigsaw piece into place. This is how it's supposed to be. Dad requested me to stay here for six months to get to know my brother. This funny, lovely guy sitting with me.

I've always believed in fate. I don't like to force things. I like drifting with the breeze.

I think that's what my dad liked too, when he was sober. And here I am, drifting into a new life.

"I want you to be in this with me," I tell him. "And I think that's what dad would have wanted as well."

He looks stupidly pleased at that. There's a pinkness to his cheeks as he smiles.

"I'd like that," he says.

I'll have to ask Hudson to recommend a lawyer. But that's for another day, we can make it official in time. As far as I'm concerned, from this moment on we're going to be working together. And I like that.

"Is that it? Any more questions?" he teases.

"Not yet." But I'm pretty sure I'll have more. They don't seem so urgent now. There's a weird peace in my heart that I never thought I'd have. Especially last night, when it felt like my world was collapsing around me.

But there's no urgent need to know everything anymore. I have enough information for now, and I know if I have more questions he'll answer them. We look at each other again, and I try to see the resemblance between us. He has freckles like me, but that's it.

It's a start.

"I do have one more question actually," I say, and he groans out loud. But this one isn't about him or me.

It's about the one thing that's been bugging me since I arrived.

"What happened to Eileen and Mylene when they went to the mainland?" I ask him. "Is that also something everybody but me knows?"

He grins. "Nope. We're all as in the dark as you. I don't think we'll ever know."

"Damn," I say, because I'm desperate to know. "I guess some secrets aren't supposed to be found out."

* * *

HUDSON

. . .

I'm working on the business plan for the fishermen's cottages when there's a knock at my office door. I should be on the mainland with Ayda at our therapy session, but after taking one look at me after I came back from Skyler's this morning, Autumn decided she'd take her instead.

Usually I'd put up a fight, but I was too tired and my muscles ached too much to deal with Autumn's stubbornness, so I let her take my kid for an 'Aunt and Niece' day on the mainland and decided to hole up in my office and actually get some work done.

The knock repeats, so I push myself out of my leather chair, trying not to groan at the knots in my back muscles. I wrench the door open, waiting for the usual onslaught about a demanding customer wanting to speak to the owner, but instead I see Skyler standing there, looking uncharacteristically uncertain as she looks up at me.

"Hey." I blink. She's never willingly come to see me. Yes, I made her come in my office, but she was here for the party, not me. It's weird how much I like that she's actually come here of her own free will. "Come in."

A smile ghosts across her lips. "Thanks." She's not wearing any makeup, and her hair is pulled back into a high ponytail. She's wearing that denim dress that buttons from neck to hem and I get a flashback to how easy it is to unbutton and reveal her lush body.

"How did your talk with Jesse go?" I ask her.

"It went well," she replies, softly closing the door behind her. "We talked a lot. He explained everything. We're good."

I smile softly at her. "I'm glad to hear that."

"I want to add him as an owner to the bar." She pulls her lip between her teeth. "I know that makes things more complicated."

"Complicated how?"

"At one point you wanted to buy it. You're even less likely to be able to if there are two of us."

I shake my head. "I don't give a damn if I own it. I just wanted it to be..." I shake my head. "I don't know. Right for the tone of the place. And it is. You've done that." Buying the bar is so far from my mind it's not funny. "It's not complicated at all."

Her expression radiates relief. "Okay, good. Because I have another favor to ask you."

I lift a brow. She never asks for anything. I like that she's willing to now. "Go ahead."

"I need you to recommend a local lawyer. I want to do this thing right. Jesse's my brother and I want him to know how much I care."

"You can use mine," I say. "I'll speak to him. I have it covered."

"You're not paying for it," she says, her eyes flashing.

The woman can read me like a book. "Of course I'll pay."

"No." She shakes her head, her jaw jutting out like she's already anticipated this. "You have to stop saving people, Hudson."

"I'm not saving you. I know for a fact that you won't have a whole lot of cash flow until the bar is up and running. And I also know that when you make a decision you want it to happen yesterday. I'm trying to help."

"I know you are. But I don't want you to."

I don't like that one bit. "So you'll let me fuck you seven ways to Sunday – if it's not in a damn bed – but you won't let me help you sort out the bar?"

"When you put it like that..." she trails off, smiling at my annoyance. I swear she gets off on riling me up. She reaches out, touching my arm. "I appreciate all you do for me. Including the sex." She pulls her lip between her teeth and I swear that's all it takes to make me hard. "And last night." She swallows. "You didn't get into bed with me."

"Because you've made it clear that you don't want me in your bed." I thought that was obvious. And I'm not an idiot enough to force it.

She tips her head to the side. There's a strange emotion in her eyes I can't quite place. "Isn't a girl allowed to change her mind?" she whispers.

"About what?" I ask, confused.

She twists her fingers. "Maybe next time we sleep together, it should be somewhere that won't cost you a fortune at the chiropractor," she says, parroting my words from a few weeks ago. She runs the tip of her tongue along her lip. "Somewhere we can wake up together."

If I thought I was hard before, now I'm almost painful. The things I could do to this woman if I had all night with her. She'd be the one needing a back specialist.

And I'd willingly pay for all the treatment.

"When?" I ask quickly.

She smiles at my eagerness.

"When you can get a babysitter, I guess."

I start to work out the logistics in my mind. Not tonight, that's for sure. Ayda is usually exhausted after therapy. And I'm also wary enough to know that Skyler probably still doesn't want the whole island knowing that I've been having bedless sex with her every chance I can get.

"Next week? Wednesday. I have a business thing on the mainland so Autumn is keeping Ayda that night instead of Tuesday. Come with me."

"Bed sex in a hotel?" Skyler murmurs, her eyes catching mine.

"All damn night. And then again in the morning," I tell her. "You should probably bring some Tylenol."

She laughs hard, her head tipping back. "Oh God, what am I letting myself in for?"

I lean forward, my lips brushing her ear. "The best damn night of your life."

twenty-five

SKYLER

"Are you sure you have this covered?" I ask Jesse. He's standing behind the bar looking like he owns the place, which he will very soon. We've spent the last week really getting to know each other and it already feels natural to be spending time with him.

But tonight I'll be sleeping in a bed with Hudson Fitzgerald. The thought makes me feel strange – excited and scared at the same time. Bedless sex with that man I could handle. A whole night in bed with him? Only time will tell.

"Of course I have it covered." He looks over at Maud, who's working the shift with him. I offered for Jesse to stay over in the apartment, but he demurred.

"Now go sort this thing out with your lawyer," he tells me. "Not that there's any need for it."

Okay, so I told Jesse a little white lie about why I'm heading over to the mainland. Not that it's really a lie – or at least that's how I've justified it to myself. I *will* be meeting with Hudson's lawyer tomorrow morning, so that I can move the bar into mine and Jesse's joint control. But of course I didn't tell him about staying the night with Hudson.

It feels too weird right now.

The ferry blasts its horn, which means its coming into port. "That's your cue," Jesse says, because he knows the schedule by heart. "Now stop worrying, I have this under control. Do you know how many times I've worked behind this bar? And at least Hudson and I won't have to carry Dad to his bed when the night is over."

I blink. "You used to have to do that?" And Hudson helped? Gah, this man needs to stop making my legs go weak, even when he's nowhere near me.

"Only sometimes. Now go, before you miss the ferry. You know it won't wait for you."

I lean across the counter to kiss his cheek, then pick up my overnight case, which is stupidly full because I have no idea what to wear tonight. Tomorrow was a cinch. I actually have a pretty blouse and skirt to meet the lawyer.

But Hudson has been completely evasive about the plans for tonight, which is very annoying when you're a woman. He's probably used to having partners with extensively suitable wardrobes – a designer dress for every occasion. I'm a Stevie Nicks wannabe with a few dirndl skirts and tops that expose way too much skin.

I hate that I'm doubting myself. I never doubt myself. This is what happens when you give in to a man who's desperate to get you into bed. The whole of your psyche gets messed up.

And yet I still hurry to the ferry, the warm early-summer wind whipping through my hair as I make it to the dock. I can see Hudson's car lining up at the gate. It's sparkling beneath the rays of the sun like it's been buffed to an inch of its life.

It takes ten minutes for the boat to offload the visitors, then reload the return passengers. I climb aboard with one other foot passenger, then make my way to the front, where I lean on the rail and look toward the mainland in the distance.

This is the first time I've been off the island since that rainy day I arrived. It feels like a lifetime ago. Back then I didn't know I was going to fall in love with Liberty, or that I'd find out the reason why my dad wanted me to be here. And never in my wildest dreams did I think I'd be hooking up with a grumpy rich businessman who fills out a suit like nobody else can.

There are footsteps behind me. I don't have to turn around to know who it is, because every cell in my body seems to vibrate. I can smell the low notes of his cologne. Even the cadence of his footsteps is familiar.

"Hi." He kisses my cheek. "What a surprise seeing you here." I turn to look at him, and am stupidly turned on by the smirk on his lips.

"Mr. Fitzgerald," I say, playing along. "Are you sure this boat is big enough for the both of us?"

"I think we can be civil to each other for the next twenty minutes," he muses. "Although it could be a challenge." The ocean breeze lifts up his hair, and he looks almost carefree. He's wearing a suit – of course – this one is a dark blue wool, cut perfectly to fit his broad, muscled body. He's teamed it with a lighter blue shirt and a pale red tie. His jaw is sharp, freshly shaven. Everything about this man draws me in.

My own clothes are very different. A pair of vintage

flared jeans and some old sneakers, along with an old, faded band t-shirt and a thin sweater tied around my waist. Hudson follows my gaze and a smile pulls at his lips.

"You look spectacular," he says.

Oh. I grin at him. "So do you." I tip my head to the side. "Do you wear suits to bed, too? If so I might need to prepare myself." My tone is teasing, and he rolls his eyes. We both know I've seen him in jeans, but still.

"You'll find out tonight I guess. And I'm wearing a suit because I have a meeting when we get to New York."

"New York?" I do a double take, thinking I misheard. "I thought we were going to the mainland?"

"Last time I checked, Manhattan was definitely on the mainland." His voice is teasing.

"The mainland means the town." I point at the church spire that rises above the houses ahead of us along the shoreline. "Doesn't it?" Now I'm confused. This is what happens when you don't live somewhere all your life. You take on their language but then you use it wrong.

"It can mean anything. But today it means New York."

"How long will it take to drive to New York?" I ask, folding my arms in front of me.

He smiles at how pouty I sound. "We're not driving, we're flying."

"What?" I blink. "We're taking a plane?"

He shakes his head. "A helicopter. It's a lot faster. I have to be in a meeting at two. Don't worry, there's a spa at the hotel. I thought you could try it out before the party."

"The *party*?" My brows lift so high I swear they're touching my hairline. "What party?"

"I told you. There's a business thing this evening. We just need to show our faces."

"You didn't tell me it was a party." My heart does a little gallop. "I can't go to a party."

"Why not?"

"Because..." Dear god, why is he such a *man*? "Parties require planning. I need to figure out what to wear, get my hair ready. Bring the right makeup. It takes weeks to prepare for a party. Not a few hours."

He tips his head to the side, not getting it at all. "You look good like that."

My mouth drops open. "You want me to go to a party in jeans and a band tee?"

"For somebody who doesn't care what people think you seem remarkably anxious about fitting in," he says, echoing his words of the other day. "Relax, it'll be fine. What would Stevie Nicks do?"

My mouth gapes open. "You're using Stevie against me now?" I hate that he knows it will work.

"I'm just pointing out that I want you to come to the party because you're *you*. I don't give a fuck what you wear. Now if you do, then that's a different matter and we can do something about that."

"What does that mean?" I ask, narrowing my eyes.

"It means we're going to be in New York. If you want a designer dress there are a hundred shops I can ask my driver to take you to. Or I can arrange for some dresses to be brought to the hotel."

"You want to *Pretty Woman* me up?" I ask, my brows lifting.

"No. I didn't say that. For a start, I wouldn't fucking dare."

I hate that he makes me laugh right now. But he does, and I can't hide it.

"You're so annoying," I tell him. "You could have told me that we were going to New York."

"I'm sorry. I thought it was obvious. You're meeting my lawyer tomorrow."

"I figured he came here to meet with you," I say in a small voice.

"Not unless it's an emergency. It's a lot easier to meet with him when I'm in New York for business."

That makes sense. "But the party..."

"I said we were going out for dinner," he points out.

"I figured it would be casual. Like you wouldn't want to waste too much time feeding me. You only get one night in bed with me after all."

It's his turn to scowl. It makes me want to lick his face.

"First of all, having dinner with you isn't wasting time. You don't want to be pretty womaned?" he asks, wincing at using the movie title as a verb. "Well I don't want to either. I'm not a fucking trick, Skyler. I'm not taking you out for a meal to pay you for sex."

Oh, he's annoyed now. For some reason that makes me feel better. And psychologically, I know it's not a good thing but I'll worry about that later.

"And second?" I ask, my voice low.

"Second?" he repeats, frowning.

"You said first of all. Which implies a second."

"So you're not going to point out that I'm not a trick paying you for sex?"

I manage to swallow down a laugh. "Have you ever used a prostitute, Hudson?"

"No."

"Then why would I think of you as a trick? First of all, you couldn't afford me."

"And second?" He turns my words back on me.

"Second of all..." I say, trying to think on my feet. "Maybe I don't want to share you. Maybe I want it to be just the two of us and nobody else. Maybe I have plans for you tonight that involve neither of us wearing anything and me screaming your name so loudly that the whole hotel starts to shake."

A slow breath escapes his parted lips.

"Why the fuck are we arguing about this?" he asks. "I'll just decline the party invite. It's fine."

"No." I shake my head. "We're going to this party. And then you're going to owe me big time."

"How big?"

"Huge," I say. Because I'm still pretty-womaning it.

"Okay." He nods. "But I'm still paying for your dress."

"No need," I tell him. "I'm looking forward to embarrassing you with some completely inappropriate choice of clothing."

There's that smile again. "Good," he tells me.

I reach out, tracing the waistband of his stupidly expensive pants. "And by the way, it'll be so inappropriate that you'll have a hard on all night."

* * *

HUDSON

"The projections show the investment will be fully recouped within ten months," Ria, my chief financial officer says to the shareholders around the boardroom of our penthouse offices. Once upon a time this was my domain. I'd be here every day, the first to arrive and the last to leave, as a matter of principle.

I loved the adrenaline shot that came with working in the center of Manhattan. I made more money than I ever dreamed of, and I was the person that everybody in this office looked up to.

Now all I can think about is when will this fucking interminable meeting end.

My phone beeps and I pull it out of my pocket. Skyler's name appears on the screen, along with a notification that she's shared a photograph with me.

And because right now I couldn't give a shit about whether the investment gets paid back in ten or twelve months I discreetly open up the message.

Then I thank the fucking lord I was discreet, because staring back at me is the woman I've been obsessing over. She must have just stepped out of the shower, because she's completely soaked, her hair laying in a mahogany sheet down her back, her face shining bright. She has a towel wrapped around her, and nothing else.

Maybe the 'post-massage chic' look could work for tonight? Thoughts? – Skyler xx

My thoughts right now are completely honed in on the way her breasts are pressed up by the tightly wrapped towel. And how easily I could pull it off her and kiss my way down her body.

She knows what she's doing. I know what she's doing too. She's playing. And I want to play with her. So damn much.

"Isn't that right, Hudson?" Ria asks.

I look up on hearing my name. "Repeat that, please."

"Mr. Clarke asked about the future profit ratio. I was just saying we're waiting for one more piece of information to make those projections."

"That's correct, yes." I look down at my phone.

Stevie Nicks would love it. – Hudson

I hit send and try to concentrate on this damn meeting, because people have made an effort to be here and it's my business. But I'm already regretting trying to combine business and pleasure.

Would she love this, do you think? – Skyler ;)

As soon as her reply appears on my phone I know I should ignore it. But the need to open it is like a damn fly, so persistent it's aggravating. So I look down at my phone again and slide my finger over the screen.

Fuck. She's naked. And yeah, she has her back to the mirror that she's taken this selfie in. All I can see is the smooth creaminess of her skin and the plump curves of her behind, but that's all it takes for every part of me to fire up.

"Let's take a break," I say, interrupting Ria.

Everybody sitting around the table looks at me.

"Ten minutes," I add, because none of them would dare to contradict me. "I need to make a couple of phone calls, then we'll reconvene."

Before any of them can say a word, I'm up and striding

out of the board room, storming past my assistant into my office, and closing the door behind me.

I open up my phone again, my eyes lingering on the way her back curves into a dip before flaring out again. Her ass looks perfect, so high and full. I swallow hard, because right now I need to feel her skin in my hands. My mouth on her body.

My cock deep inside of her until we're both screaming each other's names.

I hit the call button and she answers within a second.

"Aren't you supposed to be in a meeting?" she asks innocently.

"I called a break," I tell her thickly. "Somebody keeps annoying me with sexy photos."

"Annoying?" she repeats. "Noted. No more photos will be sent."

"What are you wearing right now?" I demand, ignoring her warning.

"Do you really want to know?"

"Absolutely."

"A thong. Nothing else."

"Where are you?"

"In our bedroom," she says huskily. "By the way, thank you for the massage."

"I didn't give it to you."

"But you paid for it. Which is very Richard Gere of you, by the way. What are *you* wearing?" she asks.

"Way too much."

"I'm sure your staff would disagree," she says, sounding gleeful.

"I don't really give a damn what they think," I tell her. "Send me another picture."

"Oh, so you like them, huh?" She lets out a little breath

and it does delicious things to my dick. "Tell you what, I'll video call you. That way there's no evidence on your phone."

"I could screenshot you," I say.

"But you wouldn't. Because you're a man who only works on consent." My screen lights up with a message telling me that Skyler would like to change our call from an audio to a video one. I hit accept immediately.

And then her face appears and I'm fucking breathless. She's so damn beautiful. She's smiling and she's happy and it does the stupidest things to me.

"Hi," she breathes.

"Hi." I take in her glowing skin, her wet hair. "Are you having a good time?"

"The spa was nice. But I missed you."

"Next time I'll join you," I promise.

"There's going to be a next time? Interesting." Her eyes sparkle. "So do it. Show me what you're wearing."

I roll my eyes but turn to face the mirror on my wall, flipping the camera to face it.

"You haven't even taken off your jacket or loosened your tie," she says, laughing. "You're the most uptight man I've ever met."

"I just have standards." I turn the camera back to my face and smirk at her.

"Do they include talking to naked women when you're supposed to be working?" she asks huskily.

"You're not naked. You're wearing a thong."

"Are you sure about that?" she murmurs.

My eyes are trained on the phone screen as she flips the camera around. It's pointing toward the ceiling before she slowly turns her camera to her own mirror. She takes a step back and I see her beautiful body in the reflective glass.

Every inch of her is perfect. And yes, she's completely fucking naked.

"I'll tell them we can't go to the party," I say. "We'll have room service after the first round."

It's her turn to smile. "Absolutely not. I've already decided what to wear."

"I liked the post-massage chic style," I tell her.

"I'm glad. But you haven't paid nearly enough for blindsiding me about this party. So my plan is to torture you all evening until you're barely holding onto your sanity by a thread."

"It's working so far." I love the way this woman bounces back.

I love way too much about her. I blink that thought away.

"Good. Now go back to your meeting. I'll see you when you get back," she says, making it sound almost ominous.

"Be naked. And wet."

"No can do, sorry. There's no bed related shenanigans until after the party." She turns the camera back to her face.

And I can't say I'm sorry. Yes, she has a body made for sin, but her face is so damn perfect. I like looking into her eyes.

I like *her*.

And isn't that a turnaround for the books?

twenty-six

SKYLER

"You know, we could still change our minds and head back to the hotel," Hudson says, as we drive toward the party which is being held in an achingly upscale restaurant in mid Manhattan. "I can call and cancel this."

He slides his hand over my thigh. He can't stop touching me, which I'm absolutely a fan of. I ended up wearing the dress I'd packed to have dinner with him this evening, back when I thought we would be staying right over the water from Liberty and not in the swanky hotel in New York City.

It's white and long sleeved, with a plunging neckline and a skirt that skims my calves. Perfect for a provincial dinner but somehow out of place in New York. But he can't seem to take his eyes off my cleavage and I'm here for that.

"By the way," I say, leaning to whisper in his ear. "I have something for you."

His eyes lock on mine. "Is it a million dollar ruby

necklace you borrowed from a jeweler?" he asks and I laugh. He really is taking this *Pretty Woman* thing seriously.

"Not quite." I take his hand, then put his gift into it. He opens it up and frowns, looking at the white scrap of lace on his palm.

"White lace panties," he says. "I'm not sure they go with my look."

I grin. "They didn't go with mine either. And since you've already started your collection I thought you could add to it."

His gaze dips to my dress. He gets the message, I'm bare beneath it. He slides the lace into his pocket.

"You know, the usual response to a gift is to give one back," I point out.

"I thought you didn't want me to Julia Roberts you," he replies. He's still distracted by my panties. I can tell that by the way he's shifting in his seat.

"I don't. I want your underwear."

He grins. "Shut up."

"I'm serious," I tell him. "Quid pro quo. You have my thong, I want your boxers. I have space in my purse," I point out, lifting my silver evening bag.

His gaze dips to my mouth. "Just when I think I understand you, you completely surprise me. What's so sexy about men's underwear?"

"Nothing. But what's sexy is you submitting to me."

"I'm not a submissive," he murmurs. "Quite the opposite."

"I know. That's what makes it so sexy." I'm kidding really. But there's something so intense about the way I'm feeling about this man. It helps to try to keep it light.

Because in a few hours I'll be in his bed. The one thing I

said I wouldn't do. And then I'm not sure who I'll be anymore.

We arrive at the restaurant all too quickly. The sky is getting dark and all the cars and cabs on the road have their lights on. A few of them are honking their horns, reminding me just how loud normal life is compared to life on Liberty.

"Ouch," I say, wrinkling my nose. "Can't they take a chill pill?"

"I believe those are now legal in New York," Hudson jokes, waving his driver off. I guess he'll call when he wants us to be picked up.

"Does he stay nearby?" I ask.

"What?"

"The driver. Does he just drive around the corner and wait for your call?" I've always wondered about this when watching old movies with drivers in them. I want to know their story, see what they do, not the glamorous actresses sweeping through the city.

"Like a beck and call driver? No. He'll probably go and get some dinner." Hudson shrugs. "I use a service. They work out the logistics, I just look pretty in their car."

He takes my hand and leads me through the restaurant door. As soon as we're at the Maitre d' station I start to feel a little wobbly. Nobody else in here is wearing white. Everybody's in dark colors and I stand out like a sore thumb. Maybe I should have taken Hudson's offer of a dress after all.

I tug at the low neckline, wanting to cover myself up.

"You look glorious," Hudson tells me.

"Remind me why we're here again," I ask.

"Because it's one of my investor's birthdays and he invited us."

"And his name is Daniel?"

"That's right. He's there." He points at a huge table in the restaurant, where a silver haired man is laughing and surrounded by people who stare at him adoringly. "That's Daniel, next to him is his wife."

"Which next to him?"

"The left."

"She looks younger than me."

"Welcome to New York." Hudson smiles, sliding his fingers between mine, as somebody calls out his name to greet him.

It turns out that the whole restaurant has been rented for this birthday. Hudson and I are at the main table, across from Daniel and his blonde wife, who is clad in black Dior. I try not to cling too hard to Hudson's hand as he introduces me to our fellow guests.

It's one of those parties where couples aren't seated directly next to each other. Instead, Hudson is three people down from me, and I'm between two men – one of whom is apparently Daniel's son, who looks distinctly like he doesn't want to be here. The other is Daniel's lawyer, whose wife is also wearing black.

Let's face it, all the women are wearing black. Except me.

"You're a new one," the lawyer's wife says, leaning across her husband to talk to me. "What an interesting dress."

"Thank you." I flash her a smile. From the corner of my eye I can feel Hudson watching me. I take a breath and square my shoulders. It's fine. I'm fine.

"How long have you and Hudson been dating?" she asks.

"Um... a little while." If you can count bedless sex as dating. I decide not to add that.

"Where did you meet?"

"On Liberty Island. Where Hudson has his hotel. I run the bar there."

"You're a bar maid?" Daniel's son suddenly comes to life. And I immediately wish he hadn't.

"I *own* the bar," I correct him.

"Where did you go to school?" he asks.

"High school?" I clarify. Why would he want to know that?

Everybody around us laughs at my response. "He means college," the lawyer's wife tells me.

"Oh. I um...I didn't go." I feel my face start to heat up. Hudson stands up and leaves the table and I'm wondering if he's regretting bringing me. I'm such an idiot. "Well I kind of dropped out of community college after the first semester."

"Dropped out?" the lawyer's wife murmurs. "That's novel."

"Wish I could have dropped out," the lawyer says, rolling his eyes. "I only just finished paying off my loans." He shoots me a smile and I smile back. But I still feel like a stupid fish out of water.

"Okay?" Hudson murmurs, leaning down to kiss my cheek. Where's he been?

"Of course," I say too quickly. He strokes my shoulder.

"Where's your bag?" he asks.

"My bag?" I reach down for it. "Why?" Then he takes it and slips something inside.

And I swear my body implodes. I don't even need to look inside to know. He's just put his boxers in there.

Hudson Fitzgerald is going commando for me.

I open my mouth, but no words come out. Instead I feel this stupid wave of emotion, because I know he did it to calm me. To make me feel more powerful, because that's what I need right now.

He hands me my bag back, like he's just slipped a handkerchief in there. "Isn't she perfect?" he says to Daniel's son. "I keep pinching myself to check that I'm not dreaming."

I look at his face. There's no hint of malice or humor there. He's deadly serious. He's looking at me like he's the luckiest man in the world.

And I have his underwear in my bag.

This man is so getting the best sex of his life tonight.

The lawyer and his wife are looking at me again, but this time like they're trying to work me out, not trying to work out what college I went to.

"I'm having a great time," I tell Hudson. Because suddenly I am. I have his boxers, he has my heart. It's almost a fair exchange.

"Good." He turns and walks away, and I watch him with my eyes trained on his behind. His boxer-less, perfect ass.

And it's all mine. At least for tonight.

* * *

We make out like teenagers on our way back to the hotel, and the driver kindly decides to ignore us, discreetly pressing the button to raise the screen between the front and rear seats. Hudson's hands are in my hair, on my sides, sliding over my legs, and his lips are devouring mine like we're both starved and haven't just eaten a three course meal.

It's only when the passenger door next to Hudson is opened by an equally discreet doorman that I realize we're at the hotel and have probably been stopped here for a few minutes.

I breathlessly thank the driver as Hudson leans forward to tip him, then we escape into the hotel, managing to keep our hands off each other for as long as it takes to get into the elevator.

When we step inside, the car is empty, and Hudson jabs the button for the penthouse like he hates it. As the doors close he turns to me, his eyes so dark it takes my breath away.

"That fucking dress," he says. "Do you know how hard it was not to touch you knowing that you're not wearing any underwear beneath it?"

I smile, because he's right. It's impossible to wear a bra with this dress. And of course he has my panties.

He steps forward, his jaw looking almost mean. "I had to put a napkin over my lap so nobody could see me getting hard," he says, as I step back against the elevator wall. He reaches out, his hands slamming on either side of me. Caging me in.

"That's the fun part of no underwear," I tell him. "You get to lose control."

"I damn nearly got arrested."

I grin at him. "I've always wanted to have sex with a perp."

He lowers his head until it's against mine. "You are the most annoying, aggravating, beautiful, funny woman I've ever met."

"And the first to get your underwear?" I ask.

"Without a doubt."

Oh I love that. I love it so much. "It made me hot looking at you," I whisper. "Knowing I have them."

"I want them back after tonight."

"Oh no." I shake my head. "I'm framing them and putting them behind the bar like a hunting trophy."

"I'd laugh, but I believe you," he says, cupping my face with his hand. "Jesus, I've never wanted anything in my life as much as I want you right now."

He pushes his body against me, as though to prove his point. I can feel how hard he is. It sends a shot of desire through my body.

"Then take me," I whisper.

"I will. When you're in my bed."

"It's not your bed, it's the hotel's."

"I paid for it. It's mine." He's so close I can feel the warmth of his breath on my face. His body is so tense I swear I feel every muscle tighten against me. Like he's restraining himself.

And I don't want him to be restrained. I want him to come undone.

"Are we talking about the bed or me?" I whisper.

"Definitely the bed. I don't think I could ever pay for you. I don't have that much money."

"How much do you think I'm worth?" I flutter my eyelashes at him, because this man has game.

"More than any man can afford." His lips almost brush mine. They're so tantalizingly close. Then the elevator door opens and he takes my hand, dragging me into the private lobby that leads to the living room with the stupidly perfect view over Manhattan.

But he doesn't stop to appreciate it, too intent on the door that leads to the master bedroom with it's oversized bed that I've been eyeing all afternoon. We've barely made it inside before he's scooping me up like he can't wait any longer, and is carrying me to the bed.

And then I freeze.

I know he feels it. Because he stops walking and freezes too.

I start to tremble. "Sky?" he murmurs. "What's wrong?"

"The bed."

He blinks. "Okay. Tell me what about the bed?" He frowns. "Did somebody hurt you? In a bed?"

Oh god. "No." I shake my head. "I think I just got it all built up in my mind. That if I sleep with you in a bed..." I trail off. I can't tell him, I can't.

"What will happen? You'll turn into a frog?"

My lips curl. *Don't make me laugh*. He already has the trifecta of perfection. He's gorgeous, he's grumpy, and he gave me his boxers.

I can't deal with him being any more perfect right now.

"I can't fall in love with you," I whisper, and as soon as it's out of my mouth I feel like I'm careening to the ground, even though he's still holding me tight in his arms. Slowly, he puts me down, his brows knitted as he cups my face.

"Would that be so bad?" he asks me.

"Yes."

He tips his head to the side. "Because you think I'm an ass?"

"No. Quite the opposite. You're too much," I confess. "You're rich and you're confident. You walk into a room and everybody turns to look at you. Your family adores you, your daughter thinks you're some kind of God, and I'm starting to feel the same."

He doesn't take his eyes off me as I speak. His lips are parted, like he's trying to follow along.

"I have no idea who you're talking about, but I think you have me confused with somebody else," he says. He cups my face in his warm hands. "And you are so, so fucking wrong."

"What about?" I whisper.

"I'm the one batting outside my league," he tells me.

"You're irresistible. From the moment I saw you I wanted you. Then you opened your mouth and pretty much told me to fuck off and I wanted you even more.

"Everybody loves you. My sister, my daughter. Your brother. The whole damn town. You stepped off that ferry and lit everybody's world up." He lowers his brow until it touches mine. "You're worried about falling in love with me? Well I've already fallen in love with you. I fell a long fucking time ago and I think it broke every bone in my body."

I swallow, but the lump in my throat still stays. He loves me? I can't quite understand it. And yet he doesn't look like he's lying at all.

"So let's do this slowly," he says. "Tonight is about you. I'm going to sit down on that bed and you tell me what you want. You want to put our pajamas on and go to sleep? We can do that. You want to talk all night, until I prove to you that I'm not going anywhere? We'll do that, too. Or if you want to sleep on the bed alone, then I'll take the floor. The last time I did it was the second best night of my life."

"Sleeping on my bedroom floor was the second best night of your life?"

He nods.

"Why?" I ask him.

"Because it was the first night you let me take care of you."

Ka-pow. My heart shatters into tiny pieces. I swear I can feel it scattered against my ribcage. "Stop it," I whisper.

"Stop what?"

"Stop making me fall."

"I don't know how to stop," he says. "Tell me how to."

But it's too late. I think we both know that. The tide is high and the pull is hard and no amount of swimming will ever conquer nature. "I want you naked," I tell him. "On the bed."

"Okay."

To my shock he does as I ask, taking his jacket and tie off, then unfastening his shirt. I watch as he shrugs that off too, revealing his taut, muscular chest.

His eyes are on me as he toes his shoes off. Then he flicks his fly open and my breath catches as he pulls his pants down.

He's hard. His thick length presses against his stomach as he follows my instructions and sits.

I kick my own shoes off, unable to tear my eyes away from this man who's willing to make himself vulnerable to make me feel better.

"I hate you," I tell him, pulling my dress down over my breasts, the fabric brushing against my nipples as I slide it further until I'm naked too. "I hate you for making me love you."

He exhales softly.

"You gave me your boxers," I whisper, dropping to my knees and crawling to him like a cat in heat. "Nobody's ever given me their underwear."

"How many men have you asked?" There's a hint of jealousy to his voice that I like.

"Just you."

I reach his feet and incline my head to look at him. I'm still on all fours, naked. His gaze is so intense it makes my nipples harden. Sliding my hands up his calves, I feel his muscles tense beneath my touch, until I get to his thighs, my fingers tracing every line, every sinew.

And then I touch his cock.

It's smooth and warm and so hard. I'm in love with this

part of him, too. I curl my hand around him, feeling him pulse, hearing him groan.

Then I slide my mouth over him. My heart is thudding against my ribcage, my pulse so fast I swear it's almost unreadable. I lick and suck this strong, stubborn man until he's so damn close to oblivion he's vibrating.

"Sky..."

I love the way he calls me that. I love the way he tangles his fingers in my hair, hard enough to feel it, but not so hard it hurts. I love the way he groans as I scratch his inner thighs with my nails, then move up to his balls, my mouth warm, my tongue adoring, finding a rhythm I know can take him over the edge.

This is for the boxers. For sleeping on the floor. For loving me.

"Skyler." His voice is more urgent this time. I look up and he's shaking his head. "Not in your mouth. In you."

I don't need telling twice. I'm so hot and needy. I push him back on the bed and practically climb him like he's my favorite piece of play equipment. I close my hand around him again, but this time I rub his tip against me and he presses his mouth to mine urgently, like he needs to kiss me to survive.

I kiss him back, lowering myself down on him until I'm so, so full. And yet I need more. We talked last week about not using condoms, since I'm on the pill and we're exclusive. And it adds a whole new layer of intimacy as I feel him raw inside of me.

I start to rock, kissing him, scratching him, feeling him grind against me in the most delicious way. It sends shockwaves through my body, making my movements stutter. He slides his hand down my hips, steadying my movements, making love to me in a way I don't think anybody ever has before.

I slide my fingers into his hair, my eyes open, on his, as we rock and tease and grind until we're both breathless.

"Now," I whisper. "Fuck me like you hate me."

I don't need to say it twice. He rolls me onto the bed, still inside of me, then starts to give me exactly what I need. Long, mean thrusts, his hand between us, touching me, his mouth hard against mine.

"Hudson..."

"Give it to me," he mutters against my lips. "I need you to come."

I need to come too. I'm bucking underneath him, tears in my eyes because I don't think I've ever felt this good. My nails scrape his back, my lips move to his neck, my teeth digging into him.

And then I start to convulse, white hot pleasure coursing through me. I bite him hard and he lets out a shout, his back arching as he comes hard inside of me. It's animalistic and it's almost painful and it's everything I need right now. He holds me tight against him, still spilling inside of me, as I flutter around him again and again.

It feels like minutes before I can breathe. Before he pulls out and rolls onto his side, his hand cupping my face as I try to work out what my own name is.

"Are you okay? Was it too hard?" he asks me.

I shake my head. "I'm fine," I whisper, pressing my lips against him. "More than fine. Completely fucked in the best way."

He laughs softly, pulling me against him so my head is nestled into his shoulder, his hands softly stroking my hair.

"Next time I'll be more gentle," he mumbles sleepily, his

fingers pressing softly against my scalp in little circular movements.

Maybe that's what I'm afraid of.

twenty-seven

HUDSON

Skyler stares at herself in the mirror, her mouth open as she traces the skin on her neck. "I can't believe you gave me a hickey," she says, frowning at the red mouth-shaped patch there.

I smirk, because it may have been inadvertent, but it also feels like some kind of sweet justice. Plus I like seeing the little bruise on her neck. I made it. She's mine.

"We have ten minutes until the car arrives," I remind her. My plans for a leisurely breakfast followed by a long, hot sexy shower in the double sized bathroom are out of the window. It turns out that a sleepy Skyler is stubborn as hell. She wouldn't wake up no matter how many times I kissed her back, murmured in her ear, or – eventually – played Fleetwood Mac through the penthouse's expensive stereo system.

"I don't even have a scarf to cover my neck," she grumbles, shooting me a dark look. But there's amusement there, along with something altogether hotter. "Give me that," she mutters, walking over to me and yanking my tie. It tightens dangerously around my neck.

"Are you trying to kill me?" I rasp, feeling my windpipe constrict.

"Don't tempt me. Why the hell are we meeting your lawyer so early anyway?" She succeeds in taking my tie off and knots it around her neck like a choker. It looks surprisingly effective.

Now I'm imagining curling my fingers around it while I take her from behind. Note to self, *give her all your ties.*

"It's not early. It's almost ten," I point out, unfastening my top button. "And I'd like to be back on the island before Ayda goes to bed."

At that Skyler's face softens. "Of course you do. Have you talked to her this morning?"

"We got on Facetime. I talked, she listened." That was all in the other room while Skyler was asleep. "She and Autumn are going over to the bar today to help Jesse."

"Oh." Skyler claps her hands together. "I bought her a new coloring book. It's in the drawer behind the bar. You should message Autumn and tell her."

I give her a long look. "You want me to message Autumn to tell her?" I repeat.

"Yes." Skyler nods. "It's got princesses in it. Not Disney ones, real ones. Warrior princesses. I think Ayda's going to love it."

"And if I message Autumn and tell her about it, don't you think she's going to wonder how I know it's there?" I ask, looking at her carefully.

Skyler frowns. "Oh."

"Yeah, oh." I lift my brow.

"I guess we don't want to let the cat out of the bag,

huh?" She smooths down the overalls she's wearing. She won't quite catch my eye. I check my watch, we're going to be late and I hate being late.

But still I reach for her chin, tipping it up so her eyes meet mine.

"I think the cat is already out of the bag, sweetheart. You love me."

She exhales softly.

"And I love you. So it's a matter of controlling the cat. Making sure it doesn't go feral."

She narrows her eyes. "We're not talking about a real life cat here, are we?"

I can't help but chuckle. "No. But I'm tired of hiding this. I want to be able to come to your place and see you without sneaking around like a damn teenager. I want you in my arms and in my bed."

Skyler pulls her lip between her teeth. I flick it with my thumb. "But if we go public, we need to do it right," I say softly. "On a small island like Liberty, people talk. And I have Ayda to think about." That's my biggest concern. I just need to make sure we do this right.

"Of course you do. We don't have to do this. We can go back to bedless sex."

"No we fucking can't." My phone vibrates and I know that's the driver. We still haven't checked out.

This is what happens when you spend the whole night having sex at my age. Everything the next morning goes to shit. And yet I wouldn't change a minute of it. Being inside this woman, holding her all night. It was the best damn night of my life.

"Listen," I tell her. "I just need to talk this through with Dr. Methi, okay?"

"Dr. Methi?" She frowns.

"Ayda's trauma doctor. Mine, too. I need to discuss the best way to deal with it for Ayda's sake."

"Do you think she'll be upset about us? I don't want her to be upset. I'd rather just keep things the way they are."

"I think she'll be ecstatic," I murmur. "I just want to manage her expectations. Explain that this is…" I trail off.

"That this is new," Skyler murmurs. "That we're friends but we feel a lot for each other. But I'm not her mom or a mom replacement and never will be."

I blink. "I guess. And I don't want that to have any detrimental affect on her progress." Because she still isn't talking and it's killing me.

"I think talking to her doctor is a good idea," Skyler agrees.

My phone buzzes again. "Okay, we need to go." I'm dropping her off at my lawyer's on the way to my office. I have one meeting this morning before my driver picks us up to take us to the helipad.

And then we'll be back on Liberty by tonight. She'll be back in her place and I'll be at home with Ayda.

I'm looking forward to seeing my daughter, but I hate the thought of not holding this woman in my arms while I sleep.

"I'll talk to Dr. Methi soon," I say, grabbing our luggage. "The quicker we make a plan, the better."

Her eyes meet mine. There's a warm amusement in them. She slides her fingers over the tie she's knotted around her neck.

"Whatever you say, Dracula."

* * *

SKYLER

. . .

The meeting with Hudson's lawyer takes less time than I had expected. Drawing up a contract to add Jesse as an owner of The Salty Dog is simple, though he suggested he have one of his colleagues in a different firm do it, as there's some kind of conflict of interest since he's Hudson's lawyer.

Apparently, Hudson paid for the bar renovations against his lawyer's legal advice, and he suggests *my* lawyer – the one he's referring me to – makes Hudson sign a waiver to state he has no claim on the bar at all. I couldn't help but smile that his lawyer is even more grumpy than Hudson himself.

So now I have almost an hour before Hudson and his driver are due to pick me up. I walk out of the high rise building and into the New York City streets. It's late morning but they're full of people rushing to get somewhere. The sun is beating down from the topaz blue sky, and I head toward the nearest coffee shop and order a double shot cappuccino, because after last night's bed-ful sex marathon, I need all the caffeine I can get.

"Cute outfit," the barista says when she passes me the Styrofoam cup. "I love your tie."

"Thanks." I give her a broad smile, feeling content as I take a seat by the window. I have two messages from Lee. She's sent a meme of two little girls – sisters – wearing the same dresses. The younger one is smiling at the camera, with a thought bubble coming out of her head saying 'I'm dressed like my sister.' The older one is scowling, while thinking exactly the same thing.

Under it Lee has written,
This is me every time you try to get me to wear a floaty dress.

I go to reply, but then a wave of nostalgia washes over me. I miss her face. So I hit the video call button.

She answers almost right away.

"How was your dirty night in Manhattan?" she asks. Because of course I told her about it.

"Perfect." I sigh. "I hate how perfect it was."

"Only you would hate perfection," Lee replies. She's in the kitchen, doing some dishes by the looks of it. I think her phone must be propped up on the window sill because she looks like she's at a weird angle. "So he's also a master at sex in a bed?"

A woman sipping a chai latte next to me whips her head around to look at me.

"Lee," I hiss and she laughs.

"Just say yes," she urges.

"Yes, yes he is."

"So why do you look like you just found a penny and lost a dollar?" she asks.

"He wants us to go public about our dating."

Lee's hands freeze mid wash. "Seriously?"

I nod. "Yes, seriously. He's talking about making a plan with Ayda's doctor to make sure finding out about us doesn't upset her."

Lee's brows knit together. "Is that what you want?" she asks.

I can't work out why she looks so mad about that. "I guess..."

"You guess? This is a little girl we're talking about. You can't just guess, Skyler. You have to be sure." Her jaw tightens. "This is so like you."

"Why are you so mad at me?" I ask her.

"Because you never take anything seriously," she says. A wail comes from behind her. "Oh damn. She's only been asleep ten minutes." She dries her hands off and disappears, reappearing a minute later holding Cora, doing the mom dance that all babies seem to love. "So you're really staying there?" she asks.

And then it dawns on me. She's upset with me because I'm settling on Liberty. "I think so," I say, feeling reluctant to annoy her further.

"With your new brother."

"You like Jesse," I point out. They've talked a couple of times since it all came out. Lee even mentioned coming to meet him in the flesh when she gets a chance.

"Sure I like him. I don't like that you're willing to stay in the same town as him when you're not willing to live anywhere near me or your niece."

"Lee," I whisper, trying to find the right words. I hate that she looks angry with me. I hate that she's hurt. I hate that I could never stay around long enough to show her the love she shows me. "You're my number one sister. You know that."

"I'm your only sister." But her lips twitch.

"You're my very favorite, knows all the lyrics to *Tusk*, can do French braids like a professional, big sister who's better than everybody."

"Shut up."

"Move out here," I say.

"I'm not moving out there." But she's almost smiling now.

"You can live by the ocean. Cora can grow up breathing in the salt. You and James can have bedless sex to your heart's content."

"We're not moving to the East Coast," Lee mutters. "But I'll come visit."

"Good." I blow her a kiss. "The only bad thing about Liberty is that you're not there."

She lets out a long breath. "I just want you to be happy," she says.

"I am happy. I love it." I pull my lip between my teeth. "I love him."

"Skyler..."

"I know. It's too soon. I've told myself that. And I'm pretty sure he's said the same thing to himself a billion times. But there it is. I love him, the sex is perfect, and now he wants to go public."

"Is that what you want?" Lee asks.

I nod. "It is."

Her face crumples. "My baby sister's going to settle down. On a little island over two thousand miles away from me."

"I wish you were there," I say.

"Maybe I do too," she says. "I'm happy for you, I really am. Or I will be when I get over the annoyance."

"Thank you," I tell her. I glance at my watch. "I have to go. Hudson's picking me up soon."

She nods, dipping her face against Cora's soft, downy scalp, breathing her in. "You know you'll always be my baby sister? I'll always want to take care of you."

"I know that," I tell her. "But you have other people to take care of now. And I can take care of myself."

I have been for a long time. "I love you, sis."

"Love you too." She gives me a sad smile. "Just keep being you, okay? Don't let anybody dim your light."

twenty-eight

SKYLER

"Well hello stranger," a husky female voice calls out to me as I drink my morning coffee on the deck a few weeks later. I'm sitting on one of the white-painted chairs that Autumn insisted would work perfectly with the vibe she was trying to create in the bar. Of course, she was right.

Which is why I'm smiling at her as she, Ayda, and Barney the dog walk toward me.

"Hi." I sit up. "Want a coffee?"

"Just had one." Autumn takes a seat beside me and Barney lays down at her feet. Ayda walks over to me and pulls at my sleeve.

"What is it, sweetie?" I ask her. The other day, when I was on the phone with Hudson, he explained that Ayda's speech therapist thinks there's been some improvement. He's even hopeful that a breakthrough might be imminent.

But right now she's still making gestures and I recognize this one. She wants to color. I jump up, excited, remembering the princess coloring book and new crayons I bought and stashed in the drawer behind the bar.

A minute later she's kneeling on a chair at the table next to ours, Barney guarding her, as she chooses between a dark red and a bright pink crayon to color in the first dress.

I sit down and swallow my last mouthful of coffee. In the distance I can see the ferry. Both day visitors and those staying longer are getting more common now that the warmer weather is finally here. I've had to add on extra shifts for our staff to keep up with demand.

Last week, thanks to a bout of flu that seems to be going around the island and made most of my staff ill, I had to cancel my date night with Hudson. Grumpy didn't even cover his response. I was still smirking about it later that night when I was pouring a gin and tonic, only to find him behind the bar next to me, helping me serve customers.

"What are you doing here?" I whispered. "I thought we weren't telling people yet." He'd only just met with Dr. Methi, who'd suggested that I have a session with him before he helped Hudson work out a plan to get Ayda used to having me around. I'm happy with that, I'm in no rush.

Hudson, though, is in a constant rush. "I'm spending time with you," he'd huffed, completely annihilating a pint of lager as he tried to pour it from the tap.

"Go sit down. I'll be over when I take my break." I gave him the glass that was more foam than beer. "And drink this, nobody else will."

I pull my mind away from that memory and try to concentrate on Autumn, who's looking at me like she's trying to work something out.

Before she can say anything she sneezes, only just getting a tissue out in time. "Oh God, I'm sorry." She shakes her head. "I swear I thought I was over this thing."

"You had the flu too?"

"Hasn't everybody?"

She's not far off. Most people have. Mylene had to close the coffee shop for a few days last week, and Eileen battled through because she had guests. Jesse says he had it but not badly, and I've seemed to have somehow escaped it altogether. I credit my off-island genes for keeping me safe.

"So anyway," Autumn continues. "I would have come over last week but I didn't want to spread anything." She reaches out to trace a bead of morning dew on the tabletop. "So how was your trip to the mainland the other week?"

I lift a brow. "Good."

"You manage to get that contract with Jesse sorted?"

"Uhuh." I nod, my eyes narrowing. She never makes small talk. "We both signed it this week." I also had to ask Hudson to sign the disclaimer my now-lawyer sent over. I gave him a blow job to soothe the pain of it, though.

"That's good. I was going to ask your opinion. Something really weird happened when you were away." She gets her phone out, and I'm actually intrigued. Her eyelashes bat as she looks up at me. "Did you know Hudson was over in the mainland too. The same day you were?"

"No," I say too quickly.

She gives me a smile. "Of course you wouldn't have. He was in New York and you were in..."

She waits for me to fill in her sentence but I don't. Because I know where this is going and it's nowhere good.

"So what was weird?" I ask, unable to keep my curiosity from escaping.

"When we were on Facetime I saw a pair of women's shoes on the floor in his hotel living room." She clears her throat. "Really pretty shoes, too. Do you think he's seeing somebody?"

I let out a breath. "How would I know?"

"I think you *know* how you'd know," Autumn says.

"Maybe you were mistaken. Could they have been an ornament? Or left by a previous guest?" I suggest, trying not to smile at the way she's glaring at me. God, she looks like her brother sometimes.

"I took a screenshot," she says triumphantly, holding her phone up. She zooms in on my shoes – because there's no doubt that's what they are. "They look kind of seventies, don't they?"

"Hmm." I pull my eyes away.

She puts her phone back down. "So, how long have you been sleeping with my brother?" she whispers.

I look over at Ayda, alarmed, but she's way too busy coloring to listen.

I point at her anyway. I'm not a bad person, but I'll use her to try to get out of this conversation.

But then Autumn grabs my hand and drags me up. "Come over here," she mutters, practically yanking me across the deck to the railing that separates the bar from the little strip of land that leads down to the beach. I don't fight her too hard. This is Hudson's fault. He should have hidden my damn shoes.

"So?" she asks, folding her arms across her chest.

"Have you asked your brother that question?" I say.

She rolls her eyes. "Of course I haven't. Would you?"

I smile. "Probably not."

"*Are* you sleeping with him?" she asks again.

"Yes." I'm not going to lie to her. And I trust her enough that this will stay between us. And if Hudson's angry that I confirmed it, well let him be. This is absolutely his doing.

"Oh." She blinks. "I didn't think you'd capitulate that quickly."

"Have I spoiled your plans?" I ask.

A smile pulls at her lips despite her attempts to look angry. "Kinda. I was hoping for a bit more back and forth. I'm not above resorting to blackmail."

"Sorry." I lean on the railing, feeling the breeze lift my hair. God, I love this place so much.

"So?" she asks, sounding urgent again. "When did it start?"

"I'm not sure," I say honestly. "I guess at Ayda's party."

Her eyes widen. "You were the woman in his office that Parker disturbed?"

I wrinkle my nose. "I was."

"I can't believe you've been keeping this from me. I thought we were friends."

"We are," I tell her. She looks genuinely upset. I take her hand and squeeze it. "You were always going to be the first to know as soon as we were ready."

"I was?" she asks, sounding mollified. "Good." She clears her throat again, like the frog in it refuses to leave. "What exactly do you mean by ready?"

My heart rate picks up. "I think we're going to start dating out in the open soon."

Her eyes widen. "Hudson said that?"

"Yes. He wants me to meet with Dr. Methi. For us to discuss telling Ayda."

"Oh my God!" Autumn starts to jump up and down. Her excitement is so loud it causes Barney to bark. Ayda looks up at us, her brows pulled tight. "Nothing, honey!" Autumn calls out. Then she lowers her voice. "Oh my God," she whispers it this time. "We're going to be sisters."

"It's just dating," I whisper back. "Don't get ahead of yourself."

"I'm not," she insists. "Do you know how many times

Hudson has asked somebody to meet Dr. Methi to discuss his relationship with them?"

I shake my head.

"Me either. Because it's never happened." She takes my hand and dances around with me. "Face it, it's more serious than dating. He wouldn't want you to talk to Dr. Methi about that. He's into you. Really into you. He's bound to propose in no time."

I roll my eyes at her again, because seriously, this is too much. But there's a warm feeling in my stomach that I can't ignore.

Would it really be so bad if Hudson proposed? For the first time in my life, I feel like I belong somewhere. With people I'm falling stupidly in love with. Not just Hudson but Autumn and Ayda and Jesse.

No, I don't think it would be that bad. And that's really damn scary to me.

* * *

"So you're Skyler Brown," Dr. Methi says as he leads me into his office. "Please take a seat." He points at the sofa, so I take a seat on the warm leather cushions. He sits down in the armchair opposite. "It's good to finally meet you. I've heard a lot about you."

"Thank you." I have a headache, which is annoying since I want to be present for this meeting. I'm hoping it's a result of working long hours and not me catching the flu that's still been working its way through Liberty. I don't have time for it, not when half my staff are out with it.

Autumn and Jesse are running the bar for me again today. Though I guess Jesse is running it for himself now that the bar is half his. But I'm still grateful for them both.

Of course Autumn insists that family helps family. Even though we're nowhere near that.

"I hope the things you've heard about me are good," I say to Dr. Methi. "Because otherwise it's all lies."

He laughs gently. "If it helps, I kind of knew you existed before Hudson admitted it to himself."

I blink, surprised. "How so?"

"He was behaving differently. More angry, if anything. And nothing makes Hudson Fitzgerald angrier than losing control of a situation. Or a person. Especially himself."

"You think he lost control over me?" I hate that it makes me feel warm. Because I think I lost control too, but in a whole different way.

"Absolutely. You wouldn't be sitting here if he hadn't. He's a man who doesn't trust easily. But once you're in his circle..." the doctor trails off. "Anyway, we're getting ahead of ourselves. Why don't we take a step back?"

"Okay." I nod.

He looks me in the eye. "I thought it would make sense for us to talk one on one so I can best advise Hudson how to deal with Ayda and your relationship. Before we start, I guess I should make sure you're on the same page as him."

My throat feels scratchy. "Yes, of course. I wouldn't be here if I didn't want this."

He smiles. "I'm glad to hear that. Because I have to tell you I've never seen Hudson as animated as he's been in the last few weeks."

"Is that good?" I clarify.

"Mostly. When he stopped fighting himself. So you're new to the island, right?"

"I am, but my father grew up there. He left but kept going back. He owned a bar that he left to me. I came to the island once he passed and found I'd fallen in love with it. And the people."

For the next forty minutes Dr. Methi listens to me, asking questions, giving prompts, until my whole life appears laid out before him. He doesn't look shocked when I tell him about my dad's illness, about discovering Jesse is my brother, about how Hudson and I butted heads until we were both sore from it.

"And you've never had a serious relationship before?" he asks.

I pull my lip between my teeth, feeling suddenly embarrassed. "Not really." I've dated, I even lived with a guy for six weeks once, before he very calmly told me that his girlfriend – the one I didn't know existed – was coming home and it was time for me to move out.

But I've never had somebody ask me to be in a relationship.

"Why is that do you think?" Dr. Methi asks.

"Maybe I'm not relationship material," I say. My throat feels tight.

"Hudson seems to think you are."

"For now."

Dr. Methi blinks. "Why do you say it like that?" he asks. "What does 'for now' mean?"

I take a deep breath. I feel weirdly dizzy. "I'm well known in my family for messing things up then running away," I confess, because as embarrassing as this is, I can't lie to this man. Not when he wants to make sure what is decided is in Ayda's best interest. She really is the priority here, after all.

"Tell me about a time that happened."

I do, I tell him about dropping out of college. How

furious my mom was, how I used the money I'd saved over the years to pay for a one-way ticket to Europe.

"That doesn't sound much like messing up," the doctor says gently. "It sounds like a young person trying to find themselves."

"Well it took me a long time," I say and he laughs.

"I think you just hit the nail on the head," he tells me. "It takes as long as it takes. We have this weird view in the developed world that unless you follow the same path your parents and grandparents followed that somehow you're not worthy. Do well at school, go to college, get a job, get married, and have kids." He lifts a brow. "But there's only a small minority of people that actually thrive in that environment. That's why there are so many dropouts, so many divorces, so many messed up kids."

"My mom and my sister seem to have it under control," I tell him. "It's just me. My mom thinks I have my dad's blood."

He tips his head to the side. "What do you think?"

His question takes me by surprise. What *do* I think? I mull on it for a moment, trying to get the thoughts straight in my head.

"I think that I wouldn't have wanted to live my life any other way," I say. "I don't like doing what I'm told. I don't like having to conform. And I hate being judged for that."

His smile is wide. "Good. That's what I was hoping you were going to say. Hudson is..." He looks like he's trying to choose his words carefully. "He's a man who needs to be challenged."

"He hates being challenged."

"But he needs it," Dr. Methi repeats. "I know he'd hate for me to say it, but he's not always right. Very few people are willing to point that out to him."

"I like his certainty."

"And he likes you challenging it," Dr. Methi says softly.

"He does?"

He lifts a brow. "He's asked you to be in a relationship with him. It's not something a man like him does easily. I have a feeling he likes you very much." He steeples his fingers together, still looking at me. "And I also think that you would be good for Ayda. Hudson tells me that you two already know each other."

"I met her on my first day on Liberty," I say.

"And you understand her issues?"

"I'm starting to. I'd like to learn more."

He nods. "That's what I was hoping for. It's not easy having a child with issues like Ayda. Especially not in a new relationship."

"I know." I nod. "And I think that's what I'm worried about. I don't want to be another reason she's traumatized."

"And that's why you won't be. Because you care. She's been pulled a hundred different ways in her short lifetime, and it's going to take a period of stability for her to come to terms with all she's had to deal with. She also needs to spread her wings." He smiles at me. "Something Hudson struggles with a lot. I have a feeling you'll help him with that."

"I want to," I say.

"Good." He looks up at the clock. "We're coming to the end of our session. But I'd like to see you again soon. With Hudson and Ayda. I think it would be good to have a joint session."

"Should we wait until then before we start publicly seeing each other?" I ask.

"There's no reason why Hudson can't speak with his

daughter before then. And gently introduce you into her life as more than a friend." He stands up, holding his hand out to me. "I absolutely think this could be a good thing for all of you. Just take baby steps. Use your instincts. And I'm always a phone call away."

His words fill me with warmth. I stand up, ready to shake his hand, but the sudden movement causes a rush of dizziness to wash over me. I stumble to the left, and Dr. Methi lunges to catch me before I fall onto his perfectly arranged coffee table. His arms are around me as he slowly moves me back to the sofa, setting me down.

I hate being dizzy. I hate the way it makes my stomach twist. "I'm so sorry," I tell him. "And thank you for catching me."

"Are you feeling okay?" he looks concerned. "Have you eaten today?"

"I wasn't hungry," I tell him. "But I'll grab some lunch before I catch the ferry back."

He still doesn't look happy. "Have you been feeling sick?"

"Not really," I tell him. "There's been some flu going around the island but I thought I'd escaped it."

He walks over to his desk and grabs a pad, scribbling something on it. "Here," he says, ripping the top page off and handing it to me. "Stop by my secretary and she can give you the information for the lab and how to schedule. Just to rule out any other possible symptoms." I raise a brow. "If you're going to be part of Ayda's life it's absolutely paramount that you take care of your own health."

"Of course." I nod, my cheeks pinking up as I slide the paper into my pocket. "Thank you." I'm already feeling better, more steady as I stand.

"No problem. It was a pleasure to meet you, Skyler. I hope to see a lot more of you."

This time when I shake his hand there's no dizziness at all. "Likewise," I tell him.

And after his secretary gave me all the info I need for my blood draw, I walk outside, smiling as I feel the warmth of the sun bathing my face.

Good things are happening. I can feel it.

Maybe this is what it's like to finally grow up.

twenty-nine

HUDSON

I stride into The Salty Dog and look around, my jaw tight because it's been a long day and I'm exhausted as hell.

As soon as I set my eyes on her behind the bar, laughing at something Jesse's said, I let out a long breath. Like she can sense my need for her, she slowly turns her head in my direction and our eyes connect.

I want to lift her over my shoulder like a damn caveman and get us the hell out of here. To somewhere without people or expectations.

"Hi," she breathes as I reach the bar.

"Hey." I lift the counter up, ignoring the raised eyebrows of a few locals as I make myself at home.

Not that I care. We agreed that we'd tell Ayda about us, and I've already started doing that with the blessing from Dr. Methi. And of course the word has spread that we're seeing each other. I know she's told Jesse and I've spoken to Autumn and Parker – who already knew.

But nobody else in this town is owed any explanation. I just want to hold my fucking girl.

So I do. I pull her into my arms and drop my face into her hair, breathing her in like she's more important than oxygen. Like she can sense my need, she tangles her fingers into my hair, scraping the line where it meets my neck.

"Ahem."

I look up to see Jesse staring at me.

"Don't fucking start," I say to him. If I want to hold her I will.

"Somebody's grumpy," Skyler murmurs. "What's up?"

"Hey, before you say anything else, as Skyler's brother I feel the need to lay down some ground rules," Jesse insists. All the people sitting at the bar turn to watch us.

I let out a long breath and look at Skyler for help. I don't want to do this now. How can I make it any more obvious?

"Don't look at me like that, I had to deal with your sister," she says. "You can deal with my brother."

I take her in with needy eyes. She's wearing a denim skirt and a patterned shirt, tied at the waist to reveal her taut stomach and a hint of her tattoo. Her hair is in a high ponytail and she's got a slick of lip gloss on and nothing else.

And then I look at Jesse, who has the same stubbornness to his jaw as she does.

"If you hear me out," Jesse says, looking amused at my annoyance, "you can take her out for the night. I'll close up."

"Then do it." Because as soon as he closes his mouth I'm dragging her out of here and to my car. I don't care where we go. To the hotel, to the cottages, hell I'll be content to sit with her in the car and watch the moon together. I just need to be where people are not.

"Okay." He nods, looking suddenly uncertain. Skyler looks from me to him and then back to me again, her eyes beseeching. I give her the smallest of nods.

I won't hurt your damn brother.

"Okay," Jesse says, jutting his jaw out. "In the absence of Wayne, I'm the closest thing Skyler has to a father."

"You're two years younger than her," I snap.

Skyler bites down a smile.

"And as her only male relative," Jesse continues, ignoring my interjection, "it's inherent upon me to make this very, very clear. If you ever hurt this woman," he says, looking at her. "If you so much as harm a damn hair on her head, I'll make sure you regret it. Understood?"

My lips twitch. When I look at Skyler's hers are doing the same. But I also appreciate the guts it takes to talk to me like that.

"Understood," I manage to say with a straight face.

"Good." He nods. "You can go."

I don't point out that I'd like to see him stop me. Mostly because I'm kind of impressed. It's almost rubbed the edge of my annoyance.

"Ready?" I ask her.

She nods and I take her hand, barely stopping to let her grab her purse as I march us out of the bar.

"What's got you all resting-bastard-face?" she asks me as I open the door to my car. I help her in and walk to the other side, climbing into the driver's seat.

"I got a call from my attorney," I tell her, closing the driver's door.

"What kind of call?" she asks, frowning.

I start the engine up. "One where he told me that Ayda's grandparents' lawyer sent them a letter before action. They didn't like my refusal to their request for her to stay with them every summer. So they want to take me to court."

"Oh." Skyler frowns. "They want her to stay with them in England?"

"Yes." I'm so pissed I want to fucking hit something. I thought telling them no to their request would be the end of it, not that they'd take me to court again. "I gave them an inch and they took a fucking mile. I wish I'd never agreed to let them see her at all." I put the car into drive and pull out of the space, my fingers so tight on the wheel my knuckles are white.

Skyler shifts in her seat. The movement makes her shirt collar gape open. I can see the swell of her breasts from the corner of my eye.

I put my foot on the gas, turning the corner onto the country road, deciding that we're not going to the hotel or the cottages. I'm taking her home. To my bed. I need her with me tonight.

"They'll lose though, won't they?" she asks. "Like they did before?"

"Probably." I grit my teeth. "I won the case fair and square in London. But now they're petitioning the state court here. Grandparents have more rights in the US than they do in the UK."

She puts her hand on my thigh, like she's trying to soothe me.

"Listen, I don't want to think about it right now. I just needed you to understand why I'm in a bad mood." I swing into the driveway that leads up to the Captain's House. The turret is lit up by the moon, giving it an almost eerie feeling. If she's wondering why I've brought her to my home, she wisely doesn't ask.

"I understand," she says softly. "And thank you for being so sweet to Jesse earlier."

I pull into my usual space, next to the steps that lead up to my front door. "I wasn't sweet."

"You were," she says. "You didn't call him an asshole, you didn't punch him..."

"I don't punch people."

"I know." She bites down a smile. "But thank you anyway."

I turn off the engine and let out a long breath. The annoyance is slowly seeping away. She's still in her seat, looking at me with those big, brown eyes of hers.

"I like the way you look at me," I say, my voice thick.

"That's good," she breathes. "Because I like looking at you."

I turn to her, reaching for her, pulling her against me even though there's no room in this car. "Can I take you to my bed and show you exactly how pissed off I am?" I ask her.

Her lips curl into a smile. "I thought you'd never ask."

* * *

SKYLER

His breath is warm on my back, his fingers digging into my hips as he moves thickly inside of me, both of us on our knees. We're on his bed, which is a complete concession to him, because as soon as we walked through his front door all I wanted to do was drop to my knees and make him come with my mouth.

I love that he can show his vulnerabilities to me, even

though they come covered in a outercoat of annoyance. So I let him kiss me all the way upstairs and then stripped for him while he watched, his jaw still so tight I swear the man's going to need extensive dental surgery one day.

Since we've been back from New York we've made gentle love, we've made fast love, we've had oral sex enough to curl anybody's toes, but this rough, animalistic sex hasn't been in the repertoire since then.

But now he's fucking me like he hates me again, his skin hot and taut as he thrusts inside of me, his mouth tracing the line of my neck as he lifts his hand beneath my face to turn it.

His kisses are mean and mine are meaner. I bite his lip and he growls. Then he runs his hand down my stomach, his fingers searching out the neediest part of me, and he circles there, still thrusting so hard my whole body judders with every movement.

I tighten around him, making him curse, then he flicks my clit one more time, sending me into a quivering mess of pleasure, my body convulsing around him as he holds me tight, before my orgasm sets off his own, and he spills inside of me.

"Fuck." He's as breathless as I am as he pulls out and collapses onto his back. He reaches for me, looking suddenly vulnerable again. "I didn't hurt you, did I?"

"You can stop asking me that," I say. "No, you didn't. And even if you did and I didn't stop you that means I liked it. I like it rough, you know that."

I also like it slow and sensual. I like it anyway he gives it to me.

"Thank you." He kisses my brow.

"I should be the one thanking you," I point out. He made sure I was coming before he was even inside of me.

Even on the edge, he still maintains control.

He smiles softly. "I needed this. I needed you."

The way he says it, like it's a weakness, makes my heart ache. "I'm here," I tell him, kissing him. "I'm not going anywhere."

"Good," he replies, kissing me back. "Because Ayda's staying at Autumn's which means we have all night. And I have plans for you."

thirty

SKYLER

"I owe you big time," Autumn tells me as she ruffles Ayda's hair, grimacing because she hates asking for help as much as I do.

"No you don't. I'm happy to help." I give her a beaming smile. "Seriously, go home and take care of Parker. I've got this."

"You're a lifesaver. Thank you. I'll be over before the evening rush starts to take her home. He's just being such a damn baby, and I don't want Ayda catching anything from him."

Parker has the flu that everybody's been suffering from over the past month. And Hudson is in New York for a meeting.

Autumn spoke to Hudson and asked if it was okay if I took care of Ayda for the day. He agreed it was fine. It was something he and Dr. Methi have been talking about – me spending more time one-on-one with her.

I'm pleased that he trusts me enough to let me step up.

Autumn runs back to her car and I turn to Ayda. Barney isn't with us – Autumn left him with Parker because she didn't want me to have to take care of the dog, too. So for now – until customers start to flow in and the rest of the staff arrives – it's just me and Hudson's daughter.

And she's beaming up at me like I'm some kind of Fairy Godmother.

"Want to color?" I ask her.

She shakes her head.

Hmm. I try to think of something else.

"Want to listen to some music and do silly dances like we did at your party?" I suggest as an alternative.

She nods vigorously, so we head inside the bar and we walk over to the jukebox, and I show her how it works. Then she presses the buttons herself, bringing up "Mamma Mia" by Abba. As soon as Agnetha and Anni-Frid's vocals begin, I grab her hands, and we start to dance around the tables. I sing out loud and she grins like she's enjoying herself.

After we've exhausted all the tracks on the jukebox, a few customers start to trickle in. I put Ayda on a stool at the bar with her coloring book, though she keeps jumping down to change the music then walking back again.

Maud comes in right after one. After she walks behind the bar and puts her apron on, I take my break because it's past lunchtime and if there's one thing I know about kids it's that they get hungry, so I take Ayda back to the apartment and let her choose what she wants in her sandwich by pointing at some meat and cheese.

"Milk or orange juice?" I ask her, holding up both cartons for her to choose from.

She points at the sink. "Water?" I ask and she nods. I fill

up two glasses and put them on a tray along with the sandwiches I've made for us, then we carry them out to the front deck because it's way too nice a day to be eating lunch inside.

I'll never get tired of this view. It's constantly changing. Today the ocean is a blue-green as it laps against the golden sand. There are some tourists walking around the beach. There will be even more later. The ferry has switched over to its high summer timetable, sailing twice an hour each way.

Though the bar is already busy, there are some tables left. Ayda chooses one by the door and sits down on the chair and daintily takes a bite of her sandwich. Seagulls squawk in the sky above us, a woman walks out of the bar with a soda and takes a seat a few tables down from us, and I go to take a bite of my own sandwich, only to be interrupted by the shrill sound of my phone.

Thinking it's probably Hudson, I grab it and look at the screen.

But it's Dr. Methi's name written in black beneath the glass.

He probably wants to know how it's going with me and Ayda since we talked in his office, so I accept the call, smiling at Ayda who's already halfway through her sandwich.

"Hello?"

"Skyler? It's Dr. Methi." He sounds almost solemn. "Are you able to talk for a moment?"

"Yes, of course." I glance at Ayda. She's looking around at the people sitting on the deck.

"I got your results back. They sent them to me because I wrote the original script. They should have gone to your primary physician."

"No problem." I smile because I finally managed to make my appointment earlier in the week, and I'm feeling like a real grown up. "I can send you the details for my primary if you want to send them on. Unless it's bad news, in which case..." I trail off, waiting for him to laugh.

But he doesn't.

"There's no bad news, right?" I ask softly. My heart starts to speed. No, no, no. Not when I'm finally happy, finally settled.

"It depends how you look at it," he replies.

This isn't good. This isn't good at all. Ayda is drinking her water and looking at the birds flying overhead. I ignore my sandwich, because suddenly I feel sick.

"Tell me," I whisper. "Tell me what's wrong."

"Strictly speaking, I should send this to your primary physician."

"You're also a doctor. You're allowed to tell me, right?" I lower my voice, half an eye on Ayda who is completely distracted by the birds. "If I'm sick, I need to know."

He clears his throat. "It's not like that," he tells me. "You're not sick, Skyler. The blood test shows positive HCG levels. You're pregnant."

* * *

I'm on birth control. That's all I can think when Dr. Methi ends the call, after checking that I'm okay and telling me to call him once I've absorbed the news if I need to talk things through.

But it's not the kind of news you can absorb. Not when you're sitting next to your boyfriend's daughter, who's tugging at your hand because she wants to eat your sandwich, too.

I push it toward her, trying to smile. And then, while she's distracted, I start searching for answers on my phone.

Chances of getting pregnant while taking a birth control pill – one percent. Then I see the caveat, *that's if it's taken perfectly*. Imperfectly the chances run up to five percent. It's still low. So low this shouldn't be possible.

I google again. Chances of getting pregnant while on the progestin only birth control pill – eight percent.

That's not far off from ten percent. Why didn't I know this?

I click open the webpage, frowning as I read on. The reason for the increased chances on a mini pill – the progestin only pill – is because it has to be taken at the same time every day to be effective. I vaguely remember the doctor telling me that when I was prescribed it.

And yet it's so obvious that I must have missed a pill. I need to count them. And then count them again. It's like if I can prove that I've taken them this whole thing has to be wrong.

I can't be pregnant. There's no way I missed a pill.

I'm the new, in control, reliable Skyler now. She wouldn't do something like this.

And yet I can still hear Dr. Methi's voice echoing in my ears.

You're pregnant.

"We should go inside," I say to Ayda, looking over at her. She's distracted again. I thought it was the birds but I realize she keeps looking over my shoulder, not toward the sky.

She stands and I do too. Then she leans toward me and opens her rosebud lips.

"A-mother." Her voice is raspy, but I hear her all the

same. She spoke. Oh my God, she spoke. She said mother. Did she over hear my conversation?

My eyes widen. "What did you say?" I ask her, somewhere between jubilation at hearing her voice and fear of the word she said.

She shakes her head, refusing to say it again and I try to work it out in my mind.

"Ayda, you just spoke," I whisper.

She says nothing, just looks at me, then over my shoulder again. The fucking birds. "Say it again," I whisper.

But she doesn't.

Okay, first things first. I'm going to count those damn pills and then I'm going to call Dr. Methi back. Or call Hudson. They both need to know that Ayda said a word. I start to pick up our plates, layering them on the tray. "Follow me," I tell her. "We'll get some ice cream once these are all cleaned up."

The bar door is open – Maud must be feeling the early summer heat – so I walk through, carrying the tray to the bar. I put it on the counter, taking a deep breath because I swear my head is swimming right now. For a minute I rest my elbows on the wooden bar top and try to inhale to the count of eight, just to get my heart to slow down.

"It's beautiful, huh?" Maud says, when she finishes serving the only customer at the bar.

"Glorious." I don't return her smile. Because I wish it was raining. I wish I hadn't taken that stupid blood test.

I wish I had taken my pill.

"Want me to clean that up for you?" Maud asks, pointing at the tray. "So you can get back out to Ayda?"

"Ayda's here," I say, looking down to my left, where I swear she was standing a moment ago. But there's nobody there. I look over at the tables, at the jukebox, at the dance floor where we got our groove on earlier. "Where is she?" I say quickly. "She was just here."

"She wasn't with you when you walked in," Maud says.

"Yes she was." My voice lifts an octave as I look right and left for her. "She was following me. I saw her." Leaving the tray on the bar, I run back out of the front door onto the deck, looking around the groups of people drinking and laughing, for a little girl with dark hair. But she's not there.

"Have you seen the little girl I was with?" I ask a group of men at a table nearby. They shake their heads.

"Did you?" I ask a couple who are looking through photographs on her phone.

"I'm sorry, what?" The woman looks up.

"I was here with a little girl," I say quickly. "I can't find her. Have you seen her?"

"The little dark haired girl wearing pink?" she asks, and relief immediately washes over me.

"Yes." I nod quickly. "That's her."

She gives me an uneasy look. "She went that way," she says, pointing at the stairs. "She was holding a woman's hand."

And I run.

* * *

HUDSON

I'm halfway through death by PowerPoint when my phone vibrates and I see Skyler's name flash across my screen.

I have to reject the call, even though I'd much rather be

verbally battling with her than listening to this interminable dross.

For good measure, I turn the thing off. I'll call her when I get out of here. She's done me a big favor by taking care of Ayda today and I owe her at least a huge bouquet of flowers and half a dozen orgasms.

Just as we're getting to the part of the presentation I'm actually fucking interested in – the cash flow – there's a knock at the door.

"Come in," I bellow and Carleen, my assistant, pushes it open. She looks at me, ashen faced.

"What's up?" I ask, checking my watch. This meeting is set to finish at two, when my car is scheduled to pick me up. I need to be at the helipad by half past if I want to make it back to Liberty for dinner.

And I really fucking do.

"Can I have a quick word?" Carleen asks, looking nervous.

"Can it wait?" I ask. "We'll be done in what?" I glance at the deputy finance officer. "Half an hour."

"No, it can't." Carleen shakes her head. "It's your daughter."

My blood freezes at her fear filled tone. Before the final syllable is out of her mouth I'm standing up, waving at the finance team to wait. I stride across the room and follow Carleen out of the office.

"What's wrong with Ayda?" I ask. It has to be that fucking flu. It's working its way through everybody and she's bound to get it.

"I just got a call from your sister," Carleen whispers, shifting her feet. "Ayda has disappeared. Nobody knows where she is."

Panic pulls at my stomach. "What the hell does that

mean?" I ask her. "Somebody has to know where she is. She's probably gone for a walk or something? Give me that phone," I say, seeing it off it's cradle on Carleen's desk.

"Autumn?"

"Hudson." She starts to cry. "You need to come home. We can't find her."

It takes ten minutes for the driver to get to the office building to pick me up. Another twenty before I'm at the helipad waiting on the helicopter to take me back. I spend most of it on my phone, first to Autumn, then to the police, and then I call Skyler right as the helicopter is coming in to land.

"What the fuck happened?" I ask, fury rushing through me. "You were supposed to be taking care of her." I should never have let this happen. Never.

"I know. I'm sorry." Skyler lets out a sob. "She was here. I swear she was. Then she just disappeared."

"You left her out on the deck alone?" I say, not able to keep the fury from my voice. "How could you do that?"

"I know." She inhales raggedly. "It's all my fault."

"Don't you cry on me," I tell her. "Don't you do that. Have the police scoured the water?"

Ayda can doggie paddle. I made sure of that as soon as we moved here. But her tiny body is no match for the tides around Liberty. The thought that she could be in the water... I take a deep breath, trying to push it away.

She's so fucking tiny. She can't talk. The thought of her being alone and hurt... Christ.

"The police are doing everything. They're scouring the water, they're questioning everybody who was at the bar. Two separate witnesses saw her go off with a woman," Skyler says quickly.

"A woman? Who?" I don't know if that's worse or better than her being near the water.

"They don't know. They're taking descriptions. And checking footage on the ferry to see if she's been taken to the mainland."

The helicopter comes into land, the overwhelming beating noise of the rotors drowning her out. I end the call, waiting for the pilot to let me know it's safe before I practically run over to the helicopter and climb in.

It's impossible to make calls from the helicopter. The pilot won't let me remove the ear protection he insists I wear, and even if I could I'd never be able to hear voices over the sounds of our flight. So I spend the time messaging Autumn, Parker – who's dragged himself from death's door and joined in the search – and Skyler, desperate for some kind of update, devastated when I don't get one.

A police cruiser is waiting for me when the helicopter lands at the helipad on the mainland just over from Liberty. They take me to one of their speedboats, driving us over to the island, as they debrief me, telling me everything they've found out.

"We believe a woman in her fifties took her," the detective tells me, pulling up a grainy photograph on his phone. It's from the security cameras that overlook the approach to the ferry. You can almost make out a woman driving and a tiny head in the back passenger seat.

"That's Ayda?" I ask, staring at what looks like a dark ponytail. I swallow down the bile that's rising in my throat.

"We believe so, from the reports people have made. They didn't get out of the car once they were on the ferry."

"Didn't somebody notice that my daughter was with a stranger?" I ask.

"No, sir. I'm sorry."

And of course Jesse isn't working today. He's heading to the bar this evening. My jaw tightens. "Do you know who this woman is?"

"We're trying to get a better photograph of the car so we can run the plates. We're currently working on tracking their movements once she drove off the ferry. We do have a description of her though." The detective pulls up his notes on his phone. "Around five-four, a hundred and twenty pounds. Gray hair, well dressed in a pink trouser suit. Oh, and two different people said she has a British accent."

As soon as he says the last words, my eyes pretty much pop out of my damn head. "Ayda's grandmother," I say. I can't fucking believe this.

"I'm sorry?"

"Turn the boat around," I shout, trying to stand up. "I think Ayda's grandparents took her. I have to find her."

The detective puts his hands on my shoulder. "Sir, we need to take you to the island. Try to calm down and tell me who you think it is."

"Ayda's mother was British. She died, but her parents have been contesting custody for the past two years. They refused to let me bring her home from England until a court forced them to." My blood pressure is so high I think I'm going to explode. "Now can we turn this fucking boat around?"

"You need to calm down."

My eyes widen. "My daughter is missing," I thunder at him. "If they've got her, I'll fucking kill them."

"And I can't let you do that. Which is exactly why we're going to the island," the detective tells me. "Do you have an address for these people?"

I reel off the address of the house they bought on the mainland and the detective radios it through right as we arrive at the dock. The ferry is there – they've stopped crossings while they search for Ayda – so there's a huge crowd milling around the dock and the bar. I climb off the boat, closely followed by the detectives and search for my family.

I see Autumn first. She's running toward me. "Hudson," she cries, throwing herself at me. "This is all my fault."

"It's not your fault," I tell her as she sobs against my shoulder. "You weren't even there. I think it might be Catherine Clarke."

"Ayda's grandmother? Really?" She frowns.

I nod. "They're sending an officer to their house now."

"I thought she and Dennis were in England."

"So did I," I say grimly. "I guess they decided they couldn't wait and took the law into their own hands."

The detective is talking into his phone quickly. He ends the call and looks at me. "There's no sign of them at the house," he says.

Fuck. I put my head in my hands. I was so damn sure they'd be there.

"We're putting out an Amber Alert," the detective tells me. "And we're working with Homeland Security to find out if your ex's parents are in the country."

"Skyler and Parker are on the beach," Autumn tells me, sliding her hand into mine. "They didn't know what else to do. They just want to find her."

"It would have helped if Skyler hadn't lost her in the first place," I say. I'm trying to keep my fury from rising up, but it's a struggle. I'm a ticking time bomb waiting to go off.

"Here they are," Autumn says, and I follow her gaze. Parker is there, looking like he's about to keel over. He's wearing a pair of joggers and a t-shirt, but the man looks like death. Barney is on a leash, looking as dejected as I feel.

I can't help but think that if he'd been with Ayda none of this would have happened.

And next to him is Skyler. The woman I trusted with my daughter. The woman who lost the one thing I love more than life itself. She looks as pale as Parker. Her eyes are red rimmed, her hair is a mess, and as she walks toward me I have to curl my hands into fists to stop myself from reaching for her.

thirty-one

SKYLER

My mind has been in a wild panic ever since I realized Ayda was gone. I keep going back to that moment – the one where I picked up our plates and glasses and put them on the tray. Ayda was with me, I'm sure she was.

And then she wasn't.

They say that your life can change within a heartbeat. All I can think about is that Ayda is alone, scared. And it's all my fault.

"Hudson's here," Parker says to me as we reach the jetty. He's still holding onto Barney's leash. We've spent the last hour combing the coast, looking for signs. The police have helicopters out, there are boats in the water.

But there's no sign of a little girl who can't talk but can love fiercely.

I look over at the crowd that's gathered on the dock. Everybody wants to help. The police have had their work cut out trying to take statements and listen to suggestions of where Ayda might be.

But she's nowhere. And the pain of it is like a knife in my chest.

I spot Hudson almost right away. He's taller than the cops he's standing with, still wearing his suit, his tie neatly knotted. He's talking rapidly to one of the plain clothes detectives that took my details earlier.

Then his gaze slides to me.

His expression doesn't change when our eyes meet. His skin looks gray in this light, his jaw is set grimly.

"Oh God," I whisper to myself. Because he looks broken.

"Come on," Parker says, though I'm not sure if it's to me or himself. He insisted on joining me to search the coast even though he can barely walk two feet without dissolving into a coughing fit. The man should be in bed. And he won't even let me take the dog.

"Any news?" Parker asks Autumn, who's standing next to Hudson.

She reaches out for him, cupping his face. "Honey, you need to rest. And yes, there's news." She takes Barney's leash from him, and he doesn't protest.

For a second my world stops. Please let it be good news. *Please*.

"What is it?" I whisper.

Autumn looks at me, her face full of kindness. "They think she was taken by her grandmother. They have photographs that they think are Ayda and Catherine on the ferry. She's taken her to the mainland."

Relief rushes through me. She's alive. She's with somebody she loves.

Hudson is still staring at me with that unreadable expression on his face.

"I'm sorry," I tell him. "I'm so, so sorry. She was there, then she was gone."

"They've taken her," he says, sounding as broken as he looks. "How could you not notice she was gone?"

"Hudson," Autumn says softly. "It's not her fault."

I open my mouth, trying to find the right words. But what words are there? "I'm sorry," I say again. "I was..." I can't tell him about Dr. Methi's call. I can't tell him how distracted I was. Not now. He has enough to deal with. "I was an idiot," I say. "I'll never do it again."

"Ma'am," one of the detectives looks at me. "Can we show you some photographs? See if you recognize any of them?"

I nod, so aware of Hudson's scrutiny as I look at the phone the policeman is holding out. A woman's face appears on it.

"She looks familiar," I say, my voice thin.

"You've seen her?" Hudson asks.

"Sir, please let us do our job," the detective tells him. "Where have you seen this woman?" he asks me.

And then I remember. An older, elegant woman was a few tables down from where we were eating. "She was at the bar today. She had a drink and was sitting out on the deck near us."

"Are you certain?" the detective asks.

"Yes." I nod. "I remember noticing her. She was very well dressed." I look at the detective. "That's good, isn't it?" I ask him. "If she's with somebody who loves her? That means she's safe."

"She's not safe," Hudson says. "She's with two people who made the last few years a misery. They didn't let me see her. I had to fight them. I might never get her back." He shakes his head.

Autumn shoots me another sympathetic look. But I have to look away. I can't take sympathy from her, I just can't.

Mylene and her staff arrive, carrying trays of coffees and cookies that they hand out to the policemen who take them gratefully. I can see Eileen standing on her porch, her arms folded as she watches.

"Is there anything we can do?" I ask the detective. "There has to be something."

He shakes his head and looks at his phone again, then calls over another detective. The two of them talk quietly for a moment, before they turn to Hudson.

"Can we talk over here?" the older detective says to him.

Hudson nods and follows them over. Parker sits down heavily on the wall, drinking one of the coffees Mylene brought over. And Autumn walks over to me, still holding Barney's leash.

"He doesn't mean it," she says. "He's just stressed, that's all. We all know this isn't your fault. It's not like Ayda hasn't run off before."

I'd forgotten about that. The way she'd disappeared from Autumn's care and arrived in the bar the day after I arrived on the island.

"It *is* my fault though. I should have kept an eye on her. I promised."

"You did. You thought she was following you. It's not like she's a chatterbox and you would have noticed the silence. I've been there. One moment she's there, the next she's gone."

"What if her grandmother refuses to give her back?" I whisper.

"They'll make her," Autumn says stubbornly. But we both know it's harder than that. It took so long for Hudson to get her back last time. And it damaged his daughter so much.

I swallow down the nausea that's threatening to rise up.

Hudson walks over, still not meeting my gaze. "They have a lead. They've found her car," he says quietly.

Autumn snaps her head up. "Where?"

"Thirty miles away. Near an English tea shop of all places. They think she's inside with Ayda. They're sending officers there right now. I'm heading over to the mainland."

"I'll come with you," Autumn says.

He nods.

"And Skyler," she adds.

But he shakes his head. "No, they said just family," he says firmly.

I think it's those words that finally break me.

Just family.

"I'll take Parker and Barney home," I say to Autumn. "He's too sick to drive."

She nods, touching my arm softly.

"Take him to the Captain's House," Hudson says, distracted by the detectives who are getting ready to leave. "Asher's on his way. I told him to meet us there."

"Asher's coming?" Autumn asks.

Hudson nods. "He's been staying locally, wanted to help."

The cops call Hudson's name, and he and Autumn head over to the police boat, and I take a deep breath.

This is good news. It has to be. Her grandmother loves Ayda, she would never hurt her.

Or at least that's what I pray as I walk over to where Parker is slumped over against the wall.

HUDSON

"It's going to be okay," Autumn says as we speed along the water toward the mainland. We're both wearing blue lifejackets, and sitting exactly where we were instructed, because we want to get there as soon as possible.

"Of course it is," I say, my voice tight. Because I can't think of any other option. The very fact that the police – and Skyler and Parker – were searching the coast makes my stomach twist.

I thought this island was safe. I thought she'd be protected here. But the fact is, there's danger everywhere.

"Why were you so mean to Skyler?" Autumn asks me.

I let out an annoyed grunt. I don't want to talk about Skyler right now.

"Leave it," I say. "I'm not in the mood."

"We've gotten word that your daughter is in the café safe and well," the detective says, hunkering down in front of me. "We don't want to scare her by sending in SWAT. We'll wait for them to come out."

I open my mouth to tell them to unleash the dogs of hell as long as Ayda's okay, but then I close it. They're right. I know Catherine won't hurt her. Although, she'd hurt me in an instant.

But getting Ayda out of there without causing her any more trauma seems like a sensible thing to do.

"Thank you." I nod. I can't feel relieved until my daughter is in my arms. "Will it take us long to get there?"

"Twenty minutes. We have a squad car waiting to drive

us straight there. If the timing is right, we may arrive at the café before your daughter and her grandmother come out."

I narrow my eyes. "Good."

But those twenty minutes are the longest of my life. And each one of them feels like a dagger piercing my cold fucking heart.

* * *

SKYLER

Asher arrives at the Captain's House about twenty minutes after Parker, Barney, and I get there. He and Parker hug and then he holds his hand out to me. "I think we met at Ayda's party," he says. Barney is laying by the door. He looks up hopefully when it opens, then drops his head when he sees it isn't Ayda.

"We did meet." I shake his hand. "I'm Skyler."

"Asher. Or Ash. Whatever." He takes a deep breath and looks around. "Have you heard from Hudson?"

"Not yet."

Asher has the same unreadable face as his brother. Parker is currently shivering on the sofa. I gave him Tylenol when we got back to the house, and I've made him hot tea and have instructed him to drink it.

Parker's phone rings and he answers it. I can tell by the softness in his voice that it's Autumn. Their conversation is brief, but Asher and I keep silent until it ends.

"They've had a positive sighting," Parker croaks when he ends the call. "She's safe and well, and having a fucking English afternoon tea."

Asher coughs out a laugh. "Jesus. Hudson must be furious."

Parker's gaze shifts to me then away again. "You could say that."

I let out a long breath. "Would you like a coffee?" I ask Asher. "Or another drink?"

He shakes his head. "I'm good. Go sit down. You look about as sick as Parker does."

I don't want to sit down. If I sit down I'll have to think and that's the last thing I want to do right now. Thankfully, Parker's phone rings – again – and his croaky voice cuts through the air.

"Francie. Hey."

From the corner of my eye I see Asher frown at the name. At any other time in my life I'd be interested by that.

"Nah, she was just on the phone to me. That's why you probably got voicemail." Another pause. "They think they've found her." He coughs. "Yeah, I know." He glances at me again, like she's saying something. God, I need to get a grip. I feel like I'm on the edge about to tumble over.

"Uhuh," he murmurs. "No, no need to come. It's mayhem on the island and it's only gonna get worse when Hudson and Autumn get back with Ayda. You know what he's like. He's gonna wanna hermit it up again."

Asher grabs a book from Hudson's table and starts to thumb through it. I can just about see the title – *Weather Systems of The Atlantic Ocean*. I don't bother to point out to him that he's looking at it upside down.

We're all doing what we can to keep our sanity right now. If he wants to pretend he's not interested in his sister's friend, he can have at it.

I'm pretending I never got that phone call from Dr. Methi, after all.

While Parker is talking to Francie and Asher is pretending to read maps upside down, I head into the kitchen and clean up. I check the refrigerator for supplies, because if Hudson needs to 'hermit it up', whatever that means, he'll need food in the house.

There's milk and juice and fruit and cheese. All good healthy food that a great father would have for his kid. Then I see a pack of ground beef with a day until it spoils, so I grab it and some ingredients for a chili, because there are going to be a lot of people here, and they'll be hungry, no matter what happens.

"What's going on?" Asher asks a few minutes later. "Jesus, that smells good."

I'm frying off the onions. "I'm making chili."

He tips his head. "You cook in a crisis?"

"I don't know. I'm not sure I've been in a crisis like this before," I say, adding in some spices. "And chili is about the only thing I *can* cook."

"Parker says you think this was your fault," Asher says, grabbing a carton of juice from the refrigerator and pouring himself a glass. He takes a long sip, looking at me over the rim of the tumbler.

"It *was* my fault," I tell him. "I was the one in charge of looking after Ayda. I'm the one who lost her."

"Parker also thinks it's his fault for being sick," Asher says.

I frown. "Well it isn't. He can't help being sick."

"And I'm almost certain Autumn will say it's her fault because she was supposed to be looking after Ayda."

"It's nobody's fault but mine," I say. "I think we can all agree on that one."

"She'll be okay," he says softly. For a moment he looks so much like his brother it makes my heart tighten. I know how close he and Hudson are. I want to be his friend. I want to accept his understanding.

But I can't. "Thank you for trying to make me feel better," I tell him.

He nods. Then Parker calls out his name.

"They've got her," he shouts out, his voice so thin it sounds almost transparent. A second later Parker appears at the door, his fingers gripping onto the wood to steady himself. "They've got her," he repeats, quietly. Then he crumples to the ground, his eyes hazy, his body weak.

We both run over to help him, Asher lifting one arm, me catching the other, and somehow we manage to get him back to the sofa as he starts to mumble incoherently.

"Listen, has Ayda had the flu?" Asher asks when we finally get Parker's legs up so he's laying out.

"Not yet."

Asher lets out a breath. "Okay, I'm going to take him home to the lighthouse. Put him to bed there. As much as we all love him, he's going to be no use to anybody tonight."

I really like this man. I nod at him. "Okay."

Both our phones start to beep at once. I pull mine out to see a message from Autumn.

The police have Ayda. We're on our way to pick her up. She's absolutely fine, though they want her to be looked over by a doctor. Hudson's determined we'll be back on Liberty by nightfall. – Autumn.

I look back at Asher, who no doubt got the same message.

"Okay," he says. "It definitely feels like a good plan to take Parker home. You all right to stay here?"

"I'll be fine." I nod. I need to see Ayda. I need to say sorry to her. For letting her be taken.

He sniffs. "What's that burning smell?"

My eyes widen. "Oh shit, the onions."

And I rush back into the kitchen, to the charred onions. The little black dots clinging to the pot are more proof – if I needed any – of how undomesticated I am.

I can't cook, I can't take care of a child, I can't even take care of my own birth control.

Right now all I want to do is curl up in a ball and cry.

thirty-two

SKYLER

Asher and I are sitting in Hudson's living room when we hear the car pull up. Neither of us have said a word for the last ten minutes. He's exhausted from traveling and I'm exhausted from... I'm not sure what.

I managed to find some more onions and make the chili without burning any of the ingredients the second time around, but neither of us have wanted to eat anything.

A car door slams and we both stand. My heart starts to pound against my chest. I run to the front door right as Asher opens it and I see Hudson carrying Ayda, who's fast asleep in his arms. Autumn runs toward Asher and hugs him tight. He whispers something in her ear and she nods.

"Hey." Hudson nods at his brother, still holding Ayda close. At some point he must have taken off his jacket and tie. His shirt is crumpled and unbuttoned. "You didn't have to come," he says to Asher.

"Of course I did." Asher gives his brother a one-armed

hug to avoid crushing Ayda. "Come on in. Skyler made food."

Hudson looks at me. I try to smile but I can't. The guilt is killing me. He steps inside and I get a glimpse of Ayda's face. Her right cheek is resting against his chest, her little arms around his neck. She's wearing different clothes to the ones she had on this morning and for some reason that kicks me right in the gut.

She looks so tiny. And I lost her.

"I'm going to put her to bed," he says.

"Good idea." Autumn's voice is warm. "How's Parker?" she asks Asher.

"He's fine," Asher says. "He's sleeping which is for the best."

Hudson walks upstairs with Ayda, and Autumn strides into the kitchen. "God, that smells good." She groans when the aroma of chili hits her. "Can I have some?"

"Of course."

I hang around while she fills up a bowl, then scoops a spoonful into her mouth. "So," she says, when she's swallowed it down. "Wanna hear what happened?"

I nod. Asher snorts.

"You always did love to keep us in suspense," he says.

She sticks her tongue out at him. "Well as you know, Catherine and Ayda were coming out of the café when the police swooped in. Although it was pretty peaceful, according to the cops. Catherine didn't put up a fight, didn't even look surprised to see them. Just hugged Ayda and told her to be a good girl and that her daddy would be there soon. Then she let herself be arrested." Autumn takes another spoon of chili, humming as she swallows it down. "We got there about ten minutes later. Catherine was in the cop car, Ayda was being checked over by the first responders. She's fine, by the way, but it's protocol or something." Autumn shrugs. "I've never seen Hudson run so fast. Or shake so much when he picked her up. He hid his head when he hugged her but I'd bet a billion dollars he was crying." Her eyes sparkle.

"You like the thought of that, huh?" Asher says, looking amused.

"I always like seeing my big brothers melt into mush." She pokes him. "So then he carried her over to me and told me to hold onto her. She was all smiles and huggy. I swear she just thought it was a day out. Then Hudson strode over to the car where they were holding Catherine and demanded to talk to her."

Autumn barely takes a breath before she continues. "So there was a bit of an argument, but then the cops finally opened the door and I've never seen Hudson look so menacing in his life. I don't know what he said to Catherine, but I swear her eyes were about to pop out of her face. It reminded me of when I was younger and he caught me trying to smoke a cigarette."

"You set your hair on fire, Fall," Asher reminds her. "The only thing that was smoking was the half-can of hair spray you used to use daily."

"Fall?" I frown.

"That was my nickname when I was a kid." Autumn shakes her head.

"She was constantly falling over. Bruised. Always injured. Autumn – Fall." Asher ruffles her hair and she groans.

"And this is why I used to wear hairspray. So you wouldn't do that." She shakes her hair. "Do you want me to finish this story or what?"

"Carry on." Asher gives her an indulgent smile.

"Okay then. So whatever Hudson said to Catherine. She shook her head and started tripping over herself to apologize. Apparently she swore she was always planning to bring Ayda back. That she just missed her and wanted to see her. She came over to the island to see if she could get a glimpse. And then..."

"And then she saw her chance," I finish.

"So the cops took Catherine away, the ambulance took Hudson and Ayda to get her checked over. The police wanted her clothes for evidence, so I got her some new ones and made a bit of a game of it. Oh, and Dr. Methi came to the hospital."

"You saw Dr. Methi?" I ask, my eyes widening.

"Yeah. He was cool as a cucumber. Talked Hudson down. Told him that Ayda was fine. Then we came home." She shrugs. "It's been a long day."

Footsteps come from the hallway and Hudson appears in the kitchen doorway. His eyes roam over the three of us standing at the kitchen counter. Asher has finally helped himself to some chili, and Autumn is on her second bowl.

I swallow hard at the black bags beneath Hudson's eyes. "She's asleep," he says. "I'm probably going to head up too."

"Want some food?" Autumn asks. "Skyler made chili. It's good."

He shakes his head. "You should go home when you finish. You all should." His eyes land on Asher. "Except you."

Asher grins. "That's good because I have nowhere else to stay."

Autumn finishes her second bowl in double time and loads it into the dishwasher before walking over to hug Hudson. "Call me if you need anything," she tells him.

He nods.

I stand and grab my bag. "I should go home too," I say.

Hudson's eyes roam over my face. "Wait a moment. I want to speak with you privately."

It gives me the gentlest of hopes. The memory of him burying himself in me after he got the legal notice from Ayda's grandparents sparks inside my mind. I want to offer him succor. I want to comfort him. He looks like he needs it.

After we see Autumn off, Hudson inclines his head at his home office. I follow him in and he closes the door. He turns to face me, his broad body close to mine. His mouth is pulled into a thin line.

"She's really okay?" I ask.

He nods. "According to the medical staff."

"And you?" I say softly. "How are you holding up?"

For a moment he says nothing. Then he takes a step back, like he's trying to distance himself from me.

"This is my fault," he says, taking me completely by surprise. Because if anybody isn't culpable for this whole mess it's him. He was nowhere near Liberty when it happened.

"No it isn't." I frown, reaching for him. But he steps back again, like he doesn't want me to touch him. "It's all my fault. I don't know what to say. I got distracted for a second and then..." I take a breath. "I am so, so sorry, Hudson. I will do whatever it takes to make this up to you and her."

"You told me who you were," he says, as though he can't hear me. "You told me and I didn't listen. You said you weren't reliable. That you didn't like commitment. You made it oh so fucking clear. But I thought I could change you." His gaze flickers to mine. "I never should have tried."

There's an ache in my chest where my heart used to be.

"What are you trying to say?" I ask. "I'm trying, I really am. I want to be better. I want you to trust me."

"But I can't." He shakes his head. "Don't you see, I can't? She's my daughter, Skyler. My first loyalty always has to be with her."

"I know that." My voice breaks. "And it should be."

"I can't trust you. I can't leave her with you. What kind of relationship would that be?" he asks.

"I messed up once. I won't do it again. It was a one-time situation. Something happened and I got distracted for a second."

"What happened?" he asks. "What was so important that you took your eyes off my kid?"

I open my mouth to reply, but I can't. I can't tell him about the blood test. Not now. I can barely come to terms with it myself, so I can't have him thinking I'm using it as an excuse.

"It doesn't matter," I finally say. "None of it matters. You're right, all of it. I'm not the person you need me to be." A ragged breath escapes my lips. "I should go."

He looks at me. It's clear he's in pain too. I want him to beg me to stay. I want him to tell me he understands.

But instead he nods. "It's for the best."

And that's how my heart shatters, to the soundtrack of the man I love telling me that walking away is for the best.

But I do it anyway. Wondering how the hell I'm going to survive this.

* * *

HUDSON

. . .

"What did you do?" Autumn asks, pushing her way past me into the house. It's the next morning. The weather is overcast, the dark gray skies matching my mood. I've spent the last hour on the phone with my lawyer, who's arranging for a protective order to be placed against Ayda's grandparents.

Ayda is currently laying on the sofa, watching some cartoon, laughing silently like yesterday didn't even happen. Dr. Methi said she'd be like this.

"Kids don't always understand adult relationships," he'd murmured when he walked into the hospital room. "She knows you love her and she knows her grandparents love her. Unless you start ranting in front of her about it, she'll just file it away as a nice day out."

I'm still skeptical, but somehow hanging onto that.

"What do you mean 'what did I do'?" I ask her. "Are you needing me to go through my to-do-list? Because it mostly involves talking to lawyers and organizing restraining orders, with a little dash of planning fantasy murders rolled in."

"I mean what have you done to Skyler?" Autumn says, her eyes full of fire.

"I have no idea what you're talking about," I murmur, closing the front door behind her, since she clearly isn't going to do it herself. And I'm desperately trying not to think about Skyler, or how every five minutes I pull up her name on my phone and think about calling her. "How's Parker?"

She lets out a loud huff, reminding me of how she used to throw tantrums as a kid. Asher and I would place bets for how long she'd keep them going. I always chose the longest time and I always won.

"I'm not here to talk about Parker," she says, jabbing me

in the chest with her finger. "I'm here to talk about you and what an ass you're being."

"You're going to need to be more specific." I glance into the living room. Ayda is sleepy, I can tell that from the way she looks hypnotized by the television. I feel a momentary pang for using the screen as a babysitter, but right now it's the only one I trust.

Autumn follows me into the kitchen. I walk over to the coffee machine and slide a pod in. "Want one?"

"No, I don't." She throws her hands up in the air. "Skyler's leaving the island."

"What?" I turn around, frowning. My heart starts racing.

"There. Finally a response." She tips her head to the side. "Not a great one, but still..."

"Where's Skyler going?" I ask, frowning.

"Like you care," she says, sitting down at the breakfast bar. "You're such an idiot."

"I think you already said that."

"She's leaving," Autumn says again, like she's a voice recording on repeat. "How can you stand there when I've told you that?"

"What do you want me to do? A little dance?" I try to ignore the panic in my stomach and lift the cup of black coffee to my lips. My third of the day and it's still not touching the surface of my exhaustion.

"No, I want you to chase after her. I can't believe you're being so laid back about this."

My feigned indifference is working. "If she wants to leave, she's free to do so," I say, ignoring the twist in my gut.

"What did you say to her last night?" Autumn asks. "After I left."

"I think that's between me and her," I say, taking another mouthful of bitter liquid.

"Aargh!" She shakes her head. "Tell me, or I'm gonna..." She looks around for something to annoy me with. Then she jumps off the stool and stomps over to wrench open a cupboard door. "Mess around with your cans until they're not organized by date order."

"I'm quaking."

"I'll do it, don't think I won't," she says. Then she reaches in and moves the cans inside all around, like a kid playing that cup and ball game, trying to hide which cup has the ball inside. "There," she says.

"Feel better?" I ask her mildly.

"No. Now what did you say to her? Either you tell me or I'll ask her."

"I'd prefer you didn't."

"Hudson..." She steps toward me. "I will wring your neck if you don't tell me."

I sigh. I'm going to capitulate, not because she can hurt me, but because she's annoying as fuck.

"I ended things," I say. "We're not right for each other. She said it all along and it just took me until now to realize it."

Autumn's mouth drops open.

"She agreed and left. That's it."

"That's so not it," Autumn says, her voice low. "She was upset all day. You saw her. She was so scared about Ayda and she was only looking after her to help me out. I can't believe you're blaming her for this."

"Who else do you expect me to blame?" I ask, my voice sharper than intended. "She was in charge of my daughter and she let her be taken. That's not somebody I need in my life."

"Does that mean you don't need me in your life?" Autumn asks. She blinks, looking suddenly upset.

And I hate that so much more than when she's annoying.

"Of course I want you in my life. You're my sister." It's been my life's fucking work to make sure all of my family is safe. Autumn included.

"But I lost Ayda too," she says. "Even worse, I let her wander off. She wasn't snatched from under my nose. She walked away and I didn't even notice. And it was *Skyler* who took care of her. So if you're choosing who should be part of your world on the basis of whether you can trust them to look after Ayda, then I guess I shouldn't be here."

Her eyes water up and I reach for her, but she steps away. "No," she says. "You don't get to have double standards and expect me to be your friend. You don't get to take things out on Skyler when she has nothing to do with the Clarkes and the custody battle. She was just in the wrong place at the wrong time."

She grabs her keys from her pocket. "You messed up," she says, her voice a broken sob. "And you can't even see it. Even worse, by the time you work it out it'll be way too late. She's already on the ferry. She'll be far away from the island and to god knows where." She turns on her heel. "I don't like you right now, Hudson. You hurt my friend." Before she storms out, she takes one last glance at me over her shoulder. "You just lost the best thing that's ever happened to you and you don't even know it."

thirty-three

SKYLER

"Are you sure you want to leave?" Jesse asks as the ferry approaches the mainland. He's not working today but he insisted on traveling with me when I drove to his place to ask if he could look after The Salty Dog while I was gone.

For the whole ride we've been sitting on the hood of my car. He's holding my hand, watching my face warily, like he doesn't know what to say.

"I'm sure." I nod. As soon as I woke up this morning I knew I had to get out of here. I can't think properly, I can barely breathe.

If in doubt, run.

That's always been my motto. It's kind of ironic that I'm proving Hudson's point. I haven't changed, not like I thought I had.

Still the same old Skyler who can't stay in one place for long.

"I don't like it," he murmurs as we dock. "You could

come and stay with me. Are you sure he didn't say anything to you?"

"Nothing awful. He just made it very, very clear that we're not compatible. Maybe he's right."

Jesse's jaw tightens. So does his grip on my hand. "I could come with you," he says. "I feel like I've only just found you and now I'm losing you."

I turn to look at him. Today, with his hair falling over his face, he looks a little like Dad. "You're not losing me. I just need a few days away from the island to think."

"Promise me you won't make any rash decisions," he says. "That you won't leave the area without seeing me first."

I press my lips together, because even though I'm trying so hard not to hurt anybody, it feels like every step I take causes pain to those I love. "I promise," I say, meaning it. I've booked an Airbnb on the mainland. Ironically, it's on the coast with promised 'Liberty Views.'

But I know I won't bump into Hudson there. Or even Autumn, who is so lovely but also his sister and I can't bear for her to be caught in the middle of this.

"And then?" Jesse asks. People are getting back into their cars. I can see the lines of vehicles on the road ahead, waiting to drive on just as soon as the ferry's empty. They're probably excited about a trip to the island. Playing on the beach, walking around the town. A drink at The Salty Dog.

Maybe some of them will stay at the hotel. Maybe they'll see Hudson Fitzgerald's stormy face when they're walking through reception. And they'll never know what it's like to make the tightness in his jaw dissolve into a smile. They'll never know what it's like to feel him chuckle when your head is resting on his bare chest.

They'll never know what it's like to love him.

I touch my stomach, thinking of the tiny cells that are growing there. One of the reasons why I'm leaving is so that I can think about this some more.

It's also one of the reasons why I know I can't go far. I'll need to tell him face to face about the pregnancy. And I'll need to do it soon.

And then?

Jesse's question echoes in my mind.

"I have no idea what happens after that," I say, in answer to him and myself. And for the first time in my whole life, not knowing my future makes me want to throw up.

* * *

"I have chocolate, I have chips, I have whiskey, and I also have a notebook so we can plot the demise of every asshole who's hurt you, starting with Hudson Fitzgerald."

Lee strides into the Airbnb that I rented, pulling a little suitcase behind her, looking like she hasn't just traveled across the entire US to see me.

"What are you doing here?" I ask her, taking in her warm face, her dark hair tied back in a low pony tail. She looks tired and so much like Mom it makes me want to be a child again.

To climb into her lap and sob.

"Jesse called."

"I only left him four hours ago," I say. "And I'm pretty sure you can't get here from California that quickly."

She lets go of her suitcase and cups my face with her hands, her gaze taking me in like she's trying to assess my sanity. "I booked a ticket yesterday. After you told me Ayda was missing. You sounded so alone. And then I arrived at the airport and saw I had a missed call from Jesse."

"What about Cora?" I ask.

"James has her. They're having some father and daughter time." She presses her lips together. "And we're having sister time. Possibly a sibling one if Jesse can make it over."

"You asked him to join us?" I feel stupidly touched by that. "I thought you didn't like him."

"I never said that. I just said I didn't like the fact that you'd found your home and it wasn't in California."

I give her a weak smile. "It turns out I was wrong."

"Oh honey." She pulls me into another hug. "Maybe you weren't wrong. Maybe this situation is." She takes a deep breath. "Has he called?"

I shake my head.

"That rat bastard."

"He's just trying to protect his daughter." I walk with Lee to the kitchen where she unloads the food she's brought with her. My stomach gurgles at the sight of the chips. When was the last time I ate? I can't remember.

But instead of opening them she grabs the whiskey and two glasses, pouring in a generous amount. "Giant's fingers," she says. "Two of them." She passes me one of the glasses.

I stare at it for a moment, trying to figure out how to tell her. "I can't drink this," I say, handing it back.

"Of course you can. It tastes like crap but it does the job. And I don't have to breastfeed for four days, which means I have approximately ninety hours in which to indulge in every vice I can find." She takes a long sip and then promptly starts coughing.

"Go on," she says. "The first mouthful is the worst."

I let out a long breath, looking at my big sister. The one who usually has everything together. She has a job, a husband, a house, a baby. She even did it in the right order.

"I can't drink whiskey," I say to her. "Or anything alcoholic, Lee. I'm pregnant."

* * *

It's almost ten o'clock. Lee managed one more shot of whiskey before she declared it the drink of the devil and decided to move onto sweet tea. We're sitting on the porch of the Airbnb I rented for the week, in rocking chairs that make the floorboards beneath us creek every time we move.

We're only about twenty feet away from the ocean, though there's no beach here, just cliff and water. The ocean is dark and inky, and Liberty is a little sparkling jewel among the blackness. I'm not good enough at geography to work out exactly where the Captain's House is on the island, but I know it's there and I know *he's* there.

I feel empty inside. I miss him. I think I might be mourning him.

Mourning the future I thought we'd have together.

"You know you need to tell him," Lee says out of nowhere. I thought she might be asleep. She left her house in the middle of the night to get here.

"I know." And I'm not looking forward to it. "I just need to come to terms with it first."

"How do you think he'll react?"

"I don't know," I say honestly. "I guess I see it going one of two ways. Neither of them seem palatable."

She shifts in her seat, and a squeaking sound comes from the deck boards. "Are you scared he might be mad?"

"That's option one. And he has every right to be."

"You have sex, you play the roulette table," Lee says. "He wasn't wearing a condom, was he?"

"No."

"If he was that worried, he would have been. It takes two, Sky."

"I know." I swallow hard. "And the weird thing is, that's not the worst reaction."

She tips her head, the moon above us casting a long shadow on her face. "What would be worse?" she asks, crinkling her nose.

"Him wanting us to get back together for the baby."

"You wouldn't want that?" Lee asks, like she's trying to understand me.

"No." I shake my head. "I wouldn't want that at all. I don't want his pity. I don't want this baby to have to carry that kind of burden. I feel like I've messed their life up before it's even started."

"You're keeping it then?" Lee asks, her voice soft.

I blink. "I hadn't realized it until this moment, but yes. I am."

She grabs my hand, her face lighting up. "Oh, Sky, you're gonna be the best mother."

"Are you kidding me?" I ask her. "The poor kid has the dice loaded against them from the start. I can barely take care of myself let alone a baby. And let's not even get into what happened the last time I was in charge of a child."

Lee shoots me a stern look. "That wasn't your fault. I thought we agreed on this. And you're not incapable or whatever term you're telling yourself you are. You own a business. You're a businesswoman. You have friends who love you, and don't tell me you don't because your phone has been ringing all evening with people checking in.

"That was Jesse and Autumn," I say.

"And Eileen. And Francie, whoever she is."

"Autumn's friend."

"There you go," Lee says, throwing her hands up like her point is made. "Even your friends friends love you. You've got this. You're ready. You're the strongest person I know."

"I'm not strong," I say.

"Yes you are. You know the strongest tree in the field? It's not the big one that doesn't move. One hurricane and that baby would be toppling over in a minute. It's the flexible one, the one that bends with the breeze, the one that goes with whatever flow there is. That's you. Your kid is so, so lucky to have you."

Tears fill my eyes, because it's so good to see her. I've missed her. Maybe I've missed her all my life.

"Oh God, I'm going to have a baby," I whisper, and she laughs.

"Yes you are. And you're going to be amazing at it."

* * *

HUDSON

Two days pass before I finally leave Ayda with Autumn for the morning. I have no choice, I have to go to the mainland, but it still kills me to climb into my car knowing she's with Autumn in the Captain's House.

Autumn is still not speaking to me, even though she agreed to take care of Ayda, through Parker. I tried calling her for the past few days but I've been sent straight to voicemail each time.

I'll beg for her forgiveness soon. Make peace with her.

But today I need to meet with the security company who's agreed to monitor the ferry.

I arrive at the jetty with less than a few minutes to spare. Cars are already being loaded on, and there's a procession, mostly of locals who head to the mainland each day for work. There's less of them than there used to be. Wherever possible I try to employ local people at the hotel and as casual laborers for the construction company working on the new retreat. But there's enough to make a steady stream onto the boat.

As soon as he sees my car, Jesse scowls. So he's annoyed with me too.

Join the line, pal.

Once parked on the ferry, I get out of the car, listening to a couple of old timers talking about the weather.

"Rain is coming," the man nearest me says. "I can feel it in my knee."

"Jesse," I call out.

He looks at me. "I'm busy." He turns to walk away and I follow him. I know he senses me behind him, because he finally turns and huffs. "What the hell do you want?" he asks.

"Have you heard from Skyler?"

His eyes narrow. "That's none of your business."

"I just want to know if she's okay." I put my hand on his shoulder and he shrugs it off.

"Do you?" he asks. "Do you really?"

"Of course I do. Just because we broke up doesn't mean I don't care." Truth is, I've been looking at her name on my phone for the past two days. Wanting to call her. Wanting to hear her voice. Wanting to explain to her that even though I know this is for the best it's killing me.

That I've decided that I won't have any more relationships. I'm going to be a fucking monk for the rest of my life. It's easier and it hurts a lot less.

"You didn't break up with her. You tore her fucking heart out." Jesse's eyes narrow. "I told you what I'd do if you hurt her. I told you and you still did it." He turns to look at me straight on. A man on the edge.

It takes one to know one.

"You want to hit me?" I ask him.

"So fucking bad I can taste it. I want to wipe that smug look off your face. I want to make you hurt the way you hurt her."

"Then hit me," I say, my voice thick. "Just do it."

To my immense surprise he takes me at my word. I barely have a moment to prepare myself before his hard fist connects with my jaw, sending me stumbling back. My teeth bite into my tongue at the impact, and I can taste the blood.

"Fuck," Jesse breathes. "I'm sorry."

"Now will you tell me if she's okay?" I say, the words stumbling over my bitten tongue.

He takes a deep breath. "She's okay."

"Where is she?"

A half smile pulls at his lips. "Oh no, you'd have to let me kick you in the balls for that answer."

Luckily for me, I have some sense of self preservation. "I think I'll pass on that." I touch my jaw gingerly. Fuck, it hurts.

"Want me to get you some ice?" Jesse asks. He's cradling his hand. It gives me a grim sense of satisfaction to know that he gets to suffer a little too.

"It's fine."

"You're not going to sue me, are you?" His eyes widen with alarm. "Shit, if my boss finds out…"

"I'm not going to sue you," I reassure him. "And nobody's going to find out." And because I'm not above blackmail I ask, "Has she left the country?"

"No."

I let out a long breath. "Good."

"Is it?"

"Yeah, it is." I don't know why, but it is.

"We're heading into port," Jesse says, wincing as he flexes his fingers. "Maybe I should stop fighting and actually do my job."

thirty-four

SKYLER

It's Lee's last evening here. This is the longest she's been away from Cora since she was born. We've spent the last three days taking long walks, talking about our pasts, our futures, our hopes, our dreams.

And about babies. I never realized how lucky I was to have an older sister that's already been through it all. She makes me think that I might just bring us both out of this alive.

She's made it clear that she wants me to go back with her. But I can't do that. This is Hudson's child too. Even if he doesn't want me I know he'll want to know his baby. I'm not the type of person who would make him go through court for that. He has as much right as I do to see this little one grow up.

A car is coming to pick her up at an abominable hour in the morning, but she insists on us having a goodbye party, of sorts, and tells me to invite Jesse over.

Secretly I think it's because she wants to make him promise to take care of me while she's on the other coast. But I do it anyway, and he comes.

"Was Autumn okay with managing the bar?" I ask him.

"Yep. She's on a one-woman mission to piss Hudson off." He winces. "Sorry."

"It's okay," I tell him. "I'm not going to die from hearing his name."

"Which is a good thing," Lee adds, carrying a tray of snacks out from the house onto the deck.

"What's a good thing?" Jesse asks, taking a carrot stick before he even looks at the plate. He only realizes it's a vegetable when it's on its way to his mouth. He grimaces, but eats it anyway.

He's such a boy.

"Talking about Hudson," Lee says. "Because this one here needs to do it more."

"I'm going to my therapist tomorrow, I can do it then," I remind her. Dr. Methi called this morning and let me know he has space in his schedule and wants to see me. I pointed out my insurance won't pay for him, but he says he's doing it as part of Ayda's rehabilitation.

And of course, as soon as I heard her name I agreed. I think he wants to get all the versions of the story so he can help her, which makes sense.

"To talk about somebody else. When do we start talking about you?" Lee asks.

"We've done nothing else for the past few days." I pop a celery stick in my mouth.

"Have you decided if you're coming back to the island yet?" Jesse asks. "No pressure, I just…"

"Yes." I put him out of his misery. If one thing these few days watching the island from afar has given me, it's perspective. Yes, it's small and practically owned by Hudson Fitzgerald, but I have my place there too. I have family and a business and I want to be there to run it.

And at some point we'll have to work out how to co-parent.

I inadvertently touch my stomach while I'm thinking, and Lee lifts a brow. "You should tell him," she says pointedly.

"Hudson or Jesse?"

"Both."

"Tell us what?" Jesse asks, looking from Lee to me. "You're not selling the bar, are you?"

I shake my head. "No, the bar is staying." I take a deep breath because two words have never felt so heavy. "I'm pregnant."

He blinks like I've just told him the earth is flat.

"Fuck..." He shakes his head. "I should have hit him harder."

"What?" I ask at exactly the same time Lee shouts out in celebration.

"You hit Hudson?" She puts her hands up for a high five. That's when I see the bruise on Jesse's knuckles.

"Oh my God." My eyes widen. "Please tell me you didn't."

"He was pissing me off." Jesse shrugs.

"When did you see him?" I ask, desperate to know. "Did he say anything about me?"

Lee lets out a sigh.

"He was on the ferry. He wanted to know if you're okay. I told him you were fine, no thanks to him. Shit, are you really pregnant?" He shakes his head.

"Yes, but it's early."

"Is that why he broke up with you?" Jesse's jaw tightens. "I'm really going to fucking kill him."

"He doesn't know," I say quickly. "And I don't want you telling him. You have to promise."

Jesse looks at me. "You're going to tell him, though? He has a right to know, doesn't he?" He looks as confused as I feel. And I love that he's on my side. But I'm not sure what that side is. Not yet.

"How was he looking?" I ask.

"Like he had a painful jaw."

Lee laughs uproariously. She looks like she's enjoying this way too much.

"Did he say anything else?"

"He said 'hit me'." Jesse shrugs.

"He actually asked you to hit him?" Lee frowns. "What kind of idiot does that?" She lets out another laugh, staring into the distance like she's trying to imagine it.

"I said I was going to make him pay for hurting you, and then he told me to hit him. After I did it…" Jesse looks at his knuckles. "He asked if you'd left the country."

"Oh." Is that what he wants? For me to be as far away as possible? That thought hurts more than anything else.

"I told him you hadn't. I hope that's okay."

"It's fine." I pat Jesse's hand and he winces. "No more hitting, okay? In this family we're lovers, not fighters."

"Wasn't planning on doing it again. Anyway, Autumn has a much better plan about making him suffer."

"What?" I almost laugh. "Autumn is conspiring against her own brother?"

"Oh she's mad as hell. And when she gets mad…" Jesse grins. "It's delicious. As long as you're not the one she's directing her anger at."

"I like her already," Lee says. "What's her plan?"

Jesse pulls out his phone and brings up a photo on the screen. "She's getting a thousand of these printed and putting them up everywhere," he says, turning the screen to us.

I read the words on the flyer that's got The Salty Dog branding.

> 70s Karaoke Night – Saturday July 13th
> Be Kitsch, Be Bold, Be There!
> (Free shots to every singer)

I start to laugh. "Oh my God, Hudson will hate this." After all his attempts to make the Dog into somewhere more sophisticated, Autumn is taking it right back to its roots.

"He will." Jesse grins. "It's okay isn't it? That we're planning this? She's already organized the equipment. She already put in the drinks order today and she's gotten some extra staff to help. It'll be like the opening night all over again but our style."

His eyes meet mine and I can see that he wants my approval. "The place is half yours," I remind him. "You're allowed to do what you want."

"But what I want is you there. And I want you to want it too."

"I love it," I say. "And I'll be there." And it gives me a reason to go back. Not that I needed one.

Lee's right. I belong there. My heart is there, even if it's cracked right now. Okay, it's broken and torn. But I need to get back.

"You're coming home?" Jesse says, beaming. And I nod.

"Thank god," he says, hugging me tight. Over his shoulder I can see Lee smiling at us. I give her a tentative smile back and she nods.

It makes me realize. Family isn't what somebody else tells you it has to be. It's what you make it. It's messy and it's joyful and it's sad. But it's what I've wanted all my life and I have it. Both in California and on Liberty.

And I'm not going to let it go.

* * *

HUDSON

"That looks painful," Dr. Methi says, a smile playing at his lips as he takes in the bruise on my jaw. It's burgundy with the threat of ochre, and it's tender as hell.

"It's fine," I lie.

"How did you get it?"

I let out a sigh. "I walked into a door."

"Did the door have a fist?" he asks, still smiling. He looks like he's enjoying this way too much for the amount I pay him.

"It doesn't matter." I shake my head. "Now can we talk about Ayda please?"

She's just had her session with him and she's in the outer room playing under the watchful gaze of the receptionist. She seems fine. Better than me. But she's also been edgy every time we pass The Salty Dog.

She tried to drag me in the other day and almost started crying when I wouldn't let her.

I'm not welcome there, that's for sure. Jesse's made that clear, and he's in charge.

"Ayda is doing very well," Dr. Methi says, still staring at my jaw. "But she needs a father who's doing well too."

"I'm doing fine," I say, gritting my teeth.

"You're getting into fist fights."

"There was no fight. I didn't hit back."

"You didn't?" He lifts his brow. "That's interesting."

"Is it?" I frown, because there's nothing interesting about the downward plummet my life is taking.

"It is. You don't strike me as a man who lets people hit him for no reason." He looks at my jaw again. "You're a man who always likes to be in control."

"Maybe you don't know me as well as you think you do," I say, feeling tetchy.

"Or maybe you're changing. Why did you let yourself be hit without retaliating?"

He's not letting this go. "Because it was Skyler's brother who hit me."

His smile widens.

"I'm glad that amuses you," I mutter.

"It just tells me what I already know is true."

"What's that?"

"That you're in love with this woman."

"Shut the hell up."

"And you broke up with her because you're afraid."

If I thought I was annoyed before, I'm furious now. "That's not true," I say. And then I realize I'm shouting. I glance at the door, knowing Ayda's on the other side. "Do you know how hard it was to end it with her?" I ask him. "I didn't do it for me. I did it for her. And Ayda."

Dr. Methi snickers, and I realize I've never heard him laugh before. Jesus, I want to wring his neck.

"I tried to make her into something she's not," I say. "That was wrong. She needs to be free."

"Oh, that's perfect." He writes something on the pad of paper beside him. "You've managed to justify it to yourself. How long did it take you to think of that one?"

"No time at all. It's the truth."

"No it's not and you know it. We both know it. And either you start cutting through the bullshit, or you'll be the one who's harming your daughter. Not Skyler, not Ayda's grandmother. *You*."

I open my mouth to tell him he's the one talking bullshit. That he's wrong, I'm fine. I'm doing what I can to take care of my daughter.

And then I think of her. The way she tried to apologize, over and over again. The way she cooked my family dinner. The way she looked when I told her to leave.

"I'm just trying..." I say, my voice thick.

"Trying to do what?"

I swallow, but there's a lump in my throat as big as a damn rock. "Trying to make everything right."

"And how's that going for you?"

I think of the way Ayda stared at The Salty Dog. The way she keeps trying to go in, and I know the reason why. She wants Skyler.

Fuck, I want Skyler.

I want this all to go away.

"It's all I know how to do," I tell him.

"Because somewhere along the way you learned the wrong lesson."

I look at him, feeling like I'm being punched again. "What lesson?"

"You think you can control everything. You think that if you do that, then everybody will be happy. You're afraid to let go."

"Because people get hurt when I do." There's a pain in

my chest that feels somewhere between being stabbed and having a heart attack.

"Give me an example of when that's happened."

He's making this too easy. "I let Skyler take care of Ayda and she was taken from me."

"And then what happened?"

"Then she was found and we got her home."

"And is she hurt? Traumatized? Or is she okay?" he prompts.

"She's..." I let out a breath. "I don't know."

"It ended fine. Yes, it was scary. I get that. But it could have been so much worse. We need to work on Ayda not walking off. We can do that. But her being taken? That wasn't your fault." He leans forward. "I'll say it again but louder. IT WASN'T YOUR FAULT."

"It was her grandmother's."

"YES!" Dr. Methi practically claps his hands together. "What's happening to her anyway?"

"She's being deported. It's with the authorities and British Embassy."

"Good. So it wasn't your fault. It wasn't Ayda's fault. You know who else's fault it wasn't?"

I close my eyes. "Skyler's," I whisper.

"Exactly." Dr. Methi clears his throat. "You can't control everything. And you shouldn't. Your job as a father is to lovingly teach Ayda how to take care of herself. And your job as somebody's partner... is to understand. Not try to control. Do you get that?"

Every word feels like a jab to my already painful chest. "I do," I say. "I do."

"Good." He inclines his head at the door. "I think that's enough for today, don't you?"

I nod, because yes it is. I'm a fucking idiot. A mess.

And I hurt the woman I promised never to hurt. She was so vulnerable that night and I pushed her away to protect myself. Dr. Methi is right, being in control has never been about anybody else. It's always been about me.

And it's ruining my life.

I stand and shake his hand, then go out and get Ayda from the receptionist, because I need to think about this. Really fucking think. Ayda smiles happily at me, and I hug her tight.

She pats my face with her hands, like she's trying to cheer me up, and I have to wince, because she's hit my bruise right dead center.

"Shall we go home?" I ask her and she nods. "You don't want ice cream first?" She shakes her head.

Okay then. I take her hand and we walk out into the hallway, and she's so damn jaunty as she walks it almost makes me smile. It certainly makes me distracted because it's not until the elevator door pings that I realize it's open.

And Skyler Brown steps out, looking like a cool fucking drink on a hot day.

thirty-five

SKYLER

My heart does some kind of flip as I step out of the elevator and Ayda rushes over. She throws her arms around my legs and presses her face against them. I hunker down, letting her hug my body instead, pushing the hair from her eyes so I can take a good look at her.

"Hey honey," I say. "How're you doing?"

She smiles in response.

"You look so good," I tell her. "Is that a Minnie Mouse t-shirt?" I look at Princess Minnie on her front. "I wonder if they make those in adult sizes."

I look up at Hudson, who's carefully watching the two of us. His gaze locks with mine and it's like the earth beneath my feet shatters.

"Hi," I breathe. "I'm sorry, I know you don't want me..." I look at Ayda.

"No, it's fine. She's missed you."

I look at his jaw. There's a yellowing bruise on his skin.

It looks like Jesse got him good. No wonder his knuckles were hurting. I know from personal experience what a hard jaw Hudson Fitzgerald has.

"How are you?" he asks softly.

I look at him, the man I loved. That I still love. The father of the baby growing inside of me. He needs to know. I need to tell him.

But not here, and not in front of Ayda.

"I'm doing okay." That's as much as I can tell him.

"You look good," he murmurs, taking in my white summer dress. The weather is warm, the sun kissing my skin whenever I take long walks outside. Lee left two days ago and after this session with Dr. Methi I need to go back to the Airbnb to pack up my things.

I feel peaceful, which is a strange way to feel when your world is upside down. But maybe I've always found peace in the chaos. When you're standing in the eye of the storm it teaches you how strong you can be.

"You look good too."

"Liar."

I give him a small smile. Okay, it was a bit of a lie. He looks so, so tired. And that bruise gives him a menacing edge, not that he needed it. But even so, it feels good to see him. I don't want things to be awkward between us. We're going to be connected for life even though he doesn't know it.

I want to be his friend. I want him to be mine.

"I guess I should go in," I say, pointing at the door to Dr. Methi's office. He's not charging me and I don't want to be late. "Take care of yourself, Hudson."

"You too." He parts his lips. "Will you come back to Liberty soon?"

I want to ask him if he wants me to. But that's not how

coming home works. "Yes," I say. And a smile almost pulls at his lips.

"Good."

The elevator doors go to close, and I shrug. "I'll see you around," I tell him.

"You will."

I start to walk toward Dr. Methi's office, but then two tiny arms throw themselves around my legs again. I lean down to kiss Ayda's cheek, checking that Hudson is holding the elevator door – he is.

And just as I let go of her, Ayda's mouth presses against my ear.

"Come home."

My mouth drops open. She can talk. Of course she can talk. She spoke to me on the deck that day. She said a word, how could I have forgotten that?

"Home?" I say, wanting to hear it again.

"Ayda," Hudson calls, still standing next to the elevator. "Let Skyler go."

But I hold onto her. "Hudson, she spoke," I tell him. "She just said a word."

His eyes meet mine. He looks as confused as I am. "She what?"

My heart is pounding. "We need to go into Dr. Methi's office," I tell him. "Right now."

* * *

"I've spoken to Ayda's speech therapist," Dr. Methi says, walking back into the room. Ayda is kneeling at his coffee table, coloring a picture of a fish. Hudson is sitting on one end of the sofa, I'm on the other.

My therapy session is all but forgotten about, and I'm

very okay with that. Instead of the bawling and hand-wringing I thought I'd be going through, I spent the first few minutes explaining to Dr. Methi and Hudson what Ayda had said to me, both today and on the day she disappeared.

My face flamed when I told them that she'd said "mother".

"Could she have meant Grandmother?" Dr. Methi had asked. "She was sitting near you on the deck, wasn't she?"

And that's when I realized I'd been wrong. Of course she'd been saying grandmother. She was trying to tell me Catherine was there, and I hadn't realized.

"You're doing fine," Dr. Methi had reassured me, like he knew I was second guessing myself. "Why would you have thought she was saying those words? Nobody would have."

And then I told them about her two words outside the elevator. *Come home.*

Hudson's eyes had met mine when I said it. There'd been so much emotion in his gaze. And yet it made me shift, because I don't want him to feel emotion because his daughter spoke to me.

Don't get me wrong, I'm glad she did. I'm over the moon that she's actually able to say some words. But Hudson doesn't owe me anything. I was just there, listening at the right time.

"The speech therapist would like to see Ayda tomorrow," Dr. Methi says, bringing me out of my thoughts. "She thinks this is a very significant piece of progress." He smiles at Hudson then me. "But she also says that you shouldn't get ahead of yourselves. Ayda has a long way to go yet."

"Tomorrow is fine. Can she send the details to my assistant?" Hudson asks, leaning forward. There's an animated expression on his face that wasn't there before, and I'm so happy for him.

"Already done," Dr. Methi says. He looks at his watch. "Well we have thirty more minutes," he says to me. "Why don't we say goodbye to Ayda and Hudson and you can stay for a chat, Skyler?"

"Can I just have a word with Skyler first?" Hudson asks, his voice low as he glances at me. "In private?"

Dr. Methi looks at me and I shrug to let him know it's okay.

"I'll be outside," Dr. Methi says, taking Ayda's hand and striding to the door and leaving the room. Hudson stands, and I find myself doing the same, turning to face him.

"Thank you," he says. "Thank you from the bottom of my heart."

"I should have remembered earlier," I tell him.

He shakes his head. "That doesn't matter. There were other things going on. But thank you for being the one she trusts."

I don't know why, but his words send my emotions into a spiral. Tears spring to my eyes.

"You *are* coming home, right?" he asks, as I try to get them under control.

"I'm coming back to the bar, yes." I need to make it clear. I'm not expecting anything. I'm not wanting it. And soon, very soon, I'll be honest with him about what's going on inside of me.

"I understand." He takes a breath. "I need you to know, I'm so, so sorry for the things I said to you."

"It's okay," I say quickly.

"No, it very much isn't. What I said..." He trails off, running his fingers over his bruised jaw. "It wasn't about you. It was about me. I like who you are." He shakes his head. "Dammit, I *love* who you are. I love everything about you. I love the way you see life as an adventure, not something to be protected from. I love the way I never know what to expect from you, but whatever it is, it's always magical. I love the way you make me laugh and make me think and the way you challenge every single thing I do. And most of all," he takes a breath, "I love how big your heart is. How there's infinite room for everything and everybody." His gaze is oh-so gentle as he looks at me. "I'm not asking you to forgive me. I can't forgive myself. I'm just telling you the truth. Because you deserve it."

I inhale raggedly. My heart thuds, like it wants me to let his words inside. To let them rebuild me.

But I can't.

"Hudson," I whisper.

"It's okay. I understand if you don't feel the same. I just need you to know how very welcomed you'll be on the island. Especially by me." He shakes his head. "By everybody. I'm absolutely sure if you took a poll, everybody would vote to push me out and let you back in."

"You make it sound like a reality show," I say.

"I'm trying to tell you that Ayda was right. Her words were right. Come home. To *your* home. It's where you belong."

He steps forward, his hands reaching for my shoulders. He pulls me close, not close enough that our bodies touch, but still so near that it's easy for him to drop his head and kiss my brow, right where my hairline meets my skin. Even that sends a shiver through me, like my body is waking up and remembering exactly who he is.

Oh hello, giver of orgasms, god of the unbelievable sex. I was wondering where you were.

"Okay then," Dr. Methi says, coming back in. Hudson reluctantly lets go of me, giving me the softest of smiles.

"I'll see you back on the island."

And it doesn't sound like a threat.

* * *

I pull onto the ferry the next morning, grinning at Jesse's happy face as he realizes I'm on my way back home. He walks over and I roll down the window. "Hey," I say to him. "I've got Lee on speaker phone."

"Hi Jesse," Lee calls out over the car's speaker.

"Hi Lee." He taps my car. "I'll be at the bar later," he tells me. "You don't need to work tonight."

"I want to," I say. I want things to go back to normal. Or as normal as they can be.

"Okay." He gives me a wink. "We'll catch up later."

"We absolutely will." I'm still smiling as he goes to help cast off from the dock.

"See," Lee says, her voice sounding tinny. "It's all going to be fine."

"I know." There's still that feeling of trepidation though. Since I saw Hudson at Dr. Methi's office, I've been replaying that forehead kiss over and over again in my mind. It made me realize just how much I still love him. How I'll always love him. He's the Lindsay Buckingham to my Stevie Nicks. He'll always be my one who got away.

"When are you going to tell him?" she asks.

I take a long breath. "I need to settle back in. And we have Karaoke on Saturday. I think I'm gonna need to let him calm down when he realizes we've turned his upmarket drinking establishment back into the down low and dirty local bar it always used to be."

"You're procrastinating. At this rate the kid's gonna be going to college before you finally get the guts to tell him."

I roll my eyes even though she can't see me. "I'm going to tell him," I protest.

"When?"

"Next Wednesday."

She starts to laugh. "Why Wednesday?"

"I don't know," I admit. "You just forced me to say something. And I guess Wednesday is far enough away that I don't have to worry about it yet, but close enough that he'll find out before graduation."

Lee huffs. "I don't understand why you're so afraid. Do you think he'll go ape?"

"No," I say honestly. Maybe I was afraid before, but that's because I'd been building it up in my mind. "He's a good man," I say, feeling sure about that. "He'll be calm."

"So what are you afraid of?" Lee asks.

The feeling of nausea I've been fighting for the last few days rises up. "I'm afraid he'll pity me," I say. "That he'll try to do the honorable thing and rekindle something between us, and he'll be doing it for all the wrong reasons."

Lee is silent for a moment. The ferry starts to move along the water and I look ahead, seeing Liberty in the distance.

"I hate the way you do this," she finally says.

"Do what?"

"Why can't you accept that he might want you for *you*? Why can't you see that you're a catch, whether you're having his baby or not? I wish you could see yourself the way we all see you. You're funny, you're clever, you're beautiful. You make this world such a better place. What man wouldn't want you?"

I blink at her words. "You have to say that. You're my sister."

"I'm saying it because it's true. I just wish you would believe it."

"I'm trying," I tell her. "I really am."

"You need to try harder. You're going to be a mom. And you're going to be a great one. I just wish you'd believe in yourself the way that I do."

I swallow hard. She's right. I need to be a grown up. "I'm going to," I promise. "I am."

"Good. Now go start living your life. Don't forget that James, Cora, and I want to visit soon."

"I'm banking on it," I tell her, then we say our goodbyes and she hangs up.

For the rest of the ride I sit in the car silently, thinking about Wednesday. That's when I'll tell him. And let the chips fall where they may.

"We've got this," I say, tapping my stomach softly. "Or at least I think we do." All I know is I have less than eight months to get my life together. Which actually isn't too bad a deadline.

When we dock, Jesse leans in through the window and kisses my cheek, telling me to go take a nap because I look beat. I drive off the ferry and park in my usual spot outside the bar, amazed at how busy it is. Maud is working today, and she waves at me from the porch as I climb out of the car.

"How sweet is that?" she asks me, pointing at the beach. I follow the direction of her finger to where somebody has written out words with pebbles on the sand.

You Have Never Been A Still Ocean. You Have Always Been My Storm.

"You think it's some kind of love letter?" she asks.

"Maybe we'll get a proposal in here. How romantic would that be?"

"I wouldn't get your hopes up."

"Still sweet though," Maud says.

"It is." I nod, carrying my suitcase through the bar to the private door leading to my apartment. It feels like it's been months, not days, since I was last here and when I step inside and put the bag on the floor it takes me a moment to catch my breath.

Unlike the first time I walked in here, it's clean, it smells fresh. It feels like home. I take my luggage to the bedroom and leave it there. I'll unpack later, when I'm ready.

Walking back into the bar, I grab a fresh apron and knot it around my waist, sliding behind the counter to where Autumn is smiling at me, like she's been waiting for me all this time.

"You're back," she says, grinning.

"Yes." I nod. "I really am. Now tell me, which song are you planning to sing at Karaoke, because I don't want any dupes."

* * *

Decaf coffee really is the worst. I wrinkle my nose as I swallow it down the next morning, wishing I hadn't read a whole thread on Reddit that listed everything you have to give up for nine months to have a healthy baby.

I can live without blue cheese. And avoiding liver and liver products really isn't going to ruin my life. But no caffeine? Are they serious? I sigh and take another sip of the devil's juice.

It's super early and the town is only just waking up. The first ferry of the day is waiting at the dock, and there's a mist dancing above the surface of the water as it gently laps into shore.

A seagull swoops down to pick something up from the beach, and I frown when I see there are some more pebbles there, spelling out words. They're different from yesterday. I move my eyes over the sentence, my throat tight.

You've woven a spell around me, and I never want to break free.

I look around, trying to see if the wordsmith is still around, because I swear those pebbles weren't there last night as the sun went down. But the beach is empty, save for the birds.

I let out a long breath, then pour the rest of the decaf coffee into a nearby plant, because if I have to avoid caffeine for the next eight months, I'd rather not drink coffee at all.

Or at least I'll ask Mylene if she can work her magic and make something that resembles the cappuccinos I love.

The jukebox calls to me as I walk back into the bar. I turn it on, then flick through until I find "Silver Springs" by Stevie Nicks.

And as her husky voice sings out, telling Lindsay Buckingham he could be her Silver Spring, I take a deep breath.

Because I'm starting to wish Hudson could be mine.

thirty-six

HUDSON

"Where have you been?" Asher asks as I walk into the living room, Ayda at my side. My daughter's knees and hands are covered in sand from helping me find stones.

"Out for a walk. I told you."

"At this time?" He looks skeptical. "Hey kid, you need a shower," he says to Ayda, who's somehow managed to get sand in her hair too.

I tip my head to look at him. "When are you going home?" I ask him. "Not that it's not a pleasure to have you here."

He smirks at me. "Not sure yet. Thought I'd hang around and watch the fun."

"What fun are you watching?" I ask. "Another cartoon on your TikTok feed?"

His grin widens. "Nope. I'm talking about my brother finally learning to grovel."

"I'm assuming you don't mean Wyatt."

He smiles. "Man, I'm loving it. You're so transparent. Do you think I don't know that it was you who wrote those song lyrics on the sand with rocks yesterday? They're the talk of the town."

I shrug. I don't care what he knows. "Even if you don't have work to do, I do. I'm gonna take Ayda for a shower and then grab one myself." I put a coffee pod in the machine, because after an early start like this, I need as much caffeine as I can get. "What are your plans today?" I ask. "Looking at flights back home?"

"You trying to get rid of me, bro?"

"I just don't want to stand in the way of you and your career."

The smile almost slips from his face. And I know there's more to his prolonged visit than meets the eye. But like me, Asher learned from an early age to keep his cards close to his chest.

And I can't solve everybody's problems. I'm taking Dr. Methi's words to heart. Asher is a grown up, let him sort himself out.

I have my own life to get back on track.

That's why, after some morning meetings and another visit with Ayda's speech therapist, I pack us both up in the car and drive over to the lighthouse. I park on the gravel road that leads up to it, next to Autumn's car, and once Ayda is out of her car seat we both walk up to the door.

"Okay, I need to do a bit of groveling to Aunt Autumn. You got my back?"

She nods, though I can tell she has no idea what I'm talking about. I rap the brass knocker on the huge oak door, and a minute later Autumn opens it.

"Hi." Her voice is wary. Then she sees Ayda and a huge smile breaks out on her face. "Hello sweetie," she says, hunkering down to hug her niece. "I hear you've been talking."

Ayda shrugs. She hasn't said anything more yet, but the speech therapist told me to give it time. She thinks it'll happen very soon.

"Come inside," Autumn says. "Parker is feeling better now. He's in the kitchen, if you point at the cookie jar he'll know what to do."

Ayda does as she's told, skipping through the door and into the main living area. The kitchen is at the back, in an extension to the lighthouse. Autumn designed the entire interior, and it's pretty impressive.

"So," she says, folding her arms over her chest, looking at me expectantly.

"So." I swallow. "I'm sorry."

"For what?"

To be honest, I'm not exactly sure. "For upsetting your friend."

Her eyes light up. "Have you told her that?"

"I have. But not enough. And not nearly for long enough." I take a deep breath. "That's why I'm here. I need your help to win her back."

If there's one thing I know about Autumn, it's that she likes to get involved. And she loves to help.

"I really, really need it," I say, because I know she's going to revel in this. "And I'd be so appreciative if you could."

"Will you owe me?" she asks, trying not to grin.

"Big time."

"Excellent. And you'll actually listen to me for once? Because if we're doing this, we're doing it my way."

I clear my throat. "I may have already started, but yes,

of course I'll listen. That's why I'm here. I need a woman's perspective."

"How have you started?" she asks, narrowing her eyes. I tell her about the lyrics in the sand. When I describe them her eyes sparkle.

"You're an old romantic at heart."

I clear my throat. "I'm trying. So are you going to invite me in, or am I on my own here?"

"Of course you're coming in." She grabs my hand and practically yanks me through the front door. "Parker, we're gonna need coffee, and lots of it," she calls out. "We're making plans."

* * *

SKYLER

On Saturday morning there's a new sentence on the sand.

You Are Fearless. You Are Graceful. You Are Love.

It's like an old fashioned text without a reply button.

But maybe, just maybe, this is what I need. Time to absorb, time to work out what I want.

Time to come to terms with the fact that I think the man I love is wooing me.

I grab my coat and head up to Mylene's for a palatable coffee. The shop is quiet when I walk in. The tourists aren't up yet, and since it's a Saturday the support staff are probably still in bed too. Life on Liberty only seems to come alive at lunchtime over the weekends.

"Your usual?" Mylene asks. It's only been my usual for a few days, but I nod anyway. She didn't blink when I told her I had to drink decaf for medical reasons.

I'm starting to think she knows everything that goes on in this island before anybody else does. Her and Eileen.

"Are you coming to Karaoke tonight?" I ask her.

"That's the plan," she says. "The other one can't sing, so I'm hoping she's not there."

"Eileen, you mean?"

She wrinkles her nose at my words.

I open my mouth to ask her why they can't just let bygones be bygones. But then I realize it's none of my business.

One day I'll find out the answer. But for now, I have my own problems to think about. I don't need to take on hers.

"How are you feeling?" I turn to see Jesse pulling out a chair beside me.

"I'm fine. The same way I was last night when you asked."

"Just checking." He looks at my stomach. "Uncle's privileges." He leans on the counter. "So..."

"So?" I repeat, lifting a brow.

"You told him yet?"

I tip my head to the side. "Has Lee been talking to you?"

"She might have called to ask me how you were doing. Like *really* doing."

"I'm not sure I like the two of you ganging up on me."

He shrugs. "Hey, that's what families do. So we need to talk about song choices tonight. Have you chosen what you're singing."

"Yes. Have you?"

"I have." He narrows his eyes. "Are we going to divulge? Make sure we haven't chosen the same track?"

I narrow mine back. "Are you afraid of a little competition?" Not that he should be.

He laughs. "Nope, I love it. Do you know if Hudson knows about it yet?"

"I have no idea," I say lightly. He still hasn't been near the bar.

"I hope he hates it."

"No you don't."

"I do." He grins.

"By the way, Mylene is coming to Karaoke," I say.

He looks over my shoulder at where she's busy filling the cake stands with pastries. "Hey Mylene," he shouts out. "What are you planning on singing at Karaoke?"

"'Lyin' Eyes' by the Eagles," she replies.

"Nice choice." He leans forward to me. "She'll be hoping that one gets back to Eileen."

I sigh. "What if she shows up too?"

"She won't. They have an unspoken agreement. Eileen was at the last party which means it's Mylene's turn."

"They both turned up to Ayda's," I point out.

"Yeah, but that was a mistake. Mylene got her dates wrong." He takes a sip of his coffee. "Why are you so worried about Mylene and Eileen anyway?"

"I'm not," I say. "I'm just trying to learn from them. I have this really annoying sibling..."

He rolls his eyes at me and I grin back at him.

"'Born to Run'," he says.

"What?"

"Is that what you're singing?" he asks. "'Born to Run' by Springsteen. It suits you."

"No." I shake my head.

"Good."

"Is that what *you're* singing?" I ask.

He mimes zipping his lips and I grin.

Because that's totally what he's singing. And he'll be excellent at it.

I, on the other hand, will need all the help I can get.

* * *

You Are Fearless. You Are Graceful. You Are Love.

I look at the words for one last time before the sun sets. I have a feeling they'll be gone in the morning. Maybe I should have taken a photograph, but it's too late now.

I know they're all paraphrased from some of my favorite songs. He's been listening to them. The thought sends a shiver down my spine.

The Karaoke party is well and truly underway. Right now somebody is absolutely strangling their version of "Mamma Mia", but nobody seems to mind. The bar is full of people dancing – so many of them dressed in seventies costumes. More than a few of them are authentic – probably stolen from their parents or grandparent's closets.

"You're up next," Jesse tells me. He put himself on last, mostly because he doesn't want to put everybody off. We all know he's the best at singing on Liberty.

"Okay." I nod.

"I saw the song choice," he says. "Nice."

"Thank you. You sure you don't want to sing with me?"

"And have everybody know you're the talented one in the family?" he teases. "No thank you."

"Mamma Mia" finishes and I hear my name being

called. Autumn is behind the bar and she squeals with excitement as I walk to the stage in the corner.

"Hi everybody," I say and there's a loud cheer from the crowd. I look at the DJ in charge of the karaoke machine and nod. He puts the lyrics on the screen in front of me and the music starts. I take a deep breath, readying myself for embarrassment.

And then *he* walks in and I feel tingles all up and down my body. Our eyes catch, and my mouth twitches when I realize what he's wearing.

Hudson Fitzgerald, the grumpy, uptight businessman who loves control isn't wearing his usual designer suit and sharp tie. Instead he's wearing a pair of flared jeans, tight at the hips, stupidly wide at the ankles. And a shirt so tight I can see everything, as can every other woman in the room because they're all staring at him.

He's also wearing a wig and a beard. He looks like he just got in from the seventies.

"Oh my God," somebody whispers.

I start to smile, but then the ball lands on the first word and I have to sing.

I don't know why I chose this one. It just felt right. Maybe part of me always knew that Hudson would walk in at the right minute. The first line of "You Make Loving Fun" – this one written by Christine McVie – tumbles out of my lips as I sing how sweet and wonderful he is.

And yes, I'm looking straight at him as I sing. I hit a bum note at the end and he grins.

I don't know how I get through the entire song, but somehow I do. And when I finish on a high, telling him how he makes loving fun, everybody claps and cheers, even though I'm probably one of the worst singers here.

He's waiting for me when I clamber down from the stage.

"Nice outfit," I tell him.

"I'm trying something new," he replies solemnly.

"It suits you." My lips twitch because he looks so stupidly uncomfortable it's not funny. "Lindsey Buckingham?" I ask.

"How did you know?"

"It's the beard. And the wig."

He touches the curls on his head.

"Next up we have Hudson Fitzgerald," the DJ calls out.

"You're singing?" I ask him. "Seriously?"

"Gotta go," he tells me. "Stay right there."

I'm not sure I could move if I tried. Hudson Fitzgerald is about to sing karaoke and I'm pretty sure that must mean the world is ending. He strides onto the stage, flares flapping, and takes the mic.

"This one is for Skyler. Always," he says, then the music starts and I am frozen still.

I know what song it is as soon as the first note hits. It's a Billy Joel song. "Just the Way You Are". Hudson leans into the mic and starts singing straight at me, telling me not to change.

I blink at the thick sweetness of his voice. Like honey dripping from a spoon. He can sing? Why didn't I know he could sing?

"He's been practicing this for two days," Autumn whispers in my ear. "I now officially hate this song."

"I now officially love it," I whisper.

His eyes are still trained on my face as he sings that he loves me just the way I am.

Oh god, I'm going to cry.

He's so damn heartfelt as he gets to the chorus, like he

means every word. And as he gets to the end, singing that he just wants somebody to talk to, I put my hand on my chest to still my damn beating heart.

There's a roar as he comes to the end. I'm screaming along with them, because he was that good. I look over at Jesse and he lifts a brow.

And then Hudson's in front of me, smiling and I'm smiling back.

"Can I take the fucking wig off now?" he asks and I start to laugh like I'm on the edge, probably because I am.

"Yes." I nod. "Yes, you can."

"And will you take a walk with me?" he asks, holding his hand out.

I take it, our palms pressing together as we walk out of the bar. The deck is as packed as the inside of the bar, and we have to push our way through a crowd of people to make it to the beach. It's dark and cool, and I start to shiver.

"This is why I should be wearing a suit," he says. "I could have given you my jacket." He looks down. "Do you want my shirt?"

"I'm so tempted to say yes."

He laughs softly. "Say the word and it's yours." He reaches out to stroke my cheek, his fingers warm against my skin. "I want you back. I'll do whatever it takes to win you back. I'll sing a billion more karaoke songs, dress up every single day for you."

"Even more tempted," I murmur. "The dressing up thing is hot."

"Is it?" He frowns.

"No. Never do it again."

This time we both laugh. He takes my hands in his.

"The messages on the beach?" I say. "They were you?"

"Ayda and me. Yes."

"I liked them," I tell him.

"Good. That was the plan. I have more."

"Plans or lyrics?" I clarify.

"Both."

I take a breath in an attempt to control my heart rate. "Hudson, there's something I need to tell you. Before you say anything else."

He turns suddenly serious. "Okay."

This is it. I feel sick. But he has to know. I square my shoulders and look him straight in the eye. "I'm pregnant."

Those long lashes sweep down then up again as he looks at me. "Oh thank God."

"What?" I ask, confused.

"I thought you were going to say you'd never in a million years consider getting back with me."

"Hudson." I put my hand on his chest. Damn this material is thin. I can feel the heat of his skin through it. It's completely distracting. "Did you hear me? I'm pregnant. About eight weeks or so, I think. I haven't seen a doctor yet, just had the blood test done. Dr. Methi told me. The day Ayda disappeared. I was so shocked and... I got distracted."

"You've known since then?" His brows knit, like the words are finally sinking in.

I nod.

"And you had to carry this all alone?" He looks almost sick. "I'm so sorry. I'm so sorry you had to do that."

"I think I'm going to keep it."

"Good." He nods. "That's good."

"Is it? Are you listening to me? I'm pregnant." I'm beginning to think his brain is addled from the karaoke and wig.

He grins. "I know. You told me. At least three times now. Congratulations." He pulls me close, holding me.

"Congratulations to you, too," I whisper. "Are you sure

you understand. Are you okay with this?" I don't think I'll ever understand this man.

He looks down at me, his expression full of wonder. "Of course I'm okay with it. The question is are you okay with it?"

I nod. "I am. It took me a few days, but... here I am. Not drinking caffeine, taking prenatal vitamins. Trying to work out how to tell you that I missed a birth control pill."

He starts to laugh and I'm still stupidly confused. "Are you drunk?" I ask him.

"Only on you."

I start to laugh with him, because this is all so bizarre. And he's clearly not thinking straight.

"Do you know what Dr. Methi told me the other day?" he asks.

"That your brain doesn't work properly?"

He grins. "No. He told me something I haven't stopped thinking about. That my job as a partner is to understand, not to control." He drops to his knees in front of me, putting his face against my stomach. Kissing it. "We had sex, we made a baby. I don't just understand, I love it." He looks up at me. "I love you."

My throat feels scratchy. "I love you too," I whisper.

"Take me back," he says. "Let me understand you. And not control you. Every day. Twice on Sundays."

I laugh. "Yes. Yes please."

He pulls me down to the sand, so we're both kneeling. His hands cup my face, angling it slightly so his lips can press easily against mine. His kiss is soft, sure. And so deep it makes my toes curl.

"You know I kind of like you being controlling sometimes," I whisper against his mouth. "In bed at least."

"And out of bed?"

"That's when I get to be in control." I grin at him. "Bedless sex, it's a thing."

"It is." He nods solemnly. "And I'm looking forward to the next time we try it out."

* * *

HUDSON

"Ready?" I ask Ayda, who's next to me, holding my hand. She looks up at me and nods, her face glowing.

She's going to be a big sister and she has no idea. And we won't be telling her yet. But we will when the time is right and we've talked it through with Dr. Methi.

I hit send on the message.

Look at the beach. – Hudson x

We got here an hour ago. Luckily most of the pebbles from yesterday were still here, though the ocean made a good try at moving them around. Ayda spent the first twenty minutes piling them all up and making me wait until she chose exactly the ones she wanted to use.

And then I wrote out the words. This time they're about me.

I love you. I love you. I love you.

Last night, after she'd told me about the baby, we spent the next few hours on the beach. I'd found a blanket in my car because she really was shivering by that point, but neither of us wanted to go back to the bar. We walked and talked along the coast.

She told me about the extra pill she'd counted. That she thinks we conceived the baby in New York. I told her that I may have missed the first couple of weeks of her pregnancy, but I'll be at every damn appointment she has. I'll make her drinks and food and rub her feet whenever they feel swollen.

"I'm all in. So all in it's gonna take your breath away," I told her. And I meant every word.

"So you're happy? Even though this wasn't planned and it took us by surprise?"

"So damn happy you wouldn't believe. I'm all about surprises. And taking life how it comes. Plans are..." I shook my head. "They're not needed. I like discovering my way with you better."

The bar door opens and she walks out, wearing a pair of short pajamas and nothing else. Her hair is blowing in the breeze, a dark curtain that dances against her shoulders.

And I love her. I love her. I love her.

She reads the words and puts her hand on her heart, then runs down onto the sand toward us both, a huge grin on her face.

Ayda jumps up and down when she sees her. And when Skyler is almost here, my daughter runs into her arms. Skyler swings her around and Ayda giggles. *Out loud.* It's not a word but it's close.

Every day we're getting closer.

Then I walk toward them. My girls. The beat of my heart, the reason I breathe.

My life.

I put my arms around them, and Ayda links one arm around my neck, the other still clinging to Skyler.

"Good morning."

"You're up early again," Skyler tells me.

"I'm an early riser."

"That's good because I'm a late one. And I need my coffee decaffeinated these days."

"Already done." I point at the picnic we made behind us. The same blanket I'd kept her warm with last night is laid out on the sand. On top are pastries and coffees and a hot chocolate for Ayda.

"I was joking," Skyler laughs. "Kinda."

Ayda runs over to the blanket and takes another sip of her hot chocolate, kneeling on the cotton. I slide my arm around Skyler's shoulders and she curls hers around my waist.

And together we watch the sun as she rises up from the ocean to take her place in the sky.

epilogue

SKYLER

Meet me at the fishermen's cottages. – Hudson.

I turn off my phone and smile, because this man has become so very unexpected over the past few weeks. For a start, today he told me he'd be on the mainland all day, but he very clearly isn't. Even though he knocked at my door early – the way he does every morning – with an insulated cup of decaffeinated cappuccino and a blueberry bagel, because he knows I have a thing for them right now.

I love the way he does this, even though it's out of his way most mornings. He's already asked me a dozen times to move in with him. And I will, eventually. But I need to know Ayda's okay with it.

"When she says it's all right, I'll be there with all my suitcases," I told him last week when we were curled around each other in my bed. Autumn had Ayda for the night and Hudson insisted on a 'bed night' which involved eating, sleeping, and having glorious sex in bed.

I'm all for it.

We went for my sixteen week ultrasound last week on the mainland. Which is where the baby will be born, in a beautiful hospital that Hudson insists is the best.

I cried when I saw the outline of our baby against the dark screen. He or she – because they couldn't tell – was squirming, like they couldn't bear to be still for a moment.

"She gets that from you," Hudson remarked, when the sonographer commented how active the baby was.

And then the technician added that the baby was being stubborn and I practically shouted with laughter.

"He definitely gets that from you," I told Hudson.

I have a copy of the picture on my phone. I can't stop staring at it, this perfect piece of life that Hudson and I created together. I may not know their sex, but I know I already love them fiercely, the same way I love their sister.

The little girl who now hums along to Fleetwood Mac.

I discovered her humming the other day. She was sitting in the bar while it was closed, playing with a puzzle Hudson had brought over. Stevie was on the Jukebox, singing "Landslide" and I saw Ayda's legs swinging, as she hummed along.

She's humming regularly now. And yesterday she mouthed a word at me.

It was 'no', which was kind of funny. Especially since I'd just told her to wash her hands after we'd been playing on the beach.

It takes me ten minutes to drive up to the deserted north side of the island. I park outside the cottages – which are coming along magnificently. At some point over the last couple of months Asher has taken on the main responsibilities of leading the construction. Hudson says it's because he's bugging him by being around so much that he's put him to work.

I think he secretly loves it. He now has two of his siblings here. He might be trying to let go, but it's a hard battle for him.

I love that he tries to fight it every day.

There's a flickering light coming from the beach. I grab my jacket and walk to the stairs that lead down the cliff to the sand below, and sure enough I can see that he's lit a fire.

He knows I get cold. My heart fills a little more.

When I reach the sand I see him standing there waiting for me, a smile on his lips as he holds his hand out. I take it, letting him lead me down.

And then I see it. This time it's a mini message, made with the smallest pebbles he could find. He obviously didn't want me seeing it as I was walking down the steps. But it's there, in beautiful browns and grays and blacks.

Marry Me.

"Hudson…" My voice cracks as I look at him. There's this earnest expression on his face.

"I mean it," he tells me. "Not because you're pregnant with our child. Or because you take such good care of our first child." My heart cracks when he calls Ayda mine. "But because you can't live without me. The way I can't live without you. Marry me, Skyler. Be mine."

"I've always been yours," I whisper.

He drops to his knee and takes out a ring box. It's purple and velvet and as he opens it I gasp. Nestled against the cream silk interior is a perfect sapphire, surrounded by diamonds. It's big and it's kitsch and it's so me. It makes my heart ache.

"It's beautiful," I whisper.

"So are you. May I?"

I give him my hand and he slides it onto my slender fingers.

"Now you have to move in with me," he says, his lips curling.

"Not until..."

He puts his hand up. "Wait." He grabs his phone, pulling up a video and turns it to me. Ayda is in the frame, smiling at him as he records her.

"Honey, should we ask Skyler to move in here with us? Would you like that?"

She nods, her eyes wide. "Please," she whispers.

My heart does a loop the loop. "She talked to you," I say. I turn to look at him and there are tears in my eyes. "Oh my God, she spoke to you, Hudson." I take his hands, the tears starting to fall. But they're not sad, they're not those kind of tears at all.

They're joyful and they're full of life and they have so much hope I can barely stand it.

"She did," he said.

"Did you send it to her speech therapist?" I ask breathlessly.

"Yes. She says it's good news."

She's going to talk. I know it for sure. She's going to say more words. I'm sure it'll take longer than we think and be harder than we hope but she will get there.

And so will this little wriggler inside of me.

"Do you think it's wrong to feel this happy?" I ask the man kneeling at my feet.

"No," he says seriously. "I don't think it's wrong at all. I think it's hard won and it's right. I think we'll have good days and bad days but the good will always outnumber the bad, because a billion bad days with you is better than a single good day alone."

I drop to my knees too, because I need to look at him. My grumpy, taciturn businessman with a heart of gold. I cup his face, kiss him softly, tell him I love him.

"Has everybody gone home for the day?" I ask him when our lips part.

He looks up at the cottages. "Yes. They finished an hour ago."

My mouth curls into a brilliant smile. "Then let's have some bedless sex, Mr. Fitzgerald. While it's still physically possible."

He grins, that sexy, mischievous smile that sends shivers down my spine from a thirty foot distance.

"I thought you'd never ask."

THE END

dear reader

Thank you so much for reading MUST HAVE BEEN LOVE. If you enjoyed it and you get a chance, I'd be so grateful if you can leave a review. And don't forget to check out my free bonus epilogue which you can download by typing the following URL into your web browser: https://BookHip.com/SBBGCLS

The next book in the series is ASHER AND FRANCIE'S story - join them and all the Fitzgeralds in IN CASE YOU DIDN'T KNOW.

I can't wait to share more stories with you.

Yours,

Carrie xx

also by carrie elks

THE FITZGERALDS

Must Have Been Love

In Case You Didn't Know (Coming soon)

THE SALINGER BROTHERS SERIES

Strictly Business

Strictly Pleasure

Strictly For Now

Strictly Not Yours

Strictly The Worst

Strictly Pretend

THE HEARTBREAK BROTHERS NEXT GENERATION SERIES

That One Regret

That One Touch

That One Heartbreak

That One Night

THE WINTERVILLE SERIES

Welcome to Winterville

Hearts In Winter

Leave Me Breathless

Memories Of Mistletoe

Every Shade Of Winter

Mine For The Winter

ANGEL SANDS SERIES

Let Me Burn

She's Like the Wind

Sweet Little Lies

Just A Kiss

Baby I'm Yours

Pieces Of Us

Chasing The Sun

Heart And Soul

Lost In Him

THE HEARTBREAK BROTHERS SERIES

Take Me Home

Still The One

A Better Man

Somebody Like You

When We Touch

THE SHAKESPEARE SISTERS SERIES

Summer's Lease

A Winter's Tale

Absent in the Spring

By Virtue Fall

THE LOVE IN LONDON SERIES

Coming Down

Broken Chords

Canada Square

STANDALONE

Fix You

about the author

Carrie Elks writes contemporary romance with a sizzling edge. Her first book, *Fix You*, has been translated into eight languages and made a surprise appearance on *Big Brother* in Brazil. Luckily for her, it wasn't voted out.

Carrie lives with her husband, two lovely children and a larger-than-life black pug called Plato. When she isn't writing or reading, she can be found baking, drinking an occasional (!) glass of wine, or chatting on social media.

Made in the USA
Las Vegas, NV
28 September 2025